FICTIO

I0266544

22. APR. 1978   -4. SEP. 1981

-9.

30. OCT. 1978   1-. NOV. 1981

24. NOV. 1978

                      28. A

12. MAR 1979   10. M

10/X 24 MAR 79   -3. JUN   3

20. AUG. 1980

                      LL

DETAILS OF JEREMY STRETTON

Audrey Erskine Lindop

The social problems which form the background of this thought-provoking novel are ages old yet as topical as this week's newspapers. It is a warm and human story about real people, written with sincerity and with truth.

DETAILS
OF
JEREMY STRETTON

Audrey Erskine Lindop

London

WHITE LION PUBLISHERS LIMITED

204271835

Audrey Erskine Lindop

DETAILS OF JEREMY STRETTON

© Copyright, Audrey Erskine Lindop, 1955

First published in the United Kingdom
by William Heinemann Limited, 1955

This White Lion edition first published 1972

ISBN 85617 920 5

Published by
White Lion Publishers Limited
91/93 Baker Street
London W1M 1FA
and printed in Spain

by Euredit

To
JOYCE WEINER

CONTENTS

FOREWORD

By a Consultant in Psychiatry.

I HAVE read this novel and thoroughly enjoyed it, and that is why I write this foreword to recommend it. The characters are all fictitious, but it is one of the measures of the worth of the book, that I have met them all before . . . indeed, on many occasions.

In my own special field of medical practice, it has been my fortune to have to deal with men and women who are disturbed in one way or another by problems of sexual behaviour, either on their own part or by that of some member of their own family. There are many good people whose inabilities to resist certain sexual temptations (which they may themselves abhor) cause them as much suffering as anyone can possibly endure, while there are plenty of evil people whose sex-life is normal or at least conventional. Some of the unfortunates who come to me can be made whole and clean again, and some are too weak to stand up to the rigours involved in mental treatment, while others again are either pathetically or arrogantly content with their lot.

This is a book about a subject which, I know, certain people would call objectionable . . . so that they quickly turn away from it to read about murderers, or liars, or hypocrites, or about queens who lusted after their courtiers, or about tyrants who wallowed in a succession of courtesans. No one, however, who does really read this book, can or will find it objectionable in any way, for it is written with understanding and compassion, yet without any false sentimentality; and, from a lifetime of experience in medico-psychological work, I can add that it is written with sincerity and truth.

The social problems which form the background of this novel are age-old yet as topical as this week's newspapers, which people read for so many different reasons. I do not suggest this book for the seeker after the sly titter, the cheap snigger, or the base sensual thrill, for such will find nothing in it to gratify him. But to the intelligent and cultured mind, interested not only in social problems but in a warm and human story about real people, I am confident that *Details of Jeremy Stretton* will give that satisfying return which all really good, well-written novels provide for the sympathetic reader.

Part I

JORDON STRETTON

CHAPTER ONE

THERE was nothing interesting about Margaret Stretton. With her semi-fair hair, her semi-blue eyes, and her lingering colds in the head she made only the weakest impression on her fellow beings. She was not even a subject for village gossip until she died, one hour after giving birth to Jeremy. Then, because she was twenty-one and had only been married a year, she became a topic.

The vicar's marriage to such a young girl in his forty-eighth year would have been frowned upon if Margaret had not been so obviously suitable. A quietly respectable girl, with quietly respectable tastes, her youth went uncriticised. Besides, she had a little money. The vicar's proposal was considered a wise and a sensible move. There were no romantic overtures to which the village could object or discuss. Jordon had tea with Margaret—Margaret had tea with Jordon—and they were married. But her death might prove more interesting. It might have a visible effect on the Reverend Jordon Stretton.

There were other possibilities to lend the subject spice. The Reverend Jordon was a youthful forty-eight. He was also an attractive man. A widower with a young baby might marry again. There was certain feminine speculation which was not without hope.

The village, however, was deprived of any spectacle. The Reverend Jordon read the lesson the following Sunday as if he had never been bereaved. Channock was divided into two schools of thought. One called him callous, the other courageous. It was not until the underweight baby was farmed out to the Reverend Jordon's unmarried sister that the village realised that it had in its midst a tragedy.

3

The Reverend Jordon's heart was broken. He could not bear the sight of the child. Channock made the best of it.

The organist wrote an appreciation of Margaret Stretton in the parish magazine, and the fact that it expressed sentiments towards Margaret which had never been applied to her while she lived won nothing but approval. Channock preferred that the heroine of its tragedy should be idolised. It added greater pathos to the calamity.

The organist headed the article, 'A Gap in our Hearts'. He wrote:

> 'Channock has suffered an irrevocable loss in the death of Mrs. Jordon Stretton. From the youngest to the oldest amongst us she will be missed. No longer will her gentle presence bring solace and comfort to the lonely; no longer will the needy be succoured by her tirelessly charitable energies. No longer will her unconscious beauty grace our homes, her unselfish nature ease our sorrows, her steadfastness lessen our trials.'

And he concluded by adding dramatically:

> 'Only the good die young.'

The organist would have been hard put to it to remember any distinctive quality in Margaret's personality whatsoever, had he been required to write of it in detail. But he had been the first contributor to the Margaret Stretton legend. It soon became obvious to the most obtuse that the Reverend Jordon had been passionately devoted to his wife. He could not even bring himself to look upon the child who had deprived him of her.

It was because he would have preferred to remain celibate that the Reverend Jordon had put off marriage until he was forty-eight. He would have preferred to remain alone with his calm, clear-cut ambitions for Christianity, his books and his Saxon church. He devoted every moment of his scanty leisure to rising above the flesh. But he had felt it incumbent upon him to take a wife. His parish had made it clear to him that it expected a marital example and a pattern of family life.

Margaret had satisfied his every demand. Other than God, she was the only friend he needed. She took a humble second place to God, with an uncomplaining acceptance which earned her the Reverend Jordon's profound gratitude and sincere admiration. She answered his weak passions demurely, without making him aware of his inadequacy. Married to Margaret, the Reverend Jordon was as near spiritual freedom from carnal anchors as a man seeking sainthood can become. She never let domesticity interfere, never made him feel that he was bodily or mentally tied to the mundane. She was a pale little ghost who ran his house with quiet efficiency and ease, freeing his austere soul to the beloved realms above.

When she died he was stricken to a depth of loneliness he could never have believed possible of a man who longed for solitude. But he was not a demonstrative man. His own feelings he regarded as being of second importance to those of his parishioners, and he would no more have exposed his private grief than he would have performed his personal ablutions in public.

In the vicarage, cared for by the daily help, he sat as dusk descended, wondering if there might ever come a time when he would cease to miss the calm companionship of Margaret.

But in the village he took his same easy stride about his daily business, careful that his troubles should touch no one but himself. He was a man in whom pity for others was an active force. The Reverend Jordon wrote letters, filled in forms, interviewed officials, and battled with legal problems on behalf of anyone in need. But he denied others the possibility of pity for himself. His parishioners, longing to give instead of take from him, had their charity thrown in their teeth. It was an odd contradiction of his teaching. The Reverend Jordon told them repeatedly that it was more blessed to give than to receive.

His very lack of emotion inspired Channock to invent it for him.

"I reckon this 'as broken the vicar up," observed Charlie Edwards after the Reverend Jordon had purchased an assortment of nails from his shop, with no more visible signs of breaking up than a casual observation on the sudden rise to power of Adolf Hitler in Germany.

"It's a pity it's turned him against the baby," said Mrs. Edwards. "You'd have thought the little mite would have been a comfort to him."

He had no intention of abandoning his son. The vicarage was a grave, not a nursery, and the Reverend Jordon thought it no place for a baby. When he recovered, he would take the necessary steps. He would engage a nurse and see to it that the gaunt house, so disrupted by Margaret's departure, became a home again. But for the present he must have the solitude which he needed to master his grief. He felt no animosity towards his son. He felt no compassion either. He felt nothing in those early days. He looked upon Jeremy as someone no closer and no further away than any other young parishioner. As such, he attended to his wants. The child was well fed, well clothed, and well cared for. The Reverend Jordon did not recognise his cross. He did not realise that he had already received the long-prayed-for opportunity to rise above the flesh. He was expecting to be asked to give up the things of the world, not to accept them.

Channock did its best to pierce his reserve, and when it failed it fell back upon its own imagination. It was aided and abetted by the Reverend Jordon's unmarried sister, Anita. Like Margaret, she had not caused a ripple of interest until Jeremy Stretton's birth. Flustered and unused to attention, she was flattered by the amount which was suddenly centred upon her tiny house. Visitors called, clucked over the baby, stayed to tea, and tried to 'draw' Anita out. It was not difficult. Anita led a threadbare life and hers was a nature that had longed for romance. Library

books and the occasional cinema, which had kept it alive,
were a thin diet compared to the sudden personal tragedy in
her family which had caused so much local concern. She
was not aware that she was making the most of it. She did
not intend to give a false impression when she said that her
brother could not look at his own son without tears in his
eyes; or that he appeared restless and anxious for the time to
pass during the hour a day which he spent with his baby.

At four o'clock each afternoon Anita wheeled the child
up to the vicarage. She could not have been expected to
know that one uninterrupted hour of her own company was
as much as the Reverend Jordon could support in the first
few weeks of his bereavement. She believed that it was
Jeremy's presence which caused him to look at the clock.

The village, dependent on Anita for domestic details.
went short of none. Through Anita it heard of the painting.
The Reverend Jordon sat alone with it night after night.
He had Margaret's portrait copied from a snapshot he had
taken of her at Teignmouth. The snapshot was taken on
a wet Wednesday afternoon at half-past five, and the artist
had practically nothing but his imagination on which to base
his picture. The subject appeared with pale primrose lights
in a soft head of hair, wistfully regular features, and power-
fully insistent blue eyes. The artist was the second contributor to the Margaret Stretton legend.

The village became the third. It seemed that it was the
only way left for it to show its loyalty towards the Reverend
Jordon that it should not minimise his loss—that it should
garnish Margaret's colourless memory. In time the village
came to believe in its own self-created myth. It was not
romantic to say to a guest, 'The vicar married the dullest
girl you have ever seen, and is absolutely knocked out by
her death.' It was easier to say, 'My dear, she was really
rather lovely when you got to know her.'

Everyone who had taken no notice of Margaret Stretton
whatsoever had a personal anecdote to relate of her. Her

reputation grew according to the ability of the raconteur.
But it became the fashion in Channock to have an intimate
knowledge of her. The legend was officially sealed by Major
Humphries. Quite unable to have recognised Margaret if
he had met her beyond Channock High Street, he gave
twenty-five pounds in her name to the charity she would
have most approved. As she had never been heard to
express a definite opinion upon any subject, the money went
towards the installation of inside sanitation in the British
Legion Hall, but from this gesture sprang the Margaret
Stretton Flag Day. Every year on the anniversary of her
death the villagers insisted upon each other buying small
paper dog-roses in support of any charity of which Margaret
might have approved. The choice was left to the decision
of a committee. A London newspaper gave half an inch in
'The Wanderer's Diary' to: 'Midland Village has Good
Idea'. The Wanderer then reported Channock's tribute to
a beloved member of its community.

Even so Margaret Stretton would have gone out of
fashion. It was difficult in spite of inside information to
derive much satisfaction from the vicar's stoical suffering.
It was so gallantly inconspicuous. But there was a living
baby to stimulate the interest and keep the legend alive. It
became the aim of the village to reunite the Reverend Jordon
with his son. He received signed and anonymous letters.
He received visits and telephone calls. He paid attention to
none of them. He christened the baby Jeremy Howard
Stretton, as if he had been christening it Jeremy Bagshot
Bloggs. He saw no reason why the child should not be
perfectly happy in the care of his sister for the moment, and
certainly no reason why it should be better off with him.

Then there was an incident which took the whole story
out of the romantic class of gossip and placed it in the
scandal. There was a Christmas party at the Church Hall.
The Reverend Jordon distributed presents from the tree.
Jeremy put up a podgy hand and clutched his father's sleeve.

Every witness present declared it to be the most touching example of blood calling to blood. But the Reverend Jordon brushed the child's hand away and pushed a celluloid duck into it. Jeremy Stretton howled.

It was a brusque gesture, but it was not a brutal one. It was merely an acute desire not to show favouritism. By the time the story had travelled from one end of the village to the other, the gesture had become an assault. The vicar had viciously struck his own child and left bruises on its wrist. The Reverend Jordon received a letter from his Bishop. It said that while the Bishop hesitated to interfere in so delicate a matter, in view of the many letters of protest which he had received he ventured to suggest that the Reverend Jordon might set a happier example to his flock if he showed his own son a little more open consideration.

The Reverend Jordon put his sister's cottage up for sale and installed her with the child in his own house. It seemed not only an obvious but an economical solution. Nevertheless he was well aware that by giving his sister the run of his home he was saying good-bye to peace.

Jeremy Stretton took his place in a house where the only outward sign of affection came in the wet compensating kisses of an aunt, and where his mother had become a legend.

CHAPTER TWO

HE took his place in a house where nothing and no one struck him as worthy of attention except his father. The Reverend Jordon seemed remote, magnificent and unobtainable, whereas his aunt was fussy and inescapable.

There was not much to impress him about his home except the emptiness of it when his father was out of it. The spare room smelt of mothballs, the loft smelt of apples, and the wind, catching the house at a certain corner, became somehow trapped in the rafters and knocked with a ghostly hand. A row of beech trees dripped in the summer rains, making pools on the edge of the tennis-court. Two big cedars took most of the sunlight and drew nearly all the nourishment out of the flower-beds, and the church at the end of the vegetable garden threw a curious shadow across the cabbage patch at high noon. At night, if he knelt far enough up in his bed, he could see the church windows alive with evensong, and the gas-lamp hanging under the lych-gate. He had as his chief companion his father's fox-terrier, Jack.

Channock made even less impression on him. It ran, flat and straggling, towards the river as if it were making a perpetually untidy effort to cross it. Two cottages only had reached the opposite side. The others clustered along the bank as if gathering the courage to jump. When the sun slipped behind the Leigh Hills, Channock achieved a certain rosy grace, and even the corrugated roof of the Mission Hall was softened into charm. The country swept boldly round the village. The hills loomed above it in a menacing curve like never-breaking waves that hung over but never swamped it.

There were, however, things about the Reverend Jordon which never failed to impress his small son. In church his strong, dark features were striking above his surplice. The whole ceremony, of which his father was the central figure towards which every other creature knelt, both moved and thrilled the child. He liked nothing better than going to church to watch his all-important father. He early confused his father with the God about whom the Reverend Jordon taught him in their all-too-short hour after tea. He looked forward with impatience to these times, but he prayed fervently that they might take place without his aunt. Those prayers were never answered. The Reverend Jordon was quietly gratified that such a young child should show so much enthusiasm for unworldly things.

It was not through his father that he heard the legend of his mother. The Reverend Jordon scarcely mentioned her. It was through his aunt and the village that Jeremy slowly discovered that he was the cause of some form of tragedy. The Reverend Jordon showed no lack of interest in the child. He was careful to ask after its health, to make inquiries as to weight and digestive troubles. But if he laid a hand on the child it was to search for a tooth or carry out some other necessary inspection. He seldom took his son in his arms or on his knee. He rarely had the chance. Anita was both possessive and protective towards the baby, and as his son's company invariably meant that of his sister as well, the Reverend Jordon frequently avoided his son's. Even so, it was hard to escape. His fears for the destruction of his peace and privacy were more than justified. It seemed to him that there were very few moments when Anita was not tapping at the door of his study.

All her life she had been incapable of making a decision or coming to a conclusion on her own account.

"Jordon, shall I risk taking baby down by the mill-pond? Mrs. Archer says it's stagnant, and he might catch something."

When he took up his pen to write his sermon, when he took up his books or was trying to collect his thoughts, the beloved realms above were perpetually lowered. He was constantly recalled from them. Jordon! Jordon! Jordon! Margaret would have seen that he at least received the chance to reach that outer kingdom. Margaret would have brought him the baby just at the moment when he wanted the comfort of earthly things. He would have taken the child in his arms, and his touch would have been warm. There would not have been this ceaseless tyranny of domestic interference. Anita Stretton's plump face appeared round the door with incessant queries, and sometimes without knocking she would materialise, baby in arms, at his side. "Jordon, he's soaked right through again. Do you think there is anything wrong with his poor little kidneys?"

The Reverend Jordon took the child and examined it.

"Of course there's nothing wrong with his kidneys, Anita. He should have been changed before, that's all." And often it was quicker to change the child himself than argue with Anita. The Reverend Jordon strode up the stairs, his long legs taking them two at a time, his son howling under his arm. In the nursery he balanced the child on his knee and, pins in mouth, tried hard not to wish that he had engaged a professional nurse or housekeeper instead of opening up his home to his sister.

He would not have believed that it could be impossible to find an undisturbed, prayerful moment in his own house.

"Jordon, he's bumped his little head—do you think we ought to send for Dr. Dickson?"

The Reverend Jordon pushed back his chair, took a deep breath, let it out in a sigh, and said quietly:

"Anita!—if you find the child more than you can manage we'll make some other arrangements, but I really *must* ask you not to bother me with trivial matters every minute of the day."

"But he's your *son*, Jordon."

"He may be my son, Anita, but I still have work to do— God's work, the parish work, and my own work. I simply haven't got time to do yours as well. Now do you think it would be possible for me to have ten minutes off from that baby?"

He said it with a smile and he said it gently, but Anita's plump face flushed. Tears gathered behind the sandy eye-lashes. "Sometimes I can't believe you're my own brother, Jordon, let alone a man of God." And she puffed her way up to the nursery to cover the child in her soft wet kisses. "If Daddy doesn't love you, Auntie does. He's *Auntie's* little man."

The Reverend Jordon thought at first that he might find escape in the church itself. But it hurt him to discover that it made him an object of further gossip. The vicar spending more time in the church than usual, must be doing so out of grief for his wife. Fortunately he prayed less well on his knees than he prayed in the fields, on the hillsides and in the lanes. He spent more and more time out of the house. The inhabitants of Channock met him in all weathers, followed by his old fox-terrier, Jack; on the Leigh Hills, out in the woods beyond Rendall's Farm, by Withermere, and along the winding road to Wakely, coat collar turned up, hands in his pockets, he marched more than walked. No one could have guessed that he was grieving, amongst others, for his son.

Anita confided his hardness of heart to friends. She was queen of the drawing-rooms where the Reverend Jordon's affairs came under continual discussion.

"But surely, Anita, being so close to the vicar, you could find some way of bringing him round to little Jimmy?"

"Oh, Mrs. Watson," and the pale eyes in the plump face seemed as if they had an inexhaustible supply of moisture behind them, "I've done my best, but Jordon is so obstinate. How he can treat poor Margaret's boy like that is something I shall never understand. The other day the little mite had bumped his head, he caught it on the edge of the airing-cupboard door, and when I told Jordon about it he was quite angry with me. He said I wasn't to bother him with the baby again."

By the time the account of Jimmy's knocking his head on the airing-cupboard door had travelled as far as Fletcher's Cross on the road to Wakely and back round the gasworks into the High Street, the Reverend Jordon had become guilty of violence again. The story had altered somewhat. Young Jimmy Stretton had tipped out of his pram and struck his head on a concrete step. He was suffering from concussion. When it was reported to the Reverend Jordon he threatened his sister that if she did not keep the child out of his way he would turn them both out of the house.

These tales, far from detracting from his popularity, seemed to enhance it. The Reverend Jordon was considered a fine and irreplaceable shepherd. Channock had never fared better by its priest. His extraordinary attitude towards his own flesh and blood only went to show how deeply his wounds had gone.

The Reverend Jordon had no conception that he was reputed to dislike his son. To begin with, it was true that the child was a hurtful reminder of his wife, but it was a state of mind which wore off in a matter of weeks. After that he might have made an ordinarily adequate father if Anita and Channock had let him.

CHAPTER THREE

IN spite of her disruption of his everyday life the Reverend Jordon was fond of his sister. He was aware that her unfulfilled existence and her limited experience, together with a body that no man had ever wanted, could not have made for happiness. His exasperation was mainly an instinct for self-preservation.

The Reverend Jordon was forced to develop his own defences against her. He discovered that reasoning with her only brought about further disturbances. He found that the best way to quell her was to establish a fierce unapproachability. To turn from his desk with a coldly inquiring stare invariably had the desired result. He became an expert at the hostile stare. He frequently chuckled after a particularly effective demonstration, but his son did not hear him do so. It did not once occur to the Reverend Jordon that his hostility might make an unfortunate impression upon Jimmy.

Outside the study door it sent Anita down on her knees to comfort the child with the kisses he was too polite to avoid. Channock too did its best to console him. Jimmy was a pet in the village. He was small, but exceptionally sturdy for his age. He was aware of the power in his arms and legs. He could feel the strength of his short, straight spine. He held himself unusually upright. His carriage was often remarked upon, and he had a face which turned heads in the street.

He seldom went into the baker's without receiving a sugar cake.

"Poor little chap," said the baker's wife, "you'd think the vicar's heart would melt at the sight of him."

It was the same in the sweet shop, the post office, or the greengrocer's. There was an apple or a chocolate or a special pat on the head for Jim.

"Well, sonny Jim! My word, he's growing into a big, fine boy, at any rate." And always the tone of voice suggested that he was growing into a big, fine boy in spite of extra-ordinary odds. It was the same in the vicarage drawing-room when Anita entertained her friends. The child heard strange conversations above his head, which implied that he was for some reason in disgrace.

"Are things more settled now, Anita? Has Jordon for-given the boy?"

Anita shook her head. The winter sunshine seemed to feed on her plump person, taking all the colour out of her hair and eyes and lips. "No, my dear, I can't say he has. There doesn't seem to be any way to soften him." There was a clucking of lips and Jimmy would be drawn to the visitor's side, hugged against hard tweed, or given a sympathetic kiss.

At the back of the boy's small mind there was a growing uneasiness. A long time ago, when he was a tiny baby, he must have done something wrong. It must have been a very terrible thing to do, because his father was angry with him still and gave him those crushing, hostile stares. He felt that God must be angry with him too. He dared not ask Jordon what it was, for fear of reminding him of it. But he did try to ask Anita.

"Why is Daddy always cross with me?"

"Daddy won't be cross with you any more if you do what Auntie says."

Once, just once, when Anita was out at a whist drive, the Reverend Jordon kissed him. Jimmy woke up from a violent nightmare. He had been dreaming that he had found out what it was that he had done wrong, and it was so terrible that he could not understand what it was. He was throwing himself again and again against the figure of his father, but the figure was made of stone and had no ears and no eyes.

The Reverend Jordon heard his screams and took the stairs two at a time. He found the child half hysterical. He scooped him out of bed, wrapped him in an eiderdown, and carried him below to the library fire. Jimmy held himself rigid in Jordon's arms. His eyes never left his father's face. The corners of his mouth twitched and his forehead and hands were cold and wet. Jordon put warm hands either side of his son's face. "Never mind, forget all about it and have forty winks down here with me." He lifted the child on to his lap, kicked the fire into flame with his foot, and settled back to read. But before he opened his book he pressed a light kiss on the side of Jimmy's head.

Jimmy felt the firm pressure of his father's arm, the beat of his father's heart, and a curious sensation that had no name. It was loneliness dissolving. He burrowed hard against Jordon and slept.

When Anita came back from the whist drive they were both asleep. It was her high squeak of triumph that woke them. She stood in the doorway in navy and white. "Oh, Jordon! You've come round at *last*. Everyone *will* be so pleased."

The Reverend Jordon handed Jimmy across to her as if he had been a parcel. "He's had a nightmare. You'd better see that he has something lighter for supper in future." He did not say good-night to the child.

The next morning the loneliness was back. His father had forgiven him the night before but now the anger had returned. When Anita took him down to the library after breakfast she said proudly, "I telephoned Alice Macey to spread the good news. She says you've got me to thank, Jordon, that you've discovered your son at last."

The Reverend Jordon stared, and it seemed to Jimmy the fiercest of any of the stares they had ever received. He crawled into his favourite hiding-place, the cupboard beneath the kitchen dresser. He closed the door to shut himself in and put his fingers in his ears to help him think. He must have done the terrible thing again, but he could not imagine how or when. He could not have done it in between being carried back to bed and getting up in the morning, and yet perhaps he had! Yes! That was it—he had done it in his sleep. He must have done it in his sleep the first time when he was a tiny baby. That was why he could never remember it. He shivered with terror at a sudden new fear of the dark. He battered his way out of the cupboard, desperate to get to the light. The dark cast terrible spells on you. He would never again be safe in it or safe to go to sleep. Any time he closed his eyes he might do the terrible thing.

Every night he tried to fight the fear. His battle began several hours before he went to bed. He longed to beg Anita for a night-light, but to have done that would have been to risk the Reverend Jordon's finding out that he was afraid, and that would be unthinkable. He tried to hold his eyelids open so that he would not fall off to sleep.

When Anita asked why he was so heavy-eyed in the morning he answered her by a question, "Why doesn't Daddy always kiss me?"

"Because you're a little boy."

"Why don't little boys get kissed?"

"They do, dear. Auntie kisses you, and so does Mrs. Macey. It's usually ladies who kiss little boys."

Because of the ladies of his acquaintance he thought this unfair on little boys. It was hard to explain that the Reverend Jordon's quick mark of affection was comforting and important, whereas the constant pressure of Anita's lips was an embarrassment and left a wet patch on his cheek.

"Would Daddy always kiss me if I was a little girl?"

Anita said, "Oh yes, dear, I expect so."

She was spurred on by the scene in the study. She thought it a chink in Jordon's armour. She reported the fact to her friends. They said, "Oh, my dear, persevere, persevere! You're doing such a wonderful job."

Anita persevered. The Reverend Jordon could not find a Christian excuse to be rid of her. She was devoted to the child, she was fond of himself, and she was his sister. It was no use looking longingly at advertisements in the Personal Columns:

'Gentlewoman would like run home, preferably country. Look after children and drive car.'

The Reverend Jordon's mind took one or two moments off to dwell on the unknown gentlewoman. Once he dreamed that a doctor had ordered Anita to live by the sea. He woke up with a smile on his face. He removed it at once when he recognised its uncharitable source.

Afraid that any noise or disturbances would distract the Reverend Jordon and make him even less sympathetic towards his son, Anita discouraged the child from playing ordinary boys' games. When he stumped round the house firing imaginary guns she gave him a soft toy, her own old dolls house, and a box of paints. She gave him beads to string and flowers to press, and left him with the impression that only a small boy who behaved like a small girl had the slightest hope of pleasing his father.

The Reverend Jordon, studying his son, was puzzled

sometimes by him. Jimmy seemed hard to interest in any occupation which appealed to other boys of his age. He bought Jimmy a Hornby train set, and he was surprised when it was not appreciated. The child put his hands to his ears when the train rattled round on its circular track.

"It makes such a noise," he complained.

The Reverend Jordon told Anita that he found the boy lacking in spirit. Anita thought it merely another example of her brother's intolerance.

"Oh, Jordon, you're always finding fault. The poor lamb can't do anything right. After all, he's only five."

Direct appeal failing, Anita adopted different tactics. She taught Jimmy tricks to charm his father. He recited small rhymes with Anita's intonation, picked his father flowers, and delivered them with his aunt's smile, and once, on the eve of his birthday, he appeared beside Jordon's desk and chanted after a false start, "Please, Daddy, love me for poor Mother's sake."

The Reverend Jordon spoke sternly to his sister:

"Anita, I will not have the boy brought up to feel the loss of his mother. What's the point of telling him that there is something lacking in his life? The less he is told about it the less he will be affected by the loss."

It never occurred to him to put right the implication that he did not already love the boy for his own sake. He had not grasped the implication himself.

The child was primed daily as to what he must do to earn Jordon's approval and what he must not do to increase his antagonism. And always as a prize and a promise Anita held out the hope of the Reverend Jordon's love.

"If you eat up your pudding Daddy will be pleased with you."

"Daddy's sure to love you if you're a good little boy and say your prayers."

Daddy will love you if you do do this or don't do that. Always the promise that Daddy might love him. When he was six the child demanded in a shrieking fit of temper, "Why doesn't Daddy love me *now*?"

The question threw Anita into confusion. Her friend Alice Macey was not at a loss. She went down on a pair of heavy knees in front of Jimmy and put her hands on his shoulders.

November had hung a grey blanket against the windows. He could always remember how the drawing-room looked and smelt on the day when the legend was first put into words for him.

Alice Macey had a cheerful voice: "Once upon a time Jimmy had a Mummy. She was the most beautiful Mummy that any little boy could ever have, and everywhere she went she made people happy. All the other little boys wished they had a Mummy as lovely as that."

"Study Mummy?" Jimmy asked. He was often held up in Jordon's absence to examine Margaret's portrait.

"Yes, the lovely lady in the picture was Jimmy's Mummy, and Jimmy's Daddy loved her very much, but God took her away from Daddy and gave him you instead."

"And now you see," Anita put in quickly, "why you have to be such a good little boy if you want to make Daddy love you as much as Mummy. You mustn't let Daddy be sorry that God gave you to him instead."

Alice Macey stood up and said over his head, "It's a pity he wasn't a girl, really. It would have been easier to take his mother's place."

Anita sighed agreement, "Yes. A girl could have stepped into Margaret's shoes."

Jimmy ran out of the room. There was no light under the library door. The Reverend Jordon was tramping over the Leigh Hills with his hands in his pockets, composing his Sunday sermon.

In his study the portrait of Margaret showed up in the jumping firelight. Her son stood on tiptoe and stared at it. Then he put out his tongue. It had become obvious, even to a six-year-old, that this was the cause of the icy stares. That was the terrible thing he had done. It must have been his fault that God had taken away his mother. He felt a swift jealousy towards the soft, pretty face in the picture. He hated the round blue eyes and the perfect mouth. He whispered fiercely, "Hate you. Hate you." His venom all but lost him his balance. Then he stood on tiptoe again and spelt it out, "H-a-t you. H-a-t you." But he felt something more painful than jealousy. It was envy. It hurt in his chest, in his heart, and in his head. It hurt worse than the tooth he knocked out on the bedpost. His father would love him if he looked like that. If he had a long, gentle gold-coloured face instead of a round and freckled one, if he had blue eyes instead of grey, if he had straw-coloured hair instead of brown, if he had been a girl the Reverend Jordon might have forgiven him.

Then he cheered himself up. After all, whether one was born a boy or a girl was obviously a matter of choice. It was probably not too late. He would step into his mother's shoes.

CHAPTER FOUR

"I am a girl," he announced to the Reverend Jordon as he was on his way to church across the cabbage patch.

"Are you?" said the Reverend Jordon mildly. "You don't look like one to me."

It was a disappointing start. Jimmy sat back on his heels beside the ageing fox-terrier Jack. The dog was his confidant and friend, but when the Reverend Jordon bent down to pat him on the head Jimmy felt a sense of resentment.

The thin sunshine made a fuss of the Reverend Jordon's black hair, as if it were tweaking at the lights in it, and as if it were patting the straight back, proud of the shoulders being so flat. To the small boy peeping behind the ragged

Michaelmas daisies God Himself might have walked through the lych-gate. He could have been no more magnificent figure. It never occurred to Jimmy that God would not have the same dark head of hair, the same dark and thinking eyes, the same slow smile that filled the eyes, that he would not smell of tobacco, fresh soap and a promise of security, if only one were good.

Sometimes a hand might be held out to him and the Reverend Jordon might say, "I'm going down to see poor old Mrs. Hobb. Coming?"

Then Jimmy would get up without a word, slide his own hand into the big, warm outstretched one and cling to it, his day an unbelievably bright and shining thing, that was reflected in his eyes. The Reverend Jordon matched his steps to his son's, and looking down at him could not escape a twinge of pride. There was no use denying, even to himself, that Jimmy was the best-looking child in the village. He might give the child's hand a squeeze of approval so that old Mrs. Hobb would say from the bed, which made a grey hump across her tiny cottage room:

"My word, Vicar, what's happened to your little man this morning? He looks a regular little king-of-the-castle."

But he was never safe. The next night he might do the terrible thing again and spoil it all. He had only two play-mates. Little Mary Macey, a fairly frequent visitor, was easy to manage. He simply told her that she was a queen and that he was her knight in armour who would go off and fight for her. Then he shut her in the chicken-run to protect her from robbers and had the whole afternoon to himself.

Anita seldom asked boys to the house. She was afraid that their noise might lead to disturbing the Reverend Jordon. Jimmy's only other playmate was the daily help's daughter, small, black-haired Pamela Houghton, who looked like a boy in her plain dress and thick black stockings. Pam's short hair, cut above her ears, and her sharp freckled face required no knights-in-armour. If he had shut Pam in the chicken-run she would have found a way out. He could confide in her. He could even ask her to help: "Will you tell my father I am nice?"

"Why?"

"Because he doesn't like me."

"Get out!"

She was surprised that anything which lived and breathed could fail to like Jimmy Stretton.

"I've done something terrible which made God take my mother away. If you promise not to let on I'll tell you what it is when I've found out."

While Jimmy watched from behind the summer-house Pam waylaid the vicar. She chose a morning when spring had paid a premature visit to the garden. Old leaves still blew round in sudden squalls, which the valley sucked down from the hills, but the forsythia was out against the grey front of the house, and the sun felt quite strong on the face. It made a sad little target of Pam. It showed up the under-nourished skin and the sharp bones in the face, and it increased the shabbiness of the ill-fitting clothes. She came skipping up, her shadow bobbing beside her: "Mr. Stretton, I think Jimmy's *nice*. I like him *very* much."

The Reverend Jordon dropped a hand on her head: "And I think *you're* very nice, and I like *you* very much."

Then he moved her gently out of his path and hurried towards the village.

The children watched him go. Jimmy explained bitterly, "He only likes you because you're a girl." It was obvious that he must wear a skirt. The Reverend Jordon could not be expected to recognise a girl if she was dressed up as a boy. It was no good just saying he was a girl; he must become one.

It was a new theory in Pam's world. "My mum and dad wanted a boy so much Dad said, 'If it's another girl you can chuck it overboard,' when I was born." Pam laughed shrilly at the remark her mother was for ever repeating to her.

B

" 'If you don't want to feel the flat of your father's hand, Pam Houghton, you'd better remember what he said the day you was born and put your best foot forward for him.' "

Jimmy stared solemnly at her. His mind was turning over a new idea. "Do you want to be a boy?" he asked.

"Oh, I don't mind," she said. She was not a sensitive child, and it took a lot to make her feel unwanted.

"You can be a boy if you want to," Jimmy told her.

"Don't be daft."

"You can!" Jimmy insisted. "All you've got to do is to ask the stork to take you away and bring you back a boy again."

"The *stork*!" Pam squealed at him. She was a year older than Jimmy. "Babies don't come by storks."

"Yes they do," Jimmy argued, loyal to Anita's fluttery teachings. "All we've got to do is to find the stork to take us back."

"But your mum gets a baby off of your dad, and Friday night's worst because it's pay day and he goes on the beer."

"That," Jimmy told her, "is redic'los, because I was sent here in my mother's place after she was dead, so she couldn't have been here on a Friday night."

The logic of this bewildered Pam, but failed to convince her. At seven years old there were no fairy-tales left in the mind of Pam Houghton. But she was willing to pretend that she believed him. She was willing to do anything to please him: "But where do we find the stork?"

Jimmy, always practical, bowed to the difficulties. "What I was thinking was, why couldn't we both just swap?" She stared at him. "You wear my clothes and I wear yours." Pam considered it, tongue between lips. "Then your mum and dad could have a little boy and my father could have a little girl."

"What, you mean me live in your house and you in mine?"

"No, no, just change clothes."

"My mum would kick up," said Pam.

"But why?" Jimmy said, and spread out his hands at her as he saw Anita do. "My clothes are much nicer than yours." He pointed this out with no suggestion of superiority. It was simply a question of fact.

"All right," Pam said, "but we'd better do it in the wash-house."

In the wash-house they stripped. Pam handed Jimmy a pink woollen vest with a hole in the side, a pair of navy-blue bloomers cut down from an elder sister's, a petticoat, her dress, and a sun-bonnet. Jimmy's eyes caught sight of the sharp jutting edges that Pam's shoulder-blades made in her back. "Ooh! Aren't you thin! Your bones stick out." He ran a curious hand up and down her spine and into her prominent collar-bones. "Doesn't it hurt to stick out like that?"

"You stick out too," Pam told him. "You stick out where I don't."

"Yes, but not *bony*," Jimmy argued. "You feel up my back. I don't." He took her hand and pressed it on his well-covered shoulders and back.

"No," said Pam worried, "you don't."

He helped her into his own clothes. They were too big, and she squealed with laughter as her long white legs appeared through the grey flannel shorts. Because she passed so well for a boy he imagined he made a good girl. When Pam took time off from herself to study him she slapped her hand over her mouth and laughed.

"Be quiet," Jimmy hissed at her, "someone will hear."

Mrs. Houghton heard. She came into the yard. Whenever her pinched lips opened up they reminded Jimmy of his tortoise about to bite into a lettuce leaf. But she could make an unusual noise through them. "Pam *Houghton*! Pam Houghton, where are you?" She opened the door of the wash-house and said, "Come out of there at once, Pam Houghton, and you too, young man." The children came out. Mrs. Houghton slammed the door behind them and said, "You know as well as I do, Miss Stretton doesn't like you in the——" Then she gave a mixture of a squeal and a shout, which had the raw edge of a seagull's cry.

"You've got the little boy you wanted, and my father's got a little girl. Isn't that nice all round?" Jimmy demanded.

Mrs. Houghton made no reply. Her lips snapped together so hard that Jimmy wondered that they did not bruise each other. Then she snatched the children by the hand and dragged them across the yard into the house. Pam lost her footing and was more or less pulled over the polished hall on her knees. Jimmy, trying to tug his hand away, protested, "Mrs. Houghton, Pam's vest had a hole in it, and mine hadn't, so she wasn't being naughty to change."

Mrs. Houghton halted outside the door of Anita's private sitting-room. She kept a vice-like grip on the children's hands and called out, "Could I trouble you a minute, Miss Stretton?"

Anita's voice bade her come in. Anita was sitting at the old mahogany desk in the window. She was writing out jam labels in her neat and upright hand. Mrs. Houghton used a voice which neither child had heard her use before; it was tight and grim, but it was something else—it was deeply shocked. Mrs. Houghton's first instinct was to hush the matter up. But it was too big a problem for her prudish mind.

"Miss Stretton, I don't know what you're going to say, I'm sure, but I think you ought to see it for yourself. Pam Houghton will feel the flat of her father's hand, I can promise you that. But I think the vicar ought to have a word with Master Jimmy."

Anita turned round to the three at the door. "What is it, Mrs. Houghton?" She saw only three blurred figures, and heard Jimmy say:

"I am a girl instead of Pam, that's all. Ooh, you're hurting me." And he twisted away from Mrs. Houghton. She gave his arm a wrench which he felt at the socket, and jerked him down to Anita's desk. Pam was dragged over the carpet in a sitting position. Her face was white and her eyes were alarmed, but she made no sound. Jimmy said stoutly:

"She didn't do it. I did. She *said* her mum would kick up."

"What have they done, Mrs. Houghton?" Anita asked.

"Take a look for yourself, Miss Stretton." Anita changed her reading-glasses for her long-distance ones. Then she made a noise not unlike Mrs. Houghton's. It released Mrs. Houghton's tongue:

". . . and they were *both* in the wash-house together, Miss Stretton. So they must have seen each other undress. Goodness knows how long they were with nothing on. I could hardly believe I should catch a daughter of mine out so disgusting—it's not my side of the family, I can promise you that."

Anita turned round on Jimmy, her plump face caught between her hands: "Oh, you filthy, *filthy* little boy." Jimmy had never seen his aunt angry before. "I've a good mind to give you a whipping."

"There's no shame in either of them, Miss Stretton. I heard this one laughing her head off," and she gave Pam's arm a painful tug. "It makes you go hot and cold to think of it, and they're quite old enough to know better. You didn't touch each other, did you, Master Jimmy?"

"Well, I felt her all over, because she had bones, and she felt me back because I hadn't."

Anita leaned forward and hit him. Her hand darted out like a white snake's tongue and left a sting on the side of his face. "Never, never, never do a disgusting thing like that again. It's wicked and sinful for little boys and girls to see each other undressed."

CHAPTER FIVE

THE Reverend Jordon was never told about it. Anita's prim
nature baulked at introducing such a delicate subject as
nakedness in the wash-house, however young the culprits
might have been. Also she genuinely believed that such a
deplorable incident would ruin any hope she might have of
persuading the Reverend Jordon to take a more favourable
view of his son.

The father was never given the opportunity of clearing
the matter up. Had he been told, he would have been able
to convince Jimmy that there was no reason why he should
have preferred a little girl, that Jimmy had never to his
father's knowledge been guilty of doing anything terrible
at all. Better still, his genuine astonishment at being accused
of disliking his own offspring would have dispelled every
doubt in the child's unhappy mind. He would have made
short work of the legend, too. He was still deeply attached
to his wife's cloudy memory, but that his son should
imagine himself to blame for her absence would both have
shocked and angered him. He would have made it clear
once and for all to Jimmy that he had achieved a very sound
place in his father's heart, not so much as a product of his
own flesh and blood, but as a soul which had been entrusted
to his care. The Reverend Jordon had an immense capacity
for loving the souls in his care. That he was incapable of
showing the extent of his devotion Margaret, had she lived,
could have explained even better to her child. She would
have been the most surprised woman in England if she had
known the depths of her husband's feeling for her. As it
was, they could neither of them explain to their son.

Mrs. Houghton was forbidden to mention the affair to
the vicar. Pam was not brought to play at the house again,
and Jimmy was locked in his room with no tea and no
supper. For a while he sat on his bed swinging his feet,

trying to think what was so wicked about Pam's small
undressed body. The only feeling he had was one of pity
for the little thin bones that stuck out at the back, but Anita
and Mrs. Houghton could never have been so angry for
nothing. By the time he fell asleep he was deeply ashamed.

With the outbreak of the Second World War the Reverend
Jordon had even less time for his son. He was an air-raid
warden. Except for the hour he put aside for Jimmy's
religious education, they scarcely saw one another, but
Jimmy was obviously getting beyond Anita's twittering
care. The Reverend Jordon sent him to a kindergarten.
He came back boasting of tributes and triumphs: "Miss
Wallace says I'm the most cleverest boy of my age she's ever
come across, and I heard her tell Miss Brown she could look
at my dear little face for hours."

He went round the house blowing his own trumpet as
loudly as he could in the hopes that the Reverend Jordon
would be influenced by it: "She says I'm streets ahead of
the others and I hold myself like a little king, and Mary
Macey and Johnny Stringer ought to get into their gas-
masks as well as I do, and she makes me show them how to
do it, so I must be extraon'ry good. And it's not only at
school, Mary Macey says her mother says I'm the nicest
little boy she's ever known and so I am."

The Reverend Jordon put a hand to his mouth to hide the
beginnings of a smile and said firmly, "Jimmy, we usually
leave it to other people to say how good we are. It's very
proud and boastful to go about praising ourselves." But he
said to Anita, "For goodness sake stop that child from
showing off."

Then, on a morning when a deep black frost had polished
the roads and the shrubs in the garden looked like crystal-
lised fruits, both Jimmy and the Reverend Jordon lost the
fight. A lorry, coming up the vicarage drive to deliver a
load of coal, skidded, turned and pinned the Reverend
Jordon's old fox-terrier Jack between the front wheels and

the water-butt. For a while his howls flew round and about
the house like agonised birds. Then he was silent. When
Jimmy came racing into the yard there was a crowd round
the lorry. Over the cobbles in the yard the water flowed out
of the shattered butt, tinged with an ever-increasing red.
In the middle of the collection of people his father stood,
his trousers drenched, his hands completely gloved in blood.
He was holding the dying dog. Jimmy never forgot the
sight of the old black and white body he knew so well. One
of Jack's legs hung down like a piece of meat that has been
shredded off the bone, his hindquarters had been crushed
so that his lower ribs made a bright white appearance above
his skin. Blood ran out of his mouth, oozed from his body,
and dripped down his legs. It soaked through to the
Reverend Jordon's shirt.

Jimmy put his hands up, digging the fingers into his face.
He suffered the shock in his stomach in a series of little sick
waves. The coalman said the first thing which came into
his head, "It's only red paint, sonny, don't you worry. It's
only a drop of red paint."

The Reverend Jordon stroked the dog's head with a
rhythmic hand and appeared to be talking to the animal's
eyes. There were unashamed tears on his face. Jimmy
stared at them, astonished. Then his own tears fell for Jack
and for his father's pain as well, and he cried until Anita
came cooing out to comfort him.

The accident gave him an idea. He remembered a story
that he had overheard about himself. When he was a tiny
baby he had fallen out of his pram and hit his head on a
concrete step. His father had not cared at all. Perhaps if
he had hurt himself more seriously, if he had been covered
from head to foot in blood the Reverend Jordon might have
minded as much as he had minded about Jack.

He went down to the village and called in at the iron-
monger's. Mr. Edwards leant over the counter: "Well,
young man, and what can we do for you today?"

"My father says could you let him have some paint and he'll pay when he passes."

"Well, I think we might manage that," Mr. Edwards smiled. "And what kind of paint did the vicar want, my duck? Did he give you a note or something?"

"Just red paint," Jimmy said.

"Just red paint—and any particular kind? And how much did he tell you to bring?"

"No particular kind as long as it's red, and that tin will do very nicely, thank you."

"What, you going to do a bit of patching up at the vicarage, then?" Mr. Edwards smiled at him.

"Yes."

"It's grand for the vicar to have such a handy man about the place; let's see, you must be getting on for six now, mustn't you?"

"No," said Jimmy sternly, "seven," and he hurried out, clutching the paint.

Jimmy went into the garage. He eased the lid off the tin with a penny and stirred the contents with a stick. Then he crept into the kitchen and took down the old mirror that hung on the wall. In front of it he tipped the tin of paint on to his head. He massaged the spreading red mass well into his hair, covered his face and hands, his knees and legs. The rest he poured over his shirt front and trousers. Then he went to the library, leaving red footprints behind him. He took a deep breath in front of the door, opened it, and went quickly to his father's side.

"Look!" he said, "blood!" and added happily, "I've been run over."

For a moment the Reverend Jordon started forward in his chair. He took in the sight of his crimson son and the red trail he had left across the carpet behind him. There were no tears on his cheeks and his eyes were dry. Jimmy was surprised. He had planned that the Reverend Jordon should weep. But his father's eyes glinted like frost on the grass. The Reverend Jordon had not spent a pleasant day. His hopes of a peaceful evening were ruined. Anita's reaction to Jimmy's condition was something he felt he could not endure on the day he had lost such a very old friend. He dealt with the situation himself. He took his son by the collar, forced him into a bending position, and gave him a beating on the only uncoloured portion of him.

Jimmy made no sound and the Reverend Jordon no comment. But when Jimmy went to bed that night, smelling violently of turpentine, he wept until his ears tingled. They were the last tears he was ever to shed in connection with the Reverend Jordon. His father had forfeited the power to hurt the boy's feelings. It had become clear at last that a man who was more upset when his dog was run over than when his son was run over could never be broken down. Jimmy was grieving over three deaths that night—Jack's, and his own, and his father's. For in the abrupt moment when he realised that he no longer cared what the Reverend Jordon thought of him the Reverend Jordon died for him. He felt alone in the world from then on.

PART II

JOHN OSBOURNE

CHAPTER SIX

THERE were four new names on the train list. Young Mr.
Neator checked them over, "Dove, Lowry, Bowden, and
Stretton." In five minutes the train would depart. There
were thirty-three boys on the station, including Dove,
Lowry and Bowden. They stood owl-faced and silent,
apart. There was no sign of Stretton. Young Mr. Neator
said under his breath, "Where *is* the little devil?"

Orson took hold of his sleeve: "Wouldn't that be him,
sir?"

Mr. Neator followed the direction of Orson's finger. He
saw a small mushroom coming up the platform. The mushroom carried an attaché-case and a porter beside him carried
a large suitcase. The porter handed over his charge: " 'Ere
you are, sir, 'ere's Carnera for you." Jimmy turned round
and tipped him sixpence. The porter doffed his cap: "Thank
you very kindly, sir. I tell you what I'll do, I'll invest in an
'alf a pint of wallop and drink to your very good 'ealth."

Mr. Neator was obliged to stoop down to address Jimmy:
"Hullo! You're Stretton, aren't you?"

"Yessir."

"I'm Mr. Neator. You've only just made it by the skin of
your teeth."

"Yessir."

"Did you come down alone?"

"Yessir."

Mr. Neator received a cool grey glare which tolerated, but
did not accept, friendly advances. Jimmy had come to mistrust them. He had perceived them in his father of late.
He maintained an indifference which verged on hostility
towards the Reverend Jordon and it was a defence he

adopted towards everyone else. He was not again going to risk his affections. He was armed against all further snubs. There being no point in remaining where he was, Mr. Neator straightened up and handed Jimmy over to the care of the kindly Orson.

Orson's woolly brain kept him in a low form at the Bradcombe Preparatory School. He was tall for his age and there were big bones in his ankles and wrists. He was eleven. He said, "Shall I take your little case?"

Jimmy said curtly, "No."

"It's jolly rotten, being new," Orson offered, "but some of the chaps are quite decent, and old Road Hog's jolly nice."

"Who's Road Hog?"

Orson jerked a thumb towards Mr. Neator, shepherding the elder boys into the carriage.

"There's no time now, Smiley, you should have thought of books before."

"Road Hog's got a motor-bike," Orson said enviously, "and he absolutely goes whizzing about. Once he nearly ran into Mr. Osbourne." Orson giggled, big teeth showing.

"Who's Mr. Osbourne?"

"Mr. Osbourne's the *Head*."

Jimmy opened his attaché-case. He took out an apple and brightened it up on his sleeve. Then he took out his penknife and started to peel it carefully.

"What do you do that for?" Orson asked. "Why do you save the peel?"

"I like to eat it afterwards."

"Do you always go everywhere alone?" The clumsy Orson sat opposite, fascinated by the self-assurance of the small boy whose feet could not reach the floor of the carriage.

"Never been anywhere before," Jimmy said.

"But what did you do about changing trains and things? How did you know which one to get?"

"Asked."

"How old are you?" Orson inquired.

"Eight," Jimmy answered, and added, "Nosy."

The Reverend Jordon had had a funeral to conduct, and when Anita offered to take Jimmy up to Paddington he refused: "No thanks. It looks sissy," he said. He had a dread of his aunt seeing him off. He could imagine the kisses, the tweaks at his collar and tie, and the last-minute admonitions to say his prayers. He thought it very fitting when he first realised what his aunt's initials stood for: Anita Susan Stretton! A-s-s!

The Reverend Jordon sensed his feelings. "Let the boy go off on his own if he wants to, Anita. It's good for him to find his own feet. We can put him in charge of the guard."

They both stood at the window to watch him up the path.

"He's much too early for the train," Anita said, "but he would get off at once. I think it's dreadful seeing him start off on his own like that."

The Reverend Jordon had his hands in his pockets. "I must say he's an offhand little chap. I hope he doesn't get it too rough. I tipped the guard to telephone me when he's safely on the school train."

Jimmy had given himself half an hour to spare on purpose. Pam was waiting as arranged at the end of the lane. She danced out of the hedge when she saw him. Her eyelashes were wet. "My dad says they'll beat you," she said.

"Whaffor?" Jimmy wanted to know. His accent was the despair of Anita, who never knew the amount of time he spent with Pam.

"My dad says you'll have a bad time of it. He says all new boys do at a la-di-da school. He says they're ever so cruel to you. He's been to a la-di-da one, my dad has. He used to work in the boiler-house and he says they get treated shocking."

"Let 'em just take a swipe at me," Jimmy said, and added, " 'Bye, Pam."

" 'Bye," she replied. It was miserably said.

The Bradcombe Preparatory School was a long, red, turreted house. Its position was the only point in its favour in the days before the war. It spread at a slant towards the cliff edge and it overlooked the sea from one angle and the golf links from another. A pale, beige beach snaked for miles along the cliff line. It was mined, and great wire defences barred the house from the sea. Above the school Spitfires darted in and out of dog-fights like angry mosquitoes, and air-raid sirens made welcome interruptions to classes. Only one bomb fell in the vicinity of Bradcombe, five miles away in a hayfield.

When the agent first took the Osbournes out to see the house, which had been advertised as equally suitable for nursing-home or school, John Osbourne said, "It really was the most criminal form of architecture that any age ever produced. What could you do in those damn little turrets?" He met the agent's baleful eye, and said, "It's all right, we've got to take it. The others we've seen are worse."

Bradcombe started with twenty and now had fixty-six boys, including the addition of Dove, Lowry, Bowden and Stretton.

Rosamund Osbourne handed the train list to her husband. "Neator's lot are safely in. Only Richards and the other Isle of Wight child haven't turned up yet. Well!—once more unto the breach! Happy term!" She leaned over and kissed the side of her husband's head. "No measles, no food poisoning, and no parents."

John Osbourne squeezed her hand without looking up. He was reading through a pile of time-tables, rosters, and schedules. "Bless you," he said. "You'll be pleased to hear that Mrs. Smiley has spotted a musical streak in her ewe-lamb and can we arrange for piano lessons at reduced fees."

Rosamund blew out her lips. "I'll buzz you when tea's laid on." She left her husband muttering, "If they're not careful I'll reduce young Smiley altogether."

Rosamund went into what she and John referred to as
the state sitting-room, where parents were entertained. It
was the tradition that she gave tea to the staff on the first day
of term. A photograph of Rosamund in a silver frame stood
on the console table. It was in colour and showed the sheen
of the dark auburn hair, the humour behind blue eyes, and
the sensual and possessive lips. The only differences
between the photograph and the living face were the
accumulation of tiny lines at the sides of the lips and the
eyes.

Three members of the staff were already assembled.
Rosamund welcomed the matron and the French mistress.
Only when she greeted the white-haired music master was
there a coolness in her approach. In Arthur Charron-Davies
there was something which she instinctively disliked. His
eyes seemed unable to hold a glance and his handshake
struck perpetually cold. She knew that the boys called him
'Creepy Davies' and she thought the nickname apt.

Rosamund said to the French mistress, "I'm sorry about
your room, Nancy. We'll put you back as soon as we've got
the new black-out boards."

"Dawson's got to have medicinal paraffin twice a week,"
the matron said. "His mother sent a note. But I've a good
mind to stick to senna pods. I shouldn't be surprised if we
didn't find ourselves in for an appendix there. It's more than
indigestion." Her accent was softly Scottish.

A gust of wind threw rain against the windows. "Oh,
goodness," said Nancy Hopkins, "it's started blowing up."

Mr. Neator put a smile round the door. He had a small
but pleasant face. Thick lenses made his pupils large. Poor
eyesight had exempted him from military service. He envied
the dog-fighting pilots.

"Come in, Tony," Rosamund called. "How were the
Broads?"

"Absolutely grand," he told her. "You should make
Mr. Osbourne sail."

"I know. But you'll never stop him from climbing. He won't leave his beloved Lakes. Who's on teas?"

"Beryl Gribbs. She's got a shocking cold."

"Oh, not again," said matron. "She saves them up for the beginning of term."

Rosamund picked up the house-telephone. Through it she said to her husband, "We're off, John."

When he came in he shook hands all round. "You seem to have done well on the Broads, Neator. Don't tell me you ran into sunshine."

"You don't seem to have done too badly on Cumberland mists, sir. Are *you* a cragsman yet, Mrs. Osbourne?"

"Good heavens, no. I get dizzy if I sit on a five-barred gate."

"I'm a scrambler," smiled Osbourne, "not a cragsman, more's the pity. Had a look at the scallywags yet, Matron?"

"Just the usual run-through, Mr. Osbourne."

"No dread diseases? Nothing we can blame on the parents right away?"

"Not that I could see at a glance."

"How about the new lot?"

"They seemed all right. Dove could do with a spot of fresh air. I should think he's been kept in a hot-house."

Nancy Hopkins looked out of the window. "It's going to be fresh, all right."

"I brought Carnera down with me," young Anthony Neator said.

"Oh?" smiled Osbourne. "Bowden? Papa was a middle-weight amateur boxer."

"No, Stretton. Two chamber-pots high and a chip on his shoulder. He's minute, but makes up for it with the strong silent man stuff."

"He's the dearest wee thing," the matron said. "I felt I'd like to hug him."

"You'd better not try," said Neator. "He doesn't invite

friendly advances. Poor old Orson kept wagging his tail at him and nearly got his head snapped off."

The whole room laughed at the mention of Orson. Rosamund bit carefully into a bun. The cream cascaded down her chin. "Oh, my Lord! These deadly things! I won't have my poor Orson made fun of. It's not given to us all to be brainy and beautiful, and kindness is an admirable quality."

"Oh, he's a good old wool-winder," Osbourne laughed.

"He wound my wool just *once*, John, and you've never let either of us forget it."

Osbourne said, "Oh well, drink up, Neator, and let's get down to it. We'll run through the time-sheets and I'll greet the hordes before prayers. I can't think why, but I always want to go straight down to the pub on the first day of term."

CHAPTER SEVEN

NANCY HOPKINS took charge of the younger boys. They were collected in the hall. She had read out the dormitory changes. "Mr. Osbourne will talk to you after prayers. Bowden, take your hands out of your pockets, please, and no talking in the corridors."

There were nine in Jimmy's dormitory. Orson whispered outside the door, "You're allowed to bag the bed you want. You have to go in and sit on it quick."

Jimmy pushed his way to the front. When the door was opened he took a lightning stock of the long bare room. There was one bed under the farthest window which stood apart in a small recess. Jimmy skidded across the polished floor, banged his suitcase down on it, and clambered after it. Then he knelt down to open his suitcase, turned his back on the rest of the room, and ate his apple-peel.

There was a general stampede in the room. Nancy's voice reached them, "Quiet, boys! Quiet!"

A figure loomed up behind Jimmy. Smiley stood with his hands on his hips. He was a narrow-faced boy with long ears. He used an exaggerated voice: "And what, may I ask, might *you* be doing?"

Orson called, "Stretton, Smiley's dormitory prefect. That's always the prefect's bed."

"It isn't," said Jimmy. "I got here first."

Smiley was thin and his shoulders were slight. But he was nearly thirteen and tall. He had a small, pinched-up mouth. He said, "Hop it, tadpole, if you don't want your face pushed in."

Jimmy closed his suitcase. He locked it and put the key in his pocket. Then he stood up. He swung back his arm and brought it forward to give Smiley a surprisingly hard blow under the chin. It tipped Smiley's head back, jolting his spine, and sent him in unsteady steps to slip and hit his head on the floor. He lay in a crooked line. It was the first time Jimmy had used the power in his arm, except for swinging on the branches of trees. He felt vaguely smug and pleased. A shocked silence reigned at first. Then the hubbub broke. Orson clucked like a frightened hen.

The crowd round Smiley was excited and glad.

"He's killed him!"

"No, he hasn't."

"He'll hang."

"They don't hang kids."

"Well, he'll go to prison."

"Don't be soft. Smiley isn't dead." The voice that reached the conclusion was regretful. "He's only passed out."

"Well, he'll get a B.F.O."

Jimmy demanded, "What's that?"

The crowd round the body had forgotten him. It turned round with a respectful interest to study him afresh.

"It means, 'beaters from Osbourne'.

Jimmy replied, "Who cares?"

"You won't talk like that to old Ozzy," Orson warned him. "And you know, it *was* Smiley's bed." Orson, a solicitor's only son, felt bound to put forward the facts. But he was not above tricking the case. "Look here, you chaps, we've just got to stick together. We must all say it was self-defence."

"When he comes round," said Jimmy, "I'll knock him out again."

Orson's voice was stern: "You can't hit prefects, Stretton. It's against the rules. You can't hit anybody except in boxing, and then Road Hog chooses who you hit."

Matron came bustling through the door. Her faint Scottish accent burred, "Now, boys, you'll hand over all tuck at once. Stretton! Will you be good enough to get off Smiley's bed. What do you think you're doing with your great boots dancing about on——" She broke off to stare at the floor. Then she hurried to Smiley's side. She turned back, her eyes wide and anxious. "What happened to him? Why didn't one of you come for me? Will one of you kindly find a tongue?"

Her fingers felt Smiley's pulse.

Orson attempted: "Smiley was rotten to him, Matron. Wasn't he, chaps?" There was a murmur of assent.

"Smiley was rotten to whom? Davies, fetch Mrs. Osbourne here at once. Smiley was rotten to whom?"

Jimmy said, "I bagged the bed first, and he said he'd push my face in, so I pushed his in. I'll do it again when he comes round."

Matron doubled her bulk. "Orson, take Smiley's legs, we'll put him on the bed." On the bed Smiley stirred under the cold sponge that matron squeezed on to his face. "You'll not need to think you've heard the end of this, boys," matron said. "It may still be a case for Dr. Cromer. In the meantime every boy present can consider himself in silence."

Jimmy pulled her sleeve: "It was me that took a sock at him. I was the one that pushed his face in." His voice was urgent, anxious for the credit. Matron took no notice of him.

Rosamund Osbourne, followed by Davies, came into the room. Jimmy ran up to her—"It was me."

Matron stood up. "He's coming round now, Mrs. Osbourne. They set on him, and when I came in he was on the floor with the senses knocked out of him. I think we should maybe get Dr. Cromer to have a look at him."

Rosamund turned towards the boys: "Who was responsible?"

"Keep *telling* you," Jimmy said. "I did it all by myself."

Rosamund stared down at him. "Who's this?"

"It's Stretton, Mrs. Osbourne," Orson said.

"Yes, and I found him prancing about all over Smiley's bed with his boots on," matron said. "A fine start to the term. Now then, Smiley, wait while I lift the pillow behind you. Do you feel any pain anywhere?"

Rosamund looked at Jimmy. "You're too small to have knocked out Smiley. Now, boys, Mr. Osbourne dislikes having to dig for the truth, as you know. He takes a much more lenient view if you're straightforward."

"I'm not too small," Jimmy insisted. "I got up on the bed like this, see?" He scrambled on to it and stood upright. "And he was there and I was here, so I was taller than him—and I gave him a good swipe on the nose, like this." He gave a demonstration, narrowly missing Rosamund Osbourne's nose.

Rosamund turned towards Jimmy. "Get off that bed at once. What have you got to say for yourself? Is this the way you usually behave at home?"

"Don't like sleeping in the middle of a room. My bed's in the corner like that at home. I want this bed."

"Your likes and dislikes are not in the least important here, Stretton," Rosamund told him sternly, "at Bradcombe

you'll do the same and be treated the same as anyone else.
You're a very naughty little boy indeed to have behaved
like that to Smiley. You'll have to come up before Mr.
Osbourne, which is a great disgrace on your first day at
school. Orson, until Smiley's recovered, you're to take over
the dormitory prefect's duties, and immediately after prayers
bring Stretton down to Mr. Osbourne's study."

CHAPTER EIGHT

HE could not see Mr. Osbourne at prayers. Those in disgrace stood right at the back of the hall, in the charge of a
prefect. There was no one in disgrace on the first day of
term except Jimmy.

He and the reproachful Orson stood with their backs
against the partition in school hall while Mr. Osbourne's
clear and easy voice took prayers and followed it with an
address.

During the address Jimmy found himself with the most
unexpected longing for the vicarage. Even Anita's fussy
questions seemed preferable to an interview alone with Mr.
Osbourne. As for the end council house in Alma Row,
where Mrs. Houghton's family of six lived in four rooms,
and Mr. Houghton went down on his knees to teach Jimmy
to box, it seemed little short of heaven. He felt his eyes
pricking at the memory of the cosiness of Alma Row and
the unquestioning admiration of Pam. Judging from the awe
on his room-mates' faces, an interview with Mr. Osbourne
was not to be envied.

He held himself even straighter and affected a shrilly un-
concerned whistle. Orson in panic nearly nudged him off
his feet. It seemed to Jimmy that every one of the fifty-
four heads in front turned round to stare at him. There was
a murmuring at the top of the hall and an impromptu

inquiry as to the cause of the disturbance. A few words were caught: "New boy at the back, sir, whistling, sir," and then Mr. Osbourne's voice, deep and effortless, "I'm already receiving Stretton afterwards. The matter can be taken up then."

Jimmy felt better on tiptoe. It had never occurred to him to worry about his lack of height before, but in the big, yellow-lit school hall he felt no taller than Orson's ankles.

Smiley had soon recovered. There was nothing to report to Dr. Cromer except a sore chin and a severe case of wounded vanity. The symptoms of that were not visible yet. Rosamund had reported the event to her husband: "Darling, you'll have to jump right into the term with two feet immediately after prayers. There's an offender already."

Osbourne was guarding a light to his pipe. "For God's sake! Not dead on the starting-line. You know I never hear anything but rape and murder cases until I get back in the groove."

"It's neither of those. It's assault. Stretton's knocked Smiley out."

"Good for Stretton," Osbourne said.

"Don't be ridiculous, John. It's disgraceful. Smiley went out cold."

Osbourne threw the dead match into the grate. "You're not serious, Ros? You don't mean the thing I saw going upstairs with Orson? It'd fit into Smiley's pocket."

"It stood on Smiley's bed in its boots and took a swipe at him."

"With its boots?"

"No, its fists." Osbourne sat down, put his head back, and laughed. "There's nothing to laugh at, John. It said it's not used to sleeping with other people and it wants a private room."

Osbourne's laugh shook his shoulders and chest. "Is this the parson's effort?"

"Yes, and a very precocious one. John, I do think you're taking it rather too lightly. I know what you think of Smiley and so do I—but even so."

Osbourne put his pipe in his mouth, but the laughter was still in his eyes above it. "Was Smiley hurt?"

"No. And I'm not sure but what there was of it wasn't put on. Kate found him stretched out on the floor, but you know how they play up Kate. I caught him taking a peep at me a good time before Kate pronounced him officially round—but that doesn't make Stretton's part in it any better."

"No, no, of course not. Poor old Smiley." Osbourne relit his pipe. "Didn't Mr. Stretton want a private bath-room as well?"

"John! Playtime is over. Term has started."

"All right, I'll have a word with him. But do get his gun off him before he comes in."

When Osbourne left school hall all the staff filed after him with the exception of Mr. Neator. His pleasant young voice called, "All right, Orson." Then a tradition at Bradcombe took place. An aisle suddenly appeared down the centre of the room. It stretched, formidable and straight, towards the door through which Osbourne had gone. The packed figures had made a right-about turn, stepped backwards, and faced inwards with an alarming precision. They were evidently used to it. There was an excited, expectant hush.

Orson's high treble piped a command, "All right, Stretton —forward," and he gave Jimmy a helpful push in the back to get him started. Jimmy walked down the grim parting, staring defiantly into the long line of faces like a midget general inspecting giant troops. By the time he reached the door of Osbourne's study he was not in command of his knees.

Orson whispered hurriedly, "You'll make it a million times worse if you cry. He hates squirters." Then he knocked on the door and said, "Stretton, sir."

John Osbourne's voice called, "Come in, Stretton." Jimmy found himself unable to move. Osbourne called again, "Come in, Stretton."

Orson reappeared. "For the love of Mike, don't *funk* it." He turned the door-handle and pushed Jimmy into the room. Across a grey carpet Osbourne was enthroned behind a great flat mahogany desk. Rosamund sat cross-legged by the fire. She was knitting a school scarf. She did not look up when she gave her instructions: "Go up to Mr. Osbourne's desk and stand with your hands at your side."

Jimmy passed a poodle asleep on the hearthrug on his way up to the desk.

Osbourne crooked a finger at him: "Come round here." Jimmy moved round to his side. Osbourne leant back in his chair. "Tell me what happened this evening."

"Knocked out Smiley."

"Who taught you to box?"

"Taught meself. But Pam's dad showed me."

" '*I* taught *my*self, *sir*!' And who's Pam's dad?"

"Pam's dad's my dad."

"Then Pam is your sister?"

"Haven't got a sister."

" '*I* haven't got a sister, *sir*!' How can you and Pam have the same father if she isn't your sister?"

"My dad hates me because I made my mother die and he had to have me instead. Aunt Anita said God took her away, but that's daft. It was just me being born. Anyway, I'd much rather have Pam's dad than mine."

Osbourne's eyes caught and held Rosamund's. He said quietly to Jimmy, "I see." Then he filled his pipe. "Stretton, in school there are certain rules. They are not made for the express purpose of making everybody unhappy. They are made to ensure that everybody has at least a working chance of being happy. You might not like Smiley, and Smiley might not like you—I doubt if he does, after this—but these rules, which include not knocking each other out on sight, make it possible for you to live together peacefully. That gives you an opportunity of putting up with each other and possibly getting to like it. Do you think you understand? And after all, Stretton, Smiley may be no happier at home than you are—do you think you have made him any happier tonight?"

Jimmy raised his eyes from the ground. It was the first time he had dared to take a proper look at Osbourne. His mouth opened. Osbourne was shorter and broader than the Reverend Jordon. His face was not as long, but he had the same deep brown, thinking eyes. Unlike the Reverend Jordon, he laughed with them. He had the same definitely marked eyebrows, the same black hair, the same smile that crept slowly to the corners of the mouth and consumed it. Jimmy took it for granted that this would mean that Osbourne would hate him. He felt an instinctive enmity towards every gesture, every physical reminder of his father in Osbourne.

When he had left the room, Osbourne sat back and removed his pipe. "Well?" he said to Rosamund's back. "How did you think it went?"

"Oh, fine! Except that he's only eight years old, and you treated him as if he was the Foreign Secretary and used to diplomatic relations."

"Oh, he got it all right," Osbourne said. "Pour me out a little of the schoolmaster's ruin, will you?" When Rosamund brought him a glass of whisky John Osbourne raised it to her; "Problem child!" he said.

CHAPTER NINE

THE feeling seemed physically alive in the air. Every boy could sense it, although the masters and mistresses tried to disguise it. Matron gave out the doses and distributed the tuck with no obvious signs of disturbance, but it was there. It was in every gesture they made. It was in their voices and in their faces. Something had happened.

It started with the absence of Smiley. Orson was the first to hear of it. Anthony Neator sent for him. "Orson, you are to be dormitory prefect. You can move your things to the prefect's locker in the break." Orson's bedclothes were moved to Smiley's bed and Smiley's personal belongings disappeared from his locker. So did his clothes. He did not come to class and he was not seen at breakfast. Prayers were fifteen minutes late, and were taken by Mr. Neator instead of Mr. Osbourne. The time-table was altered. Mr. Neator appeared in every class-room, "There will be no music lessons, today, boys. Mr. Charron-Davies has been taken ill. You will use the usual lesson times as practice times until further notice."

Rumours flew round in the break. 'Creepy' Davies was reputed to be suffering from a fatal disease and Smiley had caught it from him. Smiley was Creepy's favourite, and took extra lessons from him, so it was only to be expected that he should go first. There was animated speculation as to who would be next. Creepy had arrived at nine o'clock that morning the same as usual. Smith Major had seen him and spoken to him, so he must have dropped dead after prayers.

Longridge was full of possibilities: "I expect they got the body out in a trunk or something. It's bad for a place if you die in it."

It was only a matter of hours before the whole school had convinced itself that the music master was dead. By the mid-morning break it was taken for granted.

"I wonder who we'll get in poor old Creepy's place."

Creepy was despised, but not disliked. He was old, with white hair, and made no sound when he walked, but he offered boys apples and sweets. Once when Claypole could not get a piece right Creepy told him he must not be upset

by it and to comfort him asked Claypole to sit on his knee.
Claypole, a large sandy-haired boy, spread the tale gleefully
about him. He sat Clifford Minor on his knee and took off
Creepy's voice: "Now we'll never make a pianist if we're
going to lose our confidence." And Claypole jigged the
stolid Clifford playfully up and down on his lap. He
smoothed Clifford's hair and patted his hand, and hummed
a few bars of a tune, "La-tiddle-dum, tiddle-dum-de-dee—
one two, one two, one two three. It's not very difficult,
is it?"

It became a point of honour to strive for an invitation to
sit on Creepy's knee. The accepted method was to stumble
over a selected piece, put the head in the hands, and sob out,
"Oh, sir, I'm so scared of this bit. Oh, sir, I'm really scared."

The first few attempts were successful. The victor came
out of the music-room and held up a thumb to signal
triumph. He was serenaded with, "Knees up, Mother
Brown." But there came a look of suspicion on Creepy's
tired face and when Moorhead collapsed on the keys during
'The Ride of the Valkyries' he was jerked into position by
the ear.

Moorhead reported, "Phew! I've never seen the old boy
so mad. He looked just like an old white rat. He showed
all his teeth and he put his face right up close to me, and he
said he'd make me laugh the other side of my face if I tried
to take the Mike out of him. I thought I'd get a beaters from
Ozzy."

Smiley was indignant when he was asked what had
happened to him in a lesson with Creepy. "Nothing of
course. I haven't got time to muck about like you kids."

But Smiley was always well off for tuck, and he seemed to
be able to get hold of it out of hours.

In Osbourne's office the sun struck the centre of the
carpet. In its fall from the window it included Osbourne's
head. It polished the black hair, and made a play on the

smoke-drifts that came from Osbourne's cigarette. Osbourne had his back to the room. He was staring down Bradcombe's straight and uninteresting drive without a trace of a smile in his eyes. He smoked steadily and in silence. Behind him there was a faint and rhythmic sound. It was almost too gentle to bear any resemblance to a human sob.

A weak voice said, "It wasn't the boy's fault. You mustn't blame the boy."

Osbourne answered without turning round. "I've every reason to blame the boy. There was an incident over a year ago which you possibly know about. It was not as filthy as this, but it was filthy enough. I gave both Smiley and the boy concerned a second chance. The other boy was older, but was undoubtedly enticed by Smiley. He showed a genuine sense of shame and was disgusted with himself. He benefited by his chance and when he left we were able to be sure that there had never been another incident connected with him. Smiley has obviously not benefited, and furthermore has no intention of doing so. Mr. Neator, had you any suspicions concerning Smiley and Mr. Charron-Davies before what you discovered this morning?"

"No, sir. I knew that the lesson should be in progress and when I heard no sound coming from the music-room I simply opened the door to see what had happened."

"I see. Thank you."

Between Osbourne and Anthony Neator, Arthur Charron-Davies sat. He looked frail in his worn black suit, and his shoulders were narrow. He had a thick head of white hair above a dry and faded skin, and his features were long and sharp. His age showed in his eyes and his mouth. He was weeping resignedly, in tight little sounds like a cough. His pale hands were still in his lap, and his thin ankles were encased in black boots. He said, "I do try. I don't like it —I don't like to do it." No one answered, and no one looked at him, not even Smiley, tear-stained and sullen in the corner. He stood up, his boots creaking, and shuffled towards Osbourne. "You don't know what it's like. You can't know what it's like. I *do* fight it—I've fought it all my life."

"I find myself disinclined to discuss it with you, Mr. Charron-Davies," Osbourne said. His voice had the cut of an east wind to it and, as though he even felt its chill himself, a shudder ran through his body. "I suggest that you save your explanations for the police."

"Police!" It was Rosamund who repeated the word. She crossed quickly from her chair by the fire and caught Osbourne's sleeve. "John, you're not going to bring in the police?"

"Naturally," Osbourne said.

"But, John! What about the school? It's much better to keep this sort of thing quiet."

Osbourne shook his arm free of her hand, "My dear girl, do you realise how serious 'this sort of thing' is? For a master to interfere with a boy is a felony and for a headmaster to keep quiet about it is to compound a felony."

Young Mr. Neator interrupted, "May I suggest, sir, that we put it up to Smiley's parents? I think it's possible that they'd prefer the matter hushed up."

"It's a matter," said Osbourne, "for the police."

Arthur Charron-Davies felt round for his hat. When he had found it he walked to the door. He stopped and turned round without lifting his head. "I did so hope and pray it wouldn't happen with you. You've been so good to me."

When the door closed behind the old man Osbourne said, "You are catching the eleven-thirty, Smiley. Matron will put you on it. Before you leave, do you wish to repeat your accusation?"

"Yes, sir."

"You still insist that there are other boys deserving this punishment as well as yourself?"

"Yes, sir."

"Are you prepared to give me names?"

"Yes, sir."

"Proceed."

"Claypole, Moorhead, Clifford Minor, Sanderson, Long-ridge, and Stretton. Particularly Stretton, sir."

CHAPTER TEN

THE boys were interviewed together, with the exception of Jimmy Stretton. Osbourne made him wait until last. He sat in matron's sitting-room trying to battle against a knocking of the heart against the ribs. It was more frightening, this intimate waiting, than the mechanical parting that appeared down the school hall when he was sent to see Osbourne first. There was something furtive and uncanny about this private imprisonment with matron.

He stared defiantly out of the window. A clear December sunlight struck the hills and toasted them a gentle golden-brown. Winter claimed the valley in between, and a soft slate-grey predominated.

Matron sat beside him knitting a school scarf. "Stretton, keep your legs still. Don't fidget." Her voice was unusually severe and oppressive. Her face was extremely grave. Her needles clacked quickly and purposefully. Matron was usually bustling and friendly, and Jimmy was an open favourite. It was seldom that he could not make her smile or call him a 'bad wee man'. He tried to search her face, and asked again, "But what's he want to see me for? I haven't done anything wrong."

"Mr. Osbourne has a name, Stretton. You'll be good enough to use it. The idea of it, calling him 'he'."

"Mr. Osbourne hates me," Jimmy said gloomily. "He's always hated me."

"What nonsense is this, now? Mr. Osbourne has never hated anyone, and if he's angry you may be sure he's a reason for it. If you want him to think well of you there's an easy enough way to bring that about. You've only to be an ordinary nice and decent boy and learn to behave yourself."

There they were again: the conditions imposed by dark-eyed people upon those who wished for their regard. If you're good, Mr. Osbourne might like you—if you're decent, he might think more kindly of you—if you do do this or don't do that, Mr. Osbourne may or may not finish up by admiring you. If you do this and that, daddy might like you! Jimmy knew only too well the outcome of efforts like those. You did everything in your power—you worked, you struggled, you plotted and planned and pleaded. You thought you were gaining a little ground, and you lost it. One night you were kissed and the next morning you were stared at more icily than ever. At the end of it the dark-eyed person was as unmoved towards you as if you had never tried to win his respect at all. He cried when he saw his dog covered in blood, but when he saw you covered in blood he simply took a stick to you with a hard and a bright dry eye. It was pointless trying to make any impression. Dark-eyed people hated you. There was nothing you could do to get past that. "What have I done, Matron? Matron! What have I done?"

"Be silent. And if you've no better thoughts to keep you company, say your tables inside your head."

In Osbourne's office the other five boys stood shoulder to shoulder in front of the desk. Osbourne's voice had an intimidating effect on the boys. It was not the usual brusque attack; it was a wary, careful questioning, which sent a ripple of apprehension down every spine. It was obvious that Creepy had split after all about having the Mike taken out of him. But what became an even more awful possibility which afflicted every boy in turn was the thought that their baiting of him might have brought about his death. Creepy was old, and brittle. He could easily have had a weak heart. Osbourne's voice, judge-like and calm, seemed to confirm the dread.

"Have any of you boys had anything to do with Mr. Charron-Davies during a lesson other than learning music from him?"

There was an embarrassed, cautious silence. One or two tongues came out to lick lips. One foot turned over and jigged on its side. Another put a toe on a rose in the carpet. Several faces turned fiery pink. Osbourne licked his own lips. "Moorhead?"

"Um—n—no, sir—not really, sir."

"Longridge?"

"No, sir, not really, sir." And so on until the end of the line.

Osbourne said, "You boys are lying." And started from the beginning again. "Moorhead?"

"We didn't mean it, sir—it was only a rag."

"A rag?"

"Well, sort of, sir. We didn't mean to do poor old Creep —er, Mr. Davies, in, sir. It worked at first, and then he got mad."

"What worked?"

"Well, sort of ragging him, sir." The effort had crumpled Moorhead's forehead. He was becoming a dried-up source.

Osbourne switched to Claypole: "It's been reported to me that you've been seen with Clifford Minor on your lap and that you were stroking his hair and squeezing his hand. Is this correct?"

"Yes, sir. Well—yes, sir."

"Where did this disgustingly unmanly exhibition take place?"

"In the dormitory, sir, I think, sir. Or it might have been in the common room."

"In the *common* room? In front of the other boys? Did you ever go to any further lengths than this with Clifford Minor?"

"Lengths, sir?"

Osbourne attacked Clifford Minor: "Have you ever repeated this revolting performance with Mr. Charron-Davies?" Clifford Minor gulped. "I want the truth, and I intend to get the truth in the end, so you might just as well spare yourselves a more painful form of investigation."

"I tried, sir," confessed Clifford Minor, "but it didn't come off."

"You *tried*?" Osbourne heard himself repeating.

"Yes, sir. But when it got to my turn he twigged it and he wasn't having any."

"Twigged what?"

"That we were ragging him, sir."

Osbourne sat back with a puzzled line between his eyes. Sanderson took a step forward. He was ten, and he spoke up bravely: "We know it was jolly rotten of us, sir, but we didn't mean to kill him. We didn't know he'd got a weak heart. He tried to make Claypole soppy with him—and it seemed sort of—well, it seemed funny. And when Claypole did it with Clifford for us we all laughed, sir, we couldn't help it, because they looked so funny. And then we bet each other we could make Creep—er—Mr. Davies, ask us to sit on his knee. It was only a rag, sir. We didn't mean to kill him."

Osbourne said, "Thank you, Sanderson. Which of you succeeded in extracting this invitation from Mr. Davies?" Four sheepish hands went up. "Am I to take it that this was simply and solely a matter of being *invited*, that there was never any question of *doing* what Mr. Charron-Davies asked?"

Longridge was broad, and he came from the north. There were still traces of it in his accent, which Bradcombe had not yet conquered. "We should have looked proper daft, perched up on old Creepy's lap, sir." And he grinned at the picture. There was a general intake of breath at the use of the nickname. Osbourne made no comment on it. "What

did you think of Mr. Charron-Davies?" There was a conference of eyes. "You may tell the truth. I shan't blame
you."

"We thought he was rather sissy, sir, and some people
thought he was bats."

Again there was an intake of breath and again Osbourne
made no comment. In fact Sanderson, the most observant
of them, noticed that the tension had slackened. Osbourne's
whole attitude seemed less forbidding and strained. It was
an intangible softening, but it was better than nothing.

Osbourne said, "Mr. Charron-Davies is not dead. He is
merely tired, and he has gone away for a rest. You may go
now, boys. Tell matron to send me Stretton."

That was all. No beaters, no tick-off; just question after
question and a let-off. They had not killed poor old Creepy
after all. The boys went skipping out of Osbourne's study.

When matron pushed Stretton into the room, Smiley was
in it also. Osbourne sat back in his chair and lit a cigarette.
Osbourne said, "The five boys you named, Smiley, are
refreshingly innocent. Now let's hear what you have to
say against Stretton." The tension was back in Osbourne.
He thundered, "Take your hands out of your pockets at
once, Stretton. Keep your arms at your sides, and stand up
straight."

It was impossible for Jimmy to stand any straighter. He
knew it, and shot a quick glare of resentment towards
Osbourne. He might expect to be picked on unjustly by
Osbourne.

"Well, Smiley?" Osbourne said. "Don't forget you've a
train to catch."

Smiley shifted his weight to another foot. "Stretton got
into my bed, sir."

Jimmy's robot position snapped, "Ooh, you liar! I *never*
got into your bed. I was jumping about on top of it.
Matron saw me. She ticked me off, and so did Orson, and
Mrs. Osbourne."

Osbourne interrupted him, "Smiley isn't accusing you of taking his bed away from him this time, Stretton. That was all over and done with long ago. It's something much more serious. This time Smiley is accusing you of sharing it with him. Did you at any time get into bed with Smiley?"

"Get into bed with *him*! Whaffor?"

The boy's genuine astonishment at such an accusation eased the compression of Osbourne's lips and relaxed the stiff line of his shoulders. He said reproachfully, "What for, *sir*."

"He did get into bed with me, sir, lots of times. I told him what Mr. Davies made me do with him—and he said he'd do the same with me if I gave him some tuck."

Osbourne was not looking at Smiley. He was watching Jimmy. The boy's face was bewildered and blank. He never ceased to regret that there had been no other witness to that expression on Jimmy's face.

Jimmy pleaded, "He's telling whoppers, sir. He never gimme any tuck. He never gives anyone any tuck. Orson and the others will tell you that. He just gobbles his own and takes yours."

"And you never got into bed with Smiley or cuddled him or let him pet you in any way?"

"*Cuddled* him?" Jimmy's face screwed up. Osbourne smiled at the outraged expression. It provided all the proof that was needed.

"Very well, you may go now, Stretton."

Jimmy was caught by surprise. "Aren't I going to get a beaters, sir?"

Osbourne leant over the desk at him; he stretched his eyes. "*Whaffor?*"

Jimmy retreated several steps, then turned, and ran out of the room.

Osbourne said to Smiley, "Matron will take you to the station now, Smiley."

Later he said to Rosamund, "It wasn't hard to see through

the little swine. He was just trying to drag the others down with him. It's not surprising he was out for Stretton's blood. He can never have forgiven that punch on the nose."

CHAPTER ELEVEN

THE police were not called in. Rosamund and Neator spent an hour and a half in persuading Osbourne for the sake of the school to leave the decision to Smiley's parents. Neator was right. Their immediate response was to ask that the matter should not be brought into the open. Mr. Smiley paid a visit to the school and succeeded in gaining a reluctant promise from Osbourne that no further action would be taken.

Osbourne's conscience remained uneasy. Rosamund, growing impatient with his scruples, said wearily, "Oh, darling, I do know it's dreadful but this isn't the only school it's happened in, you know."

"I'm quite aware of that," he said. They were going for a walk before prep. The grey sky was closing in for the night and over the beach and the headland the evening threw a cold and stony light.

"I appreciate your White Knight attitude—but don't give yourself complexes about it."

"I'm not in the slightest danger of getting complexes about homosexuality," Osbourne snapped.

"Well, it exists in everyone, so we're told, or rather the possibility of it. It just depends how strong it is, I suppose."

"Rubbish," said Osbourne. "It doesn't exist in decent people."

Jimmy was looking for seagulls' eggs. The wind fidgeted in the heather above his head and below him pushed the sea into petty waves. He was balanced on a ledge in the side of the cliff. He had discovered an undetected path. It ran through the wind-bent copse of stunted trees that stretched to the east side of the house, into the dense furze. It provided a way past the wire that defended the cliff edge. It was possible at one moment to be in the full view of Nancy Hopkins on the playing-field and at the next it was possible to be out of sight. When Nancy Hopkins turned her back he often went looking for seagulls' eggs above Fisherman's Path. This was the only portion of the beach which was not mined, but it was still out of bounds to the boys. The fishermen alone knew the exact safety of its course. John and Rosamund Osbourne knew of it and sometimes risked a stroll on it. It was the wind that brought their voices to Jimmy. Their conversation had changed by then, but their mood had not.

"My good girl, you can't blame yourself for a physical disability any more than you can blame yourself if you have a club-foot. What's the good of another specialist? We know what he'll say. Why pay for the privilege of hearing it again?"

The wind dashed the voices away again, but not until Jimmy had realised that Mr. and Mrs. Osbourne must be heading in his direction. He said, "Oh, cripes!" and looked around for escape. It was impossible to climb upwards, and to go down the way he had come would deposit him neatly in front of the Osbournes. He tried to make his way along to a piece of jutting rock.

When the wind brought the voices back again they were nearer to him and no more friendly to each other.

"But, John, I know it's the biggest disappointment of your life, and your sub-conscious can't help blaming me for it."

"Oh, for the love of God don't bring my sub-conscious into it," Osbourne begged. "You read far too many of those damned psychological books or whatever they are. No wonder you can't think straight. It's you who get the complexes."

Rosamund's interest in psychology and her efforts to introduce it into school life was a bone of contention between them. Osbourne had a hearty distrust of psychology. He considered it harmful and on a par with witchcraft. He thought the analyst's meddling with the sub-conscious not only dangerous but faintly irreligious. He saw no end to the evils such a process might invoke. He thought it the antithesis of wholesomeness and the natural enemy of common sense. He believed every psychiatrist a charlatan and would have been relieved to see every one of them under lock and key.

"The fact that a man deeply wanting a son is bound to resent the wife who can't give him one isn't something you have to discover in books, John. It's obvious."

"But, damn it, I don't resent you. You resent yourself and take it out of me. It was by no means the ambition of my life. I shouldn't give it a thought if you weren't for ever dragging it up. I believe you only do it to make an excuse for a scene."

The foothold upon which Jimmy was depending dislodged and went bounding down over the rocks. He said, "Oh, cripes!" and clutched at an exposed root which hung like a sagging vein on the side of the cliff. The stone came hurtling down towards the beach. Osbourne touched Rosamund's arm: "Look out!"

She stood back as it thudded past them and lodged in the sand. "How could you accuse me of making a scene, John? You never used to say things like that to me." They stood face to face by the runaway stone. Jimmy could hear them no longer, but he could see them. There was a green scarf round Rosamund's fiery head and the collar of Osbourne's old camel-hair coat was turned up. It could only be a matter of minutes before they looked up and saw Jimmy.

"My dear girl, do you realise that you manage to pick a quarrel nearly every day of the week?"

"But you've lost interest in me, John. I know you have."

"Ros, we've been married eleven years. I'm forty-six, you're thirty-seven. I still find you very attractive, but we're bound to have lost the first passionate excitement for each other. We've got something deeper and better in its place and I prefer it. Physical excitement is bound to die down in marriage. Marriage isn't built to sustain it. The newness goes, you get used to each other, and I say you find something much more dependable and worth while. We'd both be content if you'd let us. It's absurd to try and blame the perfectly natural development of a number of years in each other's company on to the fact that I once said I wanted a son." He spoke angrily, weary of her constant bemoaning the loss of the lover in him. He considered his attentions towards her adequate and he was resentful that she could not settle down with the same easy-going acceptance of middle age as he did himself. He did not relish deceiving her, and a schoolmaster had to beware of scandal. He suppressed his occasional inclinations to stray and put everything of himself towards the school. But her jealousy was an imaginative, destructive thing. Sometimes he felt it would be more satisfactory if he gave her a justification for it. She invented reasons and her suspicions exasperated him. She could be jealous of his dog or even of the book he happened to be reading, if she thought it robbed her of his time. He did not realise that she felt life more keenly than he, and that to her he was still attractive.

It was Rosamund who saw Jimmy first. She gripped Osbourne's arm and said, "That's one of our boys."

Osbourne's voice boomed towards Jimmy, "Hold on, Stretton, I'll come up and get you."

This being precisely what Jimmy was most anxious to avoid, he continued to struggle towards the promise of a hiding-place. Below him Osbourne's camel-hair coat looked like a moving sand-patch as he clambered towards the rocks.

Jimmy redoubled his efforts and redoubled his speed. In doing so he slipped. Rosamund, shading her eyes to look at him, covered them with her hands.

At first he was conscious of nothing but the cliff-side streaking past his face. Then he felt a series of savage thrusts against his body as if vicious birds were attacking his falling form. He did not fall far as a matter of feet, but he made a jagged tour of the jutting rocks. Then he rolled down the path which the stone had taken before him, and lodged in the sand not far from it. He was an intimidating sight. Blood made tufts in his hair and spread over his face and neck. His legs and his hands were bright with it, and he was nearly obscured in a layer of clotting sand.

Osbourne, breathing heavily, ran across to him. Rosamund called, "Be careful, John! You're off Fisherman's Path. Be careful." And then shouted wildly, "Come back."

Osbourne paid no attention to her. He bent down and lifted Jimmy up. Jimmy felt a number of shooting pains about his body which made him press his lips together. Then he felt something which impressed him much more. He felt Osbourne's acute concern for him. He felt it in the arms that held him so firmly against the old camel-hair coat, in the gently investigating hands, which he realised were hurting as little as they could, and in the anxious inquiring voice. When his own were freed of blood and sand he could see the concern in Osbourne's eyes. He felt a strange excited surprise that Osbourne should care if he had hurt himself, and that he had risked running over a portion of beach which might have been mined. He was dimly remembering another occasion on which he had come to convince himself that he was really covered in blood. There was more anxiety in Osbourne's eyes than he had seen in the Reverend Jordon's when he stood before him bright red from head to foot.

"Poor old fellow," Osbourne said. "That was a hell of a tumble."

"Has he broken anything?" Rosamund called.

Osbourne was wiping Jimmy's face clean. "Do you think you could tell us where you feel worst, old chap? Does it hurt you inside when you breathe? Does it hurt anywhere when you move?"

Jimmy managed to shake his head against Osbourne's shoulder, although the whole of his body hurt inside and out. Osbourne pressed a handkerchief hard down on the gash by the side of his eye, and carried him back to Rosamund.

She said, "For God's sake, John! You had my heart in my mouth."

"I could hardly leave him there," Osbourne pointed out.

Rosamund tore a piece off the bottom of her petticoat and bandaged Jimmy's grazes and cuts. They were moving towards the path that ran up to the cliff-head. Osbourne walked steadily, carrying Jimmy, his feet sinking down in the sand. Jimmy suddenly struggled in Osbourne's arms. He had caught sight of the camel-hair coat. It was soaked to the lapels and round the cuffs with a dark and spongy stain.

"What is it? Am I hurting you?"

Jimmy said, "Your coat! It's got all red and wet." And he added belatedly, "Sir."

"Never mind," said Osbourne, "there are worse troubles at sea than my coat."

Jimmy was feeling sick by the time they laid him under the hard light of matron's sitting-room. Osbourne's poodle came dancing after them. She sprang up and barked nervously at the bundle in Osbourne's arms. Osbourne said, "Down, Susie, down." Then he shouted, "Will somebody shut this blasted dog up?"

For the first time Jimmy smiled at Osbourne. He felt more important than Osbourne's dog.

Dr. Cromer had a kindly voice: "Well, well. What have we been up to? Fallen out with a man-eating tiger?"

Jimmy had five stitches in the side of his eye, and seven

across his knee-cap. It was a painful and wearing business washing the sand from his wounds. It was Osbourne who held his hand. Jimmy gripped it with all his might. It was Osbourne who carried him up to the bed in the sanatorium, and it was Osbourne who laid him into it while matron held back the fresh white sheets.

Rosamund, standing beside them, said, "Perhaps he'll understand now why the cliffs are out of bounds."

Jimmy gave his apology to Osbourne: "I'm sorry, sir. But I do so love climbing things, and I'm getting too old for trees."

"You'd better join me in the Lakes," smiled Osbourne. "I'll teach you to cling on a bit better than that."

Jimmy lay looking up at him. He felt cold out of Osbourne's arms. He shivered inside the new sheets. Matron's voice came in between them: "You'll not find time to say Mr. Osbourne hates you any more, will you, Jimmy?"

Osbourne turned to look at her, "Does he think I hate him? I'm sorry for that."

He was seized in a startlingly powerful grip. Jimmy had shot up in bed. His strong round arms came near to throttling Osbourne. It seemed as if he could never hold himself close enough to the wearer of the comforting camel-hair coat which Osbourne had not yet removed. He burrowed into the warmth of it, into the wholesome smell of tobacco and the faint but indisputable sense of security. Osbourne felt wet eyes pressed hard against his neck, and he felt a still further surprise.

Jimmy released him, wriggled down in the bed, and covered his head with the sheets in an agony of sudden embarrassment.

Rosamund asked, "What on earth happened then?"

Osbourne replied, smiling, "He kissed me."

"Good gracious! Eight years old is too old for that sort of thing."

"Oh, I expect it was only a 'thank you'."

"He's getting a big boy now," matron agreed.

"Yes, poor little devil," Osbourne said, "he could pass for three and a half in a good light."

CHAPTER TWELVE

THE Reverend Jordon had a letter from Jimmy. It arrived on the last day of term.

> 'Dear Sir, I like it *much much best* with Mr. Osbourne. Lots of boys stay on in the hols, so please could I stay. *Please*. Your obeddent son, Jimmy.'

The Reverend Jordon put the letter at the back of a drawer. He saw no reason for Anita to be wounded by it, as he had been wounded himself.

Jimmy did not realise that he had given the Reverend Jordon no time to reply, so he jumped off the London-bound train which was taking the boys home on holiday. Anthony Neator was in charge of the group bound for Paddington.

Jimmy lurched down the shaking corridor on the pretext of going to the lavatory. He passed it without even attempting the door. He walked right to the end of the train. He was waiting until such time as the tracks should run close to a bank. He sat in an empty carriage watching the scenery slide past. When the train came to a halt at a level-crossing he opened the door and jumped. He pitched on to his head down a deep grass bank, somersaulted into a weed-choked ditch, and crawled out. He felt none of his bruises yet. He lay in the grass until the train had passed. Then he went to the signal-box. "Please could you telephone Etherton 202 and ask for Mr. Osbourne. I've fallen off the train."

He was eating an apple when Osbourne and Rosamund drove out to collect him. He saw them arrive from the window. He slipped the apple core into his shirt. When they followed the signalman up the stairs he was lying on the floor.

" 'Allo," said the signalman, startled. "He was right as rain just now."

Osbourne picked Jimmy up. The camel-hair coat had been cleaned. It came back with a notice pinned to it: 'It has been impossible to remove all the stains from this garment, although expert methods have been employed. It is thought, nevertheless, that you will be pleased with the improvement.'

Osbourne carried him out to the waiting car, "What the devil can Neator have been about? We'd better go straight to Cromer's."

Jimmy murmured, "I'm afraid I'm most terribly hurt, sir. I shan't get better for weeks and weeks. Can people stay in the san. till next term, sir?"

Osbourne said, "Cheer up, old chap. It won't be as bad as all that."

Rosamund leant forward. "Just how did you fall from that train," she asked Jimmy.

Jimmy sat up, button-bright and excited: "I leant against the door, Mrs. Osbourne, and it swung right open—and I went head over heels and plop. I spun and spun and spun. It's a wonder I wasn't dead."

"Where was Mr. Neator?" Osbourne asked.

"Oh, it wasn't his fault, sir," Jimmy said. "He was right down at our end of the train."

"Why weren't you down at your end of the train?" Rosamund asked.

"What are you getting at, Ros?" said Osbourne.

Rosamund sat back. "Never mind."

Dr. Cromer could find nothing wrong with Jimmy, but he advised that the boy should be kept in bed. "He's had a pretty good shaking up, and there might be a question of shock."

Matron had gone back to Paignton. It was Rosamund who made up the bed in the sanatorium. Jimmy took a leap into it: "Ooh, Mrs. Osbourne, the sheets are cold."

"Stretton," said Rosamund. "You do realise that Mr. Osbourne doesn't stay here all the time during the holidays, don't you? He always has a fortnight up in the Lake District, so you wouldn't see very much of him."

Jimmy said, "Yes, but it's only a fortnight, and then *he* comes back and *you* go away." His voice was triumphant and jubilant, and his eyes seemed alive with delight.

When Osbourne came to say good-night Jimmy sprang up and trapped his sleeve. "Sir, Muggeridge and Foster and Stevens and Lowry—they all stay right through the hols—couldn't I, sir? Because I've been hurt—I'm really most unfit to travel. I *am*, sir, I'm stiffening up."

Osbourne disentangled himself. "Muggeridge and Stevens's parents are in India. Foster's are out in Teheran and Lowry's are in North Africa. They have to stay here in the holidays. They haven't got homes to go to."

"Neither have I, sir, honestly, sir. My old man hates me. If you ring him up and say could I stay here he'll be only too pleased to say yes. Oh, *please*, sir, I won't be a nuisance. I can be most stroarn'ly good. I'm a pleasure to have, Pam's mum says so."

"I've yet to see it," Osbourne smiled. "Now, you bed yourself down and get off to sleep."

When he went into the study Rosamund handed him a gin and French. "My verdict is suicide while the balance of the mind was disturbed. What's yours?"

"Careless little devil," Osbourne said. "He might have broken his neck."

"I don't think it was carelessness, John. I think it was deliberate. He threw himself out of that train."

Osbourne lowered the glass from his mouth. "In the

name of God why should he? Have you forgotten his age?
Kids of eight don't do things like that."

"Surely you realise the child simply worships you, John?
You're not usually so far behind. The whole thing was
done on purpose to stay at school with you."

"You mean to tell me that that wretched boy is so miserable at home that he is willing to risk his neck in order to
stay at school?"

"In order to stay with *you*, John."

"If the child threw himself off the train rather than go
back to his father, the father must be a swine."

"Stretton can wind you round his little finger, John."
She had touched on his most stringent rule.

"You're not suggesting that I show Stretton favouritism?
You know perfectly well I am incapable of that sort of
thing."

"You were once upon a time, but you are in danger of
becoming capable of it. Do you realise that you've upheld
Stretton on every single occasion that he's come up before
you?"

"If I've upheld Stretton there's been a good reason for it.
I've treated him no differently from any other boy. Stretton's
not much more than a baby, and he's obviously been done
out of babyhood. He's naturally affectionate and he grasps
at any outlet for it. What do you want me to do? Pour a
bucket of cold water over him and command him to grow
up overnight? I'll find out about this train business,
though."

He went upstairs to the sanatorium. He found Jimmy
awake and flushed. "Hallo," Osbourne said, "not asleep
yet."

"No, sir, I tried, but I can't." Jimmy's lips were dry.
Osbourne felt his pulse. "Are you in pain, old man?"

"No, sir," Jimmy lied.

"Are you sure you feel all right?"

"Yes, sir, thank you, sir, almost, sir." Every bone in his

body ached and stabbed. He was shocked and frightened
that pretence could have turned so quickly into real pain.

Osbourne sat down on the bed, "Jimmy. Are you sure
you fell out of that train?"

"Yes, sir."

"Do you think it friendly to lie to me, Jimmy?"

"No, sir."

"Did you jump out?"

"Yes, sir."

"What made you do a terrible thing like that, Jimmy?"

"I wanted to stay here with you, sir."

Osbourne telephoned to the Reverend Jordon. His voice
was ungenerous and cold. "Your son threw himself off the
school train rather than go home to you. He's not hurt, but
he's badly shaken up."

The Reverend Jordon cleared his throat. He sounded
faded and far away on the indistinct line. "I see. Thank you.
Will you be able to keep him with you a while, then?"

Osbourne said, "Yes," and hung up.

CHAPTER THIRTEEN

AT the end of the next term it was the Reverend Jordon who
wrote:

'As you must know, it has caused your Aunt Anita and
myself considerable disappointment to feel that you have
again preferred to remain resident at school during the
holiday period. There is, I am aware, not much in the
line of recreation or companionship in Channock, and
presumably at school attention is devoted to your enter-
tainment. My work and my lack of assistance make it
difficult for me to place as much time at your disposal as I
should like, and I am not insensitive to the fact that the

vicarage with its absence of young company may be dull
for a boy of your age. It is, however, your home, and I
should be saddened to think that there might ever come
a time when you would cease to regard it as such. For
the sake of your Aunt Anita, I think it would be advisable
if you divided your holiday period between the school
and your home.'

"Wordy old blighter, isn't he?" Jimmy remarked. "Does
it say I can stay or not stay?" He was showing the letter to
Osbourne and to Rosamund.

"Don't let me hear you refer to your father as an old
blighter again," Osbourne said sharply. "It says you may
stay a fortnight here and a fortnight there. I should have
thought that was clear enough."

"Can I go home the fortnight you're away, then, sir?"

"Yes, I should think that could be arranged."

Jimmy bore his visit to the vicarage with a none too well
disguised resignation. He spent most of his time at No. 15
Alma Row, and could never hide his delight as the moment
for returning to Bradcombe approached. What time he did
spend with the Reverend Jordon was usually given over to
religious instruction. There were moments, however, when
the Reverend Jordon invited companionship. He worked
harder and at a greater pace in order to spare the time.
With a rare free hour on his hands he sat by Anita's
economical fire and asked Jimmy questions about his school
life.

Jimmy's part was restricted to disinterested answers. He
was anxious to be on his way down to Pam's. He boxed at
five-thirty with William Houghton. In the firelight he made
a stealthy check on the clock with his wrist-watch.

"Mr. Osbourne must be a remarkably fine person to have
made you admire him so much."

Jimmy said, "Yes, he's quite decent."

The Reverend Jordon recognised the embarrassed understatement of hero-worship. He smiled at it. "All right," he said. "You can run along now." He was so obviously detaining the boy.

Jimmy jumped up with alacrity and left his father for once wondering what to do with the remainder of the time he had taken such pains to have left on his hands. As with the death of Margaret, he did everything in his power to see that no one should realise that the arrangement for his son to remain at school for part of his holidays was one which occasioned him considerable personal hurt. It was an arrangement which lasted several years. Only two out of the four persons who were most closely concerned with it wished it to change—the Reverend Jordon and Rosamund Osbourne.

In the term Osbourne's preference for Jimmy was undetectable. In the holidays it was apparent to Rosamund alone. He made no noticeable distinction between Jimmy and any other boy. It was only detectable in the way that he spoke of him to Rosamund. Sometimes in the evening he put down his paper, not even bothering to identify Jimmy by name: "That little devil's language is appalling. I imagine it must be the influence of 'Pam's dad'. I can hardly believe it's the parson's."

"You ought to tell him about it, John."

"Tell him about it! I've beaten him for it."

And on other occasions, "I wonder what he'll do with his life? He doesn't seem to have a bent for the Church."

"There *are* other boys in the school, John," Rosamund pointed out.

Once, on the night before term started, Osbourne and the boys were playing a game which had become a tradition. It was a variation of hunt-the-thimble. Osbourne hid a shilling on his person, and the boy who discovered it kept the prize. They shook, jostled and half-lynched him in the search. Muggeridge clung crablike to his back, Foster inspected his turn-ups, Stevens burrowed in his trouser-pockets, and Jimmy and Lowry sat astride his knee, systematically searching his waistcoat pockets.

Rosamund brought in the tea-tray. She snapped, "Get down at once, Stretton. You're too old to sit on Mr. Osbourne's lap."

Osbourne laughed, "Why pick on Stretton? Aren't the others too old as well?"

Rosamund would have been surprised if she had been told that she was jealous of Jimmy Stretton. She was aware perhaps of a spark of resentment towards Osbourne's obvious pleasure in the boy's admiration for him, but her chief concern was that he might relax his well-known rules in connection with favouritism, and she felt it would be to his discredit if he departed from them noticeably. She could not bear the possibility of his losing respect. She was quite unaware that she resented their close companionship. It was not that she felt excluded by them, it was simply annoying to feel that there was any question of her having to be included. But she was aware of an unreasonable dislike for Jimmy, and she recognised its cause. She felt that he had stepped into the shoes of the non-existing child she had so longed for for herself and Osbourne. It was as if Osbourne had secured himself a son with no help from herself. Jimmy was missing a father, Osbourne was missing a son. Their companionship seemed a natural combination.

When Muggeridge's parents came home from abroad, when Stevens and Lowry left, and when Major the Honourable and Mrs. Tracy Foster came home on leave, Jimmy was the only boy who could still make it impossible for the Osbournes to holiday together.

Rosamund said, "Darling, do you realise we're free?"

Osbourne said, "What about Stretton?"

Rosamund said, "Let him get to know his own Reverend father. He sounds delightful on the phone."

"I thought he sounded about as human as a mechanical foster-mother."

"Then Stretton should be given the opportunity of melting his heart."

Osbourne said, "Couldn't we take the little chap with us? He'd love scrambling about in the Lakes."

Rosamund answered curtly, "No."

CHAPTER FOURTEEN

THE holiday was not a success. If the weather was fine, Osbourne climbed and Rosamund took short walks, read books on psychology, and longed for the evening to come. When it did, Osbourne read detective stories and looked forward to the morning. If it was wet, Osbourne stared out of the window grumbling about the rain. When they returned to Bradcombe they were both disgruntled and depressed.

Osbourne cheered up immediately. Jimmy was lying in wait for him. He ran up excited and out of breath. "Good evening, Mr. Osbourne. Good evening, Missisosbourne. Did you bring back the snaps of Scafell, sir, and did you get lost in the mists?"

"Tell you about it later," Osbourne smiled, "and I'll pass round the snaps in class."

"Oo, thank you, sir," Jimmy squeaked.

"You know, that boy's really keen on climbing," Osbourne observed with satisfaction to Rosamund.

At the staff tea in the state sitting-room Osbourne laughed when the cream of a bun cascaded down his chin, joked with Neator about the inevitable superiority of sailing over climbing, and accused matron of having a lover in Paignton. They had seldom seen him so unrestrained.

Matron said, "It's easy enough to see you've had a good time, Mr. Osbourne."

Rosamund told him afterwards, "It was hardly flattering

to see a man so obviously overjoyed at getting back to his work after the rigours of spending the first holiday for years alone with his wife."

Osbourne replied, "Oh, for God's sake."

Three days later five boys were sent up to him for a beating. They were Claypole, Longridge, Clifford Minor, the orderly Orson, and Stretton. Osbourne was enthroned behind the great flat desk. Rosamund sat knitting a school scarf. Anthony Neator accompanied the boys. "At first I couldn't go after them, sir. I couldn't make out where they'd got through. This lot, with the exception of Stretton, were watching the game. I was up by the wicket and suddenly saw Orson drop down in the grass. The others had already disappeared. I spotted Orson crawling off and shouted at him. He says he didn't hear, but I'm certain he did. When I went down on the beach they were clambering about on the cliffs."

Osbourne said, "Where was Stretton?"

"He was bowling, sir. He wasn't out of bounds. I just brought him along because I thought you ought to have a word with him. Apparently it was he who mapped out the escape route for them."

Orson spoke up in his patient voice: "It wasn't Stretton's fault, sir. We held a pillow on his face till his legs waved as a signal he'd tell us."

"It was only a rag, sir," squeaked Longridge. "He wouldn't tell us how to get round the wire at first. He was holding out on us, he was blacklead-swinging."

"I fancy you are somewhat confused, Longridge, between lead-swinging and blacklegging." Osbourne leant back in his chair. "Stretton, perhaps you could give a slightly less complicated account of how you were involved in this matter."

"It was where I'd got through before, sir. When I fell over the cliff, I mean. It was my private way out, and I didn't see why they should use it."

"Am I to understand that you have used it yourself since your accident?"

"Well, sir, yes, sir. Just once or twice, sir."

Orson spoke up again: "He only gave a sort of clue, sir." And Orson recited dutifully:

"White is white and black is black
And some silly sausages will find it at the back."

"If you found your way out of the grounds on those flimsy instructions, Orson," Osbourne said, "you should prove a skilled navigator in later life."

"There's a white post and a black post, sir," Jimmy explained, "just before you get there. But they were really only ragging, sir. I think they would've let me breathe in the end."

Osbourne said, "Stretton, you should know better than any other boy why it's necessary to put the place out of bounds. Any one of these boys might have hurt themselves as much as you did, or have broken their necks, and you would have helped them to do so. In future be a little more thoughtful towards the safety of others and if I ever hear of you being out on those cliffs again yourself you'll be expelled. Is that clear?"

"Yes, sir."

"Very well, you may go." The other boys received four strokes of the cane apiece.

Rosamund said quietly to Osbourne, "You're adopting a short-sighted policy with Stretton. He'll lose any respect for you he's ever had." Outside the clouds were lowering, making black clumps of the heather. The air was clinging and filled with thunder threats. "You should have beaten him with the others."

"But he was only indirectly involved. He wasn't out of bounds himself."

"He was responsible for the whole thing. He admitted to

having been out of bounds on other occasions, and as usual
he got away with it."

Osbourne lit a cigarette. Anger was close to his voice
and his eyes. "I don't think I've ever heard a more grossly
distorted interpretation of facts. Orson admitted that they
held him down."

"You're side-tracking, John. Stretton was as guilty as
the others, by implication, and you let him off."

"Very well," said Osbourne. "We'll see what Neator has
to say."

They waited for Neator in silence. When he came in
Osbourne asked him, "Neator, do you think I showed
Stretton favouritism just now?"

"No, sir, I don't."

"My wife thinks I should have beaten him. Do you?"

"I don't see how you could wallop the little blighter, sir,
for something he got away with last term. It would put him
against telling the truth, and you gave him a stiff enough
warning."

Osbourne said, "Thank you, Neator," and to Rosamund
when he had gone, "Well?"

"Tony doesn't know the facts."

"What are the facts?"

"That you are quite obsessed with this child."

"Rubbish!"

"Right from the beginning when he punched Smiley on
the nose—he didn't get punished for that." She looked
gentle in the thundery light. "You never even remonstrated
with him for going out of bounds when he hurt himself."

"Well, good God, I thought a toss like that was punishment enough."

"It obviously wasn't, or he wouldn't have gone out of
bounds again. And when he jumped off the train you
played straight into his hands. You should have sent him
back to his father. You should never have started this
business of his spending his holidays here."

"But that confounded parson asked me to keep up the arrangement."

"And you agreed only too willingly. John!" She laid her long hand on his head. "Have you ever heard me accuse you of being unfair before?"

It was true that he had not. He relied on her judgment greatly. There had been times when it had stood him in excellent stead. He sat back to think about it. "Ros, I'm sure I was right on this occasion. I swear I was right on all of them."

Rosamund shook her head. "It's not fair to him, John. He'll go through life thinking he can get away with anything he wants to. You always have listened to me, I'm closest to you, I can see you best."

He had a great fear of spoiling Jimmy. He did an unprecedented thing. He had never reversed a decision before. He sighed when he sent for Jimmy.

When Jimmy came into the room he said, "Stretton. I have decided that I let you off too lightly this afternoon. You'll get the same as the other boys."

"But I wasn't out of bounds, sir. Mr. Neator will tell you that."

"If you stand there and argue with me, my boy, you'll get double the dose." And he gave Jimmy five hard strokes.

Jimmy bent over and kept his lower lip between his teeth. There was considerable power in Osbourne's arm. Rosamund's portrait hung on the wall. It was a wispy and elfin affair in chalk. Jimmy's eyes slipped round to it. He wondered how it must feel to be Mrs. Osbourne and always to be in Osbourne's good books. He discovered that he envied Mrs. Osbourne. She could keep a smile trapped in Osbourne's eyes and she was never addressed in Osbourne's precisely timed school voice. It was this business of being a girl again. Everything went right for girls. He wondered what it was about them which gave them their extraordinary privileges. He stared at the portrait again. He did not think

he liked Mrs. Osbourne's eyes. They were too roundly blue
and too chilly. He did not mind her mouth and he liked
the curve of her neck and the soft bones where it joined the
bottom of her throat. But best of all he liked her legs. They
were long and smooth and silky. He could understand Mr.
Osbourne liking those. He would have liked to have had
legs like that himself. They made his own feel too stumpy
and short. He would have liked her shapely hands as well.
His own grew too square and too practical. He was
surprised as he gazed up at the picture to find that he hated
Mrs. Osbourne so much. It was obviously an enormous
asset to look as she looked. He wished that he had everything Mrs. Osbourne had to trap the smile in Osbourne's
eyes. There would be no unfair beaters, no tick-offs, and no
wounded feelings if you had pretty, long, silky legs. There
was another advantage too. You could shed tears when you
had to say good-bye to Mr. Osbourne with no fear of him
thinking you sissy. When he went off to the Lakes by himself for his holiday Mrs. Osbourne nearly always cried. But
nobody called her a sissy. She stood at the door with her
cheeks quite wet when Mr. Osbourne went over and kissed
her. It was a fine life, being a girl.

CHAPTER FIFTEEN

HE had forgotten Mr. Osbourne. When he came out of his
reverie Mr. Osbourne was in the middle of a sentence.
". . . and while I don't doubt my wife would be highly
flattered at your close interest in her portrait I feel I have a
right to claim your attention too. It seems to me some
considerable while since I had it."

Jimmy jumped. "I—oo I—gosh, I'm sorry, sir."

"So I should think. I'm not used to boys going off into
day-dreams when I'm in the middle of talking to them. I

don't think I know what to do with you, Stretton. You
obviously take advantage of kindness. I have a feeling that
I may have been blaming your father unjustly. I've done
everything in my power to make up for any deficiency you
might have felt in your home-life and the only way you repay
me is to threaten me with a perpetual ache in my right arm.
You don't seem to mind being beaten."

Jimmy stared down at the ground. If you said 'Yes' it
might mean you were a coward. If you said 'No' it would
be defiant and rude. You could not possibly say that to be
beaten by Mr. Neator, or anyone else for that matter, was
painful only on the spot that it happened to contact, but that
to be beaten by Mr. Osbourne hurt differently. If you said
that, it would be sissy. And if you confessed that to be
beaten unfairly by Mr. Osbourne went on hurting, it would
be even more sissy.

Jimmy was fighting a rising panic. Mr. Osbourne hated
squirters and he felt himself unbelievably starting to cry.
He fought the tears with a series of furious grimaces, grating
and clenching his teeth. Osbourne mistook it for temper.
He put down the cane he was holding. "Very well, Stretton.
Consider yourself dismissed."

Jimmy raced over the playground. From the window
Osbourne saw him and swore with his hands on his hips.
The playground was out of bounds after five. Jimmy was on
his way to a hole by the rockery. It was the successor to the
kitchen cupboard under the vicarage sink. He ran with his
head down and his fists doubled. He cannoned into Anthony
Neator, a striped scarf lying flat on the wind behind him.
Osbourne took his hands off his hips. He watched Neator
addressing the boy. Jimmy kept his head down as if he had
broken his neck. Neator put a hand beneath his chin and
stood looking into his face. Then he ruffled the already
blowing hair and they passed each other by. Jimmy made a
bolt for the rockery. Neator sauntered towards the house.

Osbourne called him in. Neator's young voice was

embarrassed. "I'm sorry, sir. I know I should have pulled him up about being out of bounds, but the poor little devil seemed so upset. He thinks the world of you, sir, and . . . and when you—well, after you beat him——" Neator broke off, even more embarrassed. "Well, he seemed so upset. He's got some sort of hide-out in that direction, and he wanted to get his crying over somewhere he couldn't be seen."

"All right, Tony," Osbourne nodded at him. "In this instance you did the right thing."

For one unaccountable moment he was jealous of Anthony Neator because there had never been an occasion upon which the latter could reproach himself for being unfair.

He was still smoking hard at the window when Jimmy streaked back across the playground. He had not spent long in tears. Osbourne tapped on the window and beckoned to him. Jimmy skidded to a standstill with fright. He said wearily, "Oh, cripes."

He came like a reluctant dog to Osbourne's insistent beckoning and gave a small tap upon the door. Osbourne was not at the big flat desk. He was sitting in Rosamund's chair by the fire. When Jimmy came in he was reassuring. "It's all right, Stretton. Mr. Neator explained that you'd had permission." Jimmy said nothing, averting his head. "Come here, Stretton," Osbourne said. Jimmy took two steps forward. "I hear that you *do* mind being beaten."

Jimmy mumbled, "Yes, sir."

"I am relieved to hear it, Stretton," Osbourne said. "I was beginning to wonder what it was you did mind about."

Jimmy began to shake. He felt it creep up the back of his sturdy legs, he felt it trembling up his spine, across his flat shoulders, and into his lips. He tried to induce a ram-rod stiffness to fight the shameful trembling off. He felt the tears jump savagely back to his eyes. He whispered, "Please, sir, could I go?"

Osbourne answered, "No."

The trembling had climbed to the top of his head. Osbourne said gently, "I think I should try to take it easy. Do you often get worked up like this?"

"No, sir."

"Did this last beating hurt you much?"

"No, sir."

Embarrassment overtook Jimmy. He was chewing his lips to pieces and distorting the line of his mouth. You could not tell him that once he had stopped you from feeling lonely because he minded when he found you were covered in blood. You could not say that he had brought back the loneliness doublefold because he beat you with a hard and dry look in his eye for something for which you were not to blame. It was best to say nothing and stare at the floor.

Osbourne held out a hand to him. "Come nearer, Stretton. Sit down." Jimmy shuffled nearer. He refused the outstretched hand. But he sat on the beaded stool which Rosamund used for her feet. Osbourne leant down to talk to him. "You think I was unfair to you today, don't you?"

"I didn't say you were unfair to me, sir."

"I'm aware that you didn't. *I'm* saying it."

The truth came out at last. It came out in a gabbled stream. "I only minded because it was you, sir, and it isn't because you beat hard, Mr. Neator beats twice as hard as you, but I expect that's because you're so old. You see, it's sissy to mind about masters, sir, everyone hates the masters —I mean some people don't think you're too bad, sir, but I don't think they'd mind if you died or anything. But I should, really I should, sir, I'd rather Mr. Neator died."

Osbourne put back his head and laughed. Then he leant forward seriously. "Jimmy, it was because I didn't want you to think me a sissy that I beat you unfairly today. Do you think you can understand any of that?"

Jimmy nodded, although he could not. But he knew that

all was well again by the smile that was trapped in Osbourne's eyes.

"Would your father let you visit the Lakes during one of the holidays?"

Jimmy might have been fired off the foot-stool. He landed in Osbourne's lap. As he clambered up Osbourne's body his voice came in breathless and unbelieving squeaks. All trace of embarrassment was gone. He had not felt so natural with Osbourne since the days of hunt the shilling.

"Oi, oi!" said Osbourne. "What do you think I am, Scafell?"

Jimmy tugged at his lapels and grabbed at his hands, "Oh, sir, could it be these hols? Could it be these hols, please?"

"Get off, you young scoundrel, you're too big to nurse!"

"I'm tons big enough to climb up Scafell, sir. Tell me about it again, sir. Oh, go on, sir, be a sport. Tell how you thought you knew better than anyone else and got stuck out all night." He wriggled himself into a more comfortable position on Osbourne's lap, with no consideration for Osbourne's shins. "Go on, sir, when you spent the night out in the mist, and the friend who came to rescue you got drunk."

Osbourne told of the time when the friend who had joined in the search for him drank all the brandy intended to thaw him. "But his breath did the trick," laughed Osbourne, "and it was me who had to carry him down and put him straight to bed."

"Can you always smell drink on people's breath, sir?"

"Always," Osbourne warned him. "So beware if you're thinking of knocking back a pint. I'll be able to tell at once. Off with you now, you'll be late for prep."

Jimmy asked with interest, "Could I smell it on your breath now, sir?"

"Certainly not," Osbourne said. He leant forward and blew towards Jimmy. Jimmy leant forward and sniffed.

Rosamund came in at that moment. She went straight out again.

CHAPTER SIXTEEN

OSBOURNE went in search of her. He found her in tears in the stationery-room. Osbourne looked at the end of a cigarette and propped himself up in the doorway. "It's always been my experience that whenever you turn out the stationery cupboard you're upset."

"Upset! I've never seen anything so disgusting in the whole of my life."

Osbourne inhaled in silence. Then he asked, "Ros, what have you got against Stretton?"

"I've got nothing against him, except that I think that he has an extremely unhealthy passion for you and I'm beginning to think that it's unhealthily reciprocated."

"Are you accusing me of infanta homosexuality on the strength of finding me with a very unhappy small boy on my knee?" Osbourne was laughing at her.

The smile in his eyes infuriated her. "Have you *ever*, in the whole time you've been at Bradcombe, taken one of the boys on your lap before in the privacy of your own study?"

"I don't think I've ever come across a boy whose home circumstances required such a gesture." He smiled at her tragic face.

"John! You do realise how much I love you, don't you?"

"My dear, on occasions, I must say I see no signs of it at all." The lights hissed high up in the stationery-room. Bradcombe was lit by gas. Osbourne trod his cigarette-stub out underfoot. "Ros, I've been thinking for some time lately that you ought to get away for a bit."

"To leave no one between you and Stretton? When I came in this evening, John, you'd just been kissing him." Osbourne laughed out loud. "You're no better than Creepy

Davies. You know what you thought of him. You know what he was! Taking boys on his knee and petting them, kissing them to give them confidence, kissing them to comfort them. Cuddling and kissing them to make up for unfortunate home circumstances." Her voice rose above the wind outside.

The smile had left Osbourne's eyes. "You haven't by any chance started the change of life, have you, Ros? I hear it can produce the most extraordinary delusions and some people do start young." Rosamund slapped his face. Osbourne said, "Stretton was trying to see if he could smell any alcohol in my breath."

It was Rosamund who laughed. Osbourne spoke quietly to her. "The kindest thing to say of you at the moment is that you have temporarily tal·en leave of your senses. I suggest you see matron and have an early night. Stretton was upset to the point of collapse, entirely due to my treatment of him. Some form of human understanding was bound to be established between us, unless I cared to be responsible for confused thinking in the boy later on."

"Did it necessitate Creepy Davies methods?"

Osbourne walked out of the room.

Rosamund did not address him until half-past three on the afternoon of the following day. He was correcting Latin papers in the green and claret study.

"John, matron tells me that Stretton says you've promised to take him climbing in the Lakes. I don't quite know how to tell you how much I hope that isn't true."

"It's absolutely true. He's extremely keen to climb."

"If you take Stretton away these holidays I shan't be coming with you. I shall go home to my parents at once." Osbourne did not look up. His dark hair seldom shone, but it was healthily thick and alive. She saw the downward drop of the lines she loved, that ran from the nose to the mouth. They made her hand catch at her throat. "John, did you hear what I said?"

"I did. And I think it's a splendid idea. I'm not too happy having to put a good face on it with someone who's accused me of having homosexual relations with one of my own boys."

Rosamund came to the desk. "You of all people, John! One of the finest, the best—the—do you realise what it means, John? Do you realise what this ghastly thing means? It's the filthiest and most abominable—you *know* what it means. In your position it means the end of everything we've ever worked for together. You saw what it meant to Arthur Charron-Davies. It shattered and finished his life. I wouldn't demean myself to pity him, but he's an outcast. He's worse than a leper. He's loathed. He was lucky he didn't get sent to prison. He would have been if Smiley's parents hadn't wanted to keep the thing quiet."

Osbourne looked up at last. His voice was sarcastic and deep. "With such a depressing example in front of me I assure you I shall exercise nothing but the utmost discretion and care."

"I'm asking you, John. I'm begging you not to take Stretton with you. I want you to send him away from the school altogether."

Before she left the room Osbourne said to her, "My dear, are you quite sure you haven't been conducting an illicit affair with Orson? You've always had your eye on him, and I must confess I should find it embarrassing to have to cite such a very much younger man."

Outside, three seagulls behind the window swooped above Osbourne's head. The gong sounded loud and dismally inside the house to summon the boys to tea.

Osbourne put up a notice in school hall. It read, 'Will any boys interested in taking part in a climbing holiday in the Lake District sign their names below? Permission must be obtained from parents first.'

Five names appeared on the list, 'J. H. Stretton. S. L. C. Moorhead. R. D. Burgess. F. Claypole. D. G. Morris.'

Easter was fine in the Lakes. Osbourne chose Grasmere as a centre, and took rooms for himself and the boys in the village. They appeared to share one all-consuming ambition in common—to be lost for the night in the mist. Osbourne started them off on Helvellyn. They set out in the morning, a chattering train in Osbourne's wake, full of hopeful speculations as to the possibilities of not returning.

"I heard of a man who was stuck out on a ledge for two months and all he had to eat was raw sheep."

"Sir," said Jimmy, "when can we climb Scafell?"

"Sir," said Moorhead, "is this what they call a tarn?"

"No," Osbourne called back.

"Why don't they call it a tarn, sir?"

"Because they know it isn't one. I should have thought it might have struck even you as being an ordinary puddle."

"Sir," called portly Burgess, "is there a place to have tea at the top?"

"What a scandalous suggestion," Osbourne said. "Is it impossible for you to take your mind off of your stomach, Burgess?"

"Can we come back through Patterdale, sir?" asked Claypole, "like you do, sir?"

"No, it's too far," said Osbourne.

"Why is it too far, sir?"

"Oh really, Claypole! I do hope we don't find your mental powers getting lower and lower the higher you climb. It's too far because it's too far."

They shot questions at him with the same pelting brusqueness as they shot stones from under their feet. Their knees and their hands and their noses were red. Their eyes were as bright as the clear Easter sky. Osbourne, looking back at them, saw Claypole punch Morris's head. "You and your daft old sheep! How did he eat through the wool?"

"He had to wait till it was rotten, see? Then it came off in tufts and he sucked the meat off the end."

"Get out! Anyway, mutton's not meat."

" 'Tis."

" 'Tis *not*."

"What is it, then?"

"Mutton of course, silly."

Osbourne smiled to himself as he anticipated the noisy scramble to catch him up. They surrounded him in a breathless bombardment, oblivious to the gracious calm of Brothers Water and the green beauty pocketed between the hills beneath the wind-harassed sky. "Sir, mutton's *not* meat, is it, sir?"

"Meat *is* mutton, isn't it, sir?"

"No, it's not, sir, is it? It's like pork, isn't it?"

Morris clamoured anxiously. "Sir, tell him that meaton's not mutt."

Sandy-haired Claypole was convulsed with laughter, showing great gaps in his teeth. He doubled up, hugging his sides. "Sir! He said, 'Meaton's not mutt!' Did you hear him, sir? He said, 'Meaton's not mutt.' "

The spoonerism so amused Claypole that it seemed as if he would never straighten up.

Osbourne stood laughing down at him. "I'm afraid we weren't far out in our fears for your mental decline, Claypole."

The earth swept round him in violent upward curves that rose to granite peaks. The young greens vied with the warm glowing tints that autumn had left behind. There was not a familiar line of it that was not beloved to Osbourne. As he stood looking out on it he felt his whole inner being revived. Helvellyn, a spreading climb ahead of him, rose blue-tipped to puncture a lead-coloured cloud. When the cloud lifted it left lagging shreds which still clung to the long black line of Striding Edge. The wind brought a soft, eager scent from the fells. Osbourne filled his lungs with it, like a man gulping water to quench a desert thirst. Jimmy was standing beside him: "Gosh, sir, isn't it wizard?"

"I have heard more poetical appreciations of it, Stretton,"

Osbourne smiled at him, "but I'm delighted you like it so much."

It was when he returned from taking the boys to see the Wordsworth museum and cottage that he found Rosamund waiting for him.

He walked quickly to where she sat in the hotel lounge. She had the straight figure that suited tweeds. She had chosen a check with a rust colour in it that followed the glints in her hair. She looked very young and sad. He smiled at her, "Hullo, Ros."

"Hullo, John."

Moorhead said, "Mrs. Osbourne, Wordsworth couldn't put the whole of his name on his attaché-case, so he jumped some of the letters on top of each other. You can see them in his house."

"They wore sun-glasses even then, Mrs. Osbourne. His didn't look half bad."

Claypole came giggling towards her. "Mrs. Osbourne, do you know what Morris said?"

"Now, now, Claypole," Osbourne interrupted, "I think we've really exhausted meaton's not mutt."

The freckled-nosed Claypole collapsed into laughter.

Osbourne took Rosamund upstairs to his room. Before he had closed the door she was in his arms. He held her and kissed her forehead. "I must say this feels a bit more like home."

"I can't think what got into me. It was a terrible thing to accuse you of."

He laughed and held her closer to him. "If I'd been guilty of that sort of thing I shouldn't be here to accuse. I'd have put a bullet through my head long ago."

"Yes," she said, "I believe you would." They swayed side to side in each other arms. "Oh! John, you never had any intention of bringing Stretton alone."

"No. I never had any intention of it."

"Why didn't you tell me you were bringing other boys too?"

"I didn't feel all that much socially inclined towards you. I'm afraid I was blowed if I would."

Her slender weight hung from his neck. She felt as small and as lonely as Jimmy had done when he sat up in bed and caught Osbourne in the quick embrace that had sent him slithering under the sheets in embarrassment. She felt very much as Jimmy had done in the tight-gripping need of her arms.

"John darling, I love you. I love you so much. I was jealous of Stretton. I do know that now."

"Mad!" Osbourne smiled at her. "Mad!"

"I thought he was giving you something I couldn't."

He took her face in his hands. "No one could give me what you do, Ros." In his arms she felt a promise of the eleven years sliding away. She sensed a new tenderness, a new need of her. It was as if something in him were groping for help and as if he had turned to her afresh and in the freshness found her young and sweet again. He kissed her on the lips. "We'd better go down now, Ros. I don't trust those scallywags."

The landlady put an extra bed into Osbourne's single room. "I'm sure I don't know what it'll be like, Mr. Osbourne. It's the one we keep by for Bob's dad." They did not sample its comforts that night. They both slept in Osbourne's narrow divan. That night it was as if the eleven years had never been.

The dream struck like a cobra's head.

CHAPTER SEVENTEEN

It woke Osbourne, sick with a nausea that came from self-disgust. In his dream Rosamund's arms had changed to Jimmy's. He felt all their weight round his neck, lonely and needing and gripping. It was Jimmy's and not Rosamund's body that he took with such newly-found delight.

When Rosamund opened her eyes in the morning he was sitting up in bed. Lack of sleep put dark patches under his eyes that matched the deep blue of his unshaven chin. He lay with his head turned to the window where the sun made a feeble effort to disperse the mist above the Lion and the Lamb. He lay with the taste of the dream in his mouth, with the sense of it in his head. He felt as if it had pumped a black and slimy poison into his veins that was slowly absorbed by his bones.

He lay slowly trying to remember the details of something he would have preferred to have forgotten at that moment. It was as if he were dragging it out of a reluctant mind in which he had forcibly buried it. He had an impression at first only of the misery it had caused him at the time; the shock and the self-dislike. It was an older boy—older than Smiley. It would have been at his public school. The boy had pestered him week after week. He knew that he had not disliked the boy. In a way he must have been attracted to him to have given in at all. But as an undistinguished fag it was flattering to have a popular sixth-former so obviously interested in him. Nor were the presents of tuck unwelcome. He remembered that it took place in a wood where the trees made a black and dense tunnel to the roadway; that Carson lay on his back in grey flannels, his blazer bright against the bank, and made fun of him for being 'sissy' and scared. He remembered his own truculent, "Well, all right," and afterwards the appalling sense of shame and disgust which the physical contact with Carson produced. When he felt it necessary to confide in someone he told his greatest friend.

"Gosh!" The boy whistled. "Old Carson tried that one with me," and he added curiously, "What did you think of it?"

"I *hated* it," Osbourne replied.

"Me too," said the other boy cheerfully. "When old Carson tried it on again I just said 'Rats!' ".

But Osbourne was not sure that he could have said 'Rats!' He lived in daily dread of Carson. He wondered if he would have the courage, alone with the burly sixth-former, to say 'No' on a second occasion, or if the jibes and the light-hearted sneers would persuade him again. It was impossible to be disgusted by Carson himself. He was so breezy, so clean and so magnificent. He had no opportunity to put himself to the test. Whether the elder boy simply lost interest or whether he had seen the effect on the younger child and judged him an unwise victim Osbourne never found out. But he did not receive a second invitation from Carson, and he received no more tuck. He was left to torture himself by wondering if he would have been able to refuse. Sometimes he persuaded himself that nothing would have induced him to undergo such a nauseating experience again—but at other times he could only doubt.

It was over thirty years ago and he had forgotten it completely until Rosamund's accusation, but now, as he lay in bed staring at a Westmorland mist, it caused him to doubt again.

"Are you all right, darling?" Rosamund asked him.

"Yes," said Osbourne. "Quite."

But even the boys saw that he was not all right. He seemed disinclined to talk and when he did he snapped at them. "What's happened to old Ozzy this morning?" Moorhead asked. "He's as ratty as old Harry."

"Here! Do you know where that comes from?"

"What?"

The boys were out in the road kicking stones at each other, waiting for the Osbournes to start off on the morning's scramble.

"There!" said Burgess. "That's where it comes from," and he pointed to the great green mound that rose up beyond the road. "Old Harry's buried in that."

"Nuts!"

"He *is*. That's where it comes from. Old Ozzy told me.

He was a Dane called Old Ari and he was jolly good at sports. He could outdo almost anybody, although he was so old. That's why you say you can run like Old Harry, and his enemies slaughtered him and he's buried in there."

"Nuts!"

The Osbournes came out of the house. Rosamund's smile went from one to the other. But Osbourne smiled at no one. As he stood tying the belt of his old camel-hair coat he frowned as he searched the sky for weather signs. He seemed suddenly thinner in the face. His voice was irritable when he addressed the boys.

The sun caught and was carried along in the windows of the bus bound for Keswick.

"Everything was grand until she came," Jimmy said under his breath. At first it was obvious to no one but Jimmy that Osbourne was avoiding him. If he dropped behind to ask a question it was answered but followed with a quick "Run on, Stretton." If he pointed out a particular view Osbourne might nod a preoccupied head. And when in excitement Jimmy caught hold of his sleeve the arm was withdrawn abruptly. At tea-time in Ambleside, when the dying light was beginning to fade out the line of the hills, the chair beside Osbourne fell quite naturally to Jimmy's lot. But Osbourne said, "Let Burgess have this one, will you, Stretton? He's better at passing round tea." It was an absurd excuse, and Osbourne knew it. There had never been any opportunity of judging Jimmy's powers of passing tea, let alone selecting Burgess's in preference. He tried hard to ignore Jimmy's puzzled eyes. But when Burgess sent a cup of tea skidding off its saucer to soak the table-cloth he could feel them boring into him.

Jimmy said over-casually to Claypole, "Do you think old Ozzy's got a down on me again?"

Claypole said, "Dunno. I say, it's true about Old Ari. Ozzy says it's a legend round here."

Each morning when he woke, Jimmy hoped that the new

day was going to be different. That it might prove that the day before was something that only took place in his own imagination. But each day made it clear that Mr. Osbourne was definitely trying to avoid him.

It was the same when they went back to school. He must have done something between the time of that exciting moment when Osbourne said, "Would your father let you come up to the Lakes?" and the day when Rosamund arrived at the Lakes. He must have done something to turn Osbourne against him. There was no longer any doubt about it. Even the other boys noticed it: "What's made old Ozzy so ratty with you?"

The dream had recurred in broad daylight. Osbourne was correcting Third Form compositions. At the end of an essay entitled 'My Walk Through the Woods' he was about to write 'Complete lack of imagination' when he suddenly wanted Jimmy. It was an indisputable physical desire for the boy. The horror that came with the realisation stiffened the fingers that still clung to his pen. Osbourne was not acquainted with the powers of direct self-suggestion or the accumulated forces of auto-suggestion. If he had thought about it at all he would have imagined it something peculiar to the Yogi. He would not have believed any directive, self-enforced or otherwise, capable of having a mental effect on him. He sat at the desk while the sweat that slid slowly down his face crept down his neck and soaked through to his collar. Into his mind came the memory of an old man's voice, wearily trying to excuse himself: "I *do* try to fight it. I don't *like* to do it." He closed his eyes when he recalled his own cutting reply to the appeal of Arthur Charron-Davies.

Rosamund studied Osbourne's face. "I believe you're losing weight, and you're so nervy and jumpy lately. What *is* the matter, darling?"

"Look, Ros, do me a favour, will you. Be a good girl and don't fuss."

Jimmy plucked up his courage. He waylaid Osbourne outside the library door.

"Please, sir, what have I done? Even Moorhead can spot you've got a down on me again, sir, and Moorhead can't usually spot anything."

"I'm not interested in Moorhead's powers of detection. I've never heard such impertinence." It was so long since Jimmy had found it hard to talk to Osbourne. It came as quite a shock to find him unapproachable again. It was not possible to explain anything to that look on Osbourne's new, drawn face. "Just because I don't spend my entire day dancing attendance upon you in particular doesn't mean that I have a 'down' on you. Do you expect me to lay out a red carpet for you whenever you come into class? How dare you suggest that I show you favouritism." Jimmy was too stunned by the sternness in Osbourne's voice to make any form of defence. As Osbourne walked away he said over his shoulder, "You ought to be ashamed of yourself, Stretton." Then he turned back from the library door. He halted in front of Jimmy. "Stretton, sometimes people do things for our own good that we don't understand. And sometimes people have troubles that we don't understand."

"Have you got troubles, sir?"

"Yes," Osbourne answered, "a few."

"You're not broke, are you, sir? Like Major Humphries at home. He drank all his money away."

Osbourne said, "No, I'm not broke, Stretton."

"Couldn't I help somehow, sir?" Jimmy asked, "I'm jolly good at getting people out of jams. I got Moorhead out of a shocking one last week." He broke off, remembering that Moorhead's problem was hardly fit for Osbourne's ears.

Osbourne smiled at him. He seemed to be talking aloud to himself rather than replying to Jimmy. "No, Stretton, thank you all the same, but I don't think that you of all people can help me out of my 'jam'." He put out a hand to

give a reassuring pat to Jimmy's head, but half-way there
withdrew it.   Jimmy stood taut with astonishment at the
expression on Osbourne's face. Something awful had happened between them. Something cold, and unclear, and dark.
Osbourne could not bring himself to touch him.   It was as if
every ounce of his strength was needed to force himself to
place his hand on the boy's strong hair. When he did so, both
his eyes were closed and on his face there was a look of
complete disgust.

Jimmy stood still several minutes after Osbourne had felt
him, clinging to the comforting folds of the coat. An agony
of bewilderment gave way to a memory faintly stirring. A
long time ago, as far off as a bird singing outside a window
can sound in the half-moments between wakefulness and
sleep, he had done something terribly wrong that his father
could never forgive. He had come to believe that it was
because he had caused his mother's death, but perhaps it was
something worse than that. Perhaps Osbourne had lately
discovered it. There must be something about him to account
for the revulsion he had witnessed in Osbourne's face.

CHAPTER EIGHTEEN

THE following morning Osbourne made an abrupt decision.
He decided to go away. He said to Rosamund, "You were
right when you told me I needed a rest. I'd like to get off at
once, Ros, if you think you could manage with Neator."

"Yes, of course, darling," she told him.

He said good-bye to no one but Rosamund and Neator.
From Grasmere he wrote to Rosamund:

'DARLING,

'Just at this moment I'm not a fit companion for you.
I'm even less fit to run a school, I'm not fit to be in charge
of the boys. I've always despised nervous breakdowns,

but I think I know now that they're not to be despised.
I've written to Neator and I've written to the bank.
Financially things are satisfactory, and if at this moment
anything were to happen to me it would be the best
moment for it to happen because I should know that I
should be leaving you well cared for. I find we can easily
afford someone to take Neator's place if he steps into my
shoes. Let Neator interview the new man. I have complete faith in his judgment.

'You would be doing me the greatest possible service
if you would go out of your way to do your best for
Stretton. I am worried more than I can possibly make
you understand that what must have appeared to him as
inexplicable behaviour on my part might have disturbed
him and harmed him emotionally. It is for this reason
that I feel myself unfit at the moment to have the development of his or any other boy's character entrusted to me.
No one knows better than you the things I believe in.
You know my principles, my ideals, my ideas. If you
could keep a personal eye on Stretton in particular and
try and guide him along the lines I should do myself if I
were there, you would be doing the most you can for me.
He must never be made to feel guilty over anything
connected with me.

'Never think that you have not been to me everything
that a wife could be. You will remain what you have
always been to me, my dearest dearest girl.'

Osbourne climbed his familiar Helvellyn. He climbed
slowly up to Striding Edge, his movements unhurried, his
breathing steady. He stood several moments looking out at
the great stretching views. Then he started to walk forward
deliberately. When he saw a girl-hiker he stopped. He said
softly, "Damn, damn, damn."

The girl was sitting down with her head in her hands.
She said, "Isn't it daft of me, but every time I get up I feel

queer. I thought I'd be here for the night. I suppose I was daft to try it. But I didn't think it was going to be bad. Every time I look down I get dizzy."

Osbourne took her hands. "You'll be all right, don't think about it. A lot of people feel like that the first time they come across Striding Edge."

The girl kept a good grip on his hands. "It's ever so high up, isn't it?"

Osbourne advised her, "Keep your eyes on me."

"Do many people fall off?"

"Not often unless the mist comes down."

"You're ever so brave on it, aren't you?" she said. "I closed my eyes when you went so near the edge. I thought you were going to jump off."

"Oh no," Osbourne said quickly, "I was just looking round." He gave the girl tea in Patterdale and put her in a bus. Then he walked over the exhilarating loneliness of Kirkstone Pass down into Ambleside and back into Grasmere. He was not expecting to see his father-in-law.

Major Brain was a small-featured man. His voice split when he talked, sounding shreddy. He sat in a chintz-covered chair in a deserted lounge.

Osbourne asked, "Are you staying here, Douglas?"

"No. Windermere. Got a car waiting outside."

"May I get you a drink?"

"No, thank you."

Major Brain had hard blue eyes. They were hostile when they rested on Osbourne. He and Osbourne had never been drawn towards one another. Moderate congeniality at Christmas time was as much as they had ever achieved.

Major Brain bore none of the tender messages Rosamund had begged him to deliver. "Daddy, first and foremost make him see how much I love him—make him feel that nothing in the world is so important to me as having him love me back. I don't care what he's done. I can forget and forgive anything he wants me to, Daddy, be *sure* and tell him that."

Major Brain said to Osbourne, "That letter you wrote to Rosamund looked as if you were angling for a separation. It upset her very much."

"I'm sorry. I did my best to see that it wouldn't."

"What *are* you after, Osbourne? *Are* you angling for some sort of separation? It was a damn queer letter to write."

"I'm not *angling* for anything."

"Do you think it a decent thing to do to walk out on a woman—and leave her to shoulder your responsibilities?"

"I merely want time to sort myself out. My nerves have taken rather a bad beating just lately, and I feel that what I need most is to get completely away from anything and anyone I've ever known." He gave Major Brain a meaning look.

Major Brain said, "Rosamund said she believed you were ill. The girl's worrying herself into fits about you. She wants you to come home and rest."

"I've just explained why that's not possible."

"You look all right to me."

"Nothing could flatter me more, Douglas."

"Look here, is there anything in these disgusting suggestions that it's anything to do with the boy?"

"What is the suggestion and who made it?"

"Dr. Cromer seems to think that the boy's got an indecent passion for you."

"Did he use those words?"

"I wasn't there when the fellow said it. I'm passing it on second-hand. Apparently the boy's been fretting for you, filthy little swine, and they got Cromer in to look at him. I hear he was a wrong 'un from the start."

"He was not a wrong 'un from the start."

"Wasn't he mixed up in that other dirty business with Davies?"

"No."

"You've only got his word against the other boy's, haven't you?"

"I only need his word against the other boy's."

"I'm afraid I told him outright that I thought him a disgusting little sissy. It's none of my business, of course, but somebody had to tell him."

"I disagree with you, Douglas. Nobody should have told him anything of the sort."

"Ros said you'd a bee in your bonnet about him and wouldn't hear a word against him. Well, all I can say is that if there is any truth in it I'm damned if I can see why Rosamund wants you back. I shouldn't care to be under the same roof with you."

"If there is any truth in what?"

Major Brain took a breath and crossed short legs in ginger tweed. "We might as well call a spade a spade. Rosamund didn't actually say so, but I gathered from her attitude that she was afraid you'd been monkeying about with the boy." Osbourne put back his head and inhaled. "You know what that means, don't you?"

"I'm not a congenital idiot, and I'm able to understand English, however insulting. I understood that Rosamund had realised her fears on those grounds were absurd."

"Apparently the doctor's opinion bore 'em out." It was cold in the seldom used lounge. From the bar came a warm and noisy chatter. "He says the boy's feelings for you are little short of damned unnatural, and it's only one jump from there to imagining that he must have had some form of encouragement in them. The boy himself is so keen to drum it in that you never favoured him, the whole thing sounds pretty suspicious. I mean to say, there's no smoke without fire." Major Brain's firm, round face crumpled up in disgust. "The boy's an obvious little nancy. He behaves no better than a lovesick girl. The whole thing's nauseating. You should have expelled him at once."

"On what grounds? That he wouldn't be safe with me about?"

Major Brain stood up. "I gather, as you haven't even bothered to deny it and put up nothing but a sickening defence of the boy, that my assumption is correct."

Osbourne lit another cigarette. "I have no intention of bothering to deny it to you. I'm extremely uninterested in your opinion of me. If it had been Rosamund who still needed convincing I should have been willing to discuss it with her."

"You realise that this sort of thing can mean the end of you with regard to the school? If you don't care for yourself you might at least think of the boy. Cromer thinks your influence on him is so damned harmful that if the boy ever sets eyes on you again it will go a long way to ruining his life."

"You'll observe that for the moment at least I have moved myself out of his way."

Major Brain walked over to him and glared down into Osbourne's strained face and tired eyes. "If me own daughter's name wasn't linked with yours I'd like to see you get your deserts. Horsewhipping's too good for you. You ought to see the inside of a gaol for ten years."

Osbourne examined his hands. "Douglas, I feel I should like to take this opportunity of telling you how much I dislike you."

"There's no love on my side, I can promise you that. Your type of man pollutes the air." And Major Brain snatched at his hat and walked out of the hotel.

CHAPTER NINETEEN

A SHOCKED depression hung over the school, in a weighty and unlifting blanket. Jimmy stared at the headlines and stared at the photographs, before matron rounded up the newspapers that the day boys had smuggled in. There was not much space devoted to Osbourne's death. V.E. Day celebrations took up most of the room, and the happy laughing faces and the dancers round bonfires made incongruously gay company for the face of the dead man.

Jimmy had had little association with death. Old Jack was the only living thing connected with him that he had felt as a loss in his life. He realised that death removed people continually, boys at school had lost parents at times, but that it should touch Osbourne seemed unthinkable. At first it was a proposition which Jimmy's brain refused to concede. But he had a cold warning of what he might feel if he were ever to realise that it was true. He shut the premonition off like a key in the door of a room that contained something more frightening than it was possible to contemplate. One day he would have to turn the handle and face the dreaded interior. He could not postpone the opening for ever.

In Jimmy's class Claypole was unusually awed and quiet-voiced. "It says in the paper there wasn't a mist."

"Well, he just must have slipped. Gosh, poor old Ozzy!" Moorhead stared moodily down at his desk. "It says it can be dangerous if somebody isn't used to climbing."

"But old Ozzy *was used* to climbing. He was absolutely tops at it."

A tall boy in glasses read out from a smuggled paper: "Schoolmaster falls to his death on Striding Edge! The dead man's hotel companions had not supposed that he intended to climb that day. For an experienced climber he was unsuitably dressed. Mr. Osbourne was wearing a camèl-hair coat and suède shoes when his body was found."

"Gosh," Moorhead said, "poor old Ozzy."

A day-boy claimed attention. "Do you know what my dad says? He says that Ozzy did himself in. He says it's quite clear if you read between the lines, because he paid his bill the day before he died as if he knew he wasn't coming back and didn't want to leave any debts.

"But he still went back that evening," Orson insisted, "so your dad's talking rot."

"No, he's not. My dad says he thinks old Ozzy meant to bump himself off that day he met the girl on Striding Edge. But he couldn't because she was there and he had to help her home. She said in the paper he went near the edge. So he had to go back to his hotel and he went off and did it the next day instead."

There followed a violent discussion about suicide. "It's a dreadful disgrace," said Burgess. "You can't be buried in proper ground and you go to Hell."

"Who says?"

"You're not allowed to do it in the Bible."

"You can be hanged for it," Claypole claimed.

"Stuff and! How can you be hanged if you're dead?"

"Still, it's against the law and you're not allowed to do it. It's like murdering yourself. It's a crime."

"It's a coward's way out," said Longridge. "It tells you that in books."

He was knocked off his feet by Jimmy. When they were separated Jimmy stood, fists clenched, fuming in Orson's restraining hold. "You call Ozzy a coward and I'll knock all your teeth out. I'll give you a bloody nose, I'll——"

"Pack it up, Stretton," said sensible Orson. "Longridge wasn't getting at Ozzy. He just meant anyone who does it. Of course Ozzy wouldn't have done himself in. What would he go and do a ruddy silly thing like that for?"

"There's something in that," admitted Moorhead. "He didn't have any reason. It's only people who don't want to stay alive like when you've got an awful disease or something."

"Perhaps he *had* got an awful disease. He looked jolly rotten just lately."

"Rats!"

"Or perhaps he'd been gambling, or perhaps he was blackmailed." Claypole's eyes widened with excitement.   "Perhaps he was in some awful jam."

Jimmy's mind travelled back to the hall on the night that he had asked Osbourne what it was that he himself had done wrong. He recalled Osbourne's quiet voice admitting to being in a jam.

Jimmy's mental defences underwent a violent contraction. From not feeling able to face the truth he had jumped to a momentarily painless acceptance of it. In the moments of hearing Osbourne accused of cowardice and crime, of hearing that he might have committed a sin which condemned his soul to Hell, anger had anæsthetised grief. There followed an even greater shock, that he and he alone perhaps was in possession of the knowledge that Osbourne had been in trouble, that he might indeed have had reason to 'do himself in'. His senses made an emotional by-pass of the dreaded realisation that Osbourne was dead. Osbourne was in need of protection and therefore lived once more. There was so much to think of, so much to fight. There was Osbourne to be saved from a 'dreadful disgrace'. There was Osbourne to be buried in proper ground, there was Osbourne to be saved from going to Hell, and therefore there was Osbourne. The anæsthetic was strong and reviving, and the pain of grief was effectively dulled. There was a campaign to take the place of mourning.

When Rosamund and Dr. Cromer interviewed him they were surprised at his composure. He knew what he had to do. He had to convince them that there was not and never had been anything troubling Mr. Osbourne. To do that he must make it appear that he was entirely in Osbourne's confidence. If he took away the reason for Osbourne's killing himself, then surely he would not be suspected. The mere fact that Dr. Cromer and Mrs. Osbourne wished to see him at all convinced Jimmy that they were trying to get some form of information out of him. His eyes were alert and his mind prepared for pitfalls.

Dr. Cromer's smile was forcedly cheerful. Rosamund

seemed unable to look at Jimmy. There were no lights in her hair. It looked dead and dry. Jimmy suddenly lost his hatred for her. She must be as sad as himself.

Dr. Cromer's hands folded, whitening his knuckles. "Stretton, we are going to ask you one or two questions and we should like you to answer them truthfully and carefully. We know that you had a great regard for Mr. Osbourne and that you must be very distressed by this terrible—accident." The slight hesitation before the word put Jimmy on his guard afresh. That was it all right. They were trying to find out through him. Upon his replies would depend the fate of his beloved Osbourne's soul. "Stretton, you have told us on previous occasions that Mr. Osbourne never showed you any favouritism."

Jimmy interrupted, "That wasn't true, sir. Mr. Osbourne *did* favour me."

There was a short silence, during which Rosamund looked at him, looked away again and Dr. Cromer licked his lips. "What makes you say that, Stretton?"

"He used to be terribly terribly nice to me. Much nicer to me than to anyone else."

"In what way did he express this—this niceness, Stretton?"

Jimmy for a moment was flummoxed. Then he remembered his purpose. "Oh well, he used to tell me all his secrets. He never kept anything back from me." He added, his voice rising, "We were absolutely the most tremendous friends. There wasn't anything he wouldn't have told me. He was so fond of me he'd have been sure to tell me if anything was wrong, and he didn't."

"Are you suggesting that Mr. Osbourne would have confided things to you which he wouldn't confide to his wife, Stretton?"

"Rather," Jimmy said. He turned round, addressing Rosamund. "I expect you thought he was in some kind of a jam, but that was all rubbish—he wasn't. He told me everything was fine."

It was Dr. Cromer who addressed him: "How is it you managed to receive these confidences from Mr. Osbourne, Stretton? Did you see him alone very often?"

"Oh yes, sir," Jimmy said happily. The silence that prevailed made a noise in the ears.

Again it was the doctor who broke it. He was solemn-voiced and grave-eyed. "Stretton, did you understand what occurred between Smiley and Mr. Davies?"

"Yes, sir. They sat on each other's laps and made love to each other for tuck."

"Did anything like that ever occur between you and Mr. Osbourne?"

"Oh *yes*, sir. Mr. Osbourne was much nicer to me than Mr. Davies was to Smiley. He made much much more fuss of me than that."

Rosamund Osbourne covered her eyes with one hand.

The doctor said, "You've admitted your very close association with Mr. Osbourne, Stretton. You're suggesting that Mr. Osbourne petted and fondled you."

The word 'fondled' suggested affection, and Jimmy was trying to claim affection. "Oh yes, sir. He often fondled me."

"In what manner?"

"Well—er—he——"

"There was an occasion on which Mrs. Osbourne came into the room, Stretton, and found you sitting on Mr. Osbourne's knee. Had you then been kissing him?"

"Oh yes, I expect so. He was always kissing me." Jimmy searched in his mind for a convincing example. He remembered the Reverend Jordon. "I had a nightmare once, and Mr. Osbourne came up and fetched me. He tucked me all up in my eiderdown and he carried me down to the study. He kept me on his knee and cuddled me all up tight in his arms. Then he kissed me and we went to sleep together until my aunt came in."

"Your *aunt*!"

"Yes, my aunt came in and then my father told her I'd had a nightmare and—I mean—Mr. *Osbourne* told her—I mean he—he didn't tell my aunt, he told matron. It was matron who came in, not my aunt." He broke off and flushed. Matron might be questioned. "No, it wasn't her, it was Mr. Neator—no, no, no, it wasn't anyone. No one came in at all."

"The boy's lying," Dr. Cromer said. Jimmy panicked:

"I'm not, I'm not lying. He was my best friend and he told me everything. He'd have told me if he'd got into trouble. He didn't, he *didn't* kill himself. Why can't he go in proper ground like everyone else? He didn't do a sin, he didn't." He put the back of his wrist to his eyes and wept.

Rosamund Osbourne left her chair. She came round to Jimmy's side. She went down on one knee before him and took his hand. "Jimmy, do you know what this means to Mr. Osbourne? You're saying very terrible things about him, and he isn't here now to defend himself. I thought you were fond of him. I thought you liked him. Why are you saying things which could hurt him so much?"

It took them very few minutes to break him down after that. Rosamund remained on one knee before him. Dr. Cromer sat silent, a cigarette unlit between his lips. They heard of Osbourne's confessing to being in trouble and of his telling Jimmy that he least of all could help. They heard of the slow hand that went out to touch the boy's hair and of the self-disgust that drew it back. They realised that there had never been any indecent behaviour between Osbourne and Jimmy, and they realised why Osbourne had killed himself.

"Don't tell anyone he was in trouble, *please*," Jimmy begged.

Rosamund said to Dr. Cromer, "Leave me alone with Stretton, please."

When Dr. Cromer left the room she took Jimmy in her arms. He wept noisily against her, releasing his grief. He had opened the door to the dreaded room, but it was a comfort to enter it with Rosamund. It was less painful than going in alone. She, too, was crying above his head. He felt himself not entirely deserted in the terrible empty room. "Jimmy, we're the two people who loved him best. We can keep him alive together. He need never be dead between us. No one dies if two people remember him. We must be friends, Jimmy, always, always. He asked me to be a friend to you. He asked me to help you. You'll let me, won't you? He wants you to know that he never blamed you for anything that happened to him. You made him happier than I did. I misjudged him and made him unhappy. But he had very high hopes for you. He'd be so proud of you if you do well in life." She smoothed back his hair and smiled at him. "We need never never lose him, Jimmy, if we keep him alive in our hearts."

CHAPTER TWENTY

WHEN Jimmy came home a week before the end of term the Reverend Jordon held out his hand, "When we've lost a very dear friend it's possible that another friend can make the loss easier to bear. I hope you can look upon me, Jimmy, as someone who might be able to fill the gap."

Jimmy took the hand that was offered to him. It seemed pointless to leave it stranded in the air. But that was his only emotion regarding his father's offer of friendship. That and a slight resentment towards him for looking so much like Osbourne.

Pam was helping Mrs. Houghton with the silver. She was tall for her age, and thin. He whispered to her, "I say, Pam. Do us a favour, will you." Pam managed to slip away from her mother's side. She was ready to do him any favour. Her black hair was still cut short round her ears. He whispered, "Meet me upstairs in my room."

He was kneeling in front of his trunk when Pam's sharp face peeped round the door. He said, "Here, lock the door behind you, quick." His clothes were strewn over the floor and the bed. At the bottom of the trunk under layers of newspaper lay Osbourne's old camel-hair coat.

"Whatever is it?" Pam asked.

"I stole it. It's Mr. Osbourne's."

Pam knew all about Mr. Osbourne. On Jimmy's short visits to the vicarage he was their main topic of conversation. She was sure of Jimmy's company hour after hour if she cared to keep on talking about Osbourne. At the end of each term she was eager for news. She felt it a personal victory when Jimmy was asked to the Lakes, and she felt it a personal defeat when Jimmy reported that Osbourne had taken a dislike to him. But she was a sensible, practical child. "It couldn't be your *hair* that he didn't like touching. Perhaps he didn't feel well in himself. Dad's face goes like that when he looks at Mum sometimes. But it's only when he's had too much beer."

"Mr. Osbourne *never* has too much beer."

Pam's eyes were round as she stared at the coat. "Stole it," she whispered, "stole it!"

"Yep. I saw matron shaking it out at the back of the house, so I went round to have a look. It was the night we were all being sent home. Matron had got all his things out on the kitchen table. She was putting them in a box or something. I hid until she went into the scullery. Then I nicked the coat off the back of the chair and hid it in my hole in the rockery. I went down and fetched it at night to pack."

Pam put out a wary hand to feel it. "It's been blooded on," she said. "What are you going to do with it?"

Jimmy said, "I don't know. We'll dry it out and hide it somewhere. Mr. Osbourne was crazy about this old coat— Mrs. Osbourne was always wanting him to get a new one but he just wouldn't. He'd be hopping mad if they'd thrown it away. I sort of thought—I'd save it for him."

They hid the old coat in the loft. It became a secret meeting-place. They visited it frequently. They lit candles and picnicked in front of it. It flung a curious shadow by candlelight from its hanger on one of the beams.

The Reverend Jordon, trying to express friendship towards Jimmy and make up for Osbourne's loss, could never understand how his son managed to disappear for so many hours at a time. He never thought of the loft.

Jimmy bore with his father's company patiently, and listened to whatever he had to say. But he reported to Pam, "I know, Dad's all right really. But I can't seem to stick the old bird. It gives me the creeps to see him fiddling around the altar and everyone kneeling behind him. It sort of makes me squirm."

Pam said severely, "That's daft."

Anita's hair had faded and she needed stronger glasses. She said frequently, "Jeremy, where *do* you pick up those common expressions? A gentleman doesn't say 'daft'."

Three weeks of public school seemed to put a world and a half between Bradcombe and Jimmy. He was bewildered and wretched at first. He was too ashamed to tell his father his feelings, and Pam was an unsatisfactory correspondent. She could not express herself on paper. He sent a postcard to Rosamund Osbourne, 'This place is jolly beastly.' He added a postscript, and underlined it, '*No one thinks I'm a sissy here.*'

Rosamund replied from her parents' home. She was giving up the school. Her letter was long and full of advice, and because she knew Osbourne so well it might have been Osbourne himself who had written. Jimmy read and re-read the letter, mouthing the words with his lips. It was a comfort to feel in touch with Osbourne. 'We must both work hard to see that you become everything Mr. Osbourne would have wanted you to be.' There was a P.S. at the bottom of

Rosamund's letter too: 'Providing you conduct yourself manfully there is no need for anyone to think you are a sissy.'

At the cost of his education he became aggressively determined to prove himself manly. He paid attention to little but gymnastics and games.

The maths master wrote on his first report, 'Stretton would do well to remember that there are fields of achievement in this world unconnected with athletics and physical feats.'

Jimmy himself corresponded frequently with Rosamund Osbourne, and the replies which were as regular and encouraging were so definitely Osbourne's replies.

'Mr. Osbourne would be very proud if he knew you had won the cup.'

'Yes, it would have pleased Mr. Osbourne enormously to know that you got in the team. Bravo!'

And sometimes:

'You know as well as I do the importance Mr. Osbourne placed on sports and anything to do with athletics, but he placed importance on other things too. Don't you think if you made a superhuman effort you could get on the right side of maths? Life isn't made up of games, and where would Mr. Osbourne have been if he had done nothing but study rugger? He wouldn't have been much use to Bradcombe or to you.'

On Jimmy's report the maths master wrote, 'There are signs of improvement. Stretton is trying.'

Rosamund scribbled, 'Bravo!'

The Reverend Jordon was proud of his son. At the end and the beginning of every term he gave Jimmy a man-to-man friendly talk, which put forward most of the viewpoints already expressed in Rosamund's letters. He was

more than gratified at the results of his talks. Jimmy was
doing very well at school. If he saw less of the boy during
the holidays than he could have wished he put it down to the
fact that he was an old man and that boys will be boys.
Anita was less complacent towards the adage. She waylaid
the Reverend Jordon. "He's seeing too much of that
Houghton girl. I found them down by the kitchen garden
eating an apple together."

"That seems a mild offence."

"But they were eating it between them, Jordon. They're
much too big for that. Alice Macey says she thinks you
must be blind. The whole village is talking about it."

"Then I'm sorry the whole village hasn't something better
to talk about." And the Reverend Jordon, still straight-
shouldered, walked past her, up past the lych-gate where the
church threw a curious shadow over the cabbage-patch.

Jimmy continued to see much of Pam. He showed her
all Rosamund's letters. They had ceased to bear an English
postmark. The letters were posted in France. Rosamund
was living in Paris. But she wrote to Jimmy none the less
regularly. They had established a mutual affection and a
great friendship through the medium of their letters. As
long as they wrote to each other Osbourne remained alive.
It made Pam feel unwanted and powerless to help. There
was little she could do to retain Jimmy's interest now that
Rosamund had such a hold over him. Rosamund was a
formidable rival. She could not write to him as Rosamund
could:

'I feel that we two have something even greater in
common than a blood relationship. I feel more like your
mother than your ex-schoolmarm! Because of you he has
not died for me, and I like to think that you feel the same
through me.'

There was a photograph of Rosamund in Jimmy's bedroom. It stood in a frame he had made himself. He explained

it with a laugh to friends, "No, she's not actually my mother. But, well, she's just as good." Rosamund sent snapshots of herself in beach clothes when she visited Cannes, and Jimmy's friends whistled their praise. Behind sun-glasses and a South of France tan Rosamund looked young enough in a snapshot to appeal to youth itself.

Pam studied the photograph secretly, and once she dared to criticise it. "She's not *really* pretty, is she?"

"Good gosh, yes. She's got ripping hair and wizard eyes." And he polished the photograph frame on his sleeve.

"But she's terribly old," said Pam.

"Old my foot!" said Jimmy. "The chaps at school think she's a smasher. And anyway, I can't stick young girls. They just giggle and go all ga-ga."

Pam had to find other means of holding his interest now that she was excluded from the Osbournes. She had to fall back on his everyday existence and she found this confusing and bewildering. She had to listen and try to keep abreast with the outcome of house matches, the results of a school match, with the all-important sayings of the omnipotent Head whose acquaintance Jimmy had never made personally, and the rigours of the dreaded field days. However she struggled she felt she was beaten, and at fifteen she buried her face in the pillow and wept half-way through the night because she had lost Jimmy through the mysterious force of the 'older woman'. She was affected even more seriously than that. In Jimmy's presence she found herself giggling and inclined to go ga-ga.

Then, three weeks before the end of the spring term, Jimmy received a visitor. When he came down to his housemaster's sitting-room Rosamund Osbourne was waiting for him. It was five years since they had met. He saw very little difference in her except that she looked more smartly dressed.

She held and kept both of his hands. His good looks had not deserted him. They were accentuated by his breadth and his newly-developed height. "Oh goodness, how you've grown, Jimmy!"

"Are you over for good, Mrs. Osbourne?" He could master the excitement he felt in his voice, but he could not keep it out of his eyes.

"No, Jimmy, I'm only here on a visit. My home is in France now. But I'm hoping you'll come to visit me."

"You bet I will, Mrs. Osbourne."

Rosamund sat down. She was dressed in black. She had only one touch of white to relieve it, the small boater hat on her head. Jimmy felt a warm admiration towards her for having worn mourning so long. He wished only that the other boys might see her. There was an air about her which he did not recall her as having possessed before. He did not know the word for it. She was poised and she looked indisputably right. And she smelt nice. The word eluding him was 'chic'. She took off a long black glove. "Jimmy, we have been good friends, haven't we?"

"I'll say, Mrs. Osbourne."

She had bared her left hand when she took off her glove. A highly-set dome of diamonds sat up to catch the light on her third finger. She was playing with it. "Jimmy, I wonder if I can ever explain to you what you've meant to me. To make you understand I must tell you how I felt about you in the beginning. I resented you, I misjudged you, and I misjudged my husband. My suspicions might even have been responsible for what happened to him. I felt you were the son I should have given him, and I hated you at first. But later, after what happened to John, when all I had left of him was his letter asking me to look after you, I felt that in passing on everything he would have wanted me to say to you I had helped him to bring you up in the way he would have wanted to bring you up himself, and that you were *our* son". Jimmy kept his eyes on her, oddly apprehensive. "I felt that between us we had carried out his wishes, Jimmy, that we had granted his last request." She broke off and stared at her ring again. "I hope what I'm going to tell you will make no difference to us. I hope you'll understand." She paused, and then said heavily, "Jimmy, I have married again." The words made no sense. He stared at her. She continued, ill-at-ease, "You mustn't feel badly about it, Jimmy. You'll like him when you know him He's a Frenchman. His name's Maurice Vavasseur. He could never take John's place in my heart completely, but he's someone very dear to me. He's some-one I felt that I could share the rest of my life with and who would make me feel less lonely."

Jimmy managed to ask her, "How long have you been married, Mrs. Osbourne?"

"Over a year, Jimmy. Eighteen months."

Eighteen months! Eighteen months of deception, of treachery. Eighteen months of writing such lines as, 'He will never be dead whilst he lives between us.' 'We must keep him alive in our hearts.' And all the time she was *sleeping* with a man called Maurice Vavasseur.

He felt that Rosamund had been guilty of treachery not only towards Osbourne but to himself. Although only in his early teens he felt old and disillusioned. He thought in his new and violent dislike of Rosamund that any other woman in the world would have behaved less badly than she had done. Neither he nor Pam would have been guilty of such a betrayal.

It struck even Jimmy that it was strange that he should have suddenly coupled himself in his mind as a girl with Pam.

Part III

LOUIS PRESNOR

CHAPTER TWENTY-ONE

WHEN he was twenty he ran away with Pam. Channock buzzed with the scandal for weeks.

It took him an hour to persuade her. They stood at the end of the garden of 15 Alma Row. They were screened from the house by the shed. The light from the parlour threw a box pattern on to the lawn; now and again a shadow passed over it. Mrs. Houghton and four other daughters were at home. Mr. Houghton was down at the 'Bull'.

Jimmy was smoking cigarette after cigarette. Pam said, "Do hide it. They'll see the glow." He turned the lighted end into the palm of his hand. There was no wind, but the night air was cold. He was wearing a camel-hair coat; his legs, long in corduroy trousers, set him several inches above Pam.

The street lamp at the bridge seemed to hang in the air, an old-fashioned lantern, still shedding a gloomy glow in the foggy air. Over the allotments the ground-mist rose. There was a television aerial on top of 15 Alma Row.

Pam's foot made a squeezing sound, pressing down on the mud. She was worrying the ground with her toe. "But supposing they don't agree to it, Jimmy?"

Jimmy blew smoke out. "They will. What else can they do? We'll tell them we're living together, and we intend to go on living together. We'll threaten them with the patter of unborn feet. Use your head, girl. What do you think they'll say? 'Go on, sin it out'? Your mother's too prudish for that sort of thing, and my old man will be caught in a Christian web. They'll let us marry all right. I shouldn't be surprised if they didn't stand over us with a shot-gun."

"But, Jimmy, I'm not your sort. Mum's always telling me that."

"Your mother's a born and benighted snob."

A scholarship to a school in Hertfordshire had left a quality in Pam's voice which both amused and pleased Jimmy. He could trace in it the squeakiness of Mrs. Houghton and the hoarseness of William Houghton. Elocution lessons had taken what was theirs and what was Pam's and disciplined it into a quaintly distinctive pitch. In Channock she had a reputation which was not entirely kind. She was known as 'quite the lady'. Her face had a sensitivity which at a certain slant could pass for beauty. There was a quicksilver essence about her which gave Jimmy a pleasant sense of power. He felt that he might play on her moods as he might play on a piano. Her response would be according to his touch. She seemed his to do with as he wished. He did not consider her happiness. He was thinking of nothing but his own.

She knew that she was going to give in to him. She would have done anything he asked. Her sole feeling was one of thankful astonishment that the miracle had come to pass. She had imagined herself quietly loving him until the end of her days. She did not put much faith in the inducement of marriage. Her mother had issued stiff warnings: "If you've got your eye on that boy of the vicar's I'll thank you to take it off. No good will come of it and that's flat. You'll get no sympathy from me and you won't get your dad to stand by you—out on the beer every night! I've got enough troubles on my hands and trouble is all you'll see out of it, I can tell you. A young man like that wouldn't put things right. All you'll get out of him is a thank-you and you'll be luckier than some if you get that. They only put things right for their own sort, they think our sort is made for the other thing."

Jimmy was smiling at Pam. "If it'll make you feel better I'll promise on my word of honour as a cad and a bounder

that we'll have a bolster between us until they sign on the
dotted line." He put a hand under her chin and lifted it.
"You're not chilled to the marrow at the thought of marry-
ing me, are you, Pam? I'll be a good cook in time. The
old man gives me an allowance and he won't cut me off
without a shilling. He's too decent for that. The most we
shall get is a homily intermingled with Biblical sparks.
The allowance isn't a fortune for one, so it won't make life
ritzy for two. But we should manage to scrape along till I
can get started. Perhaps you could come out on the side of
emancipation and help out with a job for a bit, until I'm
called to the Bar and make my fortune from succulent cases."

She had been trying to count his cigarettes. She had lost
count after six. He smoked them nervously and fast. She
smiled, looking down at her feet again. "You knew
perfectly well I'd say yes."

In the train she leant back with her eyes closed. Watching
her, Jimmy wondered what gave her face its strange
attraction, not unlike a catchy, unshakable tune. Feature
by feature there was nothing to commend her. But when
her eyes were open there was a warmly persuasive calm. It
came, he decided, from expression alone. The face in repose
was less appealing. He touched her foot with his own.
"You look sweet."

The smile filled her eyes immediately. "You paid for it
all," she said. He was hardly aware of the new ensemble.
It was carefully unobtrusive. A dark grey suit, a dark grey
beret, and an overcoat flecked with white.

From Windermere they took a taxi to Grasmere. Jimmy
breathed hard on the window, rubbing its glass with his
sleeve. "Doesn't look a day older. Good old Ambleside!"
Then he leant back and offered her a nip from a silver flask.
He knew that she felt ill-at-ease. She seemed to find difficulty
in looking down at the wedding-ring she wore. She shook
her head. "No, thank you." He drank himself. "Bless the
bride to be."

She turned to him, her profile tipped up. "They won't guess about us at the hotel, will they, Jimmy?"

"We're not going to an hotel. We've got *rooms*." He rolled the word out, and patted her hand. "It was the only place I could find with a big enough bolster."

Their bedroom had white cotton curtains and a quilted bedspread. It had a worn, green carpet, and a view which caught at Jimmy's breath. "I hope you're going to be a Lake girl," he said. "Tomorrow you shall see Wordsworth's sun-glasses, but until then you must possess yourself in patience." He sat bumpily down on the bed. "Blimey. We might just as well have taken the bolster up on Striding Edge."

Pam put two sets of plain underwear into a drawer, which stuck. Jimmy came to her aid in shutting it. She blushed when he saw the underwear. "I'm afraid I haven't got many frills."

"You've got plenty of frills," he said. "The first thing tomorrow, we must write to Dad." He lit a cigarette and blew the smoke out. Three fingers on his right hand were stained with nicotine. Since they had caught their train that morning Pam had counted twenty-five cigarettes.

Jimmy composed the letter out loud: "'Honoured Sir.' No!—pomposity takes the sting out of immorality—'Dear Dad.' Bowed but unrepentant, that's the line—'I must call to your attention the fact that I hope this does not leave you as it finds me at present, propped up in bed with a lady whom I am not yet entitled to call a wife.' How's that?"

"Silly," Pam said.

"All right—'Dear Dad. I love Pam and Pam loves me. What the devil shall we do if it means we three?' "

"Jimmy, I wish you wouldn't joke."

He sensed tears in her voice. He jumped up and put his hand on her shoulder. He turned her round towards him. "My God, you really do feel scarlet, don't you? I think that's rather sweet." He put a light kiss on her forehead.

"Jimmy," she asked, "do you love me?" She raised her blue eyes to his face.

"Good heavens, girl, would I be tossing the gauntlet into the teeth of Church upbringing if I didn't?"

"But why do you love me?" she asked.

"Women! Can't take a good thing for granted. They have to poke round and find out. Oh, darling, I haven't hurt you, have I? Oh, my sweetie, I wouldn't do that for the world. You must get used to my gaiety and fun—'Our Willie's a scream.' That's me." And he kissed the side of her head. "Let's try again on the sterner side. Because you're the only girl I've ever met who has made me feel I'd like to spend the rest of my life with her. How's that?"

She looked into his face; her eyes were wet. "If our families say 'no', you won't send me home at once, will you? You'll let us stay just a little bit longer together?" She found it hard to explain that she would be bound to suffer at the hands of her family, however short her brief taste of paradise might be, and that she wanted enough to make it worth while. If it ended here she would have nothing to remember except her new odd nervousness with him, her fear of their parents and the twenty-five cigarettes he had smoked.

"I won't send you away at all. They'll say 'yes' in the end all right."

She nestled her face against him. She pressed her lips against the lapel of the camel-hair coat and kissed it. Then she said suddenly, "Jimmy. Wasn't this where Mr. Osbourne died?"

Jimmy jerked a thumb back over his shoulder, "Up yonder. We'll pay the hallowed spot a visit if you can make it."

She was running her fingers round the back of his collar. "That old coat of his is still up in the loft."

"Is it? I haven't been up for donkey's years. I should think it's threadbare, isn't it?" She saw a thin line appear between his eyes. He seemed suddenly depressed and deflated.

"Oh, for God's sake let's get out of here. I'm sick of this little white morgue."

They had dinner at the Swan Hotel. By the time they returned to the small cold room they were hand in hand and Jimmy was cheerful again. He lay on the bed in plum-coloured pyjamas, an ankle across a bent knee. "How do you like my trousseau?"

"They're a little bit bright," she laughed.

"Oh, you'll have to shake out of striped flannel ideas. They're too blooming Channock for words."

She was grateful for the dark as she climbed into bed beside him. She could feel the colour glow high in her face. She said a quick prayer in her head. 'Oh, please let me be all right for him. Please let me be all right.'

She lay very straight and still. He put out one arm to encircle her. His free hand went up to his mouth. He gave a gigantic yawn. It seemed to course down the whole of his body. "Lord! Lord! Lord! I'm tired." He was asleep in a matter of minutes. He did not wake until the sun showed through the strands of the white cotton curtains, taking the substance out of them.

Pam had been staring at them for an hour and a half before Jimmy woke.

CHAPTER TWENTY-TWO

AFTER the fifth day she said shyly, "Thank you for what you're doing."

He was swinging the head of an ash-stick. Pam was sitting down on a boulder. She was smoking a cigarette.

"Thank you for what?" Jimmy asked her. "Playing golf with sheep's droppings?"

The sun shone down hard upon Brothers Water. The grass lay a live green over the fells. The clear peak of

Helvellyn bit into the sky and Striding Edge made a thin line beside it. Jimmy cut at the turf with his stick.

"Well, for—for not touching me at night," Pam said.

"Oh that. Well, I promised you a bolster." He leant on the end of his stick. "This is where old Wordsworth said bye-bye to his brother. I can't think where the dickens he could have been going."

Pam kept her eyes on his face. She was aware that the earth spread round her in beauty which should have claimed her attention, but if she was ahead of Jimmy she kept looking back at him, and if she was behind him she studied the shape of his head and the impressive flat breadth of his shoulder-line. She noticed that wherever she went with him women turned round to look at him. She said, "Jimmy, we haven't heard from the family yet."

"No, by God, we haven't."

"What do you think it means?"

"They probably all suffered a joint fit of apoplexy, in which case we shall have to go on living in sham sin until they recover."

The smoke blew across Pam's half-closed eyes. She made a face and stubbed out the cigarette, in a patch of lime-green moss. "Jimmy, does it mean because you're not doing anything to me at night—does it mean we really *are* going to get married?"

He turned to her laughing. "Of course it does. Do you think that because I'm leaving you unsullied I'm going to take you back to the shop and say 'I haven't damaged this, I want another one, please'?"

"I just couldn't believe you meant marriage."

"Then you're a silly little goose. Oh, of course, I didn't do it properly, did I? I didn't behave at all in accordance with your romantic ideals. Well, better late than never." He went shakily down on one knee. "Miss Houghton, unworthy and humble though I be, I beg you to be my blushing bride." He pronounced the word 'braid', and she laughed at him.

"Get up. You look so silly."

She was nervous on Striding Edge, and her voice was awed. "Is this where *he* fell off?"

"X marks the spot, I've no doubt."

She walked gingerly, in spite of herself drawn to the edge. Jimmy snatched out at her hand. "Come away, you morbid little mutt. What are you looking for? Gory remains?" After that he was silent across Striding Edge. When they struck broader ground Pam sighed with relief. "I wonder everyone doesn't fall off. Jimmy, where's Mrs. Osbourne now?"

"Oh, somewhere in France with her gigolo."

She caught sight of his face and said nothing more.

In the distance the sheep looked like white specks of bog cotton caught on the fells. The valley made a funnel of sunlight and the wind tilted the tips of tall pines. They did not speak again until they climbed down into Patterdale.

Pam lagged behind, her legs throbbing. Jimmy walked steadily ahead. He was counting the posts since he wrote his letter to his father. He was impatiently awaiting the reply. The waiting put a strain on his nerves. If the delay was too long they might fail him. It would be a dastardly act to let down Pam. But if the temptation to do so was to be put much longer in his way he feared that he would never have the courage to go through with his plans.

To propose marriage to Pam at all had been a desperately difficult step to take. The Army had pressed him towards it. The latter part of his national service had been spent in Austria. He liked the life, and would have been happy to make soldiering his career. But it carried an unexpected threat of loneliness in it, which bewildered him at first. There seemed no concrete place for him amongst his colleagues. He did not share the ceaseless desire to exchange masculine for feminine company, and the perpetual talk of women failed to make an appeal to him. He did not share the youthful preoccupation with the female sex, however innocently confined to arguing the competitive points of pin-up girls. Yet when it was hinted to him that there were others with feelings akin to his own, and that provision for congenial male company could be made for him, he failed to grasp the implication. The hint came from a corporal with a hard head of red hair and a stocky frame. Jimmy was slow to understand at first and the corporal was quick enough to change the subject when it became clear to him that Jimmy was missing his meaning. He was never approached by the corporal again. He joined in the parties involving women, but he rarely enjoyed himself. He saw no hint of a warning at first. It took some while to disturb him. He did not dislike women, but he was shy of them and uninterested in them.

It was a source of acute embarrassment to Jimmy that they seemed to find him so attractive. His indifference became an additional stimulant. It was his major complaint against women that they failed to believe in his lack of interest in them. "They're so damned sure you want them. They walk about with a price in their eyes. For my money it's ten times too high. I haven't seen a good bargain yet."

A young colleague once inquired of him, "What's the matter with you? Are you queer?"

His chin had grown firm and square. His feet and his hands were big. The breadth of his shoulders combined with his height brought a change of tactics in drunkards aggressively inclined towards him. He smoked a pipe and in a society drawing-room looked the average young Englishman at bay. Out of ten suspects he would have been the tenth to be accused of effeminacy.

He had seen few real 'queers' in his life. A waiter in an English restaurant had once caused him keen amusement. He had studied the little affected movements, the high laugh, and the quick flick of the napkin: "My word! You *have* made crumbs!" And he had not troubled to conceal his derisive contempt. It had never occurred to him to look upon the waiter as anything other than one of nature's freak

comics. He would have been surprised to have been asked
to connect the boy with any of the ordinary circumstances
attached to everyday life. That the little yellow-faced waiter
should have income-tax problems, suffer from aching teeth,
be deeply religious, or be interested in politics, never
occurred to him. These were human activities reserved only
for citizens with the obvious normality of himself. This
little creature with the tray on the flat of his hand and the
'whoops!' as he slid through the serving-doors, could only
be regarded as a joke at which his fellow-men might be
amused or unamused according to their temperament.
Several men of his acquaintance found the joke repulsive.
"My God, I can't stand them. They give me the creeps."

His knowledge and his experience of homosexuality found
no deeper base than ridicule. Now and again it was jolted
into awareness by the fragments of a memory connected
with Bradcombe. But they remained confused and incom-
plete. His knowledge was chiefly limited to the fact that
such a deviation from the ordinary channels of sexual
behaviour existed. He had seen little of it at his public
school. He had not come into contact with it amongst his
immediate Army associates except for the corporal whose
roundabout approach he had failed to grasp. He knew that
it 'went on', but where, when and how it went on was a
matter for the authorities or the occasional salacious story.
"Did you hear about the pouf who went to buy a two-way-
stretch . . ?" That it was a fact he had never considered
disputing, but that it should exist amongst his own circle of
acquaintances or in the drawing-room of sanely-occupied
persons was to his mind unlikely to a point of absurdity.
It occurred only in that curious outer ring of human life.
It lay with disaster, disablement, lunacy and close bereavement. It was reserved with misfortune for other people. It
was something which could not happen to oneself.

His ideas upon homosexuality fell into little more than
schoolboy graduations. A sissy had remained in his mind

as a boy whining for favours and crying before he was hurt.
A Smiley was a dirty little swine, and a Creepy Davies was a
dirty old swine. A pervert was a complication on a higher
plane of which he had only the flimsiest conception. He
believed it to be vaguely connected with the activities of
Oscar Wilde and therefore possibly one of the lopsided
facets of genius. A queer, a queen, a pouf, a pansy, a nancy-
boy and a fairy were variations upon the description of 'one
of those', and the whole lot spelt the waiter and 'whoops'.

It did not strike him as a question deserving serious
attention, much less consideration. When the waiter's elfin
antics ceased to divert him he had asked for his coat in a tone
of voice which he had never employed to any living creature
of either sex before.

That abnormality might lie inert in normality, that
normality should have the power to mask abnormality
without being immediately detectable to the naked eye, was
not even a thinking proposition. 'They' were all like the
waiter. It was always discernible. Their inflections, their
gestures, their walk, their clothes—it was there for the
greatest fool to observe. As a deliberate vice it no doubt
carried its own wanton delights, incomprehensible to the
healthy mind. But that it was deliberate there was surely no
question. It could only be a matter of choice. He had heard
but dismissed the theories which suggested a psychological
maladjustment in childhood as being responsible. He had
small use for the adult who blamed his peculiarities upon
circumstances in infancy. He had inherited Osbourne's
hearty dislike of the psychological. That it might not be a
matter of choice or of preference in every case; that it might
be unavoidable rather than deliberate; that it might bring
inner conflicts causing an amount of misery not easily
assessed and with it a loneliness unparalleled—never caused
him a moment's reflection. To his mind, perversion was a
crime and its adherents were criminals. In common with
other types of criminal they could not escape knowing right

from wrong. The fact that they chose to follow the wrong proved that it was preferable to them and was therefore unforgivable.

Nor did the fact that it might not be instantly recognisable disturb him. To have discovered possibilities of it beneath respectable bowler hats, distinguished uniforms, and the man in the street would have shocked but not convinced him. He would have been even less easily persuaded that it could have been found in men of his own healthy interests. He laughed at the suggestion of his colleague that he might be queer.

It was, therefore, some considerable time before he became aware that his attraction towards Josef Kliebermann was physical.

CHAPTER TWENTY-THREE

AT first it was a matter of chance meetings and nothing more. After that it became a matter of looking out for the man. Acquaintanceship proved disappointing. Josef Kliebermann's English was erratic and Jimmy's German was poor. The man was several years his senior, had a wife and five children, of whose dull antics he told interminable tales.

It was a faint resemblance to Osbourne which had first drawn Jimmy towards him. But upon closer inspection it was hard to tell where the resemblance lay. It was not in feature and not in colouring. It was something vaguely to do with the stockiness of the frame and the manner of smoking; straight-fingered and swift, and the same twist to the stub as he put it out in an ash-tray. The meetings were preceded by nervous apprehension on Jimmy's part and followed by nervous depressions hard to dispel. The broad face of Josef Kliebermann lodged in Jimmy's brain. He found, without planning to do so, that when he lit Kliebermann's cigarette or passed him a drink he was going out of his way to touch him. Even at the time of doing so he was not conscious of the action. It was only in the aftermath when he battled against the strange desire to see the man again that it struck him. It was not unakin to the horror of looking back upon himself mechanically propelled by an unseen force. It was surely not within the bounds of possibility that the figure which was manœuvring itself deliberately nearer to the person of Kliebermann could be the figure of J. H. Stretton, a not inconsiderable athlete and a soldier in uniform? But in his recollections of an evening in the Austrian's company there was no doubt that he derived pleasure from physical contact with him. There was a reassurance in Kliebermann's stocky presence, a comfort, and a vague substitute for something he had lost. It was the elusive but distinctive sense of security that had been taken from him twice.

He was powerless to argue himself out of it. He experienced a sensation which was vaguely familiar. It was loneliness. In the entire world he felt that there was no one in whom he dared confide, no one whose advice he could ask, no one whose help he could claim without incurring disgust or perhaps even penalisation.

In case it was visible to his company commander or his friends he kept himself more and more apart. Josef Kliebermann he went out of his way to dodge.

He lay on his bed at the age of nineteen, suffering from an embittering self-contempt. He sent his mind backwards, probing for a start to it. Bradcombe memories were patchy in places and clear in others. Hadn't Smiley accused him of something obscene? Could it be possible that Smiley was right? Had the filthy little devil recognised in him a kindred spirit? There must have been some reason for the boy to single him out in particular. He had forgotten the punch on the nose.

Worse still, had Osbourne suspected him? Memories of Osbourne were not confused. They stood out as if etched in relief. It might have been only yesterday that the hand went out to touch his head and was withdrawn with such obvious revulsion. No wonder Osbourne had not been able to lay a good clean hand on him. He must have known him for what he was and despised him for it. The realisation left Jimmy sick with self-loathing to the base of his spine. In Jimmy's mind the sissy, the pansy, the queer, the pouf, and the waiter acquired three other names. Incredibly, unbelievably, inconceivably enough, they were Jeremy Howard Stretton.

But it was still after all a mere matter of choice. It was not compulsory to launch out on a life of crime. The only thing to do with abnormality was to stifle it with normality. He must force himself back to the natural path and give himself no chance to stray from it. It had, after all, quite a simple solution. It needed no psychiatrist. It was a matter of making a decision. Normal men married. There was only one woman with whom such a step could be taken as far as he was concerned. When he completed his national service he would have to marry Pam.

He was a long way ahead of her on the walk down into Patterdale. He sat on a stile and smoked until she caught him up. "My goodness," she said, "I should like to have had your thoughts. They seemed to give you wings. Oh, Jimmy, d'you think there's a bus?"

He put his cigarette-end out with a strong twist on the gate-post. "We'll get a car back if you're all that knocked up. And I'll buy you a slap-up tea to revive you."

CHAPTER TWENTY-FOUR

NOBODY came to fetch them, and it was a week before anyone wrote. Then two letters arrived for Jimmy by the same post. They were from Anita and the Reverend Jordon. There were no letters for Pam.

Anita wrote a tiny, pointed hand:

'. . . broken your father's heart. I could never have believed you could have behaved so disgracefully with a girl of that class. After all your dear father has done for you, to have exposed a man in his position to such shame and humiliation strikes me as being the depths of ingratitude. I only hope that you do not intend to expose him to further indignities by bringing this girl into the house and expecting us to treat her as one of the family.'

Jimmy tore the letter across. Pam said, white-faced, "What is it, Jimmy?"

"My Aunt Anita twitters worse on paper than she does when you can hear her." He opened the Reverend Jordon's letter:

'. . . and my only regret is that you should have thought it necessary to blackmail me. I fear it says little for me as a father that you should feel bound to resort to such methods. I had hoped you looked upon me as sufficiently understanding and sufficiently your friend to have discussed the matter with me. Surely you could not have supposed that I would have withheld my consent to something which concerned your happiness? I do not deny that I consider you are both a trifle young to embark on the sacred and serious state of matrimony, but my greatest wish for you is that Pamela should bring you the blessing of true companionship which your dear mother brought to me.

'It only remains for me to say now that you may be sure that Pamela will be as certain of a welcome from me as you will be yourself, and that this house is always open to both of you.'

Jimmy tossed the letter to Pam. "All's well that ends well, Mrs. S. It's O.K. with the old man."

Neither letter gave any hint of the hostile little conference which had been held at the vicarage. In the cold drawing-room Margaret's flattering portrait sent down her patient smile on to Mrs. Houghton sitting tight-lipped on the sofa. Anita sat tight-lipped on the chair by the bureau. The Reverend Jordon sat smoking a pipe, and Mr. Houghton, groomed for the occasion, sat with his hat on his knee. He struggled with the words that his wife had put into his mouth. It was obvious that they did not originate from him. "I'm sure there is no disrespect in it, Vicar, but there's never been any talk about my family." Mr. Houghton's voice was rising and his colour was following the upward trend. He had been forbidden a visit to the 'Bull' the previous evening, and he had had to forgo his lunch-time sojourn. The matter was rankling with him. "It's not that I've got anything against the boy, Vicar. I've known him since he was a little nipper and I don't think they come any better. It's just that his sort get the idea that they can take liberties with a girl like Pam."

The Reverend Jordon knocked out his pipe. "It's evident to me, Mr. Houghton, that you're misjudging his sort. You can see from his letter that his sole object in adopting this extraordinary procedure is to force us to allow him to marry your daughter."

Mr. Houghton sat down, confused. Unaccustomed sobriety had him at a disadvantage. He was wont to say that a man needed a pint inside him if he were to be at his best with his tongue.

Anita cleared her throat. "You must see that such a union would be unsuitable. I'm sure we should be saving them considerable unhappiness, if we could think of a sensible solution."

The Reverend Jordon cut across her: "Have you anything against this marriage, Mr. Houghton?"

Mr. Houghton floundered. His wife had not rehearsed him for such an opening. She came to his rescue. "We've got to think of our girl's good name, Vicar. There's never been any trouble in my family."

"Splendid," said the Reverend Jordon, "because I've no objections at all."

They were married in Marylebone Registry Office. They could not afford a honeymoon. The Lakes had swallowed Jimmy's savings.

Pam wore the dark grey suit for the wedding. They rented two rooms in Pimlico.

Jimmy was surprisingly good in the house. Pam had never met with such consideration. If she was tired he sent her to bed and waited on her. If she was ill he nursed her with a tenderness that she had never once met in her life before. She asked with a smile that seemed to involve her eyes in a conspiratorial understanding with her mouth, "Jimmy, do you believe in miracles?"

"Nope."

"Then you're an old silly, because I do."

He was reading law at the London University. The Reverend Jordon had increased their allowance. It meant economies at the vicarage.

Pam found a job. She left the house at half-past eight every morning and took care of two children in a luxury flat. She arrived home at half-past six every evening full of their antics. "I wish you could have seen the baby's face. She sat up and held out her plate and said, 'More for Katy, more,' and Lady Parker said, 'What a little Oliver Twist,' and what do you think the baby said? She said, 'Oliver T'ist, Oliver T'ist!' Oh, it was so sweet."

Jimmy was preparing an omelette. "Witty little mite!"

Pam took off a beret and put knitted gloves beside it. "Jimmy, we will have babies as soon as we can afford it, won't we?"

He beat up the omelette and made no reply.

"I'd love a little girl like Katy, and a little boy like Tim."

Jimmy changed the subject. "Bet you forgot the frozen peas."

"Oh no, I didn't. Oh, my heavens, I'd better get them out. They'll be thawing all over my basket."

They redecorated the two flaking rooms themselves. Each wall was a different colour. They shaded from pale lilac to deep mauve, with a patterned wallpaper in between. Pam stood out against single beds. "Let's be old-fashioned," she said.

Jimmy was dreading the nights. It was easy enough on the first occasion. Pam was nervous and Jimmy was sorry for her. It was possible to be tender and laugh. But Pam became gently insistent. She lay by his side and her voice was small. "You do love me, don't you, Jimmy?"

"But passionately," he said.

"You always seem to joke."

It was easier if he drank, but Pam objected to the smell of his breath. It made an excuse to quarrel and put off a reconciliation for days. "Well, to hell with it," he said. "If a woman can't stand a single Scotch on a man's breath she can't think much of him in the first place. Can you imagine a Frenchwoman behaving like that?

Pam was instantly contrite. "Oh, I'm sorry. I must have been mad. I wouldn't care if you smelt of a whole bottle of whisky. I suppose it's because of Dad. He used to blow beer all round the house. Oh, Jimmy, I love you so much."

He took her hands from behind his neck and moved away from her. "Well it doesn't always feel like it."

It was easy to blame her for lack of response. It became the more constant excuse: "For God's sake, girl, how do you expect a man to work up any enthusiasm for you if you behave like a maiden aunt?"

Quarrels became more frequent, and the excuses began to be justified. She was apprehensive, intense, and strung up. She asked anxiously, "Was *that* all right?"

He rolled up his eyes. "Was *that* all right! What a thing to ask. The mere question makes it a hundred per cent *not* all right." Their love-making seldom ended without Pam quietly crying into her pillow.

Jimmy took a blanket off the bed and made for the drawing-room couch. "Oh, God, and I thought you were the one woman who would never make a scene."

She thought she was not attractive to him, that there were women he met who showed her up. She went to a hair-dresser and came back with an elaborate hair-style which failed to suit her.

"You look like a whippet got up as a poodle," Jimmy observed.

At supper-time they were silent usually. Jimmy read his notes on the morning's lecture; Pam tried to keep her mind occupied. Watching him closely, she wondered if it would be possible to recover her faith in the lasting powers of miracles. He worked hard at the University, and he studied late at night. Tiredness might have given an irritable edge to his voice, but it would not account for the sarcastic exasperation that she sometimes heard in it. Only boredom, mistrust, or dislike could do that. She failed to see what she had done to incur any of them so soon. There was a strong strain of her mother in Pam. She had, in spite of herself, a certain amount of prudishness, and there were times when she was aware of a vague sense of shame in the extravagance of her feelings towards Jimmy. If they read side by side on the sofa she cuddled up with shoeless feet tucked under her, and manœuvred herself closer and closer to him. If he did not make the usual protest, "Look, sweetie, I can't give full attention to the law of the land and you at the same time," she made an attempt to slip under his arm. If he did not remove it she sat cuddled up to him, blissfully content.

"I love you more than anyone in the world."

"A flattering but eccentric choice."

"I get so scared when I think how good-looking you are and how other women go for you. There isn't anyone else at the University, is there?"

"Anyone else? Of course there's someone else. You don't suppose I sit there in solitary grandeur, do you?"

"I mean a woman. Oh, Jimmy, sometimes I feel as though you can't bear to touch me. I'm so afraid that it means you love somebody else."

Jimmy freed himself from her. "That's right. Spoil a perfectly peaceful evening! Make a scene if you have to tie yourself in knots. We have so many peaceful evenings these days. We could do with a dust-up, couldn't we? Don't let's risk a let-up in the good old ding-dong routine." And he stood up and put on his hat. "Be it ever so hum-bell there's no place like home!"

It was at the vicarage that he realised that his problem was not a matter of choice. They were spending their summer holidays with the Reverend Jordon, whose quiet acceptance of her as one of his own made up completely to Pam for any discomforts she felt with Anita. There were several marked evidences of Anita's resentment. Mrs. Houghton no longer worked at the house, and as Jimmy's parents-in-law the Houghtons had to be invited to tea. Anita's absence was attributed to a forgotten appointment. But Pam had heard the telephone conversation which had made a last-minute arrangement with Alice Macey. "Really, it's too embarrassing. Jordon must face it alone. After all, if he'd put his foot down . . ."

After the oppressive tea-party, at which only the Reverend Jordon and Jimmy remained at ease, Pam gave way to a childhood sentiment. She crept off by herself to the loft. She was determined that Jimmy should not see how Anita's bad manners had wounded her. She wanted to indulge in self-pity in peace. She might even shed a few tears over

Anita's hurtful slight. She had an old friend in the great
rambling loft. It had harboured her tears before. So often
when she wanted to think about Jimmy she had gone up to
seek its seclusion. She pushed back the trap and stood up.
She breathed the old familiar smell of cardboard and leather
and ageing upholstery. The draught sucked at her candle
and blew it out. She groped her way forward and felt for a
match. Some cold and damp creature struck out at her face.
It wound a long clammy arm round her throat. She dropped
the candle and matches and called out in fright. Then she
remembered the old camel-hair coat. She had some difficulty
in managing to free her neck from the sleeve's insistent
grasp. The coat hung from its hanger still, weird and limp.
It threw the same eerie pattern across the candlelight. It was
rotten, and eaten away by moths. It smelt sour and decayed,
and felt stickily wet. She held the candle high to examine it.
The hours she and Jimmy had whispered in front of it! The
hours they had plotted and planned before it, and all the fond
care she had lavished on it seemed to have vanished into
something more distant than time. She could no longer
feel a friend in the coat. There had been a period when she
cherished it because it gave her the promise of Jimmy's
company. In a strange way she felt it had cheated her. She
felt less sure of Jimmy than ever now. They were quarrelling
day by day. There was no Mr. Osbourne to use as a method
of wheedling his attention towards her. She was surprised
when it suddenly dawned on her that she had been jealous
of Mr. Osbourne. She unhooked the coat distastefully.
When she pulled it away from its hanger she made a ball of
it and carried it into the yard. She pushed the whole coat
well down in the dustbin. Then she washed her hands.

It was not until a day or two later that she told Jimmy she
had thrown it away. She was quite unprepared for what
happened. He spoke quietly at first: "You little bitch!"

"Jimmy!" she answered him, horrified. "Don't you dare
talk like that to me. I may not be good enough for your

Aunt Anita, but that doesn't mean I'm going to stand here and be talked to like that. It was all mouldy and green. It was disgusting. The collar was eaten right through by moths."

"Nevertheless it was my property. I suppose you think you've paid me out because I don't jibber with delight at the prospect of possessing your tempting little body."

She had never heard a more viciously delivered remark. She said, shocked, "You sound so spiteful, I can hardly believe it's you talking."

At his sides his fists were clenched, but, more alarming than that, there were tears in his eyes. Pam took an impulsive step towards him, but she gave a little hurt squeak when he backed away from her. She was crying herself by this time. "But, darling, I thought you'd forgotten about it. It was ages ago, we were kids."

"Have you forgotten that it belonged to a friend of mine?"

"No, of course not, Jimmy, but——"

"Perhaps the holy state of matrimony makes you think you can do what you like with my possessions. I'm not going to forgive you for chucking away that old coat, Pam." It was said with a deliberate calm more menacing than if he had shouted. It was she who backed away from him then. She spent the night at No. 15 Alma Row. Jimmy went up to London without her.

CHAPTER TWENTY-FIVE

HE was alone with his problem again. It made oppressive and clinging company. He tried every method he knew to shake it off. He was ashamed of his treatment of Pam, but could not bring himself to write to her. He made an effort to miss her physically. He stood her photograph next to the bed. He walked about the flat searching for associations

which would build up an attraction towards her. He tipped
out her clothes and sat studying them. He fondled stockings
and suspender-belts and ran her one little glamorous night-
gown through his hands. He failed to be excited by them.
He sighed when he replaced them in the drawer. He thought
of her hair, of her lips, and her breasts, and he was unmoved
by the memory of them.

In the Underground a fat man smiled at him. Jimmy
stared through him, his thoughts far away. There was an
owlish coquetry in the pallid eyes and an indisputable
invitation in the smile. It dawned upon Jimmy's conscious-
ness that the man had been following him for some considerable distance. He turned round and said, "Cut it out."
The fleshy face failed to mask disappointment; its resignation
struck Jimmy as pathetic. He wore a black hat and a discreet bow-tie. He went to pass Jimmy: "Excuse me, please."

Jimmy said, "Oh, all right. I'll buy you a drink." He
was not yet afraid of blackmail. The fat man looked un-
attractive and inoffensive. If he was burdened with the same
suffocating loneliness, the same sense of being cut off and
the need to talk to someone with the same troubles, he
deserved several drinks.

The fat man jogged beside him. "Where are we going?"
he asked.

"Oh, I don't know," Jimmy answered. "Café Royal?
The Premier, perhaps?"

The fat man shook his head. "No," he said, "O'Shaughnessy's Bar."

Jimmy prepared to follow him. The fat man said over his
shoulder, "My name's Eddie Baines. What's yours?"

"Houghton. Jordon Houghton."

There was nothing unusual about O'Shaughnessy's Bar in
itself. It smelt of oil-cloth and had varnished panelling in a
light-grained wood half-way up the wall. Bottle-green
paint took over where the panelling stopped. It was a
stuffily Edwardian, dimly-lit bar, and it was full. Jimmy's

entrance caused a frank scrutiny which gave him a tingling
sensation beneath the skin. Eddie pushed his way towards
the bar. "What'll it be?"

"This one's with me."

"No, no," said Eddie, "my party." He said good-evening
to right and to left, but Jimmy thought he detected a nervous
apprehension in his greeting towards his presumable friends.

A hand fell on Eddie's shoulder, but the eyes of its owner
were occupied with Jimmy. "Hallo, Eddie! Nice to see you
again."

"Hullo," said Eddie. He collected two glasses of whisky
and a bottle of ginger-ale. "There's a table over there," he
told Jimmy, and pointed it out with his chin.

"Look here," said the man who had greeted him, "let me
give you a hand with those."

"No, thanks," said Eddie. "We can manage." His voice
was proprietary towards Jimmy. "Go on, get that table,
there!"

Jimmy went to pass him. He came face to face with the
interested eyes. "How do you do?" said their owner. "My
name's Simpton." He was taller than Jimmy and looked his
middle forties.

Jimmy said, "Hallo," and made for the table.

Eddie sat by him, mopping his face. "I was *darned* if I
was going to introduce him to you. You want to watch out
for him."

There were times when Jimmy was unable to understand
some of the conversation which took place about him. The
jargon was foreign and incomprehensible to him. There
seemed a language peculiar to the place.

Eddie raised his glass, "Well, here's luck!"

Jimmy saluted him, "Cheers!" He was hesitant about
questioning Eddie about the place in case he caused offence.
He said casually, "Odd sort of spot, isn't it?"

Eddie looked round the bar. "We haven't been here long.
We have to keep moving, you know. Things get hot."

"You mean the police or something?"

"Yes, dreadful, isn't it? You'd think you'd be allowed to do what you like when you grow up, but no. We had to give the 'Grey Goat' the go by. I'm sorry, because that was a free house and I can't say I like the beer in this place."

"The police aren't likely to arrive at any minute, are they?" Jimmy asked anxiously.

"Oh, no. We're safe enough here for a bit. They haven't got on to it yet. We'd have been all right at the 'Grey Goat' if it hadn't been for *some* people. There was a little group of trouble-makers that used to make the place impossible. They'd get anywhere a bad name. You know, finger-nails, lipstick—*everything*. I mean, it's not only silly, it's criminal when you think how tricky things are in any case." His eye fell on Gorwin Simpton again. He said with venom, "Still, I'd rather have people like that than *him*."

"What's so bad about him?" Jimmy asked. "He looks respectable enough."

There was an anxious note in Eddie's voice: "You don't think he's attractive, do you? I don't. And besides, he's a shocking swine. He doesn't half think the world of himself, though. He thinks he's only got to crook his little finger to get everyone running round him. He was making a play for you all right."

"Making a play for me?" Jimmy said.

"Well, goodness! Can't you tell? But don't flatter yourself too much. He makes a play for everyone. I can't think what people see in him. He took David off Peter, just for the fun of it. He's always the same—he just likes to break something up. David and Peter were together a *year*. It was all going fine, they were made for each other. Of course it doesn't say much for Peter, but he's only a kid, and Gorwin can make himself charming."

Jimmy examined Gorwin Simpton. There seemed nothing about him to occasion such excessive regard. He raised his glass when he caught Jimmy's glance.

"He lets everyone down," said Eddie. "You can't trust him an inch."

Jimmy's attention was caught by a couple beside him. Under the table their feet were entwined, but above it they seemed cool acquaintances. They were discussing the merits of central heating in recognisable English.

Eddie became wet round the collar and garrulous. "I don't know how *you* are, but *me*, I'm choosy. I wouldn't give you a thank-you for any of the punks and sallies here. Not if they came on bended knees I wouldn't say thank you for anyone here."

Jimmy looked round the bar again. Here and there were sprinkled the type into which the elfin waiter, with his 'whoops' and his flick of the napkin, had fallen, affected and slight and obvious. But more frequently there appeared the well-dressed, inconspicuous type of men, who could have walked about unsuspected in Channock. He touched Eddie's sleeve. "Those two there—are they—what are *they* doing here?"

Eddie's plump-rimmed eyes screwed up. The smoke was thick round the lights in the bar. "Who? Oh, them! The one on the right is a bank manager. He's the salt of the earth when you get to know him. He's ever so well informed. But the one on the left—" Eddie settled himself into his chair like a hen on a nest—"I think he's got foreign blood, but if that boy's not a prostitute I'm a Dutchman. He's disgusting, he goes with women, too, everyone knows it except poor old Thompson. That boy's taking Thompson for a hell of a ride. You ought to see the act he puts on. He never looks at anyone else when he's with Thompson, but I've seen him trading afterwards. It's disgusting. It makes you sick."

Jimmy's eyes travelled over the man at his side. The short moustache looked absurd in the middle of Eddie's long upper lip. His cuffs were too long and his hands were purple. Jimmy was fascinated by Eddie's outstretched fingers. It was not only the little one he held out when he lifted his glass. The second and third fingers were extended as well. Surreptitiously Jimmy tried to copy him. He found he could not support the weight. He finished his drink in one gulp and asked Eddie politely, "Are you—are you—er—involved at the moment, or whatever it is?"

The couple behind them had finished with central heating. They had reached the affairs of their friends.

". . . impossible to make a go of it with Edward. She's never heard of give and take."

"You ought to meet Henry. She's worse."

Eddie turned towards Jimmy, his smile frank. "Well, since you've asked me, no. But then, you see, it's difficult for me. I'm not just out for sex."

"Oh, I see," said Jimmy. "What are you out for, then?"

"I want *affection*," Eddie told him urgently. "I'm not like these creatures in here. I'm not a sally, I'm not a punk. I'm looking for something that *lasts*. I like a home and things in common—oh, I know sex is important, you've got to have it, it's only natural. But I don't think it's the *only* thing. You wouldn't think there was anything else in the world in here. That's all they think about, sex! I like a bit of friendship to go with it, myself. Of course it's not easy when you're hounded as badly as we are. Sauce, isn't it? Women and men can do what they like together and nobody thinks it's awful. But when it's men and men! Well, I don't see the difference, really I don't. But I do think you should have decent ideas, like me. It might be dangerous setting up home together, but it's the only way to make things last. Flitting from one to the other—well, where does that get you, I ask you? I tell you I've had some experiences."

"What sort?" Jimmy asked.

"Well, no names, no pack drill. The last thing I want to do is to throw mud at a friend. But I've been let down so badly I don't feel like trusting a single soul again. My friend

and me—I was much older than him—we were absolutely
like that."

Eddie put one fat finger across another to indicate the
close understanding of himself and his friend.

"We'll call him Jack. That wasn't his name, but we'll call
him that. We were everything to each other. Laugh! Jack
could make me laugh if I was dying. We had such a nice
little flat—I was working in London then. I'm in Berkhamsted now, wines and spirits. But it's close in a town
like that, you know. There's nowhere to go and you've got
to be careful. That's why I come up to town now and
then."

"What happened to Jack?"

"Oh, it broke up. The usual."

"What's the usual?"

"Well, he went off with somebody else. But, you see,
when you've tasted the real thing you can't make do with a
bench in the park."

"No, I suppose not."

An elderly man with a baby face appeared. "I'm on my
way to the bar. Can I get you something?"

Eddie snapped, "No, thanks. We've got perfectly good
hands and feet."

When the man was out of earshot he said ruefully to
Jimmy, "You're going to get a lot of that. You're so nice-
looking. That was the trouble with Jack."

"Eddie!" Jimmy leant forward towards him. "I want
you to tell me something. "Be frank with me. When you
—'picked me up' this evening did something about me make
you think I would be a good bet?"

Jimmy realised that the painful expression on Eddie's egg-
shaped face was a manifestation of shyness. "Oh! Well, no.
But I looked at you, and you looked at me, so I thought I'd
try it. I thought it was no good at first, but then when you
said you'd have a drink——"

"Yes, my God, I did say that, didn't I? Look, Eddie,

would you like to fill us up?" He brought out his wallet and took out a pound.

Eddie said: "Hey! I wasn't hinting. This is my party, I brought you here."

"Rubbish. But get them for us, will you? I honestly don't think I've got the courage to go up to that bar. I might get my bottom pinched."

Eddie collected their glasses. "Oh, it's quite a respectable place in that way. This isn't a street-corner crowd." His squat figure pushed towards the bar.

Gorwin Simpton slipped into his seat. "Poor Eddie! So worthy, so plain." Simpton's smile seemed to fit round his cigarette. "How long have you known our friend?"

"I set eyes on him for the first time tonight, if you must know."

"How well do you intend to get to know him?"

"I'm afraid I'm not very interested in this kind of conversation," Jimmy confessed.

Simpton leant back; his voice was easy. "There's no need to be so aggressive. I'm doing you a favour. You look pretty green to me, and it's possible that you don't know Eddie's type."

"What's wrong with him?"

"Use the eyes in your head. He's no chicken and he could hardly be defended on the score of being an oil-painting. Do you imagine he finds it easy? You'll get yourself one hell of a reputation if you're seen about with him. He has to pay for what he gets. He hangs about the streets or waits about in parks. Personal attraction being somewhat lacking, he has to pick it up where he can. He's bound to fall into some pretty foul company. That's why it won't do you much good to be seen about with him too often."

"I see."

"Well, look here. Give me a ring sometime if you feel like it. We might go along to the 'L' Club." He was about to get up when a youth danced across the room. He had straight mousy hair and grey eyes. He had a gay Cockney voice and seemed lightly alive. "Gorwin, you'll have to see me home, dear. You know I'm done in on two gins."

Simpton said, "Flick, this is Mr.——"

"Houghton," Jimmy supplied quickly.

"Mr. Houghton, this is Flick. If you can't take two gins you should stick to one."

"Hark at the preacher," said Flick. "I can't stand making rules and regulations. It takes all the fun out of things."

When they left him, Jimmy found a card beside him. It bore Simpton's name and address. He watched the two walk off. Flick's slim body was raised now and again by a series of intricate skips. He said, "Here! How long has that been going on? Is that something out of your past?"

Simpton's voice sounded patient and weary. He answered with Jimmy's phrase, "I set eyes on him for the first time tonight, if you must know."

"Well, you'd better just see it's the last time, or I might look around myself."

Eddie came back with the drinks. His puffed eyes were baleful. "I saw him. What did he say about me?"

Jimmy said, "Nothing," then jumped——

Eddie peered in the same direction. "What's the matter?"

"Who's that man in the corner? The one in the dark lounge suit talking to the chap with red hair."

Eddie looked past him. "I don't know him to talk to, but he's always in here. They say he's some sort of a doctor. Nice-looking, isn't he?" Eddie sighed. "Presnor! I think that's what his name is. Why? Do you want to meet him? He's had his eye on you all the evening. You can't keep a friend to yourself in here with everyone out on the make."

Jimmy said, "In some extraordinary way he reminded me of my father, when he was younger, of course. For a moment it gave me quite a shock."

The doctor's face was turned from him. He sat nursing a glass, his legs crossed. He seemed to be effortlessly at his ease. There was a comfortable detachment about him which suggested self-assurance and claimed confidence. He leant against the bottle-green wall behind him, deep in discussion with the man at his side. Now and again he turned on Jimmy his black and thoughtful eyes. He was shorter and much less lightly-built than the Reverend Jordon, but the resemblance was there all the same. The thought of the Reverend Jordon and of Channock and of what Channock would think of O'Shaughnessy's made Jimmy determine to go. "I'll have to beat it now, Eddie. You must come round to the flat for a drink one day, but I'm afraid I'm not open to fun and games."

"Who said I was?" Eddie demanded. "What do you think I am?"

"Yes, I know, I know, you're choosy."

"If a person can't have a drink with another person without being thought on the make—well! You must think I'm pretty promiscuous if that's the sort you think I am. I'll have you know I don't jump into bed with people the first time I see them, whatever that swine of a Simpton might have said. What do you think I do? Go around with prostitutes? I take a long time to get to know people and even then it's not always a cinch."

Jimmy, looking down at the little man drawn to his plump full height, his expression withdrawn and offended, was sorry for him. Difficulty he might have in finding a congenial partner, but Jimmy believed in his claim to being choosy. There was something sincere in the little man's air of offence, and his ruffled ginger hair. "Well, any time you're passing, drop in, Eddie."

As he passed the doctor in the navy-blue lounge suit they studied each other. The doctor was the first to look away. He returned, with a smooth rolling of the head against the bottle-green paint of the wall behind him, to continue the discussion with the man at his side. Jimmy walked swiftly away from the bar. He dropped Simpton's card down a drain. There was a curious thumping sensation in the region of his heart which gave him the unpleasant experience of believing himself about to faint. He was deliberately marshalling his thoughts into a scathing attack upon the activities of the occupants of O'Shaughnessy's Bar. 'Of all revolting spectacles! I suppose I deserved it for getting myself let in for it.' He gave a physical shudder of revulsion at the recollection of Flick. 'Sickening little swine. I suppose one should laugh at it really, it's funny enough in a way. Well, never again, Jimmy lad. Never again. I wonder what the devil a decent-looking fellow like that doctor could have been doing in a hell-hole like that? He looked just about as out of place as I did—I hope. Funny him being so like Dad.' The thumping increased round his heart. 'God in heaven, what on earth is the matter with me? I hope I haven't got asthma, or pneumonia, or cancer or something.' He rubbed the left side of his chest with his knuckles. 'Thrombosis! That's what it is. *Extraordinary* place for a chap like that doctor to go to—still, of course, lots of them didn't look the part. He's probably as queer as a coot. That red-headed chap was his boy-friend, I suppose.'

Jimmy decided to write to Pam and ask her to come back to him. The prospect of Eddie's bleak future as outlined by Simpton had deeply impressed him. Poor Eddie! He was not without his ideals, he had his standards, and he had his code. It must be wearing to keep up a deception in Berkhamsted. It was the deception that alarmed Jimmy most. The prospect of a lifetime of dodging suspicion brought a chill of instinctive despair.

A thin layer of light came under the door when he went up the stairs to his flat. He turned his key hard in the door, calling excitedly, "Pam!"

She had not yet removed her coat. "You've been living out of tins," she said reproachfully. "I just knew you wouldn't bother to cook for yourself."

He danced her round the floor in his arms. "If you were

the gent who'd come to tell me I'd won the football pools I couldn't be more pleased to see you." He kissed her eyes and her nose and her chin. "Darling, you've got to do more than forgive me. You've got to forget it. Heaven alone knows what got into me. I was unpardonably, appallingly rude, but I didn't mean a word of it. All over a moth-eaten coat!" His eyes filled with tears when he mentioned the coat.

"Oh, Jimmy, I did feel so dreadful about it. I went all over the place trying to get it back. I asked the dustman and I went to the salvage department. I'd no idea that you'd mind about it so much."

"Of course you hadn't. Why should you expect me to go raving mad? It was just that it became a sort of mascot to me. I'm very superstitious in some ways. What did you tell them at home?"

"Oh, nothing. I told Mum I couldn't stick your Aunt Anita, and that's quite true—nobody knows we've quarrelled. Your father sent his love. He's a good man, Jimmy. I really love him. I like him much better than my own father."

Jimmy said, "That's nice. I ran into a chap who looked awfully like him tonight——" He suddenly tightened his arms about her. He had the stifling sensation beneath his heart again. "Pam," he said, "Pam!" and his voice was tight with an urgent misery. "For God's sake, help me, Pam."

CHAPTER TWENTY-SIX

HE knew when he woke the next morning with Pam's gentle smile at his side. "Jimmy, if we have a baby do you think we could call it Jordon?"

"Yes, if it's a boy," Jimmy said. "It would sound a bit odd for a girl."

"Oh, if it's a girl it'll have to be Fanny. It's Mother's name. If we didn't do that she'd go mad."

"I don't care if she's taken off in a strait-jacket, no child of mine is going to be Fanny. The Americans have put an entirely different slant on the word."

He knew when he battled to concentrate in the lecture-hall. When he wandered round the portrait gallery in the lunch-hour. He knew it when the little over-blonded prostitute swung towards him on his way home every night. She took his refusals good-naturedly. She laughed when he told her, "No, thanks. I'm a saint." They had a chat every night after that.

But chiefly he knew it when he went into the tiny church without any thought to what religious persuasion its congregation might have belonged. He went down on his knees in his first prayer for years. He knew even more forcibly when he went back in the evenings to Pam. He knew he was going into O'Shaughnessy's Bar again.

It was ten days before he actually did so. During that time he frequently visited the church. He liked the cool air and the deep-lying shadows. It seemed to allay a little the loneliness and the fear. He dreaded the hour approaching when his watch told him that he must go into the outside world again—a world which would condemn and despise him for something he could not understand himself. The thought of the jostling streets outside, of the endless stream of people and the feeling that amongst the moving millions there was not one human being to whom he could turn, made him put his head in his hands. But it was not easy to pray again. Somewhere at the back of his mind there was the vague feeling that with offending his father he had even offended God. It was a paralysing loneliness in such a congested world.

He had tried to confide in Pam. She was knitting a shawl in fleecy wool. Jimmy said, "That's a bit optimistic, isn't it? It's too soon to be quite so sure."

She smiled. "No, it isn't. I *feel* sure."

He sat opposite and leant forward, his fingers clutched. A wrought-iron standard lamp shed the only light in the room. It stood at the back of Pam's chair and made a strange little halo about her head. ˙Outside, the river boats hooted like mechanical owls. Jimmy said, "Pam, do you know that there are men who are more like women? Men who get involved both sexually and emotionally with each other?"

She dropped a stitch. "Oh, drat the thing! Wait a minute, don't talk to me—there! Yes, of course I do. Mother and I saw two coming home on a bus one night. You never saw such sights. It gave me the creeps."

Nor was there any hope of assistance from someone like Eddie. Eddie had found none himself. It was obvious that he must resign himself to there being no one to whom he could turn for help.

The smoke that clung hard to the walls and ceiling of O'Shaughnessy's crowded bar had turned the cream paint ginger-brown. There was a thick sulphuric fog outside. It would provide an excuse for being late home to Pam. He looked round for Eddie and failed to see him. Dr. Presnor was not present either. He refused to acknowledge a slight sense of disappointment.

The barman was not a 'queer'. Jimmy stood studying him with interest. He seemed impervious enough to what was going on about him, but an obvious sharp eye kept a look-out for trouble. O'Shaughnessy would tolerate no one who might have brought in the police.

A voice said beside him, "Hullo. How's tricks?" It was Flick. Jimmy kept out the contempt from his voice. "Tricks couldn't be trickier, thanks. Have a drink."

"All right, I don't mind. Gin and orange."

"Has Eddie been in?" Jimmy asked. "Eddie Baines?"

"No, I don't think so. Not tonight. He doesn't come up very often. I like dear old Eddie. He's nice."

"Oh?" Jimmy asked him with interest, "I thought he was rather despised."

"Who? Eddie? Why should he be? I like poor old Eddie. He's kind. Which is more than you can say for my old Dutch at times."

Jimmy thawed slightly towards Flick. "Where is your old Dutch tonight?"

Flick raised narrow shoulders. "Under a bus, I hope." He gave a quick smile and looked shamefaced. "No, I don't really mean that, of course."

"Trouble in the love-nest?" Jimmy asked.

"You *do* sound sarcastic," said Flick.

"I'm sorry. I didn't mean to."

"Oh, it's all right," said Flick. "Everyone warned me against him—but there, you know how it is, you're so darned sure you know what's best for you, aren't you?"

"What do you do for a living?"

"Me? I'm a dresser. Theatre. I've got a peach just now. But strewth, have I 'ad some stinkers! I could write a book on swollen 'eads."

"What's Simpton do?"

"Him? Oh, he's a lawyer. He's terribly clever."

"I gather you're none too happy with him."

"Oh, I'm happy all right in bits. We don't see much of each other really—with him being a lawyer, you see, he's got to be extra careful. It's a terrible strain, I can tell you. It gets on my nerves at times." Flick explained, "All the week I look forward to seeing him, and then when I do we row. He's so scared someone's going to get on to him. He thinks that there's safety in numbers. I tell you, I can't stand it much longer. The other day we met for coffee. It was one of those quiet little dumps where you don't often see people. But his nibs has to go and see someone he knows. We were sitting there, happy as sandboys, and then up he jumps like a jack-in-the-box and goes to another table." Flick added, "Well, I mean!"

Jimmy was looking past him. Dr. Presnor had just come in. He was in the navy-blue suit again and his teeth and his collar seemed extra white against his dark hair and dark skin. His black eyes were below Jimmy's level. Dr. Presnor was not a tall man.

He crossed to the bar and greeted Flick. "Any more trouble with that shoulder?" he asked.

"It gets a bit stiff now and then. I rubbed in that stuff you told me about. It's lovely. It goes all warm and stings."

"You want to keep it up," Presnor told him. "One go of it isn't enough."

"Oh, I'll keep it up all right. Providing his nibs doesn't get tired of rubbing it in. Oh! Excuse me, I say, my manners! This is Mr. Horton."

"Houghton," Jimmy corrected. Dr. Presnor gave a nod of the head. Jimmy returned it, and moved up the bar. He could hear Flick's light voice explaining, "I don't know much about him really. I only met him the other night. It was Eddie who brought him in." Then Flick said cheerily, "Toodle-loo," and joined Jimmy at the end of the bar.

"Don't drag yourself away, Flick," Jimmy said, "if you want to stay and talk to your friend."

Flick looked a trifle reproachful. "That's a nice thing when I'm having a drink with you. I hope I'm not as rude as that." Flick accepted another gin and orange. "I say, I'd better be careful. I get ever so chatty on two. I like Dr. Presnor. He's ever so kind. He's been terribly sweet to me at times."

"Yes, I can imagine that," Jimmy said bitterly. "Where did you tell me you worked?"

"The Grand. 'Hell at the Corner', seen it? I look after Dickie Short. 'E's all right in his way, but he's a bit 'take your hats off, gents, 'ere comes the lord gawd almighty'. I suppose he can't help it really. He's only good in sexy parts. Even the nastiest critic couldn't say he was acting badly, he never acts at all, and I s'pose it does make you a bit jumpy when you can see your own hair getting thin." Flick's round, grey eyes turned towards Dr. Presnor again. "I think Presie's attractive, don't you? You know what sort of a doctor I'd like to be? Not looking after boils and things—I'd like to be the kind of doctor people just brought their troubles to."

"A sort of cross between a lawyer and a psychiatrist."

"Oh, lumme no. Not *them*. I've a friend who went to a psychiatrist once. Cost him a fortune. He used to get bad-tempered whenever he set eyes on a poodle. Can you imagine it? Crazy! But they used to get his blood up, and his wife used to breed them too. Well, this psycho-whatnot, or whatever you call 'em, worked it right back to where he was jumped on by one in his pram. Came as ever such a surprise to my friend, because he says he was sure it was an Alsatian, and he had quite a liking for them. But it didn't do anything to help him. He just hated poodles worse."

Dr. Presnor had left the bar.

"So he was back where he started, then?" Jimmy asked.

"No, because it turned out that it wasn't really the poodle he hated, it was his wife. It was all tied up with his being jumped on in a confined space. I ask you," Flick said. "Crazy! I say, I've got to get back to the theatre, I'm due there at half-past six. 'Bye for the moment, and thanks."

The fog had lifted a little outside. It hung round lit windows and lamp-posts in circling patches like ill-shapen, transparent moths. Under the old-fashioned lamp-post on the opposite pavement Dr. Presnor was waiting for Jimmy. Jimmy hurried on. It was quiet in the empty street. The footsteps were quite audible following him. Again Jimmy felt the odd hammering that seemed to come from the back of his heart. He felt fear of the man who was following him, fear and mistrust, and doubt. The doubts were concerned with himself. He knew he wanted to talk to Presnor. It was for this reason he dreaded his catching him up. He was determined to resist the attraction of Presnor. At the corner the fog gathered in an acrid tunnel. Jimmy waited, his hands in his pockets. When Presnor approached him he turned round sharply— "Take yourself off, you importuning swine." The other man fell back a pace or two as Jimmy struck out at his chin. But he recovered his balance immediately. He asked quietly:

"Why did you hit me? I don't think I've made a mistake."

"Like hell you have," Jimmy said.

"Then I apologise. Good-night." He raised his hat, smiled, and walked away.

In spite of himself Jimmy caught him up. "As a matter of interest, how often do you get yourself clocked?"

The other man was walking briskly. "I don't believe it's happened before, and, as a matter of interest, I wasn't importuning."

"What were you doing, then?"

"I was hoping you'd allow me to talk to you."

"Look, chum, if you're working up to one of those little blackmailing rackets you're going to get those lovely white teeth of yours, that I don't doubt your little friends in O'Shaughnessy's find so attractive, shoved right down your throat."

Presnor halted to light a cigarette. "I hesitate to ask you for fear of arousing your suspicions. But would you care for a drink somewhere?"

"Look here, I was in that damned bar to see what the place was like. That's all."

"That was my reason for being there too."

Jimmy was aware that he was making excuses when he tried to reassure himself that his reason for accompanying Presnor would be to see what tactics the man would adopt. They went into a bar which was crowded. "Shall we sit somewhere?" Presnor asked.

"Yes, if we sit far enough apart. I won't stand any monkey business."

Presnor smiled as he made his way to the table. "May I inform you that the homosexual is no less well-mannered than the heterosexual? He doesn't force his attentions in public upon someone he has only just met. In fact he's frequently better mannered, being subject to more restraint."

Jimmy sat down with his arms crossed. "I don't know why, but it seems doubly lousy in your profession."

Presnor inhaled and studied him. "You haven't any sympathy towards it? You don't think perhaps the whole question calls for a little understanding and tolerance?"

"It calls for a horsewhip and a fifty-years stretch, and surely there's no question about it."

"You don't feel that it might be precisely that attitude," Presnor inquired, "which is helping it to increase?"

"I can see it wouldn't be an over-welcome attitude to you. It's risky in your line, isn't it? Struck off the rolls and all that?"

Presnor's elbows were on the table. He held his tankard between his hands, "How old are you, might one ask?"

"What the bloody hell's it got to do with you?"

Again Presnor smiled. He said, "Bad language isn't necessarily a sign of virility, you know. Any one of my little friends, as you call them, in O'Shaughnessy's place will tell you I'm not one of them. Many of them are my patients. It's not always easy for them to find an ordinary general practitioner who is sympathetic towards their difficulties, and in whom they can confide."

"They can get treatment in prison, can't they?"

"Would you like to go to gaol to be cured?"

"If I were 'that way inclined'," Jimmy answered, "I'd be willing to go to any lengths."

"Rubbish!" Dr. Presnor snapped. "Any ordinary person will put up with nearly anything to avoid getting involved with the police—yourself included. If you couldn't afford analysis or any other form of treatment however much you wanted to be treated, you'd have to suffer in silence or come to accept your condition. You'd certainly make no altruistic jaunts to the local police station."

"And how do you assist?" Jimmy asked. "Let creatures like that revolting little Flip, or whatever he calls himself, weep on your shoulder? And give him a sweetie after nasty medicine?"

"Creatures like Flick," replied Presnor evenly, "frequently suffer from common ailments. They've been known to have influenza or a sudden appendix."

"It must be a comfort to them to have a doctor they can rely upon not to disclose the circumstances in which he finds the sudden appendix. Especially if it was very sudden!"

"They trust me," said Presnor, ignoring the sarcasm, "and in return those who want help allow me to try to help them and to learn from their confidences."

"Some sort of bloody research, I suppose, or fiddling about with sexy complexes."

"I'm not a Freudian analyst, if that's what you mean. I regard myself as having a limited flair for treating certain psychiatric problems, but I recognise that there are some especially difficult cases which require a full Freudian analysis. For those I advise a transfer to a colleague. I have a practice in Finchley and I have to fit in my 'bloody research' when I can. I've no special qualifications for interesting myself in this particular problem, but I have special reasons."

"I thought it was a crime, not a problem."

"Did it ever occur to you that the vast majority don't deliberately seek out abnormality? They turn to it because for some reason normality fails to satisfy their needs and forces them to look for a substitute. Don't you think there's a case for considering them unfortunate in that normality fails to provide them with what it provides anyone else?"

"What the dickens are you campaigning for? Free love for queers?" When Presnor smiled, Jimmy demanded, "Do you mean to say that if I couldn't keep my hands off a guardsman you'd think I was a deserving case?"

"It would depend entirely upon your individual circumstances."

"But I wouldn't be to blame. Is that it?"

"It's conceivable that you wouldn't be to blame for the instincts which caused your behaviour."

"I'd just be a poor mixed-up kid who can't help himself because he was scared by a poodle in early life."

"I beg your pardon?"

Jimmy repeated Flick's story. He stopped laughing at the point where the patient discovered that his hatred was due to his wife, and found Presnor's patient black eyes upon him. "I say, we couldn't call you overburdened with a sense of humour, could we?"

"No," Presnor said, "we could not. I am the first to admit that I have next to none."

"Well, well. Granted there's nothing much funny about a queer—what do you think's the answer to it?"

"I'm not sure that there ever will be a complete one, but great strides are being made towards finding one."

"Such as?"

"There are certain forms of common-sense assistance. A problem, for instance, is half solved at the moment of facing it. Then there are forms of medical assistance."

Jimmy put down his glass without drinking from it. "If you knew of someone having a personal tussle with your pet problem, what would you advise him to do about it?" He took a cigarette from Presnor's case. "Thanks."

Presnor leant forward, shielding a light. "I should advise him to go and see Ken Fleischel."

"Who's he? Not a Freudian whatnot, or one of those confounded psychiatrists?"

"Have they been confounded? Mr. Fleischel has had considerable experience of the type of case we've been discussing and not inconsiderable success."

"And charges not inconsiderable fees, I don't doubt."

"Investigations are lengthy and therefore costly. But there are excellent brains at more moderate prices."

Jimmy sat foward, his hands waving. "Look here, I'm

sorry, but I hate the whole racket. I'm simply allergic to it—
the very jargon turns me up, anxiety 'neuroseseses'—schizo-
whatnots, and all the rest of it—it simply puts my back up.
As for 'Freudian analysts'! I've really got quite a thing
about it—it makes me feel creepy and nuts. If I went to one
of your complex kings, however clever, and they so much as
breathed the word psycho-anything, I should turn from an
uncertifiable case into a certifiable one at once, with violence.
I've no doubt I've got every psychological bug that it's
possible for anyone to have. But I don't want to hear about
it." He sat back, feeling calmer. "Well, what would you do
with a chap like that?"

"I should advise him to come and see me at 17 Bina Rise,
between nine and ten a.m. or five-thirty and seven-thirty
p.m., excluding Thursdays—or by appointment."

"What good would that do him?"

"It might do him none at all. It would depend largely
upon himself. On the other hand, it might help him to know
that there was someone prepared to offer him friendship
with no form of risk attached to it. I think it might surprise
him to know what a rare thing that can be in his position.
At the worst it could be a relief to be able to confide in someone, and at the best—well, miracles do still occur, and it's
just possible that he might benefit a little."

"You are *quite* sure you've got no sense of humour?"

"Quite."

CHAPTER TWENTY-SEVEN

WHEN he returned he found Pam waiting up for him. It was
very nearly midnight. She sang out to him when he came in.
She was in the kitchenette, her apron a heart shaped check,
and a matching red and white square round her head. He
noticed that her hair was cut upwards in deep natural waves,

and that the eyes were bright under a discreet eye-shadow. She wore a new colour on her lips and her nails. She wore a starched white blouse and a stiff red skirt. There were gold hoops in her ears and her feet were in raffia clogs. She looked crisply gay and attractive.

"You look like a mass of magazine tips on how to keep a husband from straying."

"That's exactly what I am," she told him. "It took me ages to get all the things together. Of course, I couldn't quite manage to get the face and the figure—" she showed him the magazine cover. Jimmy studied the angular elegance of the model. "She looks as if she's been corseted in a drainpipe from birth. What makes you think I might be straying?"

"My mirror."

"Oh, is it magic or something?"

"No, it's just brutally frank. It says, 'Wise up to yourself, honey. No one would look at you twice.'"

"There's no society for the prevention of cruelty to mirrors," said Jimmy. "Let's smash it and get another one."

"And do away with my only truthful friend?"

"Surely you can take it from me that you're in no danger from other women as far as I'm concerned."

She put a finger on his forehead and smoothed the line of his eyebrows. "You said that rather wistfully, as if you wished it wasn't true."

He leant over and kissed her again. "Never mind what I wish. It's true."

He went into the drawing-room, picked up the telephone receiver and made an appointment with Dr. Presnor.

Presnor sat at a flat desk with his back to a window. Behind his head the sky had turned an oily yellow as the great clouds banked for rain. The pencil silhouette of a church spire thrusting upwards was half lost in the leaden light of the evening.

Jimmy put a packet of cigarettes down on the desk.

"Here I am, with my posy for teacher. I got through most of yours last night."

Presnor stood up. "How good of you. But you shouldn't have bothered, Mr. —do you want me to go on calling you Houghton?"

Jimmy, lowering himself into a chair, made a face. "How did you get on to that?"

"You looked ill-at-ease when you told me your name the other night. I imagined it wasn't your real one, that's all."

"Stretton," said Jimmy, "J. H. Stretton."

Presnor wrote it down. Jimmy leant forward. "Sorry, I've left mine behind again. Could I have one of these?" Presnor pushed the Players' Jimmy had just brought him across the desk. Jimmy lit a cigarette.

A high nursery-fender stood round Presnor's fireplace. Leather chairs were cushionless. Sporting-prints hung on the walls and a radio battery lay in a corner of a sofa. The room was congested and not over-tidy. Jimmy tipped his cigarette towards the sofa. "Is that the famous couch?"

"What couch?"

"The one people lie on and spout?"

"You wouldn't be advised to try that one, it's a mass of broken springs."

Jimmy said, "I don't know what the hell I'm here for, really. I assure you I haven't come to spout. I suppose it's the Englishman's native reserve. I'm afraid you'll draw a blank in me. I can't see myself being much help to research."

"My dear boy, my minor investigations, largely for my own benefit, could hardly be dignified with the label of research. I'm personally interested, that's all."

"Why?"

"I told you, I have private reasons."

"Private or public, people do come in here to open their little hearts to you and you send them away clean and de-sodomited, don't you?"

"There isn't a guaranteed cure," Presnor said. "And what

cures there are seldom work overnight. Certain things are successful in some cases, and failures in others. It depends entirely upon the individual. Some may be resigned or content with their condition, some fail to see why they should be cured of the only sexual satisfaction they are able to get in life—and on the other hand some suffer agonies of shame. They are made wretched and ill by the constant torture of war within the self. It's those who are most likely to benefit soonest by what I call common-sense assistance."

"What's that?"

"Some people just call it getting things off your chest."

"You're a sort of a glorified Flick doctor," Jimmy said.

"I beg your pardon."

"Flick wants to set up a sort of 'Bring your troubles to Auntie Annie bureau' with cut-price bosoms to weep on thrown in."

"There have been worse ideas."

"What on earth turns out someone like Flick?"

"Flick was the only child of divorced parents. The father ran off and left the mother. He treated her abominably, and she had a considerable struggle to bring up Flick."

"Why should that make him a pansy?"

"It might not have done, but it did. Flick violently resented the father's behaviour to the mother. He was brought into divorce court proceedings and no doubt saw his mother in the light of a martyr. He detested the man, and would hear no other side of the story but his mother's. She lavished all her devotion on him and he returned it. They were inseparable until she died."

"You'd think that would have made him go out and find himself another old mum."

"He might have done. It would have been possible for him to marry a woman much older than himself in the hopes of finding the same affection and security."

"But he 'married' Gorwin Simpton instead?"

"Through his extreme closeness to his mother and her

difficulties he associates himself with the female sex. He has identified himself with it. Are you married?" Presnor asked.

"Yes."

"Are you happy?"

"No. I love my wife and she loves me, but we are not happy. Look here, I think I should take myself off. I've a feeling I'm going to waste your time on a grand scale. I'm a tough nut to crack when it comes to heart-to-hearts."

"Just as you please," Presnor said.

Jimmy stood up and walked round the room. He peered at the prints and examined the battery. He turned round to Presnor. "Are *you* married?"

"Yes."

"Happy?"

"Yes."

"Good boy," Jimmy said. "Well, cheerio—oh, half a tick, there's something I'm itching to know."

"Ask me anything you please."

"What—and I don't want any beating about the bush—what made you think I might help in your minor investigations? You were pretty damned sure I was queer. Now I haven't got an unduly high opinion of myself, but I'd lay a million to a banana that if I met me I'm the last person I should think was queer. But I imagine there must have been something, or Eddie wouldn't have pounced on me. I've heard they can always tell."

Presnor held out a hand and fluttered his fingers. "D'you think I might have one of the cigarettes you so kindly brought me? I'm afraid I've run out." Jimmy took the packet out of his pocket and tossed it across. Presnor caught it.

"You pounced out of that fog last night and leapt on me as if I were the answer to a laboratory prayer. What is it about me that put you on to me?"

Presnor stood up and walked round to him, "I want you to look at me carefully, please."

"A pleasure, I'm sure," said Jimmy, and made a sharp clicking noise with his tongue in his cheek.

"What nationality would you say I was?" Presnor asked.

Jimmy answered without hesitation, "Well, now you come to mention it, Jewish."

"What makes you so sure of that?"

"Well—I—I don't know really. I just thought you were. You are, aren't you?"

"I am. But I want to know how you detected it. I'm not wearing a caftan, my nose is no longer than many Christian noses, and I'm no darker than any Southern European."

Jimmy ran his hand through his hair. "Oh Lord! You've got me there all right. As a matter of fact, in a way you remind me of my old man, and he is a C. of E. parson." He looked Presnor up and down, frowning. "Frankly, I haven't a clue. Something about the gestures perhaps—or—well most Jews have small bones and sensitive hands—and I see now that you've got them. And most Jews are inclined to have smallish feet—oh, hell, I don't know how I spotted it. I only know that I thought that's what you were."

Presnor told him gently, "And that must be my answer to your question."

Jimmy sat down. "Well, I haven't done anything really queer yet, if it's the smallest bit of interest to you."

"I should be very surprised indeed if you had had any homosexual experiences. I merely thought from your attitude that you might have disturbing inclinations which could cause you a great deal of unhappiness."

Jimmy looked up at him sideways. "Jews aren't psychic, are they? Or is that cats?"

"Cats."

"What *was* my attitude?"

"Aggressive. You reacted violently towards me at first, and practically within the same breath you accepted my invitation. It wasn't hard to imagine you the victim of some sort of emotional conflict."

"You must take quite a few risks. How did you know I wasn't a plain-clothes policeman trying to disguise myself as a queer?"

"Because if you had been I should have been surprised to find you so anxious to prove that you were not."

Jimmy thought, 'Hell of a fine psychiatrist, or whatever he calls himself, this one is. He can't even spot that I was attracted to him.' He asked, "Well, is there a nice quick simple remedy, like a mustard bath, or penicillin?"

"In a case like yours, when you're young, when the tendencies aren't very strong, and where there's a whole-hearted desire to be rid of them, there should be every hope of a cure. The first thing to do is to try to rid yourself of the idea that there's any disgrace in having homosexual tendencies. It won't be easy, you'll need help to understand it. But it's something I hope we might achieve together."

"No disgrace!" Jimmy echoed. "No disgrace!"

"There can be disgrace in the manner in which you direct these tendencies, in what uses you put them to, so to speak. But not in possessing the tendencies themselves. You wouldn't expect to be blamed for having an illness unless you'd deliberately chosen to be infected by it? Or, having contracted it, you deliberately passed it on to someone else?"

"Oh! You call it an illness, do you?"

"I think any abnormality, whether it's physical or mental, can be classed as an affliction if it causes suffering, don't you?"

Jimmy stared at the man, his eyes narrowing. "I suppose you're some kind of a crank."

"I expect so," Presnor said.

"It's just that I've never heard the thing whitewashed before and it comes as a bit of a surprise to me."

"You're not hearing it whitewashed now. You're being brought face to face with a problem. Certain aspects of it I condemn very heartily, and in extreme cases I think punishment is the only solution."

"Blimey! Those extremes would have to be pretty sordid."

"Yes," Presnor said mildly, "they would."

Jimmy put his head back and laughed, a habit he had inherited from Osbourne. "Lordy, lordy me! It certainly takes all sorts to make a world. I wish you could have met a man I used to know. He had somewhat different ideas on the subject. You see, my mother was some sort of a blasted raving beauty—in the village she's a kind of a legend—she's even got a flag-day. She was snuffed out by having me. And I don't think my papa was any too enchanted by the patter of my little feet. We were never the wildest buddies —and at my prep school I got fond of a chap called Osbourne. This was the man I mentioned just now. I hated his guts at first because he looked so like the old man, but later . . ."

CHAPTER TWENTY-EIGHT

HE was surprised when he realised how long and how naturally he had been 'spouting' to Presnor. It was half-past ten when he asked:

"What on earth makes my eyes water whenever I talk about Osbourne's old coat? I can't seem to help it. It's like your mouth watering when you think of a lemon."

Presnor looked at his notes. "Yes, it's occurred three times this evening. That coat played an important part in your life. He picked you up when you were injured and held you against it. It was comforting, you connected it with being wanted and cared for. In return you picked up that coat and cared for it after Osbourne had had a similar fall. You were trying to bring him the comfort perhaps he once gave to you. It was as if you were picking *him* up and caring for him. You were made to feel that there was something shameful, something sinister and disgusting in your

perfectly natural affection for Osbourne himself. It may not
have been intentional, it may have been a case of mishandling
and misjudgment, but it's possible that even now you are
ashamed of showing any outward emotion in connection
with him. You may have developed a sense of guilt regarding the actual man. But no one gave you any reason to
suppose that there was anything disgusting in showing a
regard for Osbourne's coat, the coat was an inanimate
object. The coat couldn't accuse you of being a 'sissy',
whereas Osbourne in living form might. The coat took
Osbourne's place with you. That might be why your eyes
filled with tears when you mentioned the coat. You feel
bound to suppress your feelings for Osbourne, but you feel
free to give vent to them over the coat."

Jimmy caught sight of the time. "I should think your
eyes would fill with tears if I don't take myself off. I've been
here for ages. How expensive are you?"

"It won't cost you anything," Presnor replied. "For
what it's worth, it's free. My time is yours whenever I can
spare it."

"Good God, who spread the rumour that Jews were
mean?"

"A Jew, quite possibly, as a form of insurance against
Christian avarice."

"Be careful, old boy, you're coming dangerously near to
making a joke."

"On the contrary," said Presnor, "I meant it entirely
seriously. It's just that I feel that in giving my time and my
energy free of charge to those who are genuinely unable to
afford better assistance—or who can't afford it for some
other reason—I am helping a cause which lies very close to
my heart. In a moment I think you'll see why."

Presnor went to a drawer. He opened it and pulled out
a photograph. He handed it to Jimmy. A young man
smiled out of the photograph. He had strong eyes and
strong teeth. He had deep lines at the side of his mouth. He

had a pleasant expression and a cheerful smile.

"Who is it?" Jimmy asked.

Presnor replied, "My brother-in-law, Freidel Goldstein."
He passed Jimmy a second photograph. He passed it upside
down and when Jimmy turned it over he drew in his breath:
"Oh Christ! It's rather an advanced case, isn't it?"

"Very. I thought the world of him. We were at school
together," Presnor said, "I married his twin sister."

Jimmy's hand shook slightly, holding the photograph.
"Where was this taken, the Chelsea Arts?"

Presnor shook his head. "It gave him pleasure to wear
feminine clothing. He put them on whenever he had the
chance. I thought that ridicule might jolt him out of it. In
my youth and my ignorance I thought he couldn't fail to
find himself ridiculous if he could be shown what he looked
like. People are inclined to see what they like in their
mirrors. But I thought that a photograph might act as a
sort of shock treatment. I took it myself."

"What did he say when you showed it to him?"

"He was delighted with it. He asked me to take several
copies of it so that he could distribute it amongst his
friends."

Jimmy looked down at the photograph. It was badly lit
but its sitter was clear enough. A man lolled on the side of
a bed in a woman's blouse and skirt. The hair was long and
the nails were painted. The lids of the eyes were greased
and shadowed; there was lipstick on the mouth and the
cheeks were rouged. Only the strong eyes remained to give
a reminder of the first photograph.

Presnor held out a hand. "Would you or would you not
call that a sickness?"

"Great jumping crickets, I would."

"My father-in-law was far from a help to him. At the
first signs my father-in-law, a normally kindly man, behaved
like a barbarian—from making open fun of the boy to insulting him; he finally turned him out of the house."

"Where is he now?"

"He's dead. He was blackmailed, and poisoned himself rather than face prison and disgrace."

"So that's what made you anti-prison."

"I've told you, I'm not anti-prison in some cases. But if two men are confirmed homosexuals and they're not a prey to the destructive unhappiness that it can bring about, and if they are both of an age when they can make their own decisions and be held responsible for them—then I think that the law should let them alone. I also think that *every* effort should be made to induce them to have treatment, but if they're incurable, or if they refuse, they should be allowed to abide by their own choice. It's surely a greater crime against society to lay them open to blackmail and suicide?"

"But you've got to do something about seeing youth doesn't get leapt on, haven't you?"

"Youth gets 'leapt on' by so-called normality as well. You've heard of child rapes and child murders? Do you think it less criminal for a heterosexual to assault a small girl than for a homosexual to seduce a small boy?"

"No, I suppose I don't really. They're both pretty foul."

"Exactly. The one's a no more unnatural crime than the other. And the treatment for both should be punishment, unless the medical report recommends otherwise. In my opinion the invert should only be penalised if he corrupts youth. If he can be persuaded to look upon himself as afflicted he might see it as a crime to infect others, but he should be encouraged by society to undergo treatment and to be able to receive it with no stigma attached to it. Do you realise that if your friend Osbourne had taken his symptoms to a doctor he might not have taken his life?"

Jimmy said sharply, "Osbourne did *not* take his life."

"I beg your pardon. From what you said I gathered that he had."

"Why the hell should you gather it? He had an accident while he was climbing, that's all. It could happen to anyone, couldn't it? If I've said anything to make you think——"

"You made me think of Osbourne as a very fine type of man. It seemed clear that rather than risk giving way to the feelings he had discovered in himself he put an end to his life."

"Osbourne had no 'feelings' like that," Jimmy said. "Good God, he was down like a ton of bricks on anything to do with it. I told you, I think he suspected me and that's why he despised me so much."

"And I tell you that I think he suspected himself. He's exactly the type of man—holding a responsible position in connection with youth—who would come down even more heavily like a ton of bricks on himself. Homosexual tendencies are present in all of us, you know. A fact which Osbourne, having a somewhat music-hall attitude towards the psychological, if you'll pardon the use of a word you dislike so much, would be the last to realise. It's simply a question of how forcibly those tendencies are present in us, and how they are developed by our own character and outside circumstances. Osbourne's might have been weak, he may have exaggerated their importance, or he might not. One is not in a position to tell that, but it's not hard to guess from what I hear of him that he would have condemned himself mercilessly for them. Osbourne may have had no real cause to resort to such drastic measures, but it's quite clear that he would think those the only measures open to him. The more honourable the man, the higher the standards, the more abhorrent such tendencies are to him. It's precisely Osbourne's type of man who suffers most from his own intolerant attitude towards the problem he is too ashamed to seek help or ask advice about."

Jimmy sat still, with his eyes closed.

"You might find," Presnor said, "that he had had some experience of it himself in his early life. Perhaps in his own schooldays. It might have been a dormitory affair with another boy, or it might have been seduction by a master.

Such experiences have varying effects. Some boys shrug it off so to speak and go through life unharmed by it; some develop lasting homosexual tendencies, and it has been known for others to be so disgusted by it that they develop guilt complexes which could build up over the years into horror of the thing itself, fear of any recurrence of it and severe condemnation of the self in connection with it. Osbourne's character would rather lend itself to this. He would never forgive himself for his one lapse even if it were against his will and he were not to blame. It would always be at the back of his mind as something to be on his guard against. And he would feel it even more strongly in his position as a schoolmaster. If circumstances persuaded him, or if it was suggested to him strongly enough—and that doctor and the wife obviously suspected him—that he might have reverted to 'type', it could be sufficient to develop in him a severe psychotic depressive reaction."

Jimmy said sullenly, "I thought you were going to spare me your beastly jargon."

"I apologise," Presnor smiled, "I'm not for one moment suggesting that Osbourne wasn't innocent. I deeply believe that he was. But I think it possible that he didn't believe in his own innocence, and that, in a man of Osbourne's high standards and with his fears of lowering them, would be quite enough to send him to pieces and drive him to suicide."

"I see," said Jimmy. "Thanks for the translation. Just how do you think it's helping me to persuade me that Osbourne killed himself? Probably largely through me?"

"It should help in a number of ways," Presnor told him. "It should prove to you the necessity of changing your own attitude, and it should prove something much more important. Far from despising you, Osbourne cherished you to the point of sacrificing his own life rather than run the risk of exposing you to the danger of the miseries he suffered himself. That should go a long way to restoring your self-respect."

CHAPTER TWENTY-NINE

WHEN he reached home Pam came to greet him in their little close box of a hall. She was white-faced and strained round the eyes. "Oh, Jimmy, where *have* you been?" she said. "There's a friend of yours waiting. He's been here for hours and he's drunk."

When Jimmy went into the room he saw Eddie. The little man sat plumply in camel-hair socks beside a bottle of South African sherry. He hiccuped very gently, blowing out his cheeks. His glance was half-aggressive, half-apologetic. "You said to look you up if I was passing."

Jimmy said, "I'm glad you did, old boy, I'm delighted to see you. Have a drink." He refilled Eddie's glass and filled one for himself. To Pam he said, "You get off to bed, duckie. Eddie won't be offended, will you?" When they were alone, Jimmy grinned at him. "Well, what goes on in Berkhamsted?"

"It's pretty," said Eddie, "the snowdrops are out. I went up to the castle the other day. I often go up in my lunch-hour. You might have been down by the seaside, the air was so strong and sweet, and you ought to've heard the birds."

"Yes, spring only seems to settle on the top of London," Jimmy sighed.

Eddie sat forward earnestly. "You know what?—I'm going to ask you something. Do you think you and me could be friends? I liked you the first time I saw you—remember? 'Course, I know you're married, and I don't mean to break anything up. I like your wife. I'd be happy to stay just friends. My brother left me a nice little bit. It's not much, but it's something to draw on. We might all have a day by the sea now and then—or perhaps you and me go to a theatre or concert sometimes, when your wife goes out with her girl friends. You said to look in if I was passing, you did say that because you liked me, didn't you?"

Jimmy said guardedly, "Yes, Eddie, of course. I think you're a damned nice chap." His eyes sought the clock on the mantelpiece. It was well after midnight. Eddie had the settled look of a man growing moodily drunker. "But the fact is, Pam's not feeling any too well these days, so we don't go out much, and——"

Eddie stood up. "I revolt you." He took short, measured steps to the door. His eyes were narrowed and his voice was quiet. He repeated, "I revolt you."

Jimmy stood up. "Oh, for God's sake, Eddie."

Eddie's voice rose. His plump cheeks were quivering. He spat out scornfully, "Wife isn't well! Why don't you just tell me you don't like me because I'm old and *fat*? Why don't you just *say* I'm too old?"

Jimmy walked across to him. "Shut up, for the love of Mike, Eddie. You're drunk and you'll wake the whole place up."

Eddie hit out at the hands Jimmy placed on his shoulders to steady him. "Leave me alone, you bastard. You thought I was making a pass at you, didn't you? Well, I wasn't. I asked you to be my friend, that's all. But you have to think the worst of me—you've listened to that swine Simpton. You think yourself goddamned superior, don't you? You think only *your* sort go to heaven. The kind that chases girls —the kind that sneaks out on their wives and spends their money on other women, the kind that leaves girls with babies and doesn't give a damn. You think you'll go to heaven just because you're the kind that likes girls."

Pam stood in the doorway, a dressing-gown buttoned right up to her chin. Her face without make-up seemed younger. She said, "Jimmy, you're making a noise," in the same voice which she had used to him when they were children.

Eddie ignored her and continued to shout, "You can't understand anything, can you, except about chasing girls.

Oh, you can run after a girl all right, that's different, isn't it? It doesn't matter if you're married or if you've got kiddies. You think you can do what you like. You can meet them in doorways and kiss them in parks and it isn't disgusting at all, is it?"

Pam stood looking down at the floor. "Jimmy, it would be better if your friend stopped talking, wouldn't it?"

"It certainly would. But he's not talking about what you think he's talking about."

"I know what I'm talking about," Eddie insisted, "and I reckon I'm better than you. I don't go in for numbers. I don't take the first chance I get. I'm not just out looking for nothing but sex. I want to be decent, I want to be straight. I want to meet someone and stick to them—and I want them to stick to me. I'd like to save up and buy a little pub with someone."

"What would you call it, 'The Fairies' Arms'?"

"I wouldn't be unfaithful and let someone down," Eddie's voice rose again, and he pointed a short, stubby finger at Pam. "You don't mind what she thinks, do you? You don't mind how much you hurt her? You could break her heart and you'd still feel superior, just because with you it's girls, girls, girls."

Jimmy turned helplessly round to Pam. He leant in the doorway, laughing. "You don't know how pathetically opposite this is to everything you're thinking."

His laugh inflamed both Pam and Eddie. Pam said coldly, "I'm glad it amuses you to have such a reputation, Jimmy."

Jimmy looked from one angry expression to the other, Pam's pale and resigned, Eddie's flushed and infuriated. He laughed again, but there was no sound of amusement in his voice. "Perhaps it's just as well that neither of you know what the hell either of you are talking about. You look like the sailor's dream of home," he told Pam. "The kind that makes him glad to wake up at sea, and as for you, Eddie, there's nothing so goddamned marvellous about being a ruddy queer."

Eddie walked out of the room, his short arms swinging, his head held high. He tripped in the doorway and swore. Pam managed to say good-night to him. She stood with her head bent and her fingers twisted. Her voice kept a matter-of-factness which was neither accusing nor self-pitying: "I'm afraid that was rather a give-away, Jimmy. Mr. Baines doesn't seem too discreet."

Jimmy said bitterly, "Mr. Baines was accusing me of not being able to appreciate the complicated emotions involved in being homosexually inclined." He saw that she was struggling to keep back her tears. "Eddie," he said patiently, "is homosexual. He's an invert. He's like those two charmers you saw on the bus—who gave you 'the creeps' up your spine."

She took a clean tissue out of a packet and patted her eyes with it. "I'm surprised that you associate with people like that."

Jimmy lounged in the doorway, baiting her. "You've inherited my fond mama-in-law's prudery all right. 'People like that', as you call them, frequently head society hostesses' lists. Poor Eddie is not a very impressive example, but I tremble to think how you'd fluff up with pride if I introduced you to one or two 'people like that'."

In the night he put a hand out and touched her shoulder. "Pam, I'm sorry about being a brute to you; just sometimes you get my goat." He sighed when she turned to snuggle against him. If only it might rest at that.

Three days later Pam ran in from the kitchen. She carried the morning paper. "Jimmy! Jimmy! Look! He's been arrested. They've put him in prison."

Jimmy was shaving. "Whom?"

"Your friend, the little pansy one. He's been had up on a charge of importuning. They've given him six months because it wasn't his first offence."

Jimmy snatched the paper. Towards the bottom of the page a few lines of print gave the information. Jimmy stared at it several seconds, then put it down on the edge of the bath. He continued to shave. Pam picked the paper up. "He was found in Hyde Park, trying to get off with someone. It makes you feel rather sick, doesn't it?"

"Then don't read it," Jimmy advised.

"It says he says he isn't that sort at all really, and he can't think what came over him. He'd stayed out very late with friends on Wednesday night and had a lot to drink."

"The friends," Jimmy told her, "were us."

"Oh, my goodness, how awful! They might have got hold of our names."

Jimmy screwed the cap on his shaving-cream. "Yes, wouldn't it have been dreadful," he said, "to have been connected with a pariah like that?"

"What a ridiculous thing, to say that he was drunk! As if it could excuse him for behaving like that."

"Perhaps," said Jimmy, "it might have been his way of preserving his self-respect against something he was trying to fight against. Pam, you're a Christian and reasonable girl in most ways—don't you think that if someone can't help it—and it's perfectly obvious that Eddie can't—that there should be some sort of 'tolerance' towards it?"

"I think they ought to make it a life sentence," Pam replied.

CHAPTER THIRTY

HE had not thought of his long talks with Presnor in the light of analysis. They had seemed more like argumentative and friendly discussions. Few of them had taken place in Presnor's consulting-room. The majority had been spent on the golf-course.

"I know what you're doing—" he grinned at Presnor—
"you're trying to hide the forceps. You don't want me to
feel cramped by the psychiatrist's couch."

"I enjoy golf and so do you. It seems sensible therefore
to play together. If it helps you to discuss your problem
whilst we are playing, it strikes me as being common-sense
assistance."

"I ought to know better by now," said Jimmy, "than to
try and pull your leg."

He had discovered things about himself that he found
hard to believe at first. He learned that he had always disliked the memory of his mother.

"I never even knew my mother. How can you tell I
dislike her?"

"It's not very psychic of me," Presnor pointed out. "If
one has been attached to a parent's memory one doesn't
usually start off by describing her as 'some sort of blasted
raving beauty'. It's really rather elementary, my dear
Watson. Also, you've recalled quite clearly putting out your
tongue at her portrait."

"Funny," said Jimmy, "I'd clean forgotten most of these
things until you dug 'em out of me."

He was even more surprised to find that he had been
devoted to the Reverend Jordon.

"It's possible that you first identified yourself with the
female sex when you tried to compete with your mother for
your father's affections—when you first made an effort to
assume her sex."

"Come again?"

"How else would you interpret your wishing to change
your sex and dress up as a little girl? It's possible that you've
still retained your desire to compete with women for the
affections of men and that therefore you are still identifying
yourself with the female sex."

"Oh, turn it up, chum," Jimmy said.

"This would account for your feelings of revulsion when

asked to have intimate relations with women. You think it disgusting—you think it abnormal—you think of yourself as a woman, and therefore to you sexual relationship with another woman is in fact homosexual from your point of view, and therefore repellent to you."

"Do you boys get together and work this stuff out? I mean, is there a strong party line?"

"There can be few rules, more's the pity," Presnor said. "Each case is dependent upon individual circumstances."

Jimmy found also that his eyes no longer watered when he thought of Osbourne's coat. "That's a good sign," Presnor told him. "It might mean we're removing your sense of guilt."

But Jimmy had acquired a new sense of guilt. He had discovered something else about himself which he could no longer refuse to face and which he believed he could not possibly discuss with Presnor. He was unquestionably 'in love' with Presnor. The fact shocked and deeply humiliated him. It also brought with it a sense of shame at disguising the truth. In spite of Presnor's repeated instructions to suppress nothing he went out of his way to lie and throw the man off the scent. When he was not with Presnor he missed him acutely. If he could have seen in it a hunger for physical fulfilment he believed he would have welcomed it. It would be a degrading and loathsome discovery, but it would be an explanation. It would be preferable to the mystery of an aching desire to be in the presence of a man in whom he was obviously only platonically interested. "Perhaps I'm like Eddie," he sneered at himself. "Perhaps I'm not after sex, but *love*." He felt no repetition of the incomprehensible compulsion that had forced him to draw nearer to Kliebermann. He had no uncontrollable urge to touch Presnor. He was content to be in the man's company.

He suffered from a depression which he endeavoured to dodge as if it were a tangible evil pursuing him. He moved from room to room in an effort to avoid it. He left his desk

for the bath, and his bath for a sketchily prepared meal in
the kitchen. He walked until he became dismally aware that
a route march to John o' Groats could not escape it. He
read until the print blurred late at night, trying to fight the
stifling awareness that the depression was lying between the
lines. Once he went back to the church. But it was difficult
to tell at what target to aim his prayers. He had once
prayed for help and received it. Out of the blue Presnor
came to him. Proving that amongst the moving millions
there could be a helping hand. Proving the friend in a
world of strangers. A fanatical Jew with a strong dedica-
tion, with an offer of free assistance—proving the power of
prayer. Proving nothing, nothing, nothing, but the certainty
of despair. To have found the confidant and feel unable to
confide in him, to have been offered assistance and obliged
to avoid it, to have found sympathy and be forced to
deceive it. To pray again might let loose savager ironies.
If he prayed to keep Presnor's friendship he bound himself
to his own infirmity. To pray to be released from Presnor
would be to pray for the removal of help.

There were times when he longed to go down on his
knees before Presnor himself and confess to a psychological
development which surely even Presnor could not be
expected to have anticipated. But to do that would have
obvious results. He imagined the scene. The quiet reason-
ableness of the Jew's steady voice pointing out in nightmare
technicalities the desirability of terminating the treatment.
"It's possible that your ex—excessive father love cum father
resentment has cohabitated with your mother resentment
cum ex-Osbourne obsession and brought about a psychological, schizophrenic, paranoic, dyspeptic, epileptic, diabetic
... attraction towards me which can do nothing but severely
retard your progress and cause further emotional disturbances injurious to an already unhinged personality." To
confess his feelings for Presnor to Presnor would be an
act of imbecility. But it was becoming increasingly difficult

to remain in Presnor's company and conceal the disturbing truth.

When they next met in the golf club it was drizzling with a fine and chilly rain outside, and a strong wind drove into their faces. The rain lay like a minute sprinkle of dew on Presnor's well-shaped eyebrows. On the first tee he hit a long drive.

"Read about Eddie?" Jimmy asked, one eye screwed up following Presnor's ball.

"Yes, I was sorry," said Presnor.

Up in the scrub wood a blackbird called. The afternoon lay over the course, dismal and cold. In the sky a greenish crease appeared between the clouds.

"It was my fault," Jimmy said.

"I understood he was drunk," said Presnor, "and threw discretion to the winds."

"He was. But I thought he was trying to get off with me," said Jimmy. "I didn't deal any too tactfully with him. I probably drove him out on the bat." He tried to fight the attraction he felt towards Presnor by deliberately refusing to look at the man. But the desire to do so was not unakin to the urgent desire of a child to stare at some form of human infirmity. He felt his eyes pulled towards Presnor as if they were being drawn from his head.

"I shouldn't blame yourself for what happened to Baines," Presnor told him. "It would probably have happened in any case." Presnor's eyebrows, contracting in irritation as he topped his ball, made a black triangle over his eyes. "The tragic thing in Baines's case is that he has such a strong desire to be respectable. I dare say no one would be more shocked by the Baines case than Baines."

"I suppose you think he shouldn't have been sent to prison."

"Yes."

"But you said he could get some sort of treatment in prison."

"Yes, but in his case it would have been very much better if he could have got some sort of treatment out of prison."

"What was to stop him?"

"Public opinion. With the exception of the more sophisticated circles, public opinion is against his chances of recovery. Only when the man in the street comes to accept the problem and understands that in some cases it is not criminal, can something be done. At the moment he either condemns it, ignores it or makes fun of it. But public opinion could make free clinics possible."

"You mean put de-pansying under the National Health?" Jimmy laughed.

"Why not? There should be free treatment for those who can't afford it and who want it."

"How about the ones who don't want to be cured?"

"If they're doing no harm, that's their business. If they are, it's the man in the street's."

The fine rain put a sheen over Presnor's dark skin. Looking at him, Jimmy recognised a pattern: the deep eyes of Jordon, the deep eyes of Osbourne; the deep brown thinking eyes of both of them. He asked, "Is it particularly psycho-anything to find yourself drawn towards the same type of man all the time?"

"Why should it be? Many men have their preferences in types of women, and there's not anything particularly psycho-anything about that."

"Tell me something. Why is it that with my unfortunate leanings I've never set eyes on a homosexual who has caused me the slightest flutter of my obviously perverted heart? Why am I only attracted to non-queers? I've never yet gone for a queer."

"Your sense of guilt is too active for that. It's possible that you would blame yourself less if you were drawn towards someone with no homosexual tendencies—you would feel it a greater sign of normality in yourself."

Jimmy was aware that he was making a leisurely tour of

the course in an effort to prolong the game. He made a slow follow-up to his ball. To have covered the ground quickly from hole to hole would have been to speed up his leave-taking with Presnor. He had no desire to hurry home to the depression again. In the bar he drew Presnor's attention to a man in the corner. "Don't look now, but isn't that a fellow-pervert of mine over there?"

Presnor glanced in the direction of the loudly-dressed member who was discussing his game at the top of a nasal voice which flattened his vowels. "Firstly, you're not a pervert, and secondly I should think he's more likely to be colour-blind than homosexually inclined. He just thinks a purple tie goes well with yellow checks. You mustn't expect to detect homosexuality in bad taste. Some of the best taste in the world is to be found amongst homosexuals: creatively, philosophically, intellectually, culturally, and artistically they are frequently unparalleled."

"And yet you still call it a sickness?"

"I call it an illness only in cases where it causes acute suffering."

"Isn't it worth it if it leads to such a high percentage of talent?"

"It might make a contribution to the rest of the world, but I am concerned with the patient himself. My wife's twin brother, for instance, had considerable talent, but I doubt if it compensated him for his sense of being persecuted and morally outcast."

"You don't mention your wife much," Jimmy said. "What's she like?"

"My wife?" Presnor took a photograph out of his pocket and put it on the table.

A plumply dark woman stared out of it.

"Jewish?" Jimmy asked.

"Yes."

"Any kids?"

"Two."

"What sort?"

"Boys. They're a handful, but my mother-in-law lives with us and helps us out."

"Are you a madly happy little family group—all full of give and take and blood being thicker than water?"

"Kitty and I have been married for sixteen years," said Presnor, "and it doesn't seem sixteen months."

The depression descended on Jimmy in a quick and a vicious assault. He put a hand to his chest and said to Presnor, "I wish to God you'd have a look at me professionally some day. I get a beastly sort of thumping round the heart." He discovered one eyebrow raised at him. "Oh, I'm sorry. I suppose all this complex business is professional in a way." He encountered the other eyebrow raised at him. "Oh Lord, I *am* putting my foot in it. What I mean is——"

"What you mean is, will I give you a physical examination."

"Hit the nail on the head first time."

"Come and see me tomorrow, I'll have a look at you."

CHAPTER THIRTY-ONE

HE kept purposely apart from university life. Fellow students finally gave up attempts to include him. He preferred to remain upon nodding acquaintanceship. He dared not risk male friendships and he imagined women to be possessed of an intuition which would detect his trouble. In the mornings he attended lectures and in the afternoons he worked in the library. His evenings were spent between Presnor and Pam. He did not join debating societies and he never went on pub crawls. He knew that he made morose company. His manners and his language were growing worse. Once when Presnor told him that an effective method of taking the mind off the self was to think more of others he used a word for which Presnor asked him to apologise. He was contrite and made an effort to make himself less irritable. 'Sweetness and light,' he told himself grimly, 'that's what we want from Mr. Stretton. "Every day I am growing sweeter and lighter." I must make that my waking thought!'

He presented himself punctually at Presnor's surgery. He was a little aggrieved to discover that he had to wait. He was used to Presnor's undivided attention. He had not seen him before during surgery hours. He was resentful of the four people in front of him.

"That bunch before me must have had every known ailment between them," he complained when he finally confronted Presnor. Then he opened his shirt front and said, "Listen to the thing. You ought to hear it from where you are, you won't need a stethoscope. It's pumping away like a mad thing. Do you think it's fatty degeneration of the heart?"

From the landing upstairs a foreign accent demanded. "Kitty, come and look at this hole in David's sheet." The voice which answered was softer.

"Don't tell me he's kicked it through again."

"It looks as if he's eaten it."

Jimmy raised his eyes to the ceiling as footsteps hurried across it. He thought of the voice of Kitty to whom Presnor had been married for sixteen years, and who had made it seem sixteen months. There was a guttural trace in the mother's accent. In the wife's there was none at all. It was a clear voice and sounded transparent. It gave nothing away of the woman herself. Jimmy found himself with a hurtful curiosity about that strangely private life of Presnor's which was shut off and taken up again behind the light grain of the surgery door. Above the high plastered ceiling the old Hampstead house knew a separate life. Somewhere there was a bedroom. Was it the room above, where the folk-weave curtains hung? In it Presnor would yawn and prepare for the night, put his loose change on the dressing-table, put his shoes on to trees—undoubtedly put his shoes on trees. Jimmy had never seen better-tended footwear than Presnor's—and roll into—what? A four-poster? A double divan, or twin beds? He would switch on a bedside lamp and read. That much could be taken for granted. The black eyes would travel slowly down the print. Presnor would never read fast. And what kind of woman would lie beside him? Why should he have chosen her above others? Why had he remained with her so many years content and found the time so short? He was morbidly fascinated by the shadowy possibilities of Kitty Presnor. In that bedroom he could imagine so closely, with the folk-weave bedspread to match the curtains, would she raise plump white arms to pin up wiry curls? Would she have short hair or long? The photograph Presnor had shown him was taken some years ago. Was she intelligent, witty, humorous, or was she as entirely without humour as he? What must it feel like to be Kitty Presnor, to be sure of his company; to wake in the night and know him beside her; to be able to close her eyes again in the sweetly deep security of knowing that she was his and that he was hers and that there was no disgrace in it, to be able to claim physical expressions of affection from him without incurring disgust? To be a woman had enormous advantages. He found himself abjectly jealous of Kitty Presnor. He was sighing when Presnor's voice startled him.

". . . to disturb your reflections, but I've other appointments. I asked if the pain occurred more particularly after a meal."

"Er—— Oh, sorry, I was day-dreaming. No, no, I don't think so. It just hits me any old time." He had the vague feeling of familiarity with the moment. There had been another occasion, surely, when he had been both hating and envying a woman because of the advantages gained by belonging to her sex. A man had reproached him for day-dreaming then. But he could recall nothing more about the incident.

"Slip off your coat," said Presnor.

Jimmy bared his chest and back. "I promise you it doesn't go pit-a-pat just when I see a pretty policeman."

"Breathe in." Jimmy did so. "Breathe out—in—out." The stethoscope leaped over his chest and back in a series of icy hops. Presnor found nothing organically wrong. "Everything seems pretty shipshape. It's not unlikely that you would get a form of palpitation coinciding with emotional disturbances. Have you had any reason to be over-excited or irritated?"

"Well, I had a bit of a shindy with Pam last night, but I'd been having the thumping before that."

"What was the shindy about?"

"Well, it didn't start off with a row at all. It started off the opposite. She'd found out she wasn't going to have a kid and she was pretty upset about it. I was delighted myself. I don't think we can afford those larks. I'm afraid I said some pretty beastly things to her, but I made it up to her afterwards. I put her to bed and cooked her a meal and generally behaved as if I was entertaining royalty."

"But did you behave as if you were sorry for her because you loved her and she was your wife?"

"Well, all right, supposing she did find out she'd made a mistake? It's not irrevocable. There are other opportunities, so to speak. That was what the row was about. She wanted to make other opportunities too soon."

"How soon?"

"Last night."

"And you felt disinclined?"

Jimmy sighed wearily. "I always feel disinclined."

"That's not very fortunate for her."

"I suppose you'll say it's because of this subconscious feeling I'm supposed to have that we're all girls together that puts me off."

"It's possible," Presnor said. "You'd be greatly helped, you know, if you could look upon the whole science of psychology a little less facetiously."

Presnor left a hand on Jimmy's back. Its warmth made a pleasant change from the cold touch of the stethoscope. Then both hands began to feel up and down his spine. Jimmy felt their pressure for what seemed an immeasurable moment in time. The footsteps had ceased upstairs. The Edwardian dignity of the house had an apprehensive silence as if it shared the uneasiness of the boy on the chair. For a few seconds Jimmy sat still. He was fighting a 'sudden desire for Presnor which he realised had been physical. There was only one remedy, flight, but he sat there immovable, a faintness enveloping him that threatened his chance of escape. Presnor's voice sounded far up in his head. "You're a bit stiff down the spine for a boy of your age. You'll have to take more exercise. Obviously golf's not enough."

Jimmy took a deep breath and let it out through his mouth. Then he jumped up and snatched at his coat. He was in the hall and struggling into it before Presnor had time to speak. He slammed both doors behind him. Out in the street he called a taxi. He gave the first address that came into his head, "O'Shaughnessy's Bar in Clipton Street." He had no intention of facing the university that day.

The bar was empty except for Flick. He sat disconsolately perched on a stool. He was sipping tomato juice. He smiled when he caught sight of Jimmy. "Hullo," he said, "how's tricks?" Jimmy ordered a double whisky and drank it down neat. He closed his eyes, trying to black out the memory of the sensuous pleasure he had felt at the pressure of Presnor's finger-tips. He blinked, shook his head, and asked sharply of Flick, "Well, how's the theatre world going?"

"Our show's coming off, and I'm not sorry. I've 'ad enough of Dickie Short. There was a bit of iron mould on his breeches yesterday and he didn't half create. I s'pose he's mad at the play coming off. He thinks he can bring them in."

"Have a proper drink," Jimmy invited him. "Or are you enjoying that stuff?"

Flick shook his head. "I won't say it's my favourite, but when I'm a bit upset I stick to it. I think that's how you go on the booze."

"What, by sticking to tomato juice?"

"No, silly. When you're a bit upset."

Jimmy ordered a single whisky. "I suppose it puts you out of a job if the play comes off."

"Oh, I don't mind that. I've got another one lined up right away."

"What's upset you, then? Domestic troubles?" For the first time he looked at the boy with sympathy. He dropped the contemptuous tone which he discovered himself using towards Flick. "Did Simpton walk out on you?"

"Well, no, not really. It was me that turned him out. But I think he'd have gone in any case. We'd never have made a go of it."

"How do you feel about it?"

Flick wriggled, uncomfortably perched on his stool. "Me? Oh, I feel like hell. I'm crazy about him, you know."

"I should think you're well rid of him," Jimmy said. "He struck me as a thoroughly nasty piece of work."

Flick shrugged. "Oh, he can be that sometimes, but he can be so nice when he likes. I'm really not right for him, that's the trouble, he wants a la-di-da. Everyone told me it wouldn't work, but you know what it is—love's blind. He belongs to the 'L' Club, and posh isn't the word for that place. You meet anyone from dukes to kings in there. And then Gorwin likes music and poetry and painting, and he meets all that sort there. He's got a conductor friend now."

"Bus or baton?" Jimmy inquired.

"Oh, the bandstand kind," said Flick, "but he's ever so famous and clever. I don't know what made his nibs take up with me really. It was—well, it was 'just one of those things'. He sang the words, smiling over-brightly at Jimmy.

Looking into the boy's pale face and the ash-coloured eyelashes fluttering against tears, Jimmy had a sudden stab of sympathy for him. "How about having some lunch?"

"I don't mind if I do," said Flick, "I feel rather peckish now. Where shall we go?" As he said it Jimmy realised that there were very few places indeed in which he would care to be seen with Flick. He felt the boy's grey eyes on him.

"Why don't you come back with me, Mr. Houghton? I can make quite a nice omelette."

Jimmy hesitated over the name. Then he let it pass uncorrected. "That sounds a grand idea."

Flick had a basement flat. The area railings he had painted pale green. He led the way down the stone steps. "They're an awful lot upstairs with their dust-bins. They drop bits all over the place." He made a face as he picked up a banana skin and dropped it carefully into a dust-bin marked 'Carne'. "You'd think people would have more pride, wouldn't you?" He put his key in the door and stood deftly aside to allow Jimmy to enter before him. His kitchen lay under the pavement. It was blue and white and neat. A chintz frill hung down from the ceiling to cover the meters and pipes. "I'll get the pan hot," he told Jimmy; "you go in that door on the right. There should be some cigs in the Japanese box. I'll bring you a drink in a jiffy."

Jimmy opened the door and went into the room. Flick followed him in with two glasses of sherry on a small tin tray. "It's only cooking, I'm afraid. Sit you down and make yourself comfy." Then he shuddered. "I say, I'm a nice one, aren't I? This rooms feels just like a fridge." He knelt down on one knee and put a match to the gas fire. It lit with a spluttering bang. Flick's furniture was modern and simple. He had two plain upholstered chairs, a table in a natural-coloured wood, and a small combined cupboard and

sideboard. He lifted the edge of the rug and peered underneath it for dirt. "My woman comes in on a Tuesday. It's
always the same if you're out. I have to keep after her all
the time. It's easier to do it yourself."

On the mantelpiece a plaster figure sat huddled, its head
between two upward circles which suggested its legs. Its
limbs flowed stickily into one another, as if they were made
from condensed milk. To Jimmy it had no shape. He
raised his glass to it: "Is that a bit of Simpton's culture?"

"Oh goodness, no. Gorwin's classical. He absolutely
hated it. But I'm afraid I dote on it. I can't stick old-
fashioned stuff." He picked the figure up and balanced it on
the palm of his hand. "It's just called 'Crouching figure'.
Don't you think there's something terribly cruel about the
way it's holding its poor little head?"

"I think the whole thing's wicked, but I hardly think that's
what you meant."

"No, I mean sad. Something terribly sad. Something
dreadful's happened to it—you can almost see life crushing
it. But it doesn't look frightened or hurt. It looks sad. I
think it's clever in such a few lines."

He opened a drawer and pulled out a gingham table-
cloth. He shook it and threw it across the table. It came
down like a pink and white cloud. "Anything I can do?"
Jimmy asked.

"No. You just sit there and have a nice rest. Put your
feet up and make yourself comfortable. I'll fill up your glass
in a minute."

Jimmy pulled the opposite chair towards him. He put a
handkerchief on its seat and stretched out his feet. A sense
of well-being began to soak into him. "Flick," he said,
"whether it's you or the drink or the 'crouching figure' I
wouldn't know, but I'm beginning to feel quite a lot
better."

"Never mind what it is," Flick smiled at him, "as long as
it makes you feel good."

Jimmy turned his head towards him. "When did you split up with Simpton, Flick?"

"Oh, it must be a week ago now, I suppose. We haven't had the laundry back yet. It's funny how those silly things hurt you. I think I'll feel worse packing up his clean clothes, and sending them after him, than I did when I saw him walk out of the house."

"Ah," said Jimmy, "this is where my analytical training leaps to the fore. It's undoubtedly got something to do with this substitution racket they're so fond of. Your eyes don't happen to water when you think of his pyjamas, do they?"

"No. But I shouldn't be surprised if my mouth didn't. They looked like a blooming fruit salad. It's funny for some-one with all that good taste. I don't know how he ever got off to sleep in them."

"I'm rather partial to the finer shades of mulberry myself."

"I don't mind a bit of mulberry, but when it comes to orange and black and red! I was always scared someone would set light to the house. Whatever would the firemen have thought?" He patted Jimmy's crossed feet when he passed them and made a little sound through his lips. "Fancy bothering to put a hanky under them. You won't find me fussy like that. A home's meant to live in, I say. You'll spoil your handkerchief."

When they sat down to the omelette Flick asked Jimmy, "Say 'coffee' to me in a sec or two, will you?"

"By Jove, you can cook," Jimmy said.

"I had a great friend who was a chef once. He used to give me such lovely tips. We used to sit and read out recipes until we could practically taste them."

"What happened to *him*?" Jimmy asked, and added, "Coffee!" Flick jumped up.

"Oh, ta, I'll go and get it. I'm afraid there's only cheese for afters." He called from the kitchen. "You mean what happened to the chef? Oh, there was nothing like that between us. It wasn't an affair. We were sisters."

When he came back he was carrying the coffee.

"Do you miss Simpton much?" Jimmy asked.

"'M," Flick nodded, "terribly. Still, we'd only row again if he came back, I suppose. But sometimes when I get extra lonely for him I think it's almost worth it just to hear his voice. Though he could be awful sometimes. He can be nasty in such long words."

"Were you—'in love' with him, Flick?"

"And how. He's got something all right—" Flick laughed—"and he doesn't see why a lot of people shouldn't share it."

"You mean he was unfaithful to you?"

"I don't know about *that*—but he was a shocking flirt. Oo, he was *awful*," Flick said. "I mean, you could laugh at it sometimes, no one likes being tied up to a grump, but it got too much for laughing. It was everywhere you went. It made you feel so silly and cheap. I used to say to him straight out sometimes, 'Look, who did you ask out for the evening, that little blond or me? Because if it's him I'm going home. I never think three's company.' "

"Flick, if you ran into him suddenly now, at a moment when you happened to be missing him most—do you think you could keep your hands off him?"

"Well, I should hope so," answered Flick. "It'd be a nice how-d'ye-do if I couldn't. I was brought up a bit better than that."

"But supposing you felt physically drawn to him so that you—so that you either had to touch him or run away. Supposing you were longing to touch him?"

"Well, I should 'ave to go on longing, shouldn't I? After all, if I fell in love with the Crown Jewels I should have to go on wanting them."

"So what it all comes down to is just a small matter of will power."

Flick's eyes narrowed, looking puzzled. "Well, I mean, you've got to behave yourself, haven't you? People can't go about squeezing girls in the street if the girls say 'no'. If there wasn't a law against that sort of thing his nibs wouldn't keep his hands off anybody." Flick's laugh was a trifle rueful. "He had his eye on *you* that night we first met."

CHAPTER THIRTY-TWO

ON his way home from Flick's flat Jimmy was greeted by the prostitute who looked out for him every evening, provided he passed unaccompanied. She no longer invited him home with her, but they had struck up a cheerful acquaintance. He discovered that her name was Vi Barker, and that she had a curious passion for history. Her spare time was spent in museums and particularly Madame Tussaud's. "It *fascinates* me—all those kings and queens! To think they were actually living once!"

Jimmy had lent her Stefan Zweig's *Marie Antoinette*. She stepped out of a doorway and broke into his thoughts, observing with a scowl at the raining night, "Nice weather for ducks! I'm over half-way through that book, it's wonderful. Poor thing, they didn't give her a chance. They put all the blame on her just as if she'd been the one that was supposed to be ruling; after all she wasn't the king. And anyway, if she ever did take any interest they said she was interfering. They seemed to get her all ways." Her indignation on behalf of Marie Antoinette was matched only by her enthusiasm for the chivalrous Count Fersen. "Wasn't Count Fersen brave, though? It shows you can have a real friend. Fancy Napoleon daring to make that awful remark about him. As if *he* was in a position to talk!"

Jimmy smiled. "I'm sorry, Vi, but just for the moment I've completely forgotten Napoleon's remark!"

"He said Count Fersen had slept with the Queen."

"Well, hadn't he?"

"It's never been *proved*," Vi said, shocked.

"Oh well, my apologies," Jimmy said. "Cheerio, Vi. Don't let it break your heart." He walked on briskly, wondering about her. She had still the plump polish of youth.

His own flat struck cold and unwelcoming. There was a note on the mantelpiece that the charlady had carefully printed out. 'A doctor Presnor ring up and said would you telephone him back please.' Jimmy bunched up the note and dropped it carefully into the newly-lighted fire. Before Pam returned the telephone rang three times. He let his hand hover over it. Once he touched it, but to speak to Presnor would be to go back and see Presnor again. He argued the matter with himself. Surely the least he owed Presnor was the courtesy of an apology for the morning's behaviour. He would say simply that he felt he would rather overcome his difficulties alone, or perhaps out of some deference to the man who had shown him such kindness he might say that he felt himself cured. He knew the last to be absurd, for Presnor had warned him repeatedly that he felt he was suppressing facts, and that to do this was impeding his cure. Presnor had also told him that before there was any hope of a cure, or at the worst before Jimmy was brought to some liveable understanding with his own peculiarities so that they should harm himself and others as little as possible, it would be a lengthy and painstaking business. Repeatedly he discarded the thought of telephoning, only to waver again. It kept him walking about until Pam came in.

"I rang you three times," she said. "Have you only just got in?"

"Oh, it was you ringing, was it?"

"Do you mean to say you were here all the time?"

Jimmy said quickly, "I was having a bath. What were you ringing for?"

"I thought we might go to a film," she said.

He dropped into a chair and put his feet up on the seat of

its twin. Pam placed a newspaper under them. Jimmy asked, half-laughing, "Aren't you scared that there are people who might let me do that without making me put newspaper under them? Who think a home should be a home?"

She threw her hat on to a hook in the hall. "I should think it would have to be someone with a share in a dry-cleaners who would let you behave like that."

The telephone rang. It was within Jimmy's arm length. He sat where he was and stared at it. Pam picked up the receiver. "Hullo. Yes, one minute, please." She held out the receiver to Jimmy. "For you."

"Who is it?"

"How should I know?"

"By finding out, you bloody little fool."

Pam flushed. "Darling, *please* don't use bad language to me. It's so difficult not to retaliate." Then she broke off and said into the phone, "Who is it calling him, please?" She looked up at Jimmy. "Dr. Presnor." Jimmy shook his head vehemently, and made fierce criss-cross signs with his hands. Into the phone Pam said, "I'm sorry, I'm afraid he's not in at the moment. Yes, this is Mrs. Stretton." Jimmy stood up and walked round her. He put his ear close to the receiver. He caught snatches of Presnor's conversation. "What time are you expecting him back, Mrs. Stretton?" Pam looked at Jimmy. He mouthed at her, "Say you don't know, you can't tell." Pam said into the receiver, "I'm afraid I've no idea, Dr. Presnor."

Presnor's voice asked on its easy note, "If I dropped in about nine tonight do you think I should find him back then?"

Jimmy made a quick face at Pam. He said, "Tell him I've gone away. I've gone for quite a time."

"I'm afraid he's gone away, Dr. Presnor, and I don't know when he's coming back. Yes, it was rather sudden. I beg your pardon?" Jimmy took the receiver out of her hand and replaced it sharply, cutting Presnor off. "Oh, Jimmy, that *is* rude," said Pam. Her tone suddenly changed. "Oh, my darling! What is it? You look quite queer."

Jimmy sat down in a chair and laughed. When he recovered he smiled at her. "I'm sorry, it's not at all funny really, but you said I looked quite 'queer'."

"Why don't you want to see him, Jimmy? I thought he was terribly nice."

"For God's sake, there are millions of people who are terribly nice, but you'd go batty if they all dropped in at nine o'clock tonight."

She pulled at his hands. "Jimmy, I was so upset about the baby and all the beastly things you said about it I forgot about your heart. Oh, Jimmy, Jimmy! I mind more about you than *any* baby. I love you much more than myself, but you get so spiteful sometimes. You make me say awful things back. What did he say about you, darling? Was that why you didn't want to speak to him? Were you expecting bad news?"

"He said my heart was fine."

"Swear to me, Jimmy, swear to me."

"I swear to you," Jimmy said gently, "and in view of some of the things I said last night I think it's nice of you to mind."

"Mind!" she repeated. "Mind!" She knelt at his side and put her head on his knee. He ran his hands through her hair. "Jimmy, you do know I'll always set you free if you want me to, don't you?"

"Don't set me free, please, Pam."

He took her to a theatre and kept her out until midnight. When they came home they found Presnor's card in the door.

"What's he chasing you for?" Pam asked.

"Goodness knows," Jimmy replied. "Hop into bed and I'll spoil you. I'll bring you a whacking great omelette." Jimmy took up most of the tiny kitchen. Pam put an arm round his neck. "Our quarrels aren't serious, are they? They're not worse than most married people have?"

"Judging from the couple upstairs I should think they're considerably less."

"Oh, those two are simply ghastly, we must never get like them."

She called through from the bedroom whilst she undressed. "Hasn't Dr. Presttor got a nice voice?"

"Has he?"

"Yes. Is he attractive to look at?"

"I don't know."

"What do you do, keep your eyes closed when you're with him?"

"Well, if you prefer it he's madly attractive," Jimmy said, "I can hardly keep my hands off him. That better?"

He heard Pam laugh. "Well, in that case I'd better not fall for him. It would be terrible if we were to fight over him." As she climbed into bed she called to him, "You *must* read your father's letters, darling. It's not the same thing to have an answer from me. There's another one from him today."

"Have them all bound in green calf and I'll go through them at leisure."

"I can't think why you don't. He's an angel. He wants us to go home for the week-end. Your Aunt Anita's going to Cardiff, so it's rather a heavenly chance."

To go somewhere, he felt, was imperative, but not to the vicarage accompanied by Pam. He felt that a deep change was needed. Besides, he had no wish to see the Reverend Jordon. At the back of his mind he had a dread of his father discovering his tendencies. If it meant avoiding him for ever the Reverend Jordon must not know. He carried the omelette in to Pam with her heart-shaped apron round his waist. "Here you are," he said. "Cut off the veg and two joints."

Pam smoothed a place for the tray on the bed. She slipped

one hand into Jimmy's and gave it a squeeze. "Stay here while I make a pig of myself. That's the best part of the treat."

Jimmy sat down on the bed and lit a cigarette. Hard footsteps crossed the ceiling. They heard a door jerk open and they caught each other's eyes. Jimmy began to recite in time with the man's voice upstairs: "Joo-*lee*, Joo-lee, what have you done with the soap!" Pam put her hand up to stifle a laugh. Jimmy grinned. "What the hell *does* Julie do with it? She must get up to something jolly odd with it. It disappears every night."

Pam lay back and sighed contentedly. "Isn't it wonderful just the two of us cosily snug in here and the rest of the world outside."

Jimmy's mind went to the room above the surgery in the old Hampstead house. It dwelt on the room uneasily, ashamed of its curiosity in the dark early hours. Presnor might be asleep, breathing deeply, or he might be awake with that book in his hand. Pam said, "Is it hot in here? You're sweating."

Jimmy said, "Pam. You do know, don't you, that whatever happens there'll never be any woman in the world I'd prefer to be married to than you? It's just that we're so much a part of each other and we've been like that so long that I fall out with you sometimes, but I'm really only getting at myself."

"Yes, darling, I suppose I do know that. But sometimes it's hard to tell. Do you know when I feel it most?"

Jimmy shook his head. "In those sort of funny attacks that you get when you say you need help and you won't tell me what."

Jimmy picked the tray up. "I'd better get out with this lot, I'm about to have one now."

He washed up and stacked all the crockery. He laid the next day's breakfast trays for Pam. He knew what he was doing, he was avoiding the drawing-room where the telephone sat white and smug. He said, "Will power, will power, will power, Mr. Stretton. If you want the Crown Jewels you can't have them. It's absolutely as simple as *that*."

He went into the drawing-room and lit a cigarette. He sat in the chair by the telephone. He could imagine it ringing besides Presnor's shadowy bedside. He could picture the wrist with its strong black hairs and the watch with the luminous dial on it that went out to pick the instrument up. He wondered what Presnor would say to him. "He will probably tell me to go to hell on a grand scale and send me in a bill for it, and I dare say it serves me right."

He knew that he would have to hear that voice, no matter what it said. There would be something unaccountably comforting in it, whatever words it chose. He felt rather like a small boy whose father's voice alone could dispel some hideous dream. His heart thumped as he dialled. The telephone must have given five rings before a woman said sleepily, "Yes?"

Jimmy stuttered, "I—is—is Dr. Presnor there?"

"Who is calling him, please?"

"Oh, just a very old friend."

There was a pause and a crackling noise. The telephone was passed across the bed. Presnor's voice was quiet and brusque, "Dr. Presnor speaking." He repeated it three times before Jimmy put down the receiver and sat still long after its click.

CHAPTER THIRTY-THREE

IN the morning he had made up his mind. He had never given himself a chance with women. He could not count his experience with Pam. She was obviously not attractive enough to him, and he felt it no disloyalty to her to admit the fact. He felt her an invaluable and irreplaceable friend, and he would feel lost if she left him. But he owed it to her to cure himself if he could. Presnor's 'psychological nonsense' had plunged him even deeper into the morass. He must try another remedy. For all he knew, there might be women who would be able to rouse in him the physical appreciation of the feminine person that was evidently lacking in him. He was cheered at the thought that his homosexual tendencies might be due to the fact that he had never given himself an opportunity. He believed because he wished to believe that this was more likely to be the cause of his trouble than any of the complicated reasons Presnor could supply. It was possible that a prettier girl than Pam might achieve the miracle of arousing a sexual interest in her. His circle of female acquaintances was exceptionally small. He could think of no one except Vi Barker to whom he could make an immediate proposition, with any chance of its being accepted. The thought of an affair with a prostitute was somewhat repellent to him, but he did not dislike the girl herself, and her professionalism might make matters easier. An experiment with Vi had also advantages in so much that it would not involve him emotionally and could be terminated whenever he chose. It would also exclude the formalities of wining, dining and wooing a fresh acquaintance. The more thought he gave to the suggestion of Vi Barker the more admirable he considered the choice.

He said to Pam, "Sweetie, would *you* like to pop home for the week-end? I know you enjoy coming the vicar's daughter-in-law all over the village and the change would do you good."

Pam smiled. "It's not so much coming the vicar's daughter-in-law, it's coming Mrs. Jimmy Stretton that gives me such a kick. But I'd hate it away from you."

"Go down and see the old man for me, sweetie. He's terribly fond of you. I want to have a blitz on work, and if you're not here to fuss me I can get well ahead."

She was easy to deceive. She asked no further questions. He took her by the shoulders and promised her, "We'll have a good holiday this year. We won't go down to Brighton with our buckets and spades, and we won't go down to dear old Dad either. We'll go to Grasmere and have a second honeymoon. If you recall the incident, we didn't have a real one there the first time."

"I recall every moment," she said.

He went off in search of Vi Barker. She was not in her usual doorway. He had to make four visits back to it before he discovered her there. It was raining and her ankles were splashed. She wore a fox cape, carried a check umbrella, and her feet were enclosed in a pair of plastic galoshes that reminded him of sandwich wrappers.

She greeted him cheerfully, "Hullo, handsome."

"Vi, I want a word with you."

She fell into step at his side. She was sturdily built and her calves looked strong. It was the taut smoothness of skin and flesh which gave her the polished appearance. She made an effort to protect them both with her umbrella. Jimmy's height made the feat impossible. She grinned up at him, "You'll have to bend your knees if you don't want to get wet."

"Vi," he said. "Have you got a passport?"

"Yes," she said, "I have."

"I wondered if you'd like to come with me on a short—er—holiday?"

"What about your wife?"

"She's going away herself. I thought you and I might pop over to Paris for a couple of days."

"Paris!"

"Paris," he said. "Keep walking, girl. You'll get wetter standing still. You can go and stare at the Bastille, or is that one of the ruins Cromwell knocked about a bit?"

"Don't be silly. The French knocked it down themselves. I read that lovely book again. Wasn't the French Revolution *terrible* for King Louis and Queen Marie Antoinette? For all the French, I mean—?"

"Yes, I should think it was acutely tiresome to those involved," Jimmy said.

"Do you know, I'm not sure I don't feel sorrier for Count Fersen than the Queen. It must have been dreadful for him —thinking about her like that. I always say it's worse for the ones who are left behind."

"I forget now," Jimmy said, smiling, "which of them broke my heart most."

She stood still again. "I say, this Paris. Were you really serious?"

"Deadly."

"What's the catch?"

"There isn't one."

"Why me? Why my sort, I mean? Someone like you could take anyone you liked to Paris. You don't have to pick on a professional. It's not a divorce racket, is it? Because my boy wouldn't like me to go in for that."

"I'm doing my best to avoid a divorce. Well, do you think you can make it?"

"I'll have to have a word with my boy first. What's your name?"

"Jimmy Houghton. I'll go ahead with the arrangements on the assumption that your 'boy' will say yes. He won't want to vet me, will he? I mean, he doesn't want to vet all the rest."

"No, but it's different abroad. I mean, it means missing week-end business. How much were you thinking of paying?"

"Expenses, of course, and I'll give you your full travelling allowance."

"Paris! Paris," she said. "Is there anything left of it that you can see?"

"What, of Paris?"

"No, silly, the Revolution. You know, if I had the brains and the money I'd go to college and do it properly. I would, I'm not joking. Even at my age. I wouldn't care how it

looked. I'd go to night-classes now if it wasn't my working
time. I'd like to have been a historical teacher, or write
books about history myself. Funny, isn't it, but it absolutely
gets me, anything to do with the past. My God, I do hope
Ted'll say yes. I'd go crazy if I could actually see the place
where they put the Queen in prison."

"I should think you're the first girl who's ever been lured
to Paris for a wicked week-end on the strength of a visit to
the Conciergerie."

"Ted has just *got* to say yes." Looking at her, Jimmy lost
confidence. There was a streak of artificial white hair at the
side of her head. Four ropes of grey pearls climbed her neck.
The lipstick spread over the lines of her lips. The eyelashes
projected like a row of iron railings, and the rouge was a hard
round patch worn high. A sharp perfume attacked him in
gusts as she walked, and the fox cape stood out in wet and
bedraggled spikes like a sick cat huddled before a fire. He
wondered to which hotel he could take her in Paris, and sign
the register as Mr. and Mrs. J. H. Houghton. He found,
with a quick hint of panic, that he was hoping that her 'boy'
would say no.

She turned to him, showing fine teeth. "I tell you what.
I'll say yes for him. Ted wouldn't want me to lose an
opportunity like this. He's just as keen as I am, you know."

"On what?"

"On history, and old-fashioned things. That's how we
met. In the Victoria and Albert. We're saving up to go in
for antiques. You can make a lot of money out of them, and
besides, it would be such fun. We're going to start off in a
small way at first and then branch out. Ted's got quite a
flair for finding something that looks old and no good and
then when you polish it up it's valuable. Of course with me
it's not the selling I like so much. It's the thinking about who
things belonged to and what happened to them and all that."

A policeman was heading towards them, "Is he after
you?" Jimmy inquired.

"Oh no, he's all right. I know him. I've only just paid up. Still, it might be better to say ta-ta now. I don't want to make things difficult for him. He does his best for me. But about the Paris thing, Mr. Houghton. You can take it from me that it's 'yes'."

At the airport he waited for her in a certain amount of trepidation. He was bitterly regretting what he had come to the conclusion was a bizarre and ridiculous idea. He failed to recognise her until she addressed him, "Hullo, handsome." He spun round, surprised.

"Good Lord!"

The streak of white hair had vanished, so had the wrought-iron eyelashes. She wore a tweed travelling coat and a plain grey suit. She wore gloves and shoes to match a light-brown handbag. A silk scarf was knotted round her throat and her hair was fluffed softly about her head. Her mouth was small and lightly lipsticked. She gave Jimmy a broad smile and winked. "My Ted can't stand make-up, and he can't stand my hair bleached in bits, so I darken it out for him. I thought you'd like it darkened too."

"Thank you," Jimmy said. "I must say that my taste supports Ted's."

In the plane Vi turned over the leaves of a highly-polished magazine and Jimmy pretended to sleep. In spite of her softened appearance he was still regretting the idea. He would have preferred to have played golf with Presnor. The very thought of Presnor, psychological nonsense and all, seemed nostalgically soothing compared to the effort he was about to force himself to make.

Paris was grey and wet. Vi sat with her nose pressed to the window of the taxi and Jimmy felt guilty for not bringing Pam. It seemed wrong that it should be Vi making little squeaks of excitement and not Pam. He would have enjoyed driving up to Montmartre with her at night and looking for the 'Lapin Agile'. He would have liked to have sat with her in cafés and advised her what to eat and drink. Pam's deep

capacity for enjoying herself had always been a pleasure to
him. They had done everything together for so long, and
that he should have come to Paris for the first time in his life
without her seemed as mean as creeping up to the loft in
the old days and devouring sweets behind her back. He felt
startlingly lonely for her. He decided not to look too closely
at Paris. He would re-discover it some day with Pam.

Vi sighed, "I do wish Ted was here to see it all. He told
me to remember every bit. I'm never any good at describing
things."

"We are a fine pair," Jimmy chuckled; "I was just missing
my wife."

"She hasn't walked out on you, has she?"

"No, oh no, nothing like that. But she—well, she doesn't
get much fun—and I felt a bit of a swine, for doing her out
of some."

"Couldn't you buy her something?" Vi suggested. "Am
I about her size?"

"No, she's taller. And anyhow I think she might think
it odd if I brought her a present from Paris when I'm
supposed to be in Pimlico."

Their hotel was small, inexpensive and clean. Jimmy sent
down for a bottle of Vichy water. "I'm one of those tiresome Englishmen who don't trust foreign tap water."

Vi stood at the window. "Where shall I tell Ted the
hotel looked out on?"

"We're just at the back of the Madeleine."

"I can't believe I'm here," Vi said. "I really and truly
can't." She looked out of the window, down on the street.
"Don't people hurry in France! Ooh! I smell garlic from
that little restaurant." She took off her coat and hung it up.
Their room was high and white and cold. One of the bed-
knobs rattled. Vi said, "We'd better fix that for tonight.
Could you put a bit of paper in it? Or a bit of string might
make it wedge."

Jimmy said, "Yes, I'll do something with it." He

coloured slightly. She seemed casually professional at one
moment and at the next like a schoolgirl brought out on a
treat. He imagined that she was having difficulty in bringing
her mind back to business. It so longed to escape into its
own excitements. Jimmy went out of his way to encourage
her to forget why they had come, or at least to postpone it
for as long as possible. No one was less anxious than he to
introduce a businesslike note.

"You don't want to do anything now, do you?" Vi asked.
"Because if you do—well, it's your party. So you must call
the tune."

"No, thanks," he said quickly. "Tell me about Ted.
Doesn't he mind what you do for your living?"

She looked annoyed at the question, her lips pressed in.
"He's trying to get me out of it. I was in it ages before I
met him. I was practically a kid when I started first, and
you know how it is, you just go on. Especially when the
money's good. Ted doesn't get much at present—but we're
both putting everything by, to do what I told you about.
Ted's being going straight for a long time now, but it takes
a long time to catch up."

"Straight?"

"Yes, he's only been out for a year."

"What was he 'in' for?" Jimmy asked.

"Smash and grab," said Vi. She opened her wallet and
showed Jimmy a photograph. A heavily freckled young
man stared up at him. He had a spreading, toothy grin.

"Oh, he's—he's charming," said Jimmy with difficulty.
He was powerless to imagine the spanner-faced Ted being
moved by the tragedy of a long-dead Swedish count's
passion for an ill-fated queen.

"He's a wonderful lover," Vi said. "We get on like a
house on fire. Let's have a dekko at your wife."

Jimmy passed over Pam's photograph to her. She sat
with her hands folded, soft-featured and neat. "Oh yes—
she's—she's nice," Vi told him. But he thought that her

voice lacked conviction. "You don't mind me talking about Ted, do you? Because, I mean, I won't if you'd rather not."

"No, prattle as much as you like."

"Well, it's your party, so you call the tune."

She changed into a plain black dress and carried a brightly-beaded bag. She had a well-cut fur bolero and her stockings were sheer and her seams were straight.

When they left the hotel the night air was fine and the rain had stopped.

"In the guide-book it says the Carnavalet museum has got some lovely things left over from the Revolution."

'We'll visit it tomorrow," Jimmy promised. He was glad to find something to do with her.

She squeaked, "Oh, you really are an angel. Ted always calls me Lucky Liz. He says everything comes my way, and he's certainly right on this occasion." Now and again her conscience struck her. "You are quite sure that *you're* enjoying yourself. You wouldn't rather go back to the hotel or anything, because, I mean, it's——"

Jimmy finished off for her, "Yes, I know, it's my party, and I can call the tune. Well, I feel like a breath of fresh air at the moment." A breeze blew off the Seine as they leant over the Pont Royal. "Don't look now," Jimmy told her, "but I think that great black bulk of a place on the left bank is the spot where your girl friend came to grief."

"What, the prison! The Conciergerie? Oh my goodness, it does look dreadful. Fancy her being in there. You'd think they'd have shown her a bit more respect. After all, she was every inch a queen."

"I fancy that's what annoyed them about her in the first place."

Vi turned to look at him, smiling. She observed, as a casual pleasantry, "My God, you *are* good-looking. I shouldn't think you have to whistle for it, do you? It beats me what you're doing here with me."

They dined in a small café which proved more costly than the large hotel next door, and Jimmy, determined to make the evening last as long as possible, took her to the Café de la Paix to observe Paris walking by at night. They sat in wicker-work chairs and sipped cognac. "I think this is the place," said Jimmy, "where they say you can see the whole world go by if you sit here long enough."

She picked up the ticket the waiter had put down on the table. "All those francs for just two drinks!"

"I fancy you are reading the date," he said. He had an empty sense of foreboding that Vi's chatter could never dispel. It was the depression descending in force. Pam could sometimes manage to diminish it, and Presnor could always do so—momentarily at least. Presnor seemed more than miles away. To his surprise he found other men looking at Vi. He tried to force himself to feel attracted towards her. If he failed, he would have wasted a considerable amount of money which he could very ill afford. If he failed he would face despair.

"I *am* looking forward to tomorrow," Vi said. "We might see something Marie Antoinette actually touched."

They returned to their hotel well after midnight. The night-porter gave them a heavy key, asked them if they had enjoyed themselves, and imparted the information, accompanied by a wink, that Paris was always Paris.

In the bedroom Vi said, "Isn't it queer how Madame sounds so much nicer than Mrs.?"

"Yes." He was coldly apprehensive of the little firm body she was beginning to reveal.

"Want the bath first?" she asked him.

"No," he said. "You go ahead." He longed for Pam and the consolation of a body he knew. He felt not only embarrassment but a definite repugnance towards this strangeness which was Vi. He heard her splashing about in the tiled skilful slit of a bathroom. She hummed the 'Blue Danube' for a steady five minutes and then broke into the 'Marseillaise'. "Bom ba, bom bom bom ba bom, ba bom—oh, hell's bells and little fishes!"

"What's the matter?" Jimmy called through the door.

"Slipped and wet my hair," she answered. "It always makes me mad."

She came out in a black and lemon-coloured nightgown. "Do you like it? Ted says it's indecent. I put it on because you might be the sort that likes to take them off."

"You look like a fruit salad," Jimmy grinned at her.

"I'm not so sure that you can talk. You look like a raspberry blancmange."

Jimmy was lying in bed in the plum-coloured pyjamas. He said, "Last one in turns off the lights."

"Well, of all the dirty tricks," she squeaked. She scampered across the floor and slid in beside him. The sheets struck cold in the big brass bed. "Brrrr!" she said. "It's icy!"

Jimmy moved deliberately away from her, turned over and said, "Good-night."

CHAPTER THIRTY-FOUR

THEY had to re-visit the Carnavalet. By the time the museum closed for lunch Vi had not seen a quarter of its contents. Jimmy wandered about the spacious old house, delighting in the elegant proportions and the graceful distribution of light that the vast windows spread over the well-polished floors. He smiled at Vi's face, serious in a pair of self-coloured glasses, bent over case after case. He had never seen such an expression of awe. Calamity might have struck her when the whistle blew for lunch. She had just dis-covered a cabinet containing personal relics of Marie Antoinette. She turned round to Jimmy, her voice tragic. "Oh, Jimmy! Her shoe! Look, her very own shoe! And we've got to go and leave. And, oh look, there's a piece of her hair! The actual hair that once grew on her head."

Jimmy took hold of her hand, "We'll come back again after lunch." He retained her hand as they left the museum. The shuttered and flaking façade of once well-to-do houses rose up from the narrow streets, shabby at the touch of the fingering sunlight, but with a dignity never lost.

"This is certainly a spot for Sedan chairs and powder and patches," Jimmy smiled, and added, "My God! You've got me at it."

"Oh yes," she said, her voice reverent. "You can smell it in the air." Then her conscience claimed her, drawing her mind unwillingly back to her own more recent past. "Was there anything wrong with me last night?"

"No, nothing," Jimmy told her.

"What went wrong, then? You sort of—shivered away when I tried. If there's anything special you like, you know you've only got to tell me. It probably wouldn't come new to me."

"I was just exhausted," Jimmy said. "Don't worry. It casts no reflection on you. I'm calling the tune and I'm satisfied."

She was happy to let the subject drop, happy to be free to dream again. "You wouldn't wear that sort of shoe outside, would you?"

"I shouldn't wear it anywhere," Jimmy said.

They lunched at a crowded café and sat beneath a red umbrella on the pavement of an old and mellowed square. About the ancient square there was the noon-day sense of suspended activity in all matters urgent and grave which the French luncheon-break can inspire. The buildings seemed yellow-stoned and somnolent as if far-off summer suns had been baked in them while above them a blackening sky stored a load of chilling rains.

Jimmy closed his eyes, trying to recall Vi as she stood in the London doorways, but the girl who came forward with the low suggestive 'Hullo, handsome' did not exist in Paris.

He realised that there was no sign of the semi-American accent he had heard her use before. Her impatience to be back to the museum amused him. He found her schoolgirl enthralment charming. A gentle persuasive perfume blew back to him when they walked. He sniffed at it. "Why don't you wear that always? It's much nicer than the one that you usually wear."

"I usually keep this for Ted. It's much too good for work."

In the Carnavalet he smelt it again. It lay deep in her springy bright hair. It seemed to exude from her palms and her skin. He thought he had rarely known someone who smelt so bitingly fresh and sweet. She held out her hand excitedly to him. "Look, Jimmy, look at this little sort of needle-case, and the scissors! Think of her using those!"

"I can't imagine what she'd use them for except to trim Fersen's moustache."

"He hadn't *got* one. They didn't wear them."

"Oh, I beg his pardon," Jimmy said.

In the dismal Conciergerie they followed the crowd and the guide. Jimmy whispered a passable translation of all that was being said. It was when she slipped back to the gloomy dank-walled chamber into which the Queen's cell led off, to have a final haunting look at the table-napkin reputed to have been used by her, that Jimmy turned her towards him and kissed her. It was a clumsy and ill-planned attempt. It took both of them by surprise. He stood back to look at her, dazed at the impetus which had driven him towards her and given him no warning first. He was pleased with it, filled with a hope.

She laughed, "Well, what a nice place to choose! I'm not sure Ted would approve of it. It didn't seem businesslike." Jimmy was aware of a sense of excitement struggling for power in his veins. It gathered a slow, increasing momentum that gave a promise of force to come. He had not at the

moment enjoyed the kiss, but he felt that he wanted to kiss
her again. Her eyelashes had an uptilting curl at the ends,
making them look as if feather-tipped.

"I expect lots of girls go crazy about you, don't they? I've
seen lots of women looking at you in the street. It gave me
quite a kick to be with you."

"Funny," said Jimmy. "That's how I felt when men
looked at you."

"I don't get your number," she said.

"I don't entirely get yours. Does it matter?"

"Not when you're happy," she said.

In the Café de la Paix he felt for her hand beneath the
table, and her fingers returned his pressure. He took a sip
of his cognac and closed his eyes. A herald of peace seemed
to stroll through his blood. All was well with his world.
He desired her. He grinned at her: "As it's my party
and I can call the tune, how about getting back to the
hotel?"

"All right," she said, and drank up her cognac. A party
of four blocked their way. They sat at a table in front of
Jimmy and Vi. They were discussing a cruise to Madeira.
They spoke loudly and excitedly in French. A wide fox cape
was round the shoulders of the woman immediately in front
of Jimmy. She had a neat and well-groomed head. A squat
diamond clasp to a row of pearls caught the light on the back
of her neck. She was middle-aged and well-corseted. Her
closely cropped hair was turning grey. Her gestures and
her voice were familiar to him. When she stubbed out a
cigarette she gave it a twist to the right. When she turned
her head he came face to face with the one-time Rosamund
Osbourne. For a second or two she stared. Then she held
out her hand and a smile broke out. "It isn't! It is! It
must be!"

Jimmy stood up, his heart beating. "Hullo, Mrs. Os—
Mrs.——"

"Vavasseur, Jimmy," she told him. She turned excitedly

round to the man at her side. "Maurice, this is Jimmy Stretton."

The man was broad-bodied and tiny-featured. "My dear boy, at last you've come to life. I was beginning to think Rosamund had dreamt you."

A Monsieur and Madame Delfonte were introduced, and then four pairs of eyes turned towards Vi. Rosamund held her hand out. "I did hear you were married, and I did mean to write. How do you do, Mrs. Stretton? I can honestly say that I've known your husband since he was 'so high'. In fact not as high as that." For a few seconds Vi's hand hung hesitant. Then she held it out. Rosamund sat in the chair beside her. "How long is it, Jimmy? It must be years."

"Yes, it is years, Mrs. Os—Mrs. Vavasseur," Jimmy said.

Maurice Vavasseur threw up his hands. "The stories I've heard of you! Goodness, what tales."

Rosamund patted Vi's hand. "May I use your Christian name? It seems strange to use anything else."

Vi replied, smiling, "It's Pam."

"You simply must come and see us. What are your plans for tomorrow? Whatever they are they must all be thrown over. I insist that you spend the day with us."

Jimmy answered. His voice became eager and over-emphatic. He smiled and used his hands too much. He was aware that Vi quietly watched him. "Mrs. Vavasseur, it really is most *ghastly* bad luck. But we've got to be off at the *crack* of dawn tomorrow. It's terrible after all these years. I do *wish* we'd run into each other before. I'd simply *adore* a long chat with you about old times."

"Oh but, my dear, I really can't bear it. How awful after all this time. Maurice, give him our address and our telephone number, and the next time, my dear boy, you'll be staying with us. Pam, I insist that you bring him again."

As they went out he could hear her loud voice. ". . . absolutely *devoted* to my first husband . . ."

H

Vi asked him quietly, "We aren't going back tomorrow, are we?"

Jimmy said, "If I can get the tickets changed, yes. I'm sorry you won't see Versailles or the Trianon."

In their hotel room she undressed in the bathroom. She did not appear in the chiffon night-gown. She wore a pair of plainly cut pyjamas and she had taken the make-up off her face. She clambered into bed before him and said, "Last one in turns off the lights." There was an apple in her travelling case, and she leant out of bed to grope for it. Then she settled behind a book. She inquired casually of Jimmy over the top, "I imagine you won't want me at all tonight, strictly business or otherwise."

He was putting loose change on the dressing-table. He wondered why an encounter with Rosamund had killed his so newly-born desire for Vi. He managed to smile at her: "No offence meant."

"None taken, I'm sure," she said. "It's your business, and if you like to waste your money—anyway, thanks for the most wonderful time that I've ever had. I've never enjoyed myself so much."

"Well, that's something," Jimmy said. He switched off the light and lay beside her. Her voice sounded thoughtful coming out of the dark:

"Do you think if I'd tried a bit more with you—if I'd put on a bit of a show? Would you like me to try?" she asked him. "It's surprising, you know, what can be done." She could feel him shake his head beside her. She drew up the sheets and rolled slightly away from him. "Well, I've got your number now all right."

"What's it add up to?" Jimmy asked her. He lay motionless back on the pillow. His eyes were closed and his voice was tired.

"Oh, two and two make five."

"How did you reach such a mathematical conclusion?"

She spoke evenly into the dark: "I can't think why I never

caught on before. I can tell 'em a mile off, usually. But with you I simply never thought. I only caught on tonight."

Jimmy asked her wearily, "What gave you such insight tonight?"

"It was when we ran into that woman, when you were trying to put her off—it suddenly seemed to come out. Just the way you spoke and the way you waved your hands about —well, you know how people can tell. I hadn't seen a sign of it till that moment, but then I thought—well!—that two and two make five, and I got the right answer, didn't I?"

Jimmy said, "Not far out."

CHAPTER THIRTY-FIVE

HE did not return to his own flat. He went instead to Flick's. Flick opened the door and said, "You, is it?" and shut it again in his face. Jimmy repeated the knock. There was no answer. He went to a telephone. He lounged in the booth and dialled Flick's number. Flick's voice sounded sharp on the phone. Jimmy asked:

"What have I done?"

Flick said, "Who is it speaking, please?"

"An omelette fan of yours." The telephone receiver clicked down. Jimmy returned to the basement flat. He beat a tattoo on the door. After a while Flick opened it.

"Want me to call the police?"

"What have I done to you, Flick?"

"Me? Oh, just thought I couldn't be trusted to know your right name. What did you think I'd do? Blackmail you? Complimentary, isn't it? Good-night, Mr. Jimmy Stretton."

Jimmy put a foot in the door. "How did you find out, Flick?"

"Your chum Dr. Presnor turned up. He went in to

O'Shaughnessy's and asked for you there. O'Shaughnessy
heard us fixing up our lunch together, so Presnor turns up
here. He says, 'Have you seen Jimmy Stretton?' And I say,
'Never heard of him.' Then he says, 'Tall and fair and handsome, with very deep grey eyes.' And I says, 'You mean
Jordon Houghton.' And he says, 'That's Jimmy Stretton.'
Thanks, but I don't care for false names." Flick tried to
close the door again. Jimmy put his weight against it.

"Flick, I'm so desperately miserable, for God's sake let
me in."

For a second or two Flick was hesitant. Then he stood
aside. Jimmy stepped into the blue and white kitchen and
followed Flick into the living-room. Flick took a stand in
front of the fireplace. He stood with his hands behind his
back and his chin jutted firm and defiant. But nothing could
mask the kindliness in the boy's understanding eyes.

Jimmy held out his hand to him: "I'm sorry. I suppose it
was insulting. But it wasn't only to you that I gave that
name. I just forgot to put it right. Flick, I must talk to
somebody. For God's sake take that look off your face."

The coolness was gone from Flick's voice when he
answered, "Well, what are friends for if you can't come to
them when you're in trouble?"

Jimmy found himself in a chair by the fireside. He had not
noticed Flick pulling it out. He found a cigarette in his
mouth and a match struck to light it, and a drink put into
his hand. He had not noticed Flick administering to his
comforts. It was done with undetectable speed. Flick sat
on a stool and looked up at him. Jimmy was surprised at
the ease with which he could talk to Flick. "Flick, I took a
whore to Paris. I've only just come back. I thought I could
straighten things out that way, but it just damned well
didn't work out."

Flick said, "Oh, Jimmy! You're *married*!"

"I know, but don't you see, Flick——"

"Yes, I do," said Flick, "and I think it's very naughty.

Your poor little wife stays at home and works her fingers to the bone for you and you take someone else to Paris. Gorwin was just the same. Night after night I'd come back from the theatre and knock up some nice supper for him, but who did he take to the 'L' Club? I don't always know who he took there, of course, but it certainly wasn't me."

Red-striped curtains were drawn at the window. The street-lamp shone through from outside. It made a cosy and comfortable glow in the room like a fireside let into the wall. "It nearly worked out," Jimmy told him. "The girl was rather sweet in a way. I nearly got a yen for her. Things were going fine. Then I came across someone who brought back memories of the very thing I was trying to escape. Everything went haywire after that. I couldn't have touched the girl if someone had stood over me with a gun. Flick, you know what you want. I mean you're settled—for better or for worse you've accepted yourself as what you are and you're contented with it. But, you see, I can't accept myself as I am. It's something I feel I must fight tooth and nail."

Flick's grey eyes travelled sympathetically over him, as if he might discover the source of pain in a toe or a limb. "You've got a sense of wrongdoing, that's what it is," said Flick wisely. "I've met people with that before. Not 'is nibs of course. 'E wouldn't feel a sense of wrongdoing if he was cutting his granny's throat, but then they left out his conscience when they strung him together."

"Haven't you a conscience, Flick?"

"Me? Why should I have? I don't do any harm to anyone. Of course, if people get up to tricks in the street like Eddie—well, I think that's *disgusting*," said Flick.

"Don't you think it might be possible that it wasn't Eddie's fault?"

"Well, who else's is it likely to be? Nobody egged him on, did they?"

Jimmy interrupted, "I meant—don't you think Eddie might not have been responsible for what he did?"

"Oh, you mean that he wasn't quite right in the head or something? Oh well, I suppose in that case—still, I don't go for all this forgiving madness. I think it gives sane people ideas."

Jimmy made another attempt. 'But, Flick, don't you think there's something not entirely normal about you and me?"

Flick answered cheerfully, "Well, you look all right, but I *must* be crazy. No one in his right senses would go and fall flat for his nibs. After all, I knew all about him. I knew he'd play me up." Flick sat back, cuddling his knees. He looked like a pixie garden ornament.

Jimmy said patiently, "Don't you think it a little unconventional of us to fall flat for *men* at all?"

Flick made a sudden darting lunge for a cigarette lighter on the table beside him. When he had lit it he examined the end of his cigarette. "Oh, you mean just being *queer*? Is that what's bothering you? Well, we didn't make ourselves, did we?" He gave his urchin grin. "I didn't make myself, I can tell you. I'd have made a much better job if there'd been a choice. I'd have had *real* blond hair, not just mousy lights. And I'd have had great big round blue eyes." He saw Jimmy's expression and lost his grin. "I'm sorry, I shouldn't be joking. I can see you're quite upset. But look, Jimmy, you can't help what you are or what you feel like. You can only help what you do. I mean, I think the things some people do are *awful*—everyone's got to behave themselves. That's why I'm not madly sorry for Eddie—we'd all like to break out and give way to nasty urges, but, I meantersay, where would that end up? We'd just get lower and lower until nothing was too awful for anybody to do. But there's good and bad in all kinds, Jimmy. You don't just discover it in our sort. I think prostitution's horrible when it happens with our kind, I think it's an insult to love, but then I don't think much of ladies who do it for money either. I'm told that they're very good-hearted, but there's room for a good heart in other jobs—and as for queers who do it with men *and* women for what they can get out of it or go upsetting poor little boys—well! They just aren't the sort of people you ask to tea. But then there are *plenty* of people you don't ask to tea, Jimmy—murderers, and people who hit old ladies on the head and take their savings. And people who are beastly to children and animals—but you wouldn't lump yourself in with them just because none of you were queer! Well then, just because some queers go a bit too far it doesn't mean you've got to think you're one of *them*. If what *you* do isn't hurting anyone else and it's only with someone who feels the same way—where's the harm? If you behave yourselves all right I don't see why you should be lumped in with people who don't."

"I'm afraid it might still be considered a sin, Flick. Ever heard of Sodom and Gomorrah?"

"Yes, they were burnt down, weren't they? I dare say quite rightly. They probably didn't behave themselves."

Jimmy sighed. "Well, perhaps that's the answer. 'Behave as well as you can'!" Then he said, "Flick, from the way I'm feeling just at the moment I can see it would be a fatal mistake to go back to my wife. We'd only get on each other's nerves and row."

Flick nodded sympathetically. "Well, if you're going to hurt her feelings it's better to stay away for a bit."

"Could you put me up for a while, Flick? It'd be a hell of a help if you could. I'd be able to sort myself out, and it's a grand thing being able to talk to you. I'd muck in with the rent of course."

"Oh, it isn't that—but——"

"Simpton lived here, didn't he?"

"Well—only off and on. You've got to watch out, you know, Jimmy. People have dreadful minds. Gorwin just stayed here now and again, and even then people made nasty remarks. You've got to watch out for the police."

"Just for a day or two, please, Flick."

"Oh well, I dare say we could manage that. I don't like to turn anyone who's in trouble away. Goodness knows people ought to help each other. You look simply awful, Jimmy. I don't mean that you don't look attractive, I mean sort of tired and washed out."

"I could use a good night's rest."

Flick stood up and smiled at him. "I can guess who'll have to go on the sofa with those long legs of yours—it's me!"

"Oh, I can't turn you out," Jimmy said.

"Nobody has to turn out really. It's just for the look of the thing." From an ottoman in the corner he dragged out some blankets and sheets. He made up a bed on the sofa and rumpled the pillow up. "Just in case some busybody takes it into his head to look in. You've got to look out for other things too, Jimmy. You can't always rely on your friends."

"What on earth do you mean? Blackmail?" Jimmy asked.

"There is such a thing," Flick said. He opened a door and turned on a light. "His nibs was inclined to snore a bit. I hope you're not given that way."

Jimmy followed him into a bedroom. Twin divans stood out from the wall. Beside them a bookcase ran. There was only one picture hung in the room. It was in oils, of a ballet dancer in a white and frothing skirt. Jimmy said, "But surely, when everyone knew that you and Simpton were having an affair, a sofa couldn't really have protected you, could it?"

"Maybe not," Flick replied. "But it helps."

CHAPTER THIRTY-SIX

HE slept more peacefully than he had slept for many weeks. He did not wake up from the time that his head touched the pillow until Flick brought him early morning tea.

He sat in the little white living-room and wrote out a

letter to Pam. '. . . and until I've got over this emotional
disturbance, which I don't think you'd understand if I tried
to explain, but which has nothing to do with you personally,
I think that we're safer apart. We don't want to ruin our
chances for good.'

He telephoned her when he knew that she would have
received the letter. He said merely, "Look, sweetie, don't
argue, and don't worry about me. I'll ring you up every
night." He telephoned from different kiosks and was
immune to her entreaties and tears.

He had been in the basement flat three days when the
telephone startled him out of his books. Flick was at the
theatre. It was after ten at night. A man's voice inquired,
"May I speak to Mr. Weston?"

"I'm afraid he's not back yet," Jimmy said. "Can I take
a message? Who's calling?"

"Tell him it's Gorwin Simpton, will you? And by the
way, who's that?" Jimmy replaced the receiver. He told
Flick of the call when he came in.

Flick said, "Oh oh! It's getting about, then. Isn't that like
his nibs? I do detest dogs in the manger. He's got no
more use for me himself, mind you, but if I have a friend—
that's different. He'll split himself trying to find out who
you are."

"He won't get any change out of me," Jimmy said. "I
suppose it wouldn't occur to him that there might not be
anything between us, except ordinary friendship, I mean."

"Oh, bless you, no. He wouldn't think a new-born lamb
was innocent. He'd judge it by himself."

Jimmy had been staying with Flick a week. He was
obliged to leave earlier in the morning to be in time for the
first lecture, and he was home later at night. One Thursday,
just after the nine o'clock news, they received a visitor.
Jimmy was sitting with his feet up in the chair opposite him,
a cookery book in his lap. "Well, I think where we went
wrong was the flour."

Flick had an ironing-board rigged up in the living-room.
He was pressing two of Jimmy's shirts. When the bell rang
he said, "Drat it," and stood the iron on end. He rolled
down his sleeves and said, "Look, sweetheart, if it's any
kind of busybody in uniform or out, all you say is you're
staying with me until you've made up a tiff with your wife."

"Well, that's all I am doing," Jimmy pointed out.

At the door he heard Flick call out gaily, "For crying out
loud! How's tricks?" When he came back he was followed
by Presnor. Jimmy slowly took his feet from the chair.

Presnor smiled down at him: "Well, well. Hullo, Stretton.
What a small world it is."

"Yes," said Jimmy, "cramped."

Flick folded up the ironing-board and took both the shirts
to the bedroom. He called out, "Sit you down, Presie. Make
that lazy brute give you something to drink."

Presnor said, "Your wife came to see me yesterday. She
seemed a little upset."

"She shouldn't. I phone her each night." Jimmy took a
bottle of gin from the sideboard and poured Presnor out a
drink.

"What a delightful voice she has," Presnor said.

"That's what she says about yours."

"She's a charming, level-headed girl. You're an extremely
lucky boy, Jimmy."

"Yes, aren't I," Jimmy snapped. He could imagine the
scene between Presnor and Pam. The admiration each
would awake in the other. Presnor would be impressed by
that steady calm of hers, which gave her a maturity further
than her years. The self-control that would never let her fly
off the handle, that would never let her shout hysterically at
Presnor as he had shouted at Presnor himself. Pam would
appreciate the distinctive essence of Presnor's dark masculinity. They had an easy quietness of manner in common,
those two, and they had something far more important to
draw them together. They each belonged to an opposite

sex. There was no barrier between them to prevent them from expressing their admiration. For a few savage moments he hated them both. "What did you tell my wife?" he asked Presnor.

"Nothing."

"Then what did she ask you?"

"Nothing."

Jimmy slapped the cork hard into the neck of the bottle. "For two people who are so keen on each other's vocal powers you seem to have given each other remarkably little opportunity of judging them."

Presnor chuckled. "She showed me your letter, and I said that I thought your nerves were upset and agreed that it might be a good idea for you to remain apart for a little."

Flick shouted out from the bedroom, "You don't know what an honour this is, Jimmy. Presie hasn't made a social call here for months. He didn't hit it off with his nibs. Have you run into him lately, Presie?"

"I saw him in O'Shaughnessy's a night or two ago," Presnor called back.

"Who was he with?"

"A German fellow, some sort of conductor, I think."

"Oh well, it's still on, then," answered Flick. "Surprising for his nibs. Fancy that! Lasted over a week!"

Presnor asked Jimmy, "Was it you who telephoned me about two o'clock one morning a little while ago?"

Jimmy said, "How did you guess?"

"Why did you ring?"

"Oh, I just had a nasty nightmare and wanted to hear Daddy's voice."

Flick came back with his jacket on. "Yes, you *do* have nightmares. You were trembling all over and squeaking last night. Like our old collie used to do in his sleep."

Presnor kept his eyes on Jimmy. "You'd gone away, I believe, last time that I telephoned to you."

"Yes, I took a tart to Paris." For the first time he met

Presnor's eyes. He envied the man his poise. He sat back
in the chair, his legs crossed. One hand lay completely
relaxed on the side. The odd combination of calm and
apprehension began its unquieting dispute within Jimmy.
Presnor's attraction was formidable for him. It gave him a
claustrophobic longing to get up and run from the room.

"Isn't he awful," Flick said. "He's not a bit ashamed."
He sprang up from a squatting position. "Hands up for
coffee. The 'ayes' have it. Good!" He took three little
skips to the kitchen, whistling 'Home on the Range'.

Presnor followed the boy with his eyes. "He's well rid of
that fellow Simpton."

"I gather from what Flick said that he's inclined to take
his love life lightly."

"He's inclined to do worse with it than that. Simpton's
done a lot of damage in his time. I'd like to see him under
lock and key."

"Tut, tut. Those are stern words," said Jimmy, "coming
from anti-punishment quarters."

"Unfortunately it isn't Simpton's type which ends up
under lock and key. It's much more likely to be some poor
wretch who's managed to restrain his instincts for years
whom Simpton has seduced for the sheer amusement of
breaking down his resistance. That's the type which kicks
over the traces, and finally lands up in gaol."

"Mr. Simpton sounds a charmer."

"He's a detestable man," Presnor said. "There is nothing
to admire in him at all. I know him well. He came to me
for treatment once."

"That ought to have endeared him to you, surely."

"I sent him on to Fleischel."

"Why?"

"I thought he was beyond my assistance."

"He seems to have been beyond Fleischel, too."

"He deliberately wasted Fleischel's time. He had no
intention of benefiting from treatment. The police had been

showing an interest in him. He thought that if there was any trouble the fact that he was voluntarily taking treatment might benefit him, that's all."

"Oh, I see, that's fly," Jimmy said.

"He takes a deliberate delight in breaking up affairs. He doesn't seem able to resist it. He's split up quite a few couples that I know of."

"I should have thought you'd have liked to see break-ups. It'd give you a better chance to guide the broken-hearted back to the normal straight and narrow again."

Presnor shook his head. "That sort of thing is no help in itself. It simply makes for unhappiness and distress and pushes the thing into other camps. It spreads the disease rather than cures it. Take for instance Flick. He'll only be turning to someone else." He waved a slack hand from the wrist in Flick's direction. Jimmy stretched out for a cigarette.

"In case you were getting at me, doctor mine, let me inform you that I am no more and no less than an ordinary guest. Flick is simply housing me until I can face up to my own little nest again."

"How did the Paris trip go?" Presnor asked.

"Fine. We both fell in love with Marie Antoinette's shoe."

"Was there any physical contact?"

"No, it was under a glass case."

Flick carried the coffee-pot in. "Hey, you," he said to Jimmy. "How about lending a hand?" And he beckoned behind Presnor's back.

In the tiny kitchen Flick stood with his back against the door. His voice was accusing and sharp. "You wouldn't have a soft spot for our friend Dr. Presnor by any chance, would you?"

"Good God, Presnor isn't like that."

"I wasn't worried about him. I was worried about you. I saw how you looked when he first came in. Well, I can

tell you, you won't get very far in that direction. Even his
nibs didn't stand a chance with him." Flick's voice was
rising.

"Shut up, you stupid little ass," Jimmy told him. "Don't
you realise the man can hear you?"

"That's right. Start calling me names. Well, look, Mr.
Stretton, I've got my pride and I've got my feelings, and
I'm not having any more people making eyes at each other
in *my* flat. I'm fed up with it, downwright fed up with it.
What you do outside is *your* business, but what you do here
is *mine*." He finished up shouting hysterically. Jimmy
slapped the boy on the side of the face. To have struck him
in any other manner would have seemed too brutal. He
looked as frail and as slim as a girl, with the tears standing
out in his angry eyes. He swallowed and spoke with dignity,
"After that—you're out. If anyone lifts a hand to me I'm
through with 'im. Get me? Through! I may not be good
enough for you or Mr. Simpton and his la-di-da friends, but
I've got my standards as well as anybody, and I'm afraid I
prefer a gentleman."

Jimmy pushed past him, "For the love of Mike, shut
up."

When he went into the living-room he found that Presnor
had gone. Flick followed him with three cups on a tray.
"Oh. So the bird has flown, has it? Well, good riddance to
bad rubbish, I say. Talking about Gorwin like that. I overheard what he said."

"Well, it's true enough, isn't it?" Jimmy asked.

"True or not, I won't hear it said in *my* house."

Jimmy turned and went into the bedroom. He put his
suitcase on the bed and began to pack. Flick called out,
"There's no need to carry on like Dickie Short after a bad
notice. There's no need to be so dramatic about it. You
don't have to get out *tonight*." His voice was apprehensive
and tremulous. Jimmy made no reply. He put his clothes
in his suitcase and locked it up. It still bore the tell-tale mark

of Paris. He pulled off the tie labels and took a razor-blade
to the ones which were stuck.

Flick called, "Don't bother to answer me. I like having a
chat with myself."

The razor-blade was not effective. Jimmy decided to wet
the surface. He had to walk through the living-room to get
to the bathroom. Flick let him pass with no further
comment. He sat in the chair which Presnor had vacated,
his feet curled beneath him, deep in a book. Jimmy came
back with a nail-brush and soap. He had scrubbed one label
off the suitcase when Flick followed him into the room.

"Scrubbing the filth off before you leave? It's quite safe,
I haven't polluted that."

Jimmy sighed. "Don't be ridiculous, Flick. It was damn
nice of you to put me up. But it's time I was going in any
case." Flick was silent. When Jimmy took a look at the
boy he was sobbing, his head bowed, his eyes closed, his
hands hanging slackly down at his sides. Jimmy looked
quickly away again. The sobbing continued. It was steady,
and not uncontrolled. Jimmy threw down the razor-blade.
He took a step towards Flick. "Look here, old man——"
It was too late to retreat. The boy made a quick movement
into his arms. Jimmy stood helplessly holding him; the
boy's body quivered and shook. He clung to Jimmy hope-
lessly. There was a fresh and sweet smell from his hair and
his skin. Jimmy recognised it immediately. He used the
same perfume as Vi.

"Oh, Jimmy, forgive me. I know I've been awful—I get
like that sometimes."

Jimmy patted his back repeatedly, and felt like a tender
mother trying to bring up a baby's wind. He had no idea
what to say to comfort him, and he was embarrassed by the
feel of the boy in his arms. He dared not be too conciliatory
for fear of increasing the outburst. He made his voice breezy
and light: "It's time I cleared out, really, Flick. It's got
nothing to do with what happened tonight."

Flick's fingers dug into his back. "Oh, Jimmy, don't leave me. Don't *leave* me, Jimmy. I'd die without you now."

"You haven't died without Simpton," Jimmy pointed out.

"Oh *him*! I didn't love him like I love you, Jimmy. You're the real thing in my life. I can see that now. I need you. I need everything about you. All your goodness and strength. I promise I haven't been caught on the rebound. I knew it the minute I saw you, really." He lifted his head from Jimmy's shoulder and looked with sincerity into his eyes. "I was honest about Gorwin, wasn't I? I wasn't taken in by him. I knew he was a stinker and I said so—but he did something to me and I said that too. You couldn't be fairer than that. I knew it was just infatuation. But you've broken his hold on me now. You see, I know you're *not* a stinker, and that's really what matters with me. That's how I can spot the real thing, Jimmy. This isn't infatuation, this thing that I feel for you. It's got another name, Jimmy. It's really and truly love."

"I doubt it," Jimmy said. He released himself gently. He turned Flick about by the shoulders and propelled him into the living-room. He sat him forcibly down in a chair. Then he poured a double gin into a glass, and used the rest of Presnor's tonic-water. He gave the glass to Flick. "Knock this back. You'll feel much better for it."

Flick shook his head without raising his eyes. "Jimmy, I didn't really mind about Presie. I was jealous. I do admit that. But I promise I'll never be such a little goose again." He held up a slim hand and said, "Please, Jimmy."

Jimmy sighed and took the hand. Flick pulled him down to the chair level. He slid his arms round Jimmy's waist and laid his cheek against him. "Please, Jimmy, don't leave me. *Please*."

Jimmy said wearily, "Listen, Flick." He laid a hand on the boy's head and stroked it. "I wouldn't be any good for you, I'm not any use to anyone. I'm not even much good to myself. I'm neither fish nor fowl nor good red herring, whatever that phrase might mean."

"I love you so much, Jimmy," Flick whimpered, and Jimmy felt a soft kiss on the back of his hand.

"Who was it who said if you can't have the Crown Jewels you just can't have them, and that's that?"

"You can't go *on* being brave," mumbled Flick.

Jimmy gave the hair a good-natured rumple. "You can. You don't lack guts."

"Is it really no go, Jimmy?"

"It's really no go, Flick."

Flick swivelled round in the chair and laid his head in his arms on the opposite side. "If you've got to go, could you go now, please, Jimmy. And could you go at once."

Jimmy went into the bedroom, picked up his suitcase and let himself out of the flat.

CHAPTER THIRTY-SEVEN

HE spent the night at an hotel. He put in an unrewarding day at the University and in the evening he went to see Presnor.

He threw the doctor a cigarette. "I gather you felt *de trop* last night."

"I thought I saw signs of a scene brewing up, so I made myself scarce."

"Did you hear much of it?"

"Not much."

"But you got the gist of it."

"I got the gist of it, yes."

"I thought as much, or I shouldn't be here. There's no point in hiding it now. I've left Flick's. He's a bit upset about it. I'm rather worried about him. We had an absolutely ghastly scene in the end. I hope to God he won't go and cut his throat or something."

"My dear boy, Flick's life is made up of ghastly scenes. I won't say he enjoys them consciously, but they've never driven him to cutting his throat before."

"Well, I hope you enjoy them consciously, because you're in for one right now." Jimmy took a breath, licked his lips, and said, "Do you know that if you fell over a cliff or disappeared out of my life I should feel like putting my head in the gas-oven?"

Presnor sat with his hands folded. "Yes."

"Then do you also realise that at this moment I should like nothing better in the world than to throw my arms round you—not for the immediate purposes of immoral practices, but because for some inexplicable reason it would comfort me?"

"Yes."

"Aren't you sickened by it?"

"No."

Jimmy sat back bewildered by Presnor's level tone. "Do you mean to tell me that I could have broken this pretty little piece of news to you weeks ago and all you'd have said was 'yes' and 'no'?"

"Yes."

"You wouldn't have told me never to darken your doorstep again?"

"No."

Jimmy hit his forehead with the flat of his hand. "Christ, I could have saved myself so much agony." Presnor stood up and came round to him. He laid a kind hand on Jimmy's head. Jimmy looked up, grinning sheepishly. "I'm a big boy, aren't you scared of me? I might make a grab at you."

"Always facetious," Presnor smiled. "Your feelings for me are a perfectly natural development. They're in no way peculiar to you alone. I can assure you that they were not unexpected. We call it transference when it occurs in its real sense during Freudian analysis. Yours isn't a true example of it because you were attracted to me before we had any dealings with one another. But it's possible that the mechanisms of transference took place and *accentuated* something which you already felt."

Jimmy stared at his feet and said grimly, "You won't make a pass at me, will you? I should feel like the girl in *Rain* when the parson had a go at her. All my illusions destroyed!"

"I shall try to resist you," Presnor said.

"So you're used to six-foot male patients being unable to keep their hands off you?"

"I've not studied the question in relation to height, but it's a common enough reaction. It's an accepted part of the treatment. It isn't peculiar to 'complex' kings. Gynæcologists frequently encounter the same thing amongst pregnant patients. The affections are temporarily transferred towards the person most receptive and considerate towards the symptoms while the condition lasts. It's little more than showing good faith in authority, based on affection for, and trust in, one's first authority; one's father or some father substitute."

"Well, if you knew all that, why the hell didn't you tell me and put my mind at rest?"

"My dear boy, you've been avoiding me, remember?"

Jimmy said wearily, "O.K., O.K. Now that we know my guilty secret where do we go from here?"

"We're back at the beginning again. I warned you that suppression retarded progress. We have still to convince you that there can be disgrace attached to homosexual practices depending upon how they are put into force, but not in possessing homosexual tendencies themselves," said Presnor. "As you would prefer me not to quote Mr. Fleischel, perhaps you'd mistrust Casanova less."

"Casanova," Jimmy said.

"Casanova," Presnor repeated. "A singularly uninhibited gentleman happily independent of complex kings. He gave it as his enlightened opinion that 'many things which acquire reality are first born in the imagination'."

"So you mean I might only *think* I'm homosexual?"

"That could account for your being so or becoming so. There's a pattern in all behaviour, Jimmy, and your behaviour pattern is not hard to follow. As a child you were denied the physical expressions of love and appreciation which most children get from their mothers. You had a natural need for affectionate relations with someone, and it became a necessity to you to prove to yourself that you were not despised and rejected. This was largely induced by the aunt who had the care of you. She made you feel unwanted by your father as a boy, and encouraged you to behave like a girl. You then formed the opinion that only a woman could manage to make herself loved. You wanted to imitate a woman's success in this direction, and so you directed your hunger for affection towards a male. The pattern was followed out in your admiration for Osbourne. It was even physically followed—he was black-eyed and dark-haired as your father had been—but parallel with this you had the normal boy's fear of being considered 'sissy'. Osbourne's father-in-law actually accused you of it. The damage he did was considerable. He helped to produce a major conflict in you. He heightened your fear of being homosexual, which, combined with the circumstances which were already leading you in that direction, could go a long way to establishing it as a fact. The power of suggestion is formidable. I think it might have played a great part in the undoing of your friend Osbourne himself. There is proof that your basic need was for an outlet of normal affection when you were willing to transfer your regard to *Mrs.* Osbourne after Osbourne's death. It would have been perfectly conceivable at that moment in your emotional development that your instincts would have turned into natural channels. But circumstances dictated otherwise— I've often stressed to you the importance of circumstances. It just happened that your disgust at her 'letting you down' with her 'gigolo' in France, checked your normal inclinations at rather a vital stage."

"But if all my troubles started with being dotty about dear old Dad——"

"You were not *dotty* about him," Presnor reproved him. "He was all you had and it wasn't extraordinary that you should think over-highly of him."

"Well, whatever it was in the beginning, why don't I give a damn for him now?"

"You forced your affections away from him. Your fear of being too sentimental and your feelings of being despised by him started the conflict. It was much the same with Osbourne. You were drawn to him—but you resented him. You mistrusted the pattern of black hair and black eyes as greatly as you were attracted to them. You had much the same reaction to mine at first. It probably accounts for your rebellious and uncooperative attitude towards me, at the moment," Presnor smiled.

"Well, for Pete's sake, am I always going to chase after black-eyed gents?"

"I think it unlikely," Presnor said. "Once you've realised what has been causing these feelings within you, once you realise that there *is* a legitimate cause for them, you may suddenly find yourself rid of them. A problem is sometimes three-quarters solved at the moment it's understood. Unfortunately you've not yet arrived at that moment."

Jimmy sat forward urgently. "Have it your own way. Have it any way you like. I don't believe a word of it. But I'm certainly willing to try. I'm only sure of one thing—I can't get along without you."

"No one is asking you to," Presnor pointed out.

"I don't believe you can do me the slightest bit of good— I think you talk absolute tripe—but what I do know is if you told me you couldn't do me any good I'd go right round the bend. For God's sake hang on to me. Don't let me go. Keep on nagging away with your tripe."

"It's entirely up to you," said Presnor. "You know that I'm willing to do what I can."

"And don't pass me on to that blasted Fleischel."

"Mr. Fleischel is not short of patients. I dare say he can manage without you."

"You're my straw," Jimmy told him belligerently, "and I'm a drowning man. You'll have to make allowances if I clutch at you now and again. I tell you I need you. You're all I've got. If you leave me I'm sunk. Great heavens! I'm talking like Flick."

"Not in the least," Presnor assured him. "I wonder if I'll ever convince you that each case is a different case?"

When Jimmy looked up there were tears in his eyes. "I'm sorry I've behaved like a lunatic. Put up with me if you can. You offered me friendship, don't forget."

"I shan't forget," Presnor said.

CHAPTER THIRTY-EIGHT

PRESNOR regarded him levelly. "You've walked out on your wife and you've walked out on Flick. Where are you going to stay?"

"That is a poser," Jimmy said.

"Can you afford an hotel? Or to get rooms on your own for a bit?"

"No, we're on a shoe-string enough as it is."

"Would you care to stay with me?"

Jimmy looked up at him bitterly, "Oh, sure—I'd like to pack right in with you. I don't feel safe in the great big world without my subconscious dad."

"I am serious," Presnor said. "We should be very pleased to have you if you cared to come. This room isn't used upstairs." He raised the dark eyebrows to the surgery ceiling.

"It shows what tricks one's imagination can play," said Jimmy. "I was sure that one was your room, yours and your wife's, I mean. I pictured you in there together, all married and normal, and smug."

"We'll expect you to dinner tonight. I should tell your wife where you're staying, though." He held out a hand, which Jimmy took.

"To use a time-honoured phrase," said Jimmy, "I don't quite know how to thank you."

It was Kitty Presnor who let him in. "Good-evening. I'm so pleased to see you. Louis is in the surgery. The children are in disgrace." She put a finger to her lips and listened. Presnor's voice was raised:

". . . she might have been living on the old age pension, for all you know. Out of that she may have to pay her rent and feed herself. You can see how much she would have left to buy a new hat." Kitty Presnor turned to Jimmy. She was small and dark and smiling. There was something familiar about her face, which worried Jimmy a little at first. Then he recognised it. It was the likeness to her brother's photograph. Freidel Goldstein made up as a woman had been a cruel caricature of his twin. She said to Jimmy:

"The bathroom window is a dreadful temptation to them. It juts out right over the street; they lean out and drop things on people's heads. This afternoon they threw a wet sponge on to some old lady's hat. She's threatened to sue us for it."

The door of the surgery opened and two fair-haired boys skidded across the tiled hall, swung one after the other round the newel-post, and went running two steps at a time up the stairs.

Kitty Presnor showed Jimmy into a sitting-room. Presnor was getting a decanter out. "Hullo, Jimmy," he said.

Kitty Presnor asked him, "Would you excuse me a minute, dear, I think I should keep an eye on Mamma."

Presnor said, "That would be wise." To Jimmy he

explained as he poured out a drink, "My mother-in-law is getting blind. She was a wonderful cook in her day, but now we have to see that she doesn't use Harpic instead of flour. She cooks only on special occasions. You're unlucky in choosing Kitty's birthday."

"Oh, good heavens, I hope I'm not busting in——"

"Not at all. We're delighted to have you."

Jimmy tipped down his drink. "I heard you playing the heavy father just now."

Presnor made a face. "They are criminals. That's what those two are. No psycho-therapy could help them. They should have been registered with Borstal at birth. I happen to know that their target was one of the wealthiest women in Hampstead, but one must make some sort of effort to give them a conscience."

Jimmy laughed. "They don't look very Jewish, do they?"

"I like to think so," Presnor said.

The dining-room was hot. Presnor whispered to Jimmy, "Mamma is a hypochondriac. She believes that she'll meet her death from draughts. You're safe on the first course. That is Kitty's work. Mamma Goldstein makes only the apple strudel; she was always very famous for that."

A heavily-built woman came into the room polishing her glasses. She held out a square hand to Jimmy on which gleamed a big diamond ring. She had a broader edition of Kitty's smile, but her accent was very thick. "It's nice to see you, Mr. Stretton. Minna," she said to Kitty, "you tell me what time to go out to the kitchen." She turned to Jimmy, the eyes behind the glasses beaming. "When you are getting old, Mr. Stretton, you forget the most important things in life. The time to bring out the apple strudel. Louis, tell him about my apple strudel."

Presnor was carving a chicken. "In the 'nineties it was the best in Vienna."

"In the 'nineties! What a foolish boy! It was best in the 'twenties and in the 'thirties, and it would still be the best today. You are homosexual, I expect, Mr. Stretton?"

Jimmy's breath was stopped short in his mouth. "Louis," Mrs. Goldstein demanded of Presnor, "is that for me? A smaller portion, please. Mr. Stretton, one of the saddest things about old age is that you no longer dare to be greedy. Have you been homosexual long?"

Presnor interrupted, smiling, "Mamma is just jumping to conclusions, Jimmy. She hasn't read your case history. But my theories are rife in this house and Mamma, like Mr. Casanova, has never had any inhibitions."

Mrs. Goldstein beamed on Jimmy. "Louis, only one potato, please. You couldn't have done better than to come to my boy, Mr. Stretton."

Kitty laughed. "I hope you'll notice the 'my' boy, Mr. Stretton. Mamma is always on Louis's side."

Mrs. Goldstein broke a loaf with a hole in it. She put a piece on Jimmy's plate. "Taste it. It's Jewish. It's nice?"

"Very nice," Jimmy said stiffly.

Presnor sat down at the table head. "Mamma, it is just possible that you might be embarrassing Jimmy."

Mrs. Goldstein turned round. "No! This is not possible. So? I don't believe it. Mr. Stretton looks sensible, Louis."

"I wasn't concerned with his looks, I was concerned with his feelings."

Kitty Presnor spoke up sweetly: "There's no disgrace in being homosexual, Mr. Stretton. That is, if you are, of course. Mamma takes so much for granted."

Mrs. Goldstein laid a hand on Jimmy's. "You're not mad at me, are you, for what I'm saying? After all, it is only an illness. Now me, I have fatty degeneration of the heart. Do you think I should be ashamed of it?"

"Yes," said Presnor. "I do. I think you deserve it. You eat too much in between meals."

Jimmy put down his napkin. "Mrs. Goldstein, of course I'm not 'mad' at you. I'm delighted to have it all aired." His voice was sarcastic and bright. "It makes me feel fine to know you've all got me taped." He felt Presnor's dark eyes resting kindly upon him.

Mrs. Goldstein patted his hand again. "This boy's going to get well, Louis, I have good hopes for him. He has all the right ideas."

Jimmy turned an over-sweet smile upon her. "Mrs. Goldstein, you're being too kind to me. You see—I'm not after the boys as such—I'm only after Dr. Presnor, I can hardly keep my hands off him."

Mrs. Goldstein put a spoon in her soup. "Ja? So? That is good, isn't it, Louis? It must be good if he only wants one man. My poor Freidel was wanting so many."

Kitty Presnor put bread in her soup. "It's especially good that it should be Louis. That means you've centred your affections on the man who is trying to cure you, who in reality you might look upon as your persecutor. But you love him in spite of it. That means you *want* to get better. Mamma, the apple strudel!"

"Ach, yes. I will fetch it."

Presnor sat back when she had left the room. "The suspense is quite unbearable. Last year she mixed up some pieces of onion with the apple. And we had to sit here and eat it without any expression on our faces." When the apple strudel was carried triumphantly into the room Presnor cut into it carefully. Then he looked up with relief at his wife. "It's wonderful, Mamma," he told Mrs. Goldstein.

CHAPTER THIRTY-NINE

THE Presnor household's matter-of-fact acceptance of inversion had an extraordinarily soothing effect upon him. It was a relief to shed all attempts at deception. It was helpful to feel himself somewhere where an unguarded outbreak would be tolerantly regarded as a natural develop-

·ment or an expected relapse. It removed his sense of guilt.
He felt most at home with Mrs. Goldstein. "In Germany,"
she told him, "it used to be dreadful. There were so many
sick with it, so many sick."

"Before you listened to Louis," Jimmy asked her, "what
did you think about it?"

"Think! I did not think about it. That is the terrible
thing. I was too much a 'nice girl' to have such thoughts.
Until I was married I did not know such a thing could exist.
When I found out, my Hermann was shocked." Mrs. Goldstein threw up the square ringed hands. "Shall I ever forget
how it was with my Hermann when I told him I knew! He
was a very stern man, my Hermann. He told me I was not
a fit mother for his children until I had cleaned my mind.
Think of it! We had three boys of our own and one of them
already had the sickness—but we did not know because we
were too shocked. And so our poor sickly one died of it.
If only Louis was old enough then, or if only we knew Mr.
Fleischel, but there—it is no use in looking back. It is best
to look forward and help other people not to make such a
mistake. Minna has never got over it. You know how it is
with twins."

Presnor's professional acceptance of Jimmy's feelings
towards him had removed his sense of frustration and
restored his self-respect. Every night after dinner he and
Jimmy sat together, undisturbed for hours if Presnor were
not called out, and every Saturday afternoon they played
golf. A considerable strain was removed from Jimmy. He
felt more at ease than he had felt for months. He even felt
ready to contact Pam.

He visited her on a Sunday, with a threat of fog in the
evening air. She stood up when she heard his key turn in
the lock. She said nothing when he came towards her.
She was wearing an old grey jumper and a pair of ill-fitting
slacks. Her hair was uncurled and there was no make-up
on her face. Jimmy put his hands on his hips and looked

down at her. "I see you've given up all hope of keeping the erring husband."

She managed to smile, but her eyes were nervous. "On the contrary, I just thought I'd do the opposite to every magazine hint and see if that had better results."

He said, "Rubbish. You were just sordidly caught out being a slut." He bent down to kiss her. "Hullo, Pam."

"Hullo, Jimmy," she said, but she kept her arms at her sides.

"You're looking at me as if someone had sent you an anonymous postcard to the effect that I am Jack the Ripper. What did Presnor tell you about me that day you went round to see him?"

"He just said that your nerves were a bit upset, and to leave you alone to let them rest."

"I know what a swine of a time you've had, Pam, but I promise I'm going to make up to you. It's not going to be much longer. I used not to believe in miracles, but I definitely believe in them now."

"You believe in them just when I've stopped," said Pam.

He sat down beside her and put a hand out to turn her face. "How much did you mind what Presnor told you?"

Her eyes closed. "How much did you think I should mind?" He saw moisture beneath the eyelashes.

"I didn't know, darling," he said, "but I believed that you'd mind so terribly I hadn't the guts to tell you. I know now that I made a mistake. We should have gone home together and we should have gone up to the loft. We should have lit a candle and I should have told you all about it, and you'd have helped as you've always helped."

The tip of her tongue made a tour of her lips. "It would seem that I'm the person you needed to be helped against. Dr. Presnor said the worst thing I could do was to try to force you."

"That's only temporary, sweet. It won't last. It's quite logical while I was in the throes of it—but I promise I never gave in to it, Pam—I never practised it. Not once."

·Her eyes opened. "Practised what?"

Jimmy took his hands from her face. "I never gave in to it physically. I never lived with Flick."

"Who's Flick?"

"Didn't Presnor mention Flick?"

She shook her head. "Were you in love with her, Jimmy?"

"No, I was not. And Flick is a 'he', Pam, not a 'she'."

She stared at him bewildered. He stood up. "Pam, tell me exactly what Presnor told you."

She spread her hands. "He just said that temporarily you'd turned against any form of physical relationship with me. He just said it was because of your nerves."

"He didn't tell you what it was that upset them?"

Again she shook her head. Then she stood up and came slowly towards him. "Will you tell me what upset them, please, Jimmy?"

He said, "I see that it isn't too late for the loft." He took a breath and tried to smile at her. "O.K., the candle's been lit. · Here goes. You always thought I was in danger from women, but I wasn't. I was in danger from men."

She repeated it stupidly, "Men."

"It's been known, darling," Jimmy said.

"Yes, but only for pansies and people like that. But, Jimmy, you're not—you're not . . ." She took two steps away from him, both hands at her mouth. Her eyes made a quick tour of his length and breadth, as if it were something new to her. She spoke through her fingers and shook her head. "No, Jimmy, no. I won't believe it."

"Darling, I tell you it's over now. With Presnor's help I'm through with it."

Her hands left her mouth and she backed away from him, backed until she had manœuvred the sofa between them. He dodged round the sofa and cut off her flight. He took her shoulders and then gripped her arms. He began to plead: "Pam, don't be disgusted. I shouldn't have told you." She put the crook of her arm across her eyes and stood crying without tears. He begged her, "Be angry, be shocked, be anything, but don't be disgusted. It never really came to anything. It was only inside my head."

She struggled to remove the arm from her eyes. She let it hang by her side and said to him, "How awful for you, Jimmy."

"Don't hold it against me, Pam." He felt her eyes wet against his cheek.

"It must have been my fault, Jimmy. It must have been something in me that put you off and drove you to it."

"Don't be ridiculous, darling. These things start in childhood. Everyone has it in them, you know. It just depends which way it tips. In my case—well, you remember Osbourne."

Pam's eyes widened. "Mr. Osbourne! Oh, but surely— oh, Jimmy, he should have been horsewhipped."

Jimmy whitened. "Good heavens alive, I don't mean *that*. Osbourne would rather have died—in point of fact, he did prefer to die. I thought the world of him, quite naturally. There was nothing odd in that, Presnor says. It was just that I was starved of all outward affection at home and so I pitched the whole thing on to Osbourne, and I pitched it pretty thoroughly. I never do things by halves. I went to town on thinking the world of Osbourne."

"Oh yes," she said slowly, "the coat."

"Everything might have been all right if some bungling old ass hadn't given me the idea that there was something pretty filthy in my thinking the world of Osbourne. It's Presnor who dug all this up, and you know, Pam, it is quite extraordinary, I thought I should never believe it, but it *does* help to have things dug up. You suddenly find out why you feel something, and, hey presto, the feeling's gone. I did you a grave injustice, Pam: I married you knowing all this. I thought it might put a stop to it." He saw her expression and took her hands. "Oh, sweetie, don't look like that. I'd have married you in any case, I'm sure I would. I couldn't have done without my Pam."

Pam disengaged her hands. "Jimmy, I'm terribly tired. If you're going back to Dr. Presnor's, could you go now, please?"

"Pam, you're not turning me out for good, are you? You do believe I'm cured? I tell you, I feel quite different now. That's what I came to say."

Pam put the flat of her hand on the bedroom door and pushed it gently inwards. "I should never have the courage to stay in a world where you were, Jimmy, and not ask you to come back to me whenever you felt you could." She went into the bedroom and left him staring at the grey-panelled door.

When he returned to No. 17 Bina Rise he told Presnor the outcome of the visit to Pam.

"Why couldn't you leave well alone?" said Presnor. "She was quite content with my explanation."

The telephone rang as he spoke. It was Gorwin Simpton calling Jimmy. Jimmy took up the receiver like a school-boy under Presnor's strong black eyes. He made a gesture which lifted his shoulders and eyebrows. "What on earth can he want?"

"I'm not psychic," said Presnor, "but I think I could guess."

Jimmy spoke gingerly into the receiver. "This is Stretton speaking."

Simpton's voice was brusque. "I was wondering if you could spare me half an hour or so. There's something I want to talk to you about. I thought we might meet for a drink."

Jimmy was hesitant. "Well, look here, can't you say what it is on the phone?"

"No, I should rather not."

Jimmy said, "All right," and arranged to meet him in a public-house at the end of the road. "What else could I do?" he asked Presnor helplessly.

"Keep away from him," Presnor advised. "If you must go, would you like me to come with you?"

"Good Lord, no. I'd better not take Daddy with me. What do you think it is, blackmail?"

"I shouldn't put anything past Simpton. Remember that he is a habitual pervert."

"What in the name of fortune's that?"

"It is someone who enjoys doing evil for the sake of doing it. It's someone who gets a pleasurable fulfilment in wrongdoing. Someone who would find satisfaction in destroying in you everything that we've both been building up to bring you peace."

"*En garde*," Jimmy smiled. "*En garde*."

"Don't make light of it," Presnor said. "The mere fact that you turned to me for help would be enough to spur Simpton on. He would do anything in his power to undermine my influence with you. I can't fight temptation for you, you've got to fight that for yourself."

"*En garde*," Jimmy repeated.

He felt absurdly apprehensive as he approached the small public-house with the green tiles that reached to the pavement. Inside, Simpton sat at a corner table. He stood up and held out his hand. "It's good of you to come, Stretton. I ordered you a Scotch. I hope that's all right." His grip was decisive and short.

Jimmy said "Thanks", and sat down. He had been made very conscious as they stood together that Simpton was taller than he. The saloon bar was crowded. Simpton sat back unsmiling. He had a pleasant, healthy face. His eyes appeared calm and discerning. He did his best to put Jimmy at ease. Jimmy, staring at the broadly intelligent forehead and the strong mouth and nose, could only think of highly-coloured pyjamas, the mysterious 'L' Club, and la-di-da friends. But there seemed nothing of the gay Lothario about him, homosexual or otherwise. Jimmy, who had never ridden on the proverbial nine-ten, thought of him as a typical passenger on the proverbial nine-ten.

"I hope you didn't mind me ringing you at Presnor's."

"Why should I?"

"I was afraid it might embarrass you. Presnor and I don't hit it off any too well. I thought you might have heard. He feels that I let him down rather badly."

Jimmy took a sip of his drink. "Oh?" he said. "How's that?"

"I thought once upon a time that I might put my house in order, or at least make some kind of attempt at it. I had heard great things of Presnor."

"Not substantiated?" Jimmy inquired. He had a coldly acute apprehension of hearing Simpton belittle Presnor's powers. Simpton spoke warmly in favour of them.

"I've a hell of a respect for that man. What he has to give he gives free, but tells you it isn't the best you can get. Unfortunately he sent me on to a cadaverous-faced lunatic called Fleischel."

Jimmy sat forward, interested. "You didn't get on with Mr. F.?"

"I shouldn't get on with any Mr. Fs. I hate the whole damned race of them. I've a natural prejudice against everything psychological. Some of the theories Mr. Fleischel put forward struck me as being fathered by little short of congenital idiocy. But perhaps I'm not the ideal patient."

"But you were impressed by Presnor?"

"I was impressed by Presnor as a good man. Shall I put it in that way? Because of his faith in Fleischel. I thought, 'There's a chap who's willing to forgo his fees for the altruistic reasons of passing one on to a better brain.' But when I encountered what Presnor considered a better brain I realised that Presnor must be blessed with none at all."

"He's helped me," Jimmy said. "He's helped me to a very large extent."

"I'm delighted to hear it," Simpton said.

I

Jimmy thought of Presnor's dry voice as he spoke of Simpton, "The police had an interest in him . . . he thought that by having treatment . . ." Jimmy asked carefully of Simpton, "What made you suddenly decide to put your house in order?"

Simpton replied, "The police. I'd gone a bit too far for safety, and things looked a trifle black for me."

Jimmy sat back. The frankness surprised him. He had expected almost anything from Simpton except a confirmation of what Presnor had said. "You mean you thought it could get you out of a jam with the police?"

Simpton laughed, his big shoulders rising. "My dear young innocent, you can rid yourself of that illusion. That's a gambit that rarely comes off. They've an uncanny knack of finding out whether you've done a last-minute drop on to a psychiatrist's couch. No. I was genuinely scared on my own account. The thing pulled me up with a jerk. You know what it is—you slide along in the same old groove, always going to turn over a new leaf tomorrow and the next day and the one after that. But it isn't until you really come face to face with a possible showdown that you come face to face with yourself."

"So you took treatment because you'd been shocked into feeling you needed it?"

"That's about the strength of it. I can't say it did me much good. Quite frankly, I've never heard of anybody it has helped except you."

"So you don't think there's any hope for us," Jimmy said.

"I knew one fellow that fell in with a persuasive old parson and 'got' the Church. I believe it scared him into laying off. But I think I'd rather be an invert than a religious maniac, with no wider outlook than parochial affairs. And I know another chap who went in for some kind of injection and runs round like a doctored cat. Other than that I can't honestly say that I know of anybody who benefited much by this mucking about with the mind business. Oh, I don't doubt it has a salutary effect at first, on the type who gets a kick out of talking about himself. But how long, one wonders, will it last?" Simpton banged a broad palm against his forehead. "I can't get it out of my head that there must be a perfectly simple and much more effective way to deal with the thing oneself."

Jimmy leant forward slightly. "I hadn't realised that you wanted to fight it."

"Oh Lord, yes," Simpton told him, "it gets me down at times. But I didn't bring you out to discuss our troubles. I brought you here to talk about Flick's."

"Flick's?"

"Yes. He's a somewhat sensitive young man, and I gather we both walked out on him recently."

"I never walked in," Jimmy said. "There was nothing between me and Flick."

A wariness spoke in his voice. Simpton, detecting it, laughed. "You're not in the slightest danger of a breach of confidence. After all, I'm in the same boat."

"I was in no boat," Jimmy insisted. "I simply stayed with Flick."

"Quite, quite," said Simpton evenly. "But Flick's a romantic child. I'm afraid he's taken it rather badly, coming so soon upon my desertion. He looks like death and he jumps if a feather drops beside him. I'm fond of the boy in my way, and I wondered if you'd do me a favour. I've apparently wounded his pride. He'll have nothing to do with me, and he'd no more accept money from me than fly. I'd rather like to see him go on a long holiday somewhere and not have to bother with a job for a bit. If I gave you a cheque would you let him have one of yours, and let him think the whole show was on you?"

"Good Lord, no," Jimmy said. "I couldn't do that. But I must say I think it's frightfully decent of you to want to do that for him."

For the second time Simpton smiled. "Frankly, I think

it's the least I could do. I feel pretty badly about young Flick. All that springing about like a pixy used to get on my nerves."

"I know what you mean," Jimmy said ruefully, "it used to grate on me at first."

"Yes, well, I can't answer for you of course," said Simpton "but Flick's worth ten of me."

"He's worth quite a few of me," said Jimmy.

"I'd be deeply grateful if you'd help. There's no way of doing it otherwise. Well, look here, think it over, will you, and give me a ring? Or better still, pop in here and have a noggin one night. You're bound to find me. I use this old dump as my local."

Jimmy's voice was excited when he related the interview word by word to Presnor. "I honestly think you've misjudged him, Louis. After all, it's within reason that the police thing should shake up his conscience a bit, and you couldn't call it anything but damned sporting to want to do this for Flick."

Presnor put only one question, "Why does he use the 'Grape Vine' as his local? He lives three miles away."

CHAPTER FORTY

It was three days since the meeting with Simpton. Jimmy woke up the third morning to discover that his newly-found calm had gone, and with it his newly-found confidence. The desire had returned for Presnor. The old threat of loneliness menaced again. If Presnor's friendship alone could no longer satisfy him he would be on his own in the world once more. And again there was the thought of the desirability of being a girl. He hated his masculinity. He hated his height and the breadth of his shoulders. He wished he were built on the lines of Flick. He wished that he might have small bones and a soft skin, that he might look up at Presnor instead of looking down on Presnor. He wished that he were a woman so that there could be less of an unbridgeable chasm between himself and Presnor. Surely there must be taller men with whom he could feel less masculine. He remembered that he had to look up to Gorwin Simpton.

He was playing golf with Presnor that afternoon. He dreaded it more than he had dreaded any previous contact with Presnor. He felt an inexplicable warning of violence within himself.

It sat like some dark bird of ill omen on his shoulder. Its close company was oppressive and eerie. When for a moment he felt it leave him, a sun-bright mental picture took its place. It appeared in his head as distinct and as detailed as a lit-up stage on which the curtain had suddenly risen. The scene hung static in his brain. It remained long enough for him to stare at it. In the scene Presnor lay half-hidden a few feet from the twelfth hole on the golf-course. His head and his shoulders fell at a strange angle from his feet and Jimmy knew that he was dead. He knew also that it was he who had killed him. He stood by the body as calm as the green of the course that rolled ahead of him. He had strangled Presnor with his own hands and he was repeating out loud, "I'm free now. I'm free."

The dark bird had returned to its perch on his shoulder when he and Presnor set off for their game. Spring made an erratic rash across the golf-course. Crocuses grew in sheltered spots, and under trees snowdrops were sprinkled, looking in the distance like a handful of careless salt.

He was dreading that sheltered twelfth hole. At the sixth hole he was silent. At the eleventh hole he felt the end of endurance approaching. His heart beat a suffocating drum in his breast. The twelfth hole was obscured from the club-house. The copse sheltered it, fringing the view-line with cedars and pines. When they drove towards it Jimmy's

heart ceased to hammer. It made only the normal, undetectable beat. His brain cleared from the fuddled miseries that
had been denying him speech. He heard himself say clearly,
calmly, "The weather report said rain." He was no longer
understandably conscious when he made his attack upon
Presnor. His brain was a fighting blank. He felt the blows
that broke out against his own body only as dull pains somewhere far up in the spring clouds that fluffed above him.
Presnor was forty-five years old, Jimmy was not yet twenty-
one. There were two long struggling minutes before Presnor
pinned Jimmy beneath him with a force that bruised Jimmy's
bones. His voice was unemotional and soft: "When a Jew's
foolish, he's an idiot. When he's good, he's a saint, and
when he's strong, he's very strong." Then Presnor released
his grip.

Oddly enough, at the moment Jimmy had no recollection
of the morning's premonition. He feared only that he had
broken out and made an indecent assault upon Presnor. His
brain refused to recall for him the details of the attack.
Presnor was standing over him. "Get up and pull yourself
together. Your friend Simpton is directly responsible for
this."

Jimmy asked wearily, "What's he got to do with my
making an indecent assault upon you?"

Presnor brushed down Jimmy's shoulders and back as if
he had been a disobedient schoolboy rolling in the mud,
"You've made no such thing upon me. You merely gave
physical expression to a mental conflict, and I must say I
wish you could have chosen somewhere where I have not
been a member for twenty-five years. It's sometimes very
difficult to give a psychological explanation to a golf club
secretary."

Jimmy forced himself on to his feet: "I must say even I
should find it a bit difficult to accept one for this."

Presnor told him irritably, "To you at the moment,
Simpton symbolises freedom and self-indulgence. I symbolise

the opposite. I am frustration, self-control, and restraint.
Yet I stand for what you really want. Simpton stands only
for what you think you want—but his is the easier offer of
the two and you resent me because I stand in your way of
accepting it. You took escapism to extremes and tried to
cheat your own conscience. You made an attempt to get
rid of me. You were in point of fact," Presnor added,
vigorously dusting his elbows and knees, "momentarily
inclined to murder me."

. Jimmy was silent several seconds. Then he eased his
shoulders back. "I see what you mean about the secretary.
Let's give him a break and leave him in the dark. You've
certainly got it in for Simpton."

"Simpton's a pathetic enough case in his way. He's one
of the perpetually frustrated, the permanently dissatisfied.
But he isn't my patient. If he were I might want to protect
him from you. As it is I'm determined to protect you from
him. That was one of the reasons why I wanted you under
my own roof: I felt we'd have trouble with Simpton."

On the way back to the club-house Presnor talked quietly
and earnestly. "We had reached a point together where you
were beginning to benefit, and that of course wouldn't suit
Simpton."

"Oh, look, for God's sake," Jimmy said, "how does he
know what point we've reached? I've not set eyes on the
man more than twice."

"Simpton's still in touch with Flick. They meet in
O'Shaughnessy's Bar. Flick is an inveterate chatterbox. He
would have told Simpton that you'd never yet indulged in
homosexual practices, and of how you were trying to fight
against it." He turned and noticed the position of Jimmy's
right hand. "Have you that sensation round the heart again?
It'll pass off. It's emotional. We'll walk more slowly. That
would be sufficient incentive for Simpton. Besides, he was
attracted to you the first time he saw you. I was there, and
that fact was obvious."

"For God's sake, I didn't hurt you, did I, Louis? I'd rather slit my throat than do that."

"There's no need for such extremes. You gave me a little more exercise than I had planned, that's all. Simpton's type isn't peculiar to inversion, and I feel I can never repeat that strongly enough. He could be the type who could resort to every cunning ruse to seduce a young and an innocent girl, especially if she happened to spurn his attentions. It's a deliberate and a malicious marking-down of a sexual prey. It's a delight in corruption for corruption's sake which brings this type of pervert to his chief satisfaction."

"O.K., O.K., O.K.," said Jimmy. "But I still don't see how he could make me knock you about, except by remote control."

"And there you have it," Presnor said. "In that short interview Simpton did his best to control whatever faith you had in me, and in case that should drive you to a greater authority, he took care to sow the seeds of destruction into whatever faith you might have had in Fleischel. Do you realise," said Presnor insistently, "that Simpton has deliberately tried to exclude you from every form of known assistance? There's no more effective weapon than ridicule. He has struck at religion through the 'persuasive old parson' who got hold of an invert and kept his nose to a churchy grindstone. Therefore implying that the man's alternative to homosexual practices is a narrow life of organising jumble sales and carrying round collection plates. He was careful not to say that in the revival of this obviously unhappy creature's faith the 'persuasive old parson' has probably helped beyond measure in the solving of his personal problems. He struck at the physical methods of assistance by quoting the friend who ran round like a doctored cat. He did not point out that this form of treatment was in its infancy, and that great strides were already being made in it. He struck at psychiatry through Fleischel and me. I have myself helped several people to come to terms with their condition and Fleischel has had many distinguished successes. But much more cleverly Simpton struck at us through a device which he knew would appeal to you most. Your own dislike and mistrust of psycho-therapy."

"But the man's not a magician," Jimmy wailed. "How the devil could he know how I feel about it?"

"My dear boy, you're always howling it down. Simpton could have heard you in O'Shaughnessy's or got it from Flick. There are no perfect methods of assistance as yet, but Simpton has gone out of his way to see that you don't avail yourself of what there is. He's done more than that. He's tried to persuade you to take the very course which he knows is most likely to fail: the seeking of a remedy in yourself. To fight it yourself without help and advice will be bound to fail and that's what he wants."

"Well, if he's done all that to get me," Jimmy said, "it's certainly pretty flattering."

"He's done all that to get you, and it depends what you think is flattering. Have you also thought of the danger in accepting a cheque from a practising homosexual of Simpton's type and substituting it with a cheque of your own to pay off another practising homosexual? Don't you see the excellent opportunities for blackmail?"

"Good Lord, I never thought of that! Do you think that's what he was getting at?"

Presnor shook his head. "No, as a matter of fact I don't, although it's the sort of trick he might easily play to get hold of you. I think the money for Flick was merely a means of making you sympathetic towards him."

"Well, it didn't particularly," Jimmy said, "so there's no harm done."

Presnor stood still, his voice irate. "But, my good boy, there *is* harm done. His influence so undermined your faith in the prospects of recovery that within a matter of days from the meeting you withdraw your confidence from me. It has reopened the conflict and caused such an emotional

I*

disturbance in you that you give way to a violent expression of it this afternoon. Do you call that 'no harm done'?"

Jimmy said, "Look, I think I'm going to take myself off to a newsreel. I want to calm myself down before I face your family; after all, I did try to tear up their meal ticket."

Presnor made no serious objections and they travelled home separately. When Jimmy arrived back at the house in time for dinner the family were entertaining a guest. He was not a prepossessing man. Thick lenses gave his eyes an owl-like protrusion and his cheeks were sallow and over-thin. He was slightly built and short. He sat on the arm of a chair discussing atomic ray-guns with Presnor's youngest son.

"Jimmy," said Mrs. Goldstein, "I want you to meet a great friend of ours, Mr. Fleischel."

Jimmy withdrew the hand he was about to offer to Fleischel. The small man appeared not to notice it. He said, "Mr. Stretton. Perhaps you could tell young David whether an atomic ray-gun would kill outright or just sizzle off all the flesh. I'm afraid it's not much in my line."

Young David wriggled round on his heels towards Jimmy. "In the serial I'm reading it's only the crooks who've got hold of the gun. Steve Jackson and his bunch haven't got one yet."

Jimmy ignored the boy, speaking to Presnor: "Might I have a word with you outside?" Presnor stepped out into the hall with him. He was holding a glass of sherry.

Jimmy put on his coat. "Thanks for the tactful introduction."

Presnor asked, "What are you talking about?"

Jimmy pulled down his scarf and snatched up his hat and his gloves. "I see that I've become such a problem case that you're passing me on to Fleischel, or called Fleischel in for advice. Well, thanks, but I see what Simpton means. He looks as batty as a coot."

Presnor's voice remained even and quiet. "You think I invited Ken here in a professional capacity on your behalf?"

"Bit of a coincidence, isn't it? Just after I've broken out?"

"Ken is here on a social visit. Other than that you're staying with us, he knows nothing about you at all. Why should he? He frequently comes to see us. Until I came in myself this evening I didn't even know that he was dining with us tonight. Surely my wife is allowed to invite whom she pleases to her own house?"

"Naturally," Jimmy said, "and I hope you'll apologise for me. Make any excuse you like. But I could no more stay in the room with that little crackpot than fly."

"Don't be a fool, Jimmy," Presnor said. "I tell you Fleischel is not here for your sake."

"See you later," Jimmy said, opened the door, and went out.

The night was warm, but he shook in his overcoat. He cursed himself miserably for making a scene, for being a hysterical idiot. He had no idea what to do or where he was going. And yet at the back of his mind he did know. He knew that he was going to the 'Grape Vine'.

Simpton sat at the same small table. He raised surprised eyebrows when Jimmy came in. "Hullo, I'd given you up."

CHAPTER FORTY-ONE

HE believed that he had an iron band round his head. The fact that his own dead-ended finger-tips felt over his forehead and scalp and found nothing but hair and skin in the search failed to destroy the illusion. He believed that he had an iron band round his head. He opened swollen-lidded eyes and stared at a French-grey ceiling. He heaved over in the hopes of shifting a solid ball of nausea that was pressing on his stomach, and came face to face with a pencil-written note, 'Eno's in the bathroom cupboard.' The note was signed, 'G.S.' He discovered that he was lying in a big Empire bed. He was wondering who he was and why, when he remembered the 'L' Club. It came into his congested brain like flattened wisps of smoke sucked into a hole by a draught: the star-painted neon-lit 'L' sign, the soft voice inquiring for membership, the darkly-glowing interior with its claret-red carpets and slate-blue walls, his surprise at the sight of three mink-coated women, his pride at being introduced to celebrities; a schoolboyish, pleasurable pride. And he seemed to remember a discussion that took place in a little quilted corner with a gilded wall behind. He must have been already drunk when he reached the 'L' Club. He remembered feeling dizzy in the 'Grape Vine'. 'I didn't go home to Presnor's,' he thought dully. 'I didn't go home all night.' He remembered falling asleep on a shoulder in a taxi. And he recalled that about the shoulder there was a comfortable sense of security, and that the shoulder belonged to Simpton. Then he recalled a sofa and somebody's arm round his waist. Someone who had a soft and persuasive voice. "If Sir Owen Godfrey and Rodorevsky can master their consciences, don't you think yours could be overcome too?" And a big warm hand tipped up his chin. After that there was a blank. It dawned upon Jimmy slowly that he must be lying in Simpton's bed. Beside him a second pillow was crumpled. With an effort that seemed to jar even the nerves in his teeth he set to work to remember what had happened during the blank. When he did so, his senses were momentarily paralysed with shock. Then oddly he felt relief. He no longer felt the sense of rebellion. It was replaced by a sense of liberation, such as a soldier might feel when he forces himself to accept defeat. He felt an agreeable resignation seeping into his heavy brain. No more struggles with himself, no more striving to prevent Presnor from despising him, no more efforts to keep Pam's respect, no

more fears of being found out by his father. He had fought.
He had lost. He was relieved to accept defeat. When
Gorwin Simpton returned to the big mansion flat at half-
past·six in the evening, Jimmy was still in bed. "My God,"
said Simpton, "you certainly know how to nurse a hangover."

Jimmy rolled on to one elbow. "I must have had quite
a load on me last night."

"You didn't do too badly," Simpton told him. "You'd
better have a hair of a dog." He returned with a selection of
drinks on a tray. "What did you think of the 'L' Club?"

"They seemed rather an intellectual bunch. But I don't
remember much about them. Who was it that we were
with?"

"Sir Owen Godfrey and Rodorevsky. Godfrey's a big
noise in politics. He's all right when you can get him off
them."

"What were we talking about?" Jimmy asked. "I seem
to remember being terribly earnest."

"We were discussing the rights of man."

"What sort of conclusion did we reach?"

Simpton raised his glass to him. He looked mountainous
standing beside the bed. "We decided that human frailty
being what it is, it is not reasonable to expect anyone to
resist temptation for ever. Cheers!"

No one except Simpton saw Jimmy during the next two
weeks. Not even Jimmy saw himself clearly until one morning when he got up at half-past twelve after a party that had
entered the early hours. He stood with his hands on his
hips surveying the room. Every door was ajar. A cup of
cold tea stood on the mantelpiece. Two cigarette packets
had been dropped on the floor when the contents were transferred to Simpton's gold case. The bath water remained in
the bath. Simpton's dress-clothes lay across an arm-chair,
the sleeves hanging like a figure collapsed from a shot in the
back. A pair of futuristically decorated pyjamas made a

bright pattern on the floor where Simpton had stepped out
of them. Glasses and cigarette-ash littered the drawing-
room. The rims of Jimmy's eyes felt like pneumatic tyres.
The roof of his mouth and the back of his throat felt burnt
out. His head throbbed and his neck ached. He poured
himself out a glass of Fernet-branca. He tried to remember
the row that had taken place the night before. Sir Owen
Godfrey, Rodorevsky, the little soldier with the M.C. and
bar, and—oh yes—the square-faced man who came with
Flick. The row was over Flick. Jimmy sat staring at the
disordered shell that had housed the scene. Square-face and
Flick came late.

Jimmy was arguing over Henry Moore with Rodorevsky.
Simpton was talking to Sir Owen. Simpton was soft-voiced
and amiable. Simpton scarcely drank. He had never experienced a hangover. Flick was quiet at first. He came tripping
across with his hand held out, a smile in his friendly eyes.
"Hullo, Jimmy darling, how's tricks?" And then added
with pride, "This is Bill." Square-face shook hands and
made a series of grunts. They seemed to form the major
portion of his conversational powers. After one gin Flick
grew confidential. "What do you think of his nibs's
pyjamas?" After his second drink he became sentimental.
He slid a hand into Jimmy's and squeezed it. "No bones
broken, darling. I wish you every happiness, really I do. I
never bear anyone a grudge. I say if someone can make a
go of something I can't, then good luck to them. I'm
terribly fond of Bill. I'd do anything not to hurt him."
Jimmy, looking at Square-face, thought that a charging
rhinoceros would have a small chance of rousing emotion
in him. "Bill's had a bad time too," Flick said. "He got in
with a tout. He's being blackmailed. Dreadful, isn't it?
When you think of the sort of people there are about! Well,
Jimmy, here's to you both!" And to Jimmy's acute embarrassment he stood up with an unsteady glass in his hand
and drank to Jimmy's and Simpton's health. Then he

crossed the room to carry on a similar conversation with Simpton.

Jimmy was left to Square-face, and found they had nothing in common. He longed for Flick to release Simpton so that he might come back and claim Square-face again.

At half-past eleven Flick fell quietly off to sleep and was carried out over Square-face's shoulder. As they manœuvred their way through the door he woke up. He lifted his head and smiled drowsily at Jimmy: "No bones broken, duckie, no bones."

Jimmy put a hand to his head. So it was not Flick who had created the row. Yet somehow it was connected with him. He re-heard a voice unnaturally raised, accusing Simpton of flirting with Flick. An angry voice, spiteful and uncontrolled: "Well, you spent practically the whole bloody evening jammed up in a corner with him. You were doing everything but holding his hand. If you feel like that about him why the hell did you ever leave him? Don't let *me* keep you apart."

It was not Sir Owen Godfrey's voice, and it did not belong to Rodorevsky. They had followed out Square-face and Flick. Besides, Jimmy realised instinctively that neither Sir Owen or Rodorevsky would be capable of behaving like that. He re-heard Simpton's voice, weary and patient, "Oh, put your head under the tap, you ill-bred pup." Incredibly, impossibly, it must have been Jimmy's own voice—raised in that effeminate whine. Jimmy lay back with his head still. He had not seen Simpton that morning. A ring at the bell sent pain through his eyes. He heaved himself up, cursing the charlady for forgetting her keys. He wrapped his dressing-gown round him and pulled the cord tightly round the waist. He discovered that he smelt strongly of perfume. There were traces of powder round his collar. He tugged the door open, yawning. The Reverend Jordon stood there. There seemed to be two assertive sections of white about him, his collar and his hair. In between them his face was little wrinkled, and his eyes were black and clear. His shoulders and back were still straight.

Jimmy said, "Good God Almighty, Father!"

"What an extraordinary form of address," the Reverend Jordon smiled. He followed Jimmy into the drawing-room. He side-stepped Simpton's pyjamas and sat in a chair facing the evening clothes. He lit a cigarette and explained his presence. "A Dr. Presnor came to see me."

"Good God! All the way down to Channock?"

"All the way down to Channock," the Reverend Jordon repeated. He bent down and picked up a white silk evening scarf. He laid it on the arm of his chair. "I thought it was very good of him to come such a distance, and as I'm perfectly aware that you never read my letters I thought it was not much good writing to you. By the way, where is your host? He's not under one of these interesting heaps himself, is he?" The Reverend Jordon waved a hand round the clothes-strewn room.

Jimmy smiled. "No, he's in the country. He goes down to his people each week-end."

The charlady appeared in the doorway, thin and reproachful. "Oh, my word, the mess!"

"This is my father, Mrs. Martin," Jimmy said, as the Reverend Jordon stood up and smiled.

"Well, I can tell you one thing, sir," she said to him, "this how d'ye do isn't Mr. Stretton's fault. A tidier gentleman than him I've never come across. It's Mr. Simpton that's the terror. I always say that if Mr. Simpton was stuck on a desert island in his birthday suit he'd manage to leave it about."

Jimmy said, "Marty, knock us up a cup of coffee, will you?"

"I don't mind making it my way, but I'm not touching that Venetian pot."

"It's Viennese, Marty, not Venetian. And it's a percolator, not a pot."

"I don't mind what it is, Mr. Simpton thinks the world of it, and whatever I do with it the coffee comes out wrong. I'll boil up a drop in a saucepan."

When she had gone Jimmy went to the window. He said, with his back to the Reverend Jordon, "Well, Father, I suppose you've come to preach."

"Oh, dear me, no. I'm on holiday."

"I see. You've come up to be broad-minded and big."

"I've come up to see you, Jimmy. Dr. Presnor feels that he can do no more for you himself while this friend of yours is working against him."

"So he sent you up instead?"

"There's no 'instead' about it. I wanted to see you, Jimmy."

"Why the sudden interest? You were never too keen on me, were you?"

"So I am told. But I happen to know that the opposite is true. Dr. Presnor tells me that I caused you to feel unwanted."

"Wasn't it something to do with Mother? It can't have been much of an exchange."

"I'm afraid you were rather misled, Jimmy. There was a lot of silly talk in the village, and I'm not sure that your Aunt Anita handled that particular situation any too wisely. Gossip can cause much damage. People who fail to mind their own business invariably mishandle other people's At first I admit you were a reminder of your mother's loss, but after that you were nothing but a very great consolation for it."

Mrs. Martin came in with the coffee. "If you ask me, that saucepan makes it better than that old Venetian pot."

Jimmy drank a cupful of black coffee. The Reverend Jordon said, "Naturally your Aunt Anita had most to do with you, because a woman is better at handling small babies. But I don't mind telling you that there were occasions when I changed your nappies with not inconsiderable skill."

"I hope you didn't tell Presnor that. It would throw out his calculations."

The Reverend Jordon put down his cup. He sat forward, his hands clasped between his knees. Jimmy was surprised at the youth in his movements. He had worked out that his father must be approaching his seventieth year. "I've never been a demonstrative man, Jimmy. I find it hard to express myself. But that doesn't exclude me from feeling. Very deep feeling. You know that you were important to me; I was very grievously at fault. I can only ask you to forgive me, if it isn't too late."

"Good God, take a look at me, Dad," said Jimmy. "What have I got to forgive?"

The Reverend Jordon opened his hands and looked into his palms. "I promise you that I tried to put your happiness before mine when it was so apparent that you preferred Mr. Osbourne to myself. It caused me considerable pain. Mr. Osbourne was a very fine man, Jimmy and, if Dr. Presnor's right, he appears to have given his life for you. Don't you think of that sometimes now?"

"Often."

"Jimmy, if it means anything to you any more, I love you very dearly. I've always been proud of you and I shall continue to be proud of you."

"Not much cause for it now," Jimmy said. "Nevertheless, I'd like you to know that I'm not making a permanent nest here. Simpton's getting rid of some undesirable tenants upstairs, and I'm moving into their flat. Pam's going to live in with the Parkers—the people whose kid she looks after. We're putting our stuff into store next week."

"When did you last take Holy Communion, Jimmy?"

"Heaven alone knows, Dad. But it wouldn't have made any difference, would it?"

"It would have made a very considerable difference, and it will do so in the future. I think you've no conception of the help it will be. I want you to come home with me. Oh,

I haven't come to force you. You'll be twenty-one next week." He smiled into Jimmy's eyes. Jimmy thought of Simpton's remark: "A persuasive old parson who kept his nose ground to the Church." "It won't be long before I retire. I thought we might travel a bit together. It's ages since I've been abroad."

"Dad, can't you see I've changed? Can't you see it's too late?"

"Too late at twenty-one? Think about it, Jimmy. It would give me such pleasure to have you home. When you leave here I want you to promise me that you'll come for a short time at least."

"You seem certain I'm going to leave here."

"I hear the gentleman concerned is on the fickle side and that no friendship with him lasts very long."

"Dad, don't believe everything you hear about Simpton. Presnor's got his knife into him. He's none of the things Presnor says. He's just never found the right partner before. He isn't at all promiscuous. He's just never been understood."

"Has he found the right partner now, do you think?"

"Yes, I think he has. He's a lawyer, you know. We've got a lot in common. We like the same food and we like the same jokes. I put up a pretty good fight against it, Dad, but no one can be expected to resist temptation for ever."

"Rubbish," the Reverend Jordon said. "It isn't reserved for homosexuals. Plenty of ordinarily married men feel the urge to be constantly unfaithful to their wives—plenty are. But on the other hand many control it. Countless women whose instincts no doubt are to become wives and mothers don't get the opportunity. But they make something of their lives without it. I personally don't happen to be troubled with a desire to chase young girls round the pulpit, but if I were I should have to control it. There is such a thing as control, you know. Plenty of people have desires which run outside the conventional acceptance of normal society."

Jimmy stood up by the window again. "I suppose you only think of homosexuality as something to do with public lavatories and street corners. It never occurs to you that real love between men might exist."

"On the contrary, I am perfectly aware that there can exist a very noble devotion. But I think it's rather less the rule than otherwise."

"I wish you could have met a couple who were here last night. One's a politician and the other's a composer. They've never had a cross word between them. Each one puts the other before himself and I should say that they were completely and entirely happy. I don't think they muck about much—there's more to it than that, you know. I've yet to see a man and his wife as unselfish together as those two. They've been together for three and a half years."

"It's rare, though, isn't it," the Reverend Jordon asked, "for an affair to last as long as that?"

Jimmy kicked a hassock into place and sat on it, looking up into his father's face. "How come the vicar of Channock knows so much about the wicked ways of the world?"

The Reverend Jordon laughed. "Youth always imagines that old age is ignorant. The vicar wouldn't be much good to Channock if he didn't know anything about the ways of the world, would he? You took the easy way out, Jimmy, when you let this man Simpton put you against Dr. Presnor. You got tired of battling, as most of us do. But just because you happen to have failed to resist temptation once doesn't mean to say that you won't succeed in resisting it the next time. There is always a next time, you know: The mercy of God is infinite, and so is God's forgiveness. His tenderness towards the truly repentant is limitless. There is such a thing as trying again, you know, and trying again after that. There is no such thing as failure, as long as one's game to try."

Jimmy said defiantly, "Some people think it ought to be legal. That they ought to change the law. How does *that* strike parsonical ears?"

" 'Parsonical' brains, Jimmy, have been concerned with the problem long before you knew it existed. At the moment I feel, with many others, that the attitude of the law might—and I only say 'might'—be working against the interests of youth rather than acting as a protection for it. There's a tendency for the older man to go to the younger boy because he could intimidate someone younger into secrecy. He'd be more likely to run the risk of blackmail with an adult. But if the adult were willing and he was legally entitled to give his consent there wouldn't be any risk of blackmail. There would be a risk only with someone *under* the age of consent, and that in itself might prove a protection."

"Tell me something, Dad. Quite apart from all this heavy broad-mindedness, how shocked were you about me?"

"I was more than shocked, Jimmy. I was bewildered, I was appalled and I was bitterly ashamed of you."

Jimmy spoke dryly, disturbed by the quiet emphasis of the Reverend Jordon's level voice: "How does that two and two make four with what you've just said about knowing the ways of the world?"

The Reverend Jordon met his eyes, "It doesn't. Do your sums always come out right?"

"No, Dad, I can't say they do. Why didn't you cut me off with the proverbial shilling?"

"Dr. Presnor led me to believe that it would hardly be helpful."

"He bulldozed you into Christian tolerance towards me, did he?"

"He certainly bulldozed me into remembering that charity begins at home."

Jimmy put out a hand for a cigarette. "What's the matter with him? Is he some sort of a medical saint?"

"No, I don't think so," the Reverend Jordon smiled. "He came down to Channock with the deliberate intention of wounding me as deeply as possible and he succeeded. He apologised for his brutality afterwards."

Jimmy paused with a match lit. "Good grief! I didn't know he had it in him."

"Oh yes, he has it in him," the Reverend Jordon said. "Quite rightly, I think, in this case. He seems to have a savage resentment against parents who mishandle their children's upbringing. He appeared to think me guilty of every known form of selfishness towards you."

"How did he break the happy news?"

"He asked me if I was aware that homosexuality was a modern problem or whether I could only visualise it in Biblical terms. Then he gave me a modern example on the spot. He told me that my own son had become a practising homosexual and that I could largely blame myself for it."

"It stinks of downright sadism," Jimmy said.

"No. I think it only stank of downright indignation. He feels so very strongly about the importance of home influences, and my sins of omission towards you were very grievous. Also I think he came prepared to meet with a good deal of self-righteousness, and in that he proved correct. I've told you how I felt at first."

"Yes, bewildered, appalled and bitterly ashamed, and I for one don't blame you. How long did it take him to change all that?"

"I think we changed it together," the Reverend Jordon said. "When I presented my side of the story he conceded that my sins might have been due to misunderstanding rather than mishandling. That softened him, and when I realised how good he had been to you—that softened me. We parted on excellent terms."

"Channock would gossip its head off if I came back, Dad. It's not good for a parson to have a nancy boy for a son. You must see I couldn't come home now."

The Reverend Jordon stood up. "The almond blossoms

are out. They're a lovely sight, and your Aunt Anita's gone to Cardiff. It seems an ideal time."

Jimmy stood up with him. The Reverend Jordon stepped towards him and kissed him. For a moment Jimmy clutched at him. Then he released him. "You see. Can't keep my hands off anyone, can I? That interfering swine of a Presnor knew what he was about when he sent you, Dad. You've been very easy to face."

"Don't you think he deserves a kinder description? He seems to have done everything in his power to help you, and to have asked nothing in return but that you should be helped."

"I think the world of him, Dad. I went down on my knees and prayed for his help, and a fat lot of use I made of it."

The Reverend Jordon put a hand on his shoulder. "If you went down on your knees and prayed, Jimmy, you'll find that you've been helped in spite of yourself."

There was a sharp tinkling crash from the kitchen. "That," said the Reverend Jordon, "will be the Venetian pot. She couldn't get the better of it, so she decided to smash it."

CHAPTER FORTY-TWO

WHEN the Reverend Jordon left, Jimmy ran himself a bath. He reddened his skin in his efforts to rid himself of the faint smell of perfume that clung to him. He left the bathroom clean and neat, and packed his belongings.

"Hallo!" said Mrs. Martin. "You off for good, then?"

Jimmy said, "Yes, Marty, off for good!" and repeated the last word wryly.

Mrs. Martin stood blowing on the prongs of a fork she was polishing up on a cloth. "Well, I'm not one to speak out of turn as a rule, but I can't say I'm sorry. Of course,

it's none of my business, but they say funny things about
Mr. Simpton and I shouldn't like to think of a nice young
man like you with a father like that——"

Jimmy interrupted her, "I'll miss you, Marty, you make
a wonderful cup of coffee!"

"My Bert says they all ought to be——"

"Horsewhipped?" Jimmy finished for her.

She was struck by his powers of intuition. "Well, it's a
funny thing you should've said it like that, but those were
the *very* words he used!"

"The world's full of Berts," Jimmy told her, "and they
seem to have a fondness for that solution."

He picked up his suitcase and called a taxi. It felt strange
to be going back to the little flat in Pimlico. It seemed an
age since he and Pam had redecorated it with such enthusiasm. As he put in his key a reproachful stillness seemed
to seep under the door. The small box of a hall had a life-
less quality as if no one had breathed in it for a very long
time. The drawing-room struck chilly and smelt of soot.
The furniture stood labelled for departure. The carpets
were rolled up and the books roped together. There was a
silent accusation of desertion in the inanimate objects.
Jimmy walked round them, fingering them, feeling absurdly
that his touch might mollify them. He read some of the
labels in Pam's characterless little round hand: 'Store. Store.
Channock. C/O Lady Parker.' She was taking few things
to her new address: small personal treasures, a few favourite
books and a sewing machine. The articles bound for
Channock were gifts from the Reverend Jordon.

The telephone rang, startling him. For a moment he
could not locate it. Then he discovered it busily insistent
behind the rolled-up carpet. A woman's voice asked, "May
I speak to Mrs. Southcott?"

"Who?"

"Is that Harold?"

"No, I'm afraid you've got the wrong number."

"Oh! I'm sorry, I dialled it right."

"It doesn't matter at all," said Jimmy. "I should get on to the supervisor." He was anxious to keep the voice as long as possible within the lonely room. He thought with a lingering wonderment that it was the last human being to whom he would ever speak. The voice died away with a click in his ear. He held the receiver several seconds before he replaced it. Then he dragged a small table into the centre of the room and reconnected the standard lamp.

He sat down and wrote a letter to Presnor:

'I've made a decision at last. I'm afraid it's not one you're likely to approve of, but I think it's the only way out. It wouldn't be possible to thank you for all your kindness, so I don't intend to try. Nor would it be possible to tell you how much your friendship has meant to me. Do you think you could take it as read? Father came to see me. You've trained him well. He never mentioned the word "sin" once. He talked to me rather as if I'd sprained my ankle in a rugger scrum. Thanks a lot for sending him. We cleared quite a few things up. I'm afraid it hasn't worked out how you hoped, but I think I've never admired him as much as I admired him today. I believe he'd have been willing to have me home if I'd insisted on going to church in a feather boa. I don't believe he would ever despise me, and I don't believe he ever did. He seemed quite unshaken by the fact that I'm queer. And that's not too bad going for a parson. Of course, he probably doesn't realise that it won't be long before I'm as obvious to the naked eye as Flick or a waiter that I once sneered at in a café. I catch myself out saying "Whoops" when I carry a tray—and you missed a nice bit of research work last night. Someone was shrieking at the unfortunate Simpton like a jealous parrakeet. It was me! If that's how it's going to take me I'm better off out of the way. I couldn't trust myself not to let Father

down. Supposing I turned into a parrakeet in Channock!
I couldn't bear it for him or for Pam. They both deserve
better breaks than that. Pam has gone off to the Parkers'.
Would you see her through this for me? I dare say she'll
need some help.

'As for me, I can't stand being chained to a self I detest.
If I was like Rodorevsky and Sir Owen I wouldn't dislike
myself. Even "his nibs" doesn't behave like a parrakeet.
Even Flick is not without his dignity. But I appear to
have none, which you must admit is a depressing discovery. Perhaps it's because people like Owen and
Rodorevsky have come to terms with it and know
how to manage their lives. They set a good example
in their way. Perhaps it's because I can never come
to terms with it and don't seem able to conquer it that
I am such a misery to myself and everyone else. I'm
one of the anchorless in-betweens. One can scarcely
blame "his nibs" for being fed up with me. It can't be
much fun to have a conscience-stricken neurotic on your
hands. I think he's beginning to see my nuisance value!
You will, I am sure, be kind enough to say my mind was
unbalanced. It makes a difference to consecrated ground
or something, doesn't it? And I feel I owe Father that.
He wasn't in the least condescending. It's rotten luck
that he should turn out a son like me. Curiously
enough, on this question of dignity, he seemed to
impart a bit to me. He seemed to restore my self-
respect. At least one doesn't feel one's departing this
world an absolute out-sider if a man like that doesn't
despise one. As for you, Louis—can you have Jewish
saints?

'If you see him, tell him I felt rather like Mrs. Martin
and the Venetian pot. I couldn't get the better of it so I
decided to smash it.'

He addressed the letter to Presnor and put it on the

mantelpiece. Then he went into the kitchen. He tested the taps of the gas stove and listened for a few seconds to the familiar hiss. The smell set the nerves of his stomach fluttering. He said aloud, to control them, "I don't suppose it's much worse than the dentist kind." From shelves and the bottoms of drawers he collected a pile of newspapers. He felt a dull apprehension more than fear. He tore the newspapers into strips, damped them and pressed them hard round the frames of the window-panes. A cartoon on the back of one of them caught his eye and he was glad of the respite to read it. He had never been able to wrap up garbage without reading the print underneath. Pam always said that it took him longer to throw away tea-leaves than anyone else she knew. The thought of Pam brought a sharp remorse. He wished fervently that he had taken her back to Grasmere. Surely to God he could have put up some form of pretence. If only for a fortnight he might have convinced her that she had truly tasted happiness. He had given her nothing worth while to remember. He stuffed up the second window and the mouse-hole beneath the sink. He tried desperately to remember the Reverend Jordon's fireside teachings. Dimly he recalled a God of love. It seemed immeasurably important that he should remember the teaching clearly. There was a Bible somewhere which had been the Reverend Jordon's first gift. Jimmy had not opened it once since his school days, but Pam insisted that it should lie on the table beside his bed. Pam read the Bible consistently. Jimmy often teased her for being a 'pious little piece'. He had used it as a stand for his early morning cup of tea. It raised the cup to a comfortable height for his sleepy reach. It bore several rings from the saucer. It might just be possible that the Bible had not been packed. It might lie with Pam's personal treasures—C/O of Lady Parker—or it might be bound for Channock. It would certainly not be marked for 'Store'.

He found it in neither group. It lay open at the fly-leaf

beneath Pam's curled-up hand. The Reverend Jordon's strong writing showed up through the fingers.

For an instant the shock was impeded by the astonishing fact that she had been in the flat all the time. He had felt so alone in the silence of it that he would not have believed that it was possible that another human being could have been present without his being able to sense it. His second swift thought was the telephone. It had rung and he had answered. Why had she slept through the sound of his voice? Then he took in the glass and the empty aspirin bottle—the meaning of the softly limp angle of the body on the bed, and the thing that she had done.

He all but disconnected the telephone by the force with which he snatched it up. Presnor answered his call at once. He said nothing when Jimmy let him in. He went into the bedroom and closed the door. Jimmy stood dreading his reappearance.

There was no expression on Presnor's face when he told Jimmy, "She was fortunately very amateurish. She was no more than heavily asleep. She's had an emetic and she'll be perfectly all right in the morning. You'd better go in and see her, and after that let her sleep. Oh—and Jimmy. She says that she was so tired that she must have miscalculated the dose. She's very insistent that it was an accident."

Jimmy was out of the room ten minutes, during which Presnor found and read the letter addressed to himself on the mantelpiece.

When Jimmy came back he avoided Presnor's eye. "She —she thought it was all her fault, of course. She thought she was wrong for me. That's why she did it. We're going away for a bit and then we're going down to visit Dad. I've promised her that."

"A change will do her good," Presnor said.

"It was nearly a grim coincidence," Jimmy told him.

Presnor was folding the letter. "Yes," he said, "so I see."

He replaced it in the envelope and put it in his pocket.

Jimmy said, "Actually, Louis, I know it sounds mad but I think that writing that letter sort of pulled me up. Lord knows why it should—I was probably just funking the gas oven really. I was going to go through with it because I thought it was too late and that cowardice on top of everything else would be too much of a good thing. And then I found Pam had beaten me to it and I had to get hold of you. The shock of Pam pulled me up even more, but the letter had sewn a few doubts before then." He put up a hand and rubbed his forehead as if he were physically trying to straighten his thoughts. "I don't quite know how to explain it—but I suddenly *believed* what you've been telling me all along. Up till then I'd only told myself I believed it. I realised that there really need be no disgrace in having homosexual tendencies which you can't help, but that the disgrace lay where you said it lay—in what you do about them. I know what clinched it. Dad. He made me believe you because he believed you. He admitted that he was full of Christian understanding towards the thing itself until it touched him personally, but when it did he was ashamed of me. Then after you'd had a go at him—and incidentally I hear it was some go—he made an effort and sincerely applied it to me. Somehow that helped me to feel a bit less ashamed of myself and I thought it might be worth trying again."

"That isn't surprising," Presnor said. "A man you've always thought had no use for you suddenly proved that you mean a lot to him at a time when you expected him to have even less use for you. It's bound to make you feel it's worth trying again."

"You knew that, of course. That's why you got after him."

"He 'got after' himself," Presnor said.

"Well, I'm willing to do anything I can, Louis. But that's more or less where we started, isn't it?"

Presnor smiled. "Not quite. You have your father back, you have your wife back, and you're a long way to getting your self-respect back. That's hardly where we started. We're ready to solve the last quarter of the problem now."

"It might be sticky going at first, Louis."

Presnor answered, "I think it will."

Jimmy looked up and met Presnor's eyes. "I know I've been a hell of a nuisance to you and I may have seemed ungrateful—but you did offer me friendship, don't forget."

"I shan't forget it," Presnor said.